Her Wolf

OTHER TITLES BY SAPIR A. ENGLARD

Cloak of the Vampire Series

Cloak of the Vampire

Blood of the Gods

Dance of the Phoenix

The Millennium Wolves Series

The Millennium Wolves

His Haze

Alpha of the Millennium

Ghosted Soul

Painted Scars

Stand-Alones

One Night

Desperate

Her Wolf

SAPIR A. ENGLARD

Published by Montlake, Seattle

www.apub.com

Amazon, the Amazon logo, and Montlake are trademarks of Amazon.com, Inc., or its affiliates.

EU product safety contact:
Amazon Media EU S. à r.l.
38, avenue John F. Kennedy, L-1855 Luxembourg
amazonpublishing-gpsr@amazon.com

ISBN-13: 9781662536427 (paperback)
ISBN-13: 9781662536410 (digital)

Cover design by Faceout Studio, Addie Lutzo
Cover image: © BROKER/Moritz Wolf, © fotograzia / Getty Images; © Dmitr1ch, © Inna Vlasova, © huasheng huang, © its_vadim_k.photo, © Golden Shrimp, © Watachyo, © Dewin ID / Shutterstock

Printed in the United States of America

To Mom, Eden & Gil
This book wouldn't have seen the light of day if it
weren't for you.

CHAPTER 1
CONVICTIONS

The Hallowing Hour was scheduled for publication this upcoming Thursday, and my column wasn't ready.

Staring at the old dusty laptop, I wondered if my writing conveyed the discrepancy between the police statement regarding the recent killing on Sunset Boulevard and what I had actually witnessed on-site.

According to the police, the killer was a deranged man on the run called Richard Berkins, who, after losing his wife and children to a terror attack, lost his mind and began hunting down those he believed involved.

When I visited the crime scene a few days ago, however, I saw what the police seemed to have missed.

A shadow mark.

I pulled up the image I took on my phone and studied it for the nth time. At first glance, it looked like a little puddle of water from a nearby leakage, or a recent rain. But when I'd crouched near it and *really* looked at it, I could tell it wasn't actually water. It was a liquid resembling water, sure, but it lacked the transparency and shine water had. Instead, it was a muted dark color, like a barely there shadow.

This wasn't my first time seeing a shadow mark. I'd seen them a few times before, at different locations and crime scenes I inspected.

I looked up from my phone at the world map I'd hung on the wall of my small living room. It was full of pins in different colors, stuck into different places all over the world. Most pins were red, some were blue or green, and a few were black.

Shadow marks were uncommon—especially in populated areas. That I'd found one only a few miles away from home was a miracle—or a curse—in and of itself.

Nibbling my lip, I returned my gaze to the laptop and pushed my glasses up my nose. This piece was important. It was key, in fact, to my own personal investigation. And yet I felt as if my writing wasn't good enough. That it didn't relay the message I wanted it to.

These are your insecurities speaking, Drew, I told myself as I rose to my feet and climbed over the piles of papers spread all over the floor. Unfortunately, knowing I had insecurities didn't help me fix them.

Grimacing, I put on my dark peacoat, fastened my logger boots, and wrapped a scarf around my neck as I grabbed my keys and wallet and headed out the door.

When in doubt, drink a beer.

North Hollywood wasn't a dangerous neighborhood, but it still had its fair share of unhoused. Outside my dump of an apartment building was home for two homeless men called Caveat (a pseudonym, I presumed) and Johnny. Currently, Johnny was sleeping on the staircase leading up to the front door, while Caveat was smoking pot right near the entrance gate.

I skipped over Johnny and gave a little wave to Caveat, who returned it along with a toothy grin (though most teeth were missing). "Tired, ain't ya," he said, his dopey eyes lingering on my face.

Shrugging, I handed him a five-dollar bill. "As usual, Cavi," I retorted with half a smile, "go buy yourself some water."

He blew me a kiss, which resulted in a cloud of weedy smoke engulfing my face. "Yer a doll, Drew."

The moment I was out of his sight, I let my fake smile slip and hurried down the road to the convenience store. Sometimes, I wished I had Caveat's endless optimism. Even though his life was a literal dumpster fire, he still managed to shoot me a genuine smile and look on the bright side, in an almost innocent, childlike manner.

I used to be the same up until eight years ago, when the ugly truth hit me in the face.

This world had no bright side.

There was a bleeding dog slumped against the back door of my building.

Normally, I would've entered through the front. But in the fifteen minutes since I'd left to buy a beer, Caveat had decided to join Johnny in sleeping on the stairs, effectively blocking the entrance.

So I took the back door.

And found a bleeding dog.

Although calling the beast a dog was quite the understatement. It was no fluffy Maltese or even a slender Doberman. It was huge and would've probably been almost as tall as I was if it were conscious and standing on all fours—and I was five-eight.

I slowly approached the animal, my boots squeaking softly against the asphalt, and the closer I drew, the more details I registered under the barely luminous streetlight. There was a splash of blood in the middle of the door, trickling down into a pool under the dog, as if the poor thing had been thrown against it before going limp on the ground.

My heartbeat quickened in both worry and fear. Who was the psychopath who attacked the poor dog? And who could be strong enough to throw such a humongous beast like this at the door?

I crouched near the dog's head, staring at its snout, my heart still racing. I knew close to nothing about dogs, though I liked them enough to watch random cute dog videos on my phone. But while I was no expert, I could tell that this dog's sharp, narrow snout and general facial features seemed similar to a Siberian husky. Or a wolf dog.

Whatever breed it was, however, didn't matter, since it was currently lying in its own puddle of blood, probably near death.

What the fuck should I do?

The dog shifted, only an inch, making me tense, and I saw its eyes, a pair of brilliant arctic blue, open to exhausted, pained slits. It was only for a moment, though, because the dog closed them and let out a soft sigh, almost a whimper, as it grew still once more.

My heart pounded in my ears as I stared at the poor thing. I couldn't leave it out here. While I was pressed for time when it came to finishing up my column, it could wait. I wasn't so heartless as to leave an injured animal out to die.

Standing up, I took out my phone and searched for 24/7 vet care in the area. I called the first one I found.

"LA Metropolitan Emergency Vet Care," a woman answered.

"There is a wounded dog outside my building." I got straight to the point. "Can you—"

"We don't take in strays." She cut me off before I could even finish the sentence. "If you want veterinary care for the dog nonetheless, you must pay a deposit of three hundred dollars, and then sign that you will pay the additional costs for the rest of its care."

My jaw dropped. "Excuse me?"

"It's as I said, ma'am," the woman responded impatiently. "Now, if you want to proceed, I can send you the files over—"

I hung up and called the next vet hospital on the list.

Unfortunately, the man on the other end of the line, while nicer, said basically the same thing.

Angry now, I shoved the phone back into the pocket of my peacoat and looked at the dog, helpless. If I could get it into my apartment, I could at least try and bandage its open wound. But the dog was colossal, and most likely heavier than the weights I used to lift back when I was frequenting the gym, so even if I wanted to bring it into my apartment, I couldn't.

Unless . . .

I grabbed my phone again and dialed Chase. After a few rings, a lazy voice drawled, "The fuck you want, Colter?"

Unfazed by my neighbor's attitude, I asked, "Are you home?" *Please be home.*

"No," he replied, to my dismay. "Why? Feeling lonely?"

I tapped my foot on the ground, annoyed at his suggestive tone, as I said, "I have a dying dog outside the building's back door, and I want your help to bring it inside my apartment. Can you come help me or not?"

As if I'd flipped a switch, Chase's voice turned dead serious. "I'll be there in ten."

Hanging up, I sat down near the dog's head as I waited for my neighbor to arrive and, hesitantly, reached out my hands to its matted fur. The dog did not stir, but I could feel the tension in its heavy muscles when I petted its dirty coat. Even unconscious, the dog did not put its trust blindly in a stranger.

As the minutes ticked by, I kept petting the dog, sliding my fingers through its fur until I saw its eyes open again, this time fully, and it stared right at me.

Feeling it tense further under my hands now that it was awake, I kept up the monotonous petting of its fur and looked straight into its eyes as I said in as soft and soothing a voice as I could muster, "Don't worry, doggo. I called for help. I'm not going to let you die." I paused and grimaced. "Not under my watch."

Obviously, I knew the dog couldn't understand me, but I hoped the tone of my voice at least would have a calming effect. Or the conviction of my words.

I'd had enough death in my life to last a fucking lifetime. I refused to let another living being die while I could help it.

The dog kept on staring at me unblinkingly, and I stared back. It almost seemed as if it understood what I'd just said, because I could feel the tension in its body ease a bit.

My own tension did not subside, however, because the dog did not seem to be doing well. "Try to stay conscious until help arrives, okay?"

The dog's head slightly bobbed, and I could swear it was trying to nod.

I scoffed inwardly at my silliness. While it was human nature to personify animals, it didn't mean they were actually, well, human.

And yet something about this dog felt a little different.

Car lights came into view from the entrance of the narrow alley, making me whip my head in that direction. I recognized the Cadillac that came to a stop not that far away from me and saw the tall, muscular silhouette exiting the car and heading in my direction.

The streetlight hit Chase's face when he neared. "This is the dog?" he asked, looking down at the beast in disbelief.

"I know," I murmured, rising back up to my feet. "It's huge. Now let's get it inside."

Chase frowned but nodded.

While I wasn't looking, the dog had fallen unconscious again. Chase rolled it onto its stomach and, taking a deep breath, lifted it.

Or tried to.

"Fuck!" he yelled as he let the dog go, stepping back, his chest heaving. "How much does this fucker weigh?"

My eyes widened. "Don't you lift, like, hundreds of pounds on a regular basis?"

My neighbor glared at me. "I do," he spat, "but this one is even heavier than that. Damn." He scrunched his nose. "It hurts my pride."

Since Chase's only sources of pride were his bodybuilder muscles, it made sense. "Maybe we can call Jackson?" I suggested, uneasy now, especially since the slight fall from Chase's arms made the dog's bleeding worsen.

"I'll call him," Chase replied, hissing a curse before he called another friendly neighbor from the top floor.

A few minutes later, Chase and Jackson, a fit man in his early sixties, carried the dog inside the building and up the flight of stairs to my apartment.

Throughout the whole ordeal, they contorted their faces and strained their muscles as if the weight was far more than they could bear—which was extremely surreal to witness, considering both sported quite the muscular frame. Especially Chase.

But soon those thoughts fled my mind as I shoved the door to my apartment open, watching the two men entering quickly with the dog and the trail of blood the poor animal left in its wake. I immediately switched on the lights before kicking the door closed and instructing, "Spread that blanket on the sofa and put the dog there."

My apartment might've been on the smaller side, but somehow, with the two large men and the huge dog, it suddenly felt claustrophobically tiny, especially with the blood and shoe prints covering the papers on the floor.

The dog barely fit on the blanketed sofa, and in the bright lights of the living room, I could finally make out the color of its fur—a dark, burnished bronze, which stood out strikingly against the faded green cushions of the sofa.

For the first time since I found it, I thought the dog was absolutely, tragically beautiful. Possibly the most beautiful dog I had ever seen, even. The realization would've struck me dumb if it weren't for the fact the dog was continuing to bleed without an end in sight.

While Chase and Jackson plopped themselves on empty spots on the floor and the old couch respectively, fighting to catch their breath, I hurried to the kitchen, got the first aid kit, and returned to the living room, opening it over the coffee table. I found bandages, and, before I could think twice about it, I began dressing the dog's wound.

I had to use the entire bandage roll before the blood stopped soaking through.

"Fuck," I breathed out as I sat down on the floor, sweating from the exertion.

"Well," I heard Jackson murmur, "I always said your curiosity will one day bring upon your doom."

I huffed, wiping the sweat off my forehead. "This is not *my* doom, though."

"No, it's mine," Jackson sighed, and when I turned my head to the middle-aged man, he gave me a bemused smile as he grabbed his waist, seemingly in pain from the effort. "You got something to read while I rest?"

I was about to reply when Chase snorted and interjected, "I wouldn't recommend it, Jack. *The Hallowing Hour* is hardly a literary read. Unless you want to dive into another one of dear Drew's conspiracy theories."

If I'd had the energy, I would've glared at him, but I was used to Chase's jibes, and not just his either. Everyone thought I was a complete kook, writing about the supernatural.

What none of them understood was that I *knew* all of it to be true. Like I knew that puddle of water on Sunset Boulevard was in fact a shadow mark. Like I knew the Seaside Massacre in Malibu a couple of months ago was perpetrated by ghouls, and that the disappearances of young boys up in Portland were the result of succubus attacks.

The supernatural was real.

I just wished I wasn't the only one aware of that fact.

CHAPTER 2
A WARPED WOUND

You've probably already read the headlines.

Another killing. Another "lone madman."

Another official statement that ties a bloody bow on something that feels unfinished.

We're told Richard Berkins snapped. That he's grieving, dangerous, and delusional. Maybe he is.

But the thing about delusions is—they don't usually leave behind physical evidence.

And they don't stain the sidewalk with a residue the rain won't wash away.

There's a story underneath the story. There always is.

I paused, my fingers freezing over the laptop keyboard, as I heard a slight shifting noise coming from the sofa. I looked at the time and saw it was almost four o'clock in the morning.

Leaving the desk, I walked to the sofa and crouched, looking at the dog, whose arctic-blue eyes were open after long hours of unconsciousness. Probably due to pain. The fact was that I was no medic, let alone a vet, and thus my medical skills were severely lacking.

"Hey," I said now, as the dog's eyes latched on to me, narrow and full of mistrust. Or so I interpreted the look he was giving me. "I need to check your wound, so it might hurt a little. I apologize in advance."

The dog bobbed its head slightly, as if it understood me. I wondered if it was just in my head. What were the chances of me finding some sort of a supernatural creature right outside my apartment building? If there was one thing I'd learned about supernatural beings, it was that they hid themselves very well. Too well, even.

Still, unease burrowed into my gut as I gently unwrapped the bandages from the dog's back. After Chase and Jackson helped bring the animal into my apartment and left, I'd launched myself into work while the dog was resting. I had forced myself to focus on the job I needed to do and put all my questions in the back of my mind.

Now, those questions rose to the surface and multiplied when I exposed the dog's back, cleaned the dry blood with antiseptic wipes, and saw something I hadn't earlier that night.

The wound looked like someone had carved the dog's back with a knife. It had to have been methodical because the carvings were precise, creating a certain shape.

I disposed of the bloodied wipes and turned on the flashlight on my phone to see the shape of the wound better. It looked like someone had scratched a deformed star into the skin. One line ran vertically straight down the middle, while the other six crisscrossed it, with one of them having a little wave to it, contrasting with the symmetry of the others.

Returning my gaze to the dog's, who seemed to peer at me with its piercing eyes, I couldn't help but ask, "Who did this to you?" even though I knew it wouldn't be able to tell me.

A low growl came from the dog's throat, making my eyes widen. It looked away, leaning its head on its large front paws, as if it didn't feel like responding to me.

My heart pounded in my ears as I stared at it—or rather, him. This dog gave off a masculine energy I couldn't quite put my finger on, but my gut told me it was a male.

Which, in and of itself, made my suspicions grow. "I see," I murmured as I grabbed a new bandage roll from the first aid kit sprawled open on the floor and began re-dressing his strangely shaped wound.

Silence reigned in the room as the dog let me care for his injury, but once I was done, he raised his head and turned to look at me again, his gaze so full of . . . *something*. It almost looked like he was trying to send me a silent message.

I sat down on the floor and stared back at him. "You know, I work as a columnist for an online magazine called *The Hallowing Hour*."

The dog kept on staring at me unblinkingly, and I held his gaze, heart racing. "I write about the truth my human brethren refuse to acknowledge." I paused, tensing, before I added, "Such as supernatural phenomena."

No reaction, as if the dog was containing himself on purpose.

Scowling, I pointed at his wounded back. "I can tell a sigil from a random shape, even if I don't understand its meaning."

Still no reaction. Instead, the dog seemed almost bored with me.

But I refused to let him win. "You're not just a dog," I concluded, despite my incredulity over the idea that I had really come by a supernatural creature by pure chance. "The question is, what *are* you?"

The dog cocked his head, like dogs did when they heard an interesting sound. But his doglike behavior didn't work on me. His brilliant eyes were far too intelligent and sentient for him to be a normal dog.

And I wasn't born yesterday.

"You don't have to confirm it for me to know the truth," I told him, narrowing my eyes as he suddenly leaned his head back down and closed his eyes. "I'll still take care of you."

Because—supernatural creature or not—the dog needed help. And from my extensive research of the supernatural, I knew gaining his favor would be beneficial for me in the long run.

One thing I learned early on was that the supernatural repaid what they owed, be it good or bad.

The first rays of sunlight spilled into the living room as I finished up the article and submitted it just in time. Now I was free to do some personal research.

Pulling a thick notebook from the desk drawer, I opened it, pushing my glasses up my nose, before I glanced at the sofa. The dog was fast asleep. I let him be, for now; I was definitely going to grill him about his true identity when he felt better later.

But for him to feel better, I needed to find out the nature of the sigil carved into his flesh.

I returned my gaze to the notebook. Throughout the years since my revelation that humans were not the only rational inhabitants of this earth, I'd documented the various supernatural instances and markings I'd found. Markings like the knife-carved shape on the dog's back I'd titled sigils.

Certain aspects needed to be present in a marking for me to recognize it as a sigil. They were usually shapes created by intersections of lines, dots, and sharp corners. As for their effect, which I had deduced must be magical in nature, I could only guess based on the related context.

Unfortunately, that was the extent of my knowledge about sigils. But I did copy every one of them I encountered into my notebook and guessed their meanings.

For instance, the most common sigil I'd found was what I called the Safety Spiral. It was a spiral made of dashes instead of a solid line, with three small dots trailing off the end like raindrops. I had only ever found this sigil in places of business, like restaurants or clothing shops. I interpreted it as a protective charm of sorts, like those religious blessings some people believed in.

Now, I copied the shape of the wound on paper and tried to find some sort of meaning. The straight y-axis line appeared in some other sigils as some sort of a base to the shapes, but that was the only similarity I could find. I had never seen multiple lines crisscrossing like that, and that single wavy line concerned me, seeing as it broke the symmetry I'd noted in almost every other sigil.

I flipped through the notebook, still trying to find marks that could resemble this one, but there was something utterly unique about the sigil carved into the dog's flesh. Perhaps it was a personalized sigil? I didn't know if that was even a thing, but I already knew not to quickly jump to conclusions when it came to the supernatural.

Everything was possible when the supernatural was involved.

Sighing, I closed the notebook and tried looking up the sigil on Google. Of course, the search engine found nothing of importance.

A knock on the door made me jump ten feet high in my chair. "Jesus," I murmured as I strode through the living room and looked through the peephole. Seeing it was Chase, I unlocked the door and opened it, glaring at him. "You gave me a fucking scare."

Chase smirked. "Good morning to you, too, Sunshine."

Scowling, I moved aside to let him in. He walked inside and made a beeline to the sofa, where the dog was now awake, tense, and watching Chase like a hawk. "Hello, Big Boy," my neighbor now said, crouching near the dog's head with a somewhat strained smile. "Aren't you a beauty?"

Chase was right. The dog *was* beautiful, with his shimmering bronze coat and brilliant eyes. He was also humongous enough, and *sapient* enough, to have raised my suspicions about his true nature in the first place.

The dog bared his teeth at Chase, but my neighbor kept on smiling, though his dark eyes flared. "Don't worry, I just wanted to come by and see how you're doing," he told the creature before he rose back up and turned to me with a self-deprecating sigh. "He doesn't seem to like me."

I narrowed my eyes. "How did you know he's a *he*?"

My neighbor shrugged. "Just a feeling," he said nonchalantly. "I would've double-checked, but I fear Big Boy here won't let me anywhere near his balls."

Of that I was convinced too. "He doesn't seem extremely friendly," I agreed, closing the door and approaching Chase and the dog, whose eyes now snapped to me. "Though to be fair, I don't think he's a dog at all."

"Oh no," Chase groaned, rolling his eyes and pinching the bridge of his nose. "Here we go again."

I scowled. "I'm being serious, Chase. He is not a mere dog. I'm sure of it."

He let out an exaggerated sigh and sat down on the empty couch. "Do you mind making me some coffee?" he asked. "If I'm being forced to listen to your crazy talk, I should at least pump myself up with caffeine."

Still scowling, I obliged nonetheless. Chase was probably the only friend I had, even if I didn't appreciate him calling me crazy. Still, he deserved his coffee, especially after his help yesterday.

He wasn't the first to call me crazy, nor would he be the last.

Once I finished brewing his coffee in the old secondhand machine, I also made a mug for myself and headed back to the living room, handing him his cup. "Thanks," he said, leaning back and putting his legs on the coffee table while sipping the coffee, glancing at the dog for a brief second before resting his gaze on me. "Now, what kind of *interesting* idea did you come up with?"

"It's not an idea," I immediately corrected, frowning. "Nothing I say is a mere idea. The supernatural is *real*, Chase."

I could see my neighbor fighting not to roll his eyes as he murmured skeptically, "Sure. Whatever you say."

Huffing, I sipped my coffee and sat down on the couch, looking at the dog, who was watching me now. "Anyway," I said, having no intention of getting into another argument with Chase about the existence of the supernatural, "I need to call in a vet, now that it's morning. I think the dog needs professional care I can't really provide."

The dog seemed to tense, his brilliant eyes freezing over.

"Isn't a vet house visit expensive, though?" Chase inquired, unaware of my staring match with the alleged animal. "Why don't you just call animal control or something?"

Without looking away, I replied, "Because I told him I would take care of him."

Chase was quiet for a moment before he said, "It doesn't solve the money issue, though."

He was right. Veterinary care was extremely expensive. Up until a few months ago, I'd had a cat. I'd adopted him when he was a little kitten and raised him on my own. But the cat was diagnosed with prostate cancer—which was extremely rare in cats and often diagnosed when it was at an advanced stage, which was exactly what had happened in my cat's case.

Treatment for that wasn't just experimental but also astronomically expensive. I couldn't afford it. So, I had a few choices: surrender my cat, let him wither in my arms, or have someone adopt him from me, someone who could afford the treatment.

In the end, I swallowed my ego and chose the latter, handing my cat over to my filthy rich ex-boyfriend, whose only redeeming quality was his love for cats—and my cat specifically.

It had been one of the hardest decisions of my life.

Looking at the dog now, I felt the pang of sorrow hit me deep. I didn't want to give up another stray animal I found. Sure, I suspected the dog wasn't *just* a dog, but whatever he was, he was still a living being currently under my care.

"I'll do whatever it takes to cover the costs," I said, the resolution settling down in my gut and squeezing it. I tore my eyes away from the dog to look at Chase. "Even if it means taking on a side job."

Chase gave me an odd look. "Are you sure?"

"Yes," I answered without hesitation, because I was. I was never surer of anything in my life.

I'd let my sisters down eight years ago when I failed to protect them.

I'd let my cat go when I couldn't afford his medical treatment.

I was sick and tired of being incapable of caring for those I cared about. And while I'd only met this dog last night, I cared about his well-being. I needed him to make it, to heal.

It was hard enough to live with myself as it was. The least I could do was lessen some of the horrible guilt I would feel for the rest of my life.

CHAPTER 3
WILD NEW WORLD

After Chase left, I spent the rest of the morning looking for vets who did house visits. They all asked for atrocious prices, and in the end, I settled on the one who seemed most sympathetic to my situation and offered a 10 percent discount for a first-time dog mom—her words, not mine.

By the time I made an appointment for later in the afternoon, the dog had fallen asleep. I crouched by his head and watched his body rise and fall with his deep breathing. Now that his piercing arctic-blue gaze wasn't following my every move, I allowed myself to put my hand over his shimmering bronze fur.

He felt so soft, like touching a fluffy cloud. I stroked down his sides, careful to avoid the wounded area, and felt his muscles, tense even in his sleep, relax under my touch. I'd never felt something as soft as him.

There was also a distinct smell to him that made me take a deep breath, inhaling the scent. He smelled like freshly cut grass or the damp earth after a rainy night.

It made me want to borrow my head into his fur and breathe him in.

But I had no time for this. I had to work if I wanted to afford the vet's visit—and also keep a roof over my head and food on the table.

Reluctantly, I withdrew my hand and headed to the desk, settling behind it on the broken, worn chair and flipping the laptop open.

First things first: My article regarding the Sunset Boulevard killing was approved. That meant I would see the money in my account tomorrow.

Next, I began researching for my personal project. I wanted to find more murder cases similar to the one on Sunset Boulevard. Shadow marks appeared only at violent crime scenes, after all.

Unlike with sigils, I didn't quite understand the point of shadow marks.

Seeing nothing noteworthy in the news—no new crimes that raised my supernatural-acute alarm—I decided to shift gears and start working on my next piece.

After seeing the unknown sigil on the dog's back, I had found yet another mystery to look into. Besides, it'd been a while since I wrote about sigils.

Most people don't look at a knife wound and think, magic, I typed. But I do.

From there, I let my fingers lead the way, and for the next few hours, all I did was type, look in my sigils notebook, and contemplate a name to call the sigil on the dog's back.

During breaks, I poured water into a bowl and held it for the dog to drink. I was worried he hadn't eaten or drunk in a while, so I was determined to get him to consume what he needed to, if he wanted to survive.

The dog hesitated at first, refusing to drink the water from the bowl in my hands, but after I told him, "You don't want to die from dehydration, do you?" he seemed to relent and drank the bowl dry.

Then, after simple online research, I found I could feed him some meat and rice, in case I didn't have dog food available. When I checked how much dog food cost, I opted to go for the chicken thighs and simple white rice.

Again, the dog seemed unhappy when I brought the plate to his snout. But this time, I didn't need to convince him to eat, because his hunger seemed to do him in, and he cleaned the plate in less than a minute.

After I got myself some rice and chicken, too, and sprinkled them with salt and some other spices so they had a better taste, I sat on the couch, facing the dog, who narrowed his eyes at my plate.

I found myself smirking. "I don't know what you are yet," I informed him, "so I'm treating you like a regular dog for now. Meaning you can't have spices."

If the dog was human, I would've thought my words pissed him off. He had that kind of look.

After taking a bite of the chicken thigh, I pointed my fork at him and said, "You know, if you're capable of human speech, you can simply tell me what you are."

The dog growled in response, but for some reason, I didn't find him threatening. Usually, such a humongous dog growling at me would've made me think twice about my safety, but something about him put me at ease.

Maybe it was the fact he was currently too incapacitated by his wound to actually do anything to me.

"Obviously, you understand me," I deduced, taking a bite of the rice. "Now the question remains, how can I get you to communicate with me?"

This seemed to annoy him, because he made an irritated huff, and leaned his head down on his large paws and closed his eyes. But his tail was flicking back and forth sharply, like my cat's used to do when he was agitated.

I wondered if it meant the same for dogs.

After lunch, I got back to my computer, and instead of continuing to work on my new article, I made a slight detour and searched for canine supernatural creatures online before pulling out my thick folder from the desk drawer.

The list was longer than I thought.

Opening the folder, I looked through my own lists. Much like with sigils, I documented all kinds of supernatural creatures I believed—or rather, *knew*—were real and walking among us, along with the evidence I'd collected for each.

I had mermaids, sorcerers, succubi, and even Harpies, among many others. But when it came to the canine types, there were only three I had listed.

Hellhounds, Aralez, and werewolves.

Hellhounds referred to the creatures who served the guardian of Hell, according to many mythologies. They were mostly known as the helpers of Cerberus from Greek mythology, but whether Cerberus, or even Hell, was real, I had yet to find proof. As for hellhounds, though, there was plenty of evidence. What they actually *were*, I didn't know. I simply named them hellhounds because, according to certain sightings, especially in the Nordic countries, they looked like large dogs with demonic horns.

The Aralez, on the other hand, were creatures from Armenian mythology, depicted as winged, doglike creatures who descended from the heavens to lick the wounds of fallen heroes. According to the testaments I had found, there were reports of terminally ill people who were visited by a large canine-ish creature during one night, and the next day, they were completely healed. Those people, coincidentally, were all very altruistic, helping their communities while seeking no compensation for their good deeds. Thus I named those creatures the Aralez.

Werewolves were self-explanatory, really: creatures who were part wolf, part human. They were quite popular in modern literature, movies, and shows, and there were thousands of people online who claimed to have seen one. There were countless "witness statements" about different kinds of werewolves: those who looked like a nightmare standing on two feet, with fur covering their limbs and sharp teeth, or black wolves with golden eyes and piercing fangs.

Throughout the last several years of researching the supernatural, I had learned one thing for sure: Ironically enough, when so many people thought something was real, yet all proofs contrasted with one another, the odds were that something might not actually be real at all.

And even if werewolves *were* real, and I went by the descriptions of those online who claimed to have seen one, the dog didn't exactly fit any of them—except, perhaps, for his size.

As for hellhounds and Aralez . . . well, I highly doubted he was either of those. He was far too pretty to be a hellhound—not to mention the lack of demonic horns, or the fact he was in the States rather than in Norway or something—and yet his temperament didn't feel like it could belong to an Aralez.

If I was going by my own personal lists, he didn't fit anything. But searches online showed me plenty of different options, and since I knew that I didn't even scratch the surface when it came to my supernatural investigations, any of those options could be plausible.

A knock on the door made me jump, snapping me out of my deep thoughts. "Shit," I murmured as I rose to my feet, ignoring the dog's stare as I headed to the door and opened it.

There stood a woman in medical gear, holding a black briefcase. She gave me a friendly smile and said, "Miss Colter? I'm Dr. Alicia Danvers."

"Oh, hi, yes," I said, blinking rapidly as I returned to reality after my hours-long session staring at the laptop. "Come on in."

I moved aside, letting the vet inside, and closed the door behind her. She fixed her bushy dark hair into a ponytail and peered at the sofa, where the dog was staring at her with a low growl. "I'm guessing this is the dog in question?"

"Yeah," I said, moving to crouch by the dog's head. "Feel free to check him and see what you can do."

Dr. Danvers nodded and put the briefcase down before she crouched next to me by the dog's head. He seemed to really hate it, because his growls grew louder, and he began baring his teeth.

But Dr. Danvers didn't seem fazed. Not by his behavior, at least. "He's the most stunning dog I've ever seen," she said, her dark eyes roaming over him in curiosity and wonder. "But I've never seen one this large. A Saint Bernard mix? No." She shook her head, then frowned as she pulled out a stethoscope from her briefcase. "He doesn't seem like an ordinary dog, though."

Before I could tell her about my suspicions, she held her hand up to tell me to be quiet and checked the dog's side. His growls were now really loud, to the point I could swear the sofa itself was moving from their vibrations.

I was half afraid he would literally bite the good doctor's head off, but thankfully, she withdrew from him and rose to her feet. "You said the wound's on his back, right?" she asked, a frown on her face.

"Yes," I replied, frowning as well. What was she thinking about?

Dr. Danvers reached with her hand toward the wound, or rather, the knife-carved sigil on the dog's back, but before she could even touch the skin, the dog seemed to have been pushed over the edge.

It all happened so fast. In one blurry moment, the dog jumped off the sofa and backed away from Dr. Danvers, his back hunched, his hair standing on end, and his teeth fully bared.

His growls were no longer merely loud. They were literally making the floor shake.

Dr. Danvers stood there, frozen, watching the dog with wide eyes. I couldn't take my eyes off the dog, either, but more out of worry. Because I could see a trail of blood flowing out of his wound and down his side, and dripping on the parquet floor.

"Jesus," Dr. Danvers now said, turning to look at me. "I don't think I can treat him. And neither should you."

I glanced at her, shocked. "What the fuck do you mean, you can't treat him?"

"Miss Colter," she said slowly, carefully, her voice dropping to a whisper. "It's not a dog."

Huh?

She swallowed hard before returning her gaze to the beast and said, "It's a wolf."

CHAPTER 4
WOLF IN DOG'S CLOTHING

"I'm going to call animal control," Dr. Danvers said, pulling out her phone once she put a safe distance between her and the wolf.

Heart screeching to a stop, I grabbed her wrist, tensing. "Please don't," I said when she gave me a confused look. "Let me take care of this."

She frowned. "It is my duty to report the presence of a wild animal, Miss Colter," she said calmly, gently taking my hand off her. "He's a danger to you."

I shook my head. "But he hasn't hurt me—"

A knock on the door cut me off. Grimacing, I pleaded with her to wait and strode to the door, pulling it open.

Chase stood at the entrance with a smile that immediately disappeared when he saw my face. "What's wrong?"

I let him come in and closed the door behind him before I introduced him to Dr. Danvers. "She wants to call animal control," I said, a tad too accusingly. Logically, I knew the good doctor was simply doing her job. But the thought of having the wolf taken away from me was enough to bring me to a panic. "He might be a wolf, but you saw for yourself he was harmless!"

Chase looked at me, then at the wolf, before he finally landed his gaze on Dr. Danvers, who was clutching her phone hard, as if it was a lifeline.

"Dr. Danvers," he said calmly, his voice surprisingly authoritative. "My name is Chase Kerrigan, and I work for a wildlife preservation nonprofit called the Foundation for Apex Restoration & Territory."

I tensed even further, trying not to show any surprise on my face. Especially now, when I saw Dr. Danvers's eyes light up in recognition. "Oh, I see," she said, before she let out a relieved sigh. "Then you'll take him to one of your facilities, I assume?"

Chase nodded with a reassuring smile. "It is my job, after all."

"Good," Dr. Danvers said, quickly packing up her briefcase before turning to look at me. "Then I'll take my leave for now. I'm sorry this is the outcome, Miss Colter. I know you truly care for the wolf."

I gave her a fake smile. "That's fine. Thank you for your help."

It was only when Dr. Danvers was gone that I turned to Chase and hit his shoulder. He shot me a shocked look. "I deserve a 'Thank you, Chase, dear.' Not to be hit!"

"You lied to her," I said, folding my arms as I glared at him. Chase's real occupation was project management in a cybersecurity company.

To my surprise, Chase said, "And who do you think owns this nonprofit?"

I paused, blinked, and let my arms fall as my cheeks grew hot. "Oh."

"Yeah, *oh*," he said, scowling. "And I wasn't lying when I said I will take care of the wolf."

I grimaced and turned to look at the wolf for the first time since he almost attacked Dr. Danvers. He was lying on the floor, seemingly exhausted, and yet his brilliant eyes were open, and they were almost glowing with the intensity of his fury as he glared at Chase. His teeth were slightly bared too.

This was the first time in eight years I had come across a supernatural being in the flesh—and I was completely sure that was what he was, now, considering he was supposed to be a wild wolf and yet acted human enough for me to suspect him of being a werewolf.

Never before did I think a supernatural being would simply find its way to me like this after I'd been searching for any proof of its existence. It might be my once-in-a-lifetime chance to get an "in" to that world—and finally find out what happened to my sisters.

I couldn't let Chase take him away.

"No," I said slowly, drawing both Chase's and the wolf's gazes, but my eyes rested on the arctic-blue ones of the half animal. "He's going to stay here with me until he gets better."

Chase let out a frustrated sigh. "And this is exactly why I need to take him, so he can get fixed—"

He yelped suddenly when the wolf stood up from his repose and walked toward him. Or rather, *stalked.* Like a predator measuring up prey. Showing his teeth, a murderous energy spreading in my far-too-small living room.

Chase froze, and I stared in utter amazement when the wolf put himself between Chase and me, as if to protect me from Chase, and let out a furious growl.

My neighbor watched with a deep frown, tense, and silence stretched thin as he stared at the wolf like he was trying to read its mind. My muscles were locked tight as my mind reeled, trying to make sense of what was happening, when Chase suddenly raised his hands and sighed again. "Fine. I give up. You can die for all I care."

Before I could ask Chase what the hell this was all about, he left my apartment, slamming the door shut behind him.

I looked down at the wolf, who now turned to look at me. "It seems like you offended him," I informed the possible werewolf.

Still baring his teeth, I swear he was smiling.

I stared at the dog—or wolf, rather—as he reclined on the sofa, his back freshly bandaged, his eyes closed, and his body heaving in deep sleep. I was at a loss as to what to do now.

Dr. Danvers, to her credit, had tried her best, but aside from leaving me some bandages before she left, she was of no use.

Chase hadn't been much help either.

Later, I received the request for payment. Dr. Danvers charged me the mandatory three hundred bucks (after discount, by the way) for her visit, which put a huge dent in my already frail bank account. Now I was broke with a still-injured . . . wolf.

Right. This was a wolf. Or rather, perhaps, an honest-to-God mythological creature right before my eyes. It made sense now that it had a bronze coat, which wasn't very wolflike.

Exhaustion seeped deep into my bones from the last twenty-four hours. I wanted to go to bed, since I hadn't really slept since finding the wolf, but I was reluctant to leave the creature alone in my living room.

Especially since I had come to the conclusion he wasn't just an animal.

So I took my glasses off, grabbed my patched quilt, and huddled down on the couch. Since I was a light sleeper, I would wake up if he made any sound.

But despite how tired I was, sleep refused to come. My head was too full of thoughts and worries. What should my next steps be? Even though I was wary of the wolf, I didn't want to leave him to rot on the street. I had vowed to take care of him, and I didn't go back on my word. But then again, he was still injured, even after all the fuss earlier. Yet given how he reacted to both Dr. Danvers and Chase, it didn't seem feasible to let him near another stranger . . .

Though wasn't I a stranger as well?

Why did he find *my* presence acceptable? Because I saved him? But was that enough to gain his trust?

My thoughts ran in circles late into the night, when the darkness finally came, and I fell into a restless slumber.

I woke up with soft fur in my face.

At first, I thought I might still be dreaming. Then I realized I wasn't hugging a huge stuffed animal but rather a wolf who was cuddling with me, his head leaning against my head.

Apparently, at some point during the night, I'd rolled off the couch to the floor along with my quilt, and the wolf saw it as an invitation for a cuddle session.

It should've terrified the bejesus out of me that a fucking *wolf*, potentially a supernatural wolf, was cuddling with me, and it definitely would have—had it been any other wolf.

But this wolf . . . I couldn't explain it, but he felt *safe*. Even when he was growling and baring his teeth at Dr. Danvers and Chase, I wasn't scared he would hurt me but rather scared he would hurt *them*.

And it wasn't just because he was injured and incapable of hurting me, I realized now as I nuzzled closer to his fur. Obviously, he was feeling better if he got off the sofa to cuddle with me on the floor, meaning he could've easily torn my head off if he'd so wanted. No, it was something else, without logic. Something more intrinsic. Like a gut feeling, but deeper, more definite.

I simply *knew* he wouldn't harm me.

That understanding made me feel a sudden burst of affection toward the creature. Whether he was an actual wolf, a werewolf, or something else, *more*, I liked him. I liked him so much, in fact, that in my mind, he was worth every dollar I spent on the vet visit—and for someone as stingy as I was, that meant something.

I let him go a little to raise my head and look at his sharp, wolfish face. As if feeling my gaze, he opened his own beautifully brilliant eyes and tilted his head down, staring back at me. There was something in his expression, a glint of emotion. I was sure of it.

Perhaps he liked me too.

My heart skipped a beat at the thought. When was the last time I thought someone—or in this case, some*thing*—actually *liked* me?

A very long time ago, a little, sad voice replied.

A sudden buzzing noise made me jolt and the wolf tense. But both of us relaxed when I realized it was my phone ringing, still on the couch. Reluctantly, I caressed the wolf's fur and whispered, "I have to get it," before I pulled away from his fuzzy heat and stood up.

When I grabbed my phone and saw who the caller was, however, any warmth I had felt fled my body in a cold rush. Taking a deep breath, I glanced at the wolf, who was staring at me with unblinking eyes, and looked away, answering the call with a soft "Hey, Mom."

"Drew," my mother's voice whispered in my ear, ever timid. "It's . . . good to hear your voice."

The hesitance in her voice was not lost on me. "Yeah," I said, feeling as though a bone had gotten lodged in my throat. Grimacing, I walked to the kitchen, too agitated to sit down. "How are you and Dad?" I asked as I brewed myself a cup of coffee.

"We are all right," she said quietly. "Preparing for . . . the charity fair."

I would've laughed if I didn't have the ominous feeling this call was going to take a turn for the worse. "That's nice," I said curtly, not knowing what else to say.

Silence stretched over the line. Much like me, Mom didn't know what to say either.

But I couldn't take it any longer, so I cleared my voice and asked, "Did something happen?" Because for what other reason would she call me?

I heard her intake of breath before she replied. "Do you remember my friend Karen?"

Of course I remembered Karen. She and Mom had been friends since before I was born. They'd tried to make me and Karen's daughter, Emilia, who was one year older, become friends. Unfortunately for them—but fortunately for me—they failed.

"Yes, Mom," I said, irritated now. "Why would you think I'd forget Karen?" Did she really think so badly of me?

That was a stupid question. Yes, she did.

"No, that's not . . ." Mom sighed, then perked up. "Anyway, Karen's husband, Jerome, is looking for a content w-writer . . ."

Her hopeful voice trailed off, and I could see her face in my mind. Big brown eyes that I'd inherited sparkling with wishful thinking, clapping her hands together as though in a prayer.

Anger bubbled inside me, my hands fisting over the kitchen counter. "I have a job," I said.

"So?" She sounded genuinely confused, and for her, it *was* confusing—writing for an obscure magazine wasn't a job befitting a Colter.

"Mom," I gritted out, my voice rising. "Despite what you and Dad think, *The Hallowing Hour* is a *legit* magazine, and I write about *real* things."

"Drew." Her voice turned irritated, and I could practically hear her rolling her eyes. "Just consider the possibilities—"

"I'm not considering anything," I snapped, "so don't call me about this shit ever again!"

I hung up and would've thrown the phone against the wall if it didn't ring again. Knowing that ignoring the problem wouldn't make it disappear, I answered with a snippy "What?"

"You will consider the job offer this time." Dad's voice came through, low and livid. "It's not up for negotiation."

His tone of voice made me snarl, "If you think you have a say in my life, Dad, then you're sorely mistaken."

Dad did not like hearing that, because he resorted to his favorite method of dealing with me: yelling. "*Everyone thinks you're a nutcase!*" he practically screamed at me. "*You know what it's like reading your deranged column in that sham of a magazine, knowing all of our family and friends laugh about you—about us—behind our backs, and even in our face?!*"

I couldn't help it; I barked out a humorless laugh. "I thought we were over it by now, but it seems you can't let it go," I said, feeling bitter. "Let me make some things clear: The magazine is not a sham, and my column is not *deranged*. I have a platform to share the truth about this world, and that's exactly what I'm doing!"

"This is what I'm talking about!" Dad sniped. "There is no 'truth' about this world, Drew! It's all in your head, and you refuse to snap out of it!"

My body started shaking with fury. "Oh, so I imagined the shadow monster who kidnapped Willow and Julianna, then," I spat, so angry I wanted to hit something.

"And as we tell you over and over again, your trauma made you see something that's not there, Drew!" Dad yelled. "So snap out of your stupid delusions and start working as a legit writer at a legit company!"

We both knew this wasn't what it really was about. My parents only cared about their reputation in high society. I was like a thorn in their side. They were always asked about me, and they were ashamed to tell everyone what I was up to.

Once upon a time, it used to hurt, thinking that my parents thought me a kook and were embarrassed by me. Now, I just wanted them to stop caring altogether.

Seething, I said, "If you ever offer me a job again, I'm going to block your numbers, so don't call me unless you have something to say worth listening to."

And like with Mom, I hung up, only this time, I was far angrier, and sadder too.

Because this fight with my parents repeated itself every few months. And it seemed they still weren't willing to respect my decisions or my occupation. They never actually said it, but they, too, believed I was a madwoman for my beliefs—or rather, my convictions.

And they poisoned Thayer, my older brother, against me too.

A wet nose nudged at my hand, and I whipped my head to the side. The wolf stood next to me, so big he reached the counter, and butted at my fisted hand, his bright eyes somewhat soft. Sympathetic, even.

Him trying to cheer me up made my lips wobble and tears rise to my eyes. I reached for his head and hugged his soft, warm neck. "Thank you," I whispered, tightening my hold on him.

The wolf, of course, didn't reply. But he leaned deeper against me, as if he was hugging me back.

And while I stubbornly refused to let my tears fall, because my parents were not worth such sentiment from me, his warmth comforted me nonetheless.

CHAPTER 5
THE SHADOW MARK

Living with a wounded wolf for a pet felt surprisingly, domestically normal.

Over the last three days, the wolf and I had developed a routine. We woke up in the morning, I made myself coffee and brought him a bowl of water, then I checked on his wound, the sigil, which refused to disappear and would probably scar. But at least the wound was gradually healing, and he was no longer bleeding whenever he moved around.

That meant that while I was working on my laptop, the wolf was roaming about the apartment. It felt like such a small space for a huge, magnificent being like him, but the wolf didn't seem to be bothered by the disproportion. He sniffed every nook and cranny, and he seemed especially fond of my bedroom, where he sometimes lay down on top of the bed, even when I wasn't there, or on piles of both washed and unwashed laundry.

As for the wolf's needs . . . Well, he seemed to visit the bathroom when I wasn't looking, and so far, I didn't need to take him out for walks or anything like that. So my theory that he wasn't exactly only a wolf was strengthened. But since I didn't want to break our somewhat temporary blissful life, I didn't mention it and pretended he didn't have needs to begin with.

We also went to sleep together every night on my bed. I slept much better while snuggled up to him, and the wolf seemed to simply enjoy my presence, which made me feel ten feet tall every time I thought about it.

Thank God my landlord wasn't the type to make surprise visits, or I would've been in trouble.

If it had been up to me, I would've stayed holed up in my apartment for a few more days, but unfortunately, my refrigerator was starting to look depressingly empty, and I needed to restock. Since ordering groceries online was much more expensive than physically going to the store, I was forced to choose the latter.

So on the fourth day after I found him bleeding outside my building's back door, I told the wolf, "I'm going out for a bit. Be good, okay?"

The wolf headbutted my hand as if to say *Of course*, and the fondness I felt for him was so overwhelming, I found myself reaching for him and hugging him tightly.

"I don't want to leave," I murmured into his fur. "I want to stay here and cuddle with you all day."

And not just because he was important to me. I was hoping that if we got closer, he would finally show his true colors and tell me who, or what, he was.

He leaned his body against me as if to agree, but then he butted his snout against my side, forcing me to lean back. He gave a small lick to the palms of my hands that made me almost smile before he turned his back to me and padded to my bedroom, as if telling me to get the whole going out thing over with.

And he wanted me to believe he was merely a wolf. *Right.*

Grabbing my keys and wallet, I reluctantly left the apartment, locking the door behind me before departing.

Since it was morning, Johnny, the homeless man who liked sleeping on the front stairs, was nowhere to be found. Caveat, however, was loitering near the entrance gate as he usually did, and the smell of fresh pot hit my nose at full power.

When he saw me, Caveat smiled toothily and waved. "Yo, Drew! Where ya been?"

I waved back. "I've been busy," I replied as I came to a stop before him. "Are you good, Cavi?"

He nodded, jittery, obviously from whatever type of pot he was inhaling. "Been seeing a pack o' some dogs 'round here," he told me. "Thought ye might like it."

I frowned. Stray dogs weren't uncommon in this neighborhood, but a pack of them? "It does sound interesting," I said, feeling my investigative tendencies rising to the surface, especially since I had an alleged "dog" back home. "What do they look like? Are all of them the same breed?"

Caveat shrugged. "No 'dea," he said, wriggling his brows. "But I did good, didn' I? Ye can write 'bout some gang of shape-shifters or somethin' else as crazy as you like."

His words made me remember the conversation with my parents a few days ago, and I began walking away, turning my back to him. "I'm not crazy," I said, annoyed that Caveat, of all people, dared to call *me* crazy. "One day, you will all learn the truth, and I'll be the one who says, *Told you so.*"

"Ha!" Caveat barked from behind me. "That's what all crazy people say!"

I ignored him, like I ignored everyone else. Because I knew I was right. I *knew*.

Even if everyone else, homeless men included, begged to differ.

With three plastic bags full of groceries, I climbed the road leading back home. Thankfully, I didn't see anyone I knew on the way; I was in no mood to interact with people.

All I wanted was to be back in my apartment and nuzzle my face in the wolf's fur. Which reminded me, I needed to give him a name. I couldn't keep calling him "the wolf" all the time.

But I had a feeling that the wolf already had a name, and I simply had yet to learn it. I mean, even supernatural creatures had names, didn't they?

When I reached my apartment building, Caveat and Johnny were both loitering by the gate. I had no intention of talking to them, since I was still sullen from my earlier chat with Caveat, so I rounded the building, heading to the back door.

Once at the back, however, I realized I hadn't returned here since the night I found the wolf. The door had been cleaned, so no blood remained there, or on the asphalt. There was a little puddle of water near the bottom of the building's downspout.

I was about to completely dismiss it when the sun suddenly rose brightly over the alley, peeping from beyond the neighboring building. As if they had a life of their own, my eyes were drawn to the little water puddle, and when I realized the sun wasn't reflected in it—that nothing, in fact, was reflected in it—I froze.

Slowly, I lowered the grocery bags to the ground and took a couple of steps to stand above the puddle. It was small, in the shape of a normal water puddle, but its color was dull. Dark.

It wasn't a little puddle after all.

It was a shadow mark.

Right where the wolf had been lying a few days ago, bleeding.

Heart racing against my rib cage so loudly, I wondered if Caveat and Johnny could hear it from all the way over at the main entrance, I crouched down, studying the puddle.

Back on Sunset Boulevard, there had been too many people around for me to do anything other than take a picture of the shadow mark.

But here I was alone, with full access to one. The second one that had appeared in a matter of weeks.

That could not be a coincidence. I didn't believe in coincidences anyway. Not with the supernatural roaming free.

Adrenaline boiling under my skin, I pulled a water bottle out of the grocery bag and emptied it on the asphalt behind me, away from the mark. Then I dipped the bottle opening into the shadow mark, letting the odd, murky liquid flow inside.

I scooped up as much of the shadow mark as I could, until all that was left were a mere few drops I couldn't quite capture. Then I capped the bottle, carefully put it in the grocery bag, and rushed inside the building, heading to my apartment.

Throwing the door open, I didn't see the wolf anywhere and assumed he was in my bedroom, napping, but I didn't care at the moment.

I had actually managed to bottle a shadow mark.

Finally, *finally*, I had tangible proof of the existence of the things. And now I could try and research the liquid and find out more about it . . .

After I quickly put all the groceries away in their rightful places, I took out the bottle. The shadow mark liquid inside it had the color of a dull grayish brown. The curious part of my brain wondered what would happen if I touched it. Something told me, however, it wouldn't be wise to do that. I didn't know what the shadow mark actually inflicted, or if it inflicted anything at all. I only knew it appeared at murder crime scenes, which was ominous enough as it was.

But still, it was tempting. Perhaps just a little drop?

I pulled my dark-brown hair into a ponytail, pushed back the sleeve of my right arm, and uncapped the bottle on top of the kitchen counter. Then, slowly, and very cautiously, I pushed my index finger into the bottle, reaching for the liquid—

"*Stop!*"

The sudden growl from behind made me jump. Unfortunately, my finger was still in the bottle, and before I could stop, it caused the bottle to topple off the counter.

I watched as it fell, almost in slow motion, and was about to instinctively reach out to catch it . . . until a pair of muscular arms wrapped around me from behind, caging me and my arms and pulling me back as the bottle hit the floor and the liquid splashed out of it everywhere.

My heart was like a drumbeat in my chest. Cold sweat dripped down my face. My body was shaking, as if I was cold, despite the heat blasting against my back, where I pressed against a hard something I later realized was an extremely muscular—and bare—chest.

Once the shock dissipated, I struggled against the arms, and they immediately fell back, letting me go. Once I was free, I whirled around to see who had just dared not only to trespass into my home, but also to both lay hands on me *and* get rid of crucial evidence.

What I saw made my jaw hit the floor alongside the shadow mark and the bottle.

Because in front of me stood an actual honest-to-God Greek god. An Adonis with a halo of auburn curls and a square-jawed face with a red, faint five-o'clock shadow that made his outrageously light-blue eyes even more prominent on his absurdly gorgeous face.

But then my eyes roamed down to the bare chest sporting pecs that made my mouth dry, along with the toned, corded arms I had just felt around me. My gaze dipped even lower, though, to the trail of dusty hair leading down to a symmetrically cut V, then to his . . .

My eyes locked on the atrociously attractive man's bare member before I forced them away, down to his muscular thighs, attached to his long, lick-worthy legs.

Feeling like an absolute pervert, I blinked, stepped back, felt the counter digging into my spine, and held on to it for support because I suddenly felt weak in the knees. I raised my eyes back to the man's face. He seemed full of worry and anger, which made me think he must be a combination of Adonis and Ares, the god of war.

Instead of kicking the nudist Greek god out of my home, all I could do was blurt, "What the hell?"

The man's brilliant arctic-blue eyes caught mine and held. "Where did you find this portal?" he asked in a voice as rich as dark chocolate, with a faint accent.

I opened and closed my mouth like a fish. My brain was seriously malfunctioning. I didn't know what to say, or how to act, or . . .

He strode closer to me, and I tensed for a moment, thinking he might be attacking me because I was standing there, stupidly frozen, but then his large, warm, golden palms cupped my face as he searched my eyes. "Hey," he said quietly. "Please answer me. Where did you find a portal?"

Instead of answering that, I mumbled, "Who the fuck are you?"

He stared at me for a few long moments, before he let his hands fall from my face. "Lucien," he said, voice low. "I'm . . . Lucien."

My brain seemed to catch something my consciousness still didn't, because I found myself spluttering, "You're the wolf."

Why are you so surprised, Drew? I reprimanded myself as I stared at the man, shocked. *You already knew the wolf was of supernatural origin!*

Yet thinking something and witnessing it firsthand were two very different things.

And seemingly reading my mind, the man, Lucien, gave me half a smile that turned him from an already drop-dead-gorgeous man to an absolutely, devastatingly panty-dropping one, and said, "Yes. I'm your wolf."

CHAPTER 6
DUMBSTRUCK

Since I didn't have clothes for him, I handed the man a bathrobe so he could cover his far-too-distracting nakedness and sat him down on the couch while I faced him from the sofa.

"Lucien," I murmured now, staring at him, tasting his name, mimicking the way he said it, which wasn't *Lu-shen*, but rather *Lu-see-en*. A French name, said in a barely there French accent. "You are a werewolf."

He leaned back, putting his arm on the armrest and spreading his legs, which gave me a peek at his strong inner thighs, covered by that golden skin. "Yes," he confirmed, watching me with those brilliant eyes, similar to the wolf's but far more lethal than the animal ever could be.

"Prove it," I said now, folding my arms and feeling my cheeks heat up under his piercing scrutiny. "Change shapes in front of me."

"We call it shifting," he told me, his lips twitching, "since my kind belongs to the shape-shifter category."

My eyes widened in wonder. It wasn't like I didn't think shape-shifters existed. There were enough people who seemed to believe so, and while I had yet to find concrete proof—until now—I did believe it was true, though I refused to write about anything I couldn't confirm. And I'd already speculated he was a werewolf, so that didn't surprise me.

I just felt absolutely dumbfounded that I was actually given proof this time.

Heart beating fast, I watched as he silently rose from the couch and took off the bathrobe. My face was immediately on fire, and I looked away. "Why are you stripping?" I asked far too breathlessly for my liking.

"Because I don't want to tear the robe," he replied somewhat dryly. "Now, please look, or it would defeat the purpose of shifting."

Taking a deep breath, I returned my gaze to his breathtaking face, refusing to let my eyes roam down, and watched.

It started with his eyes. One second, they were just human eyes, then the next, they weren't anymore. They were wrong. The pupils quaked. The irises were too bright. It looked like something ancient and powerful was watching me back from inside his skull.

Then his skin started to move. Not like a twitch or shivering—more like it was *peeling*. I heard something pop, then crack, followed by a whole series of sharp, wet crunches that made my stomach clench. His back bowed, his fingers bent the wrong way, and his legs snapped forward like his bones were being rewritten in real time.

Fur shot out of him in fast bursts, spreading like wildfire over his shoulders, chest, and arms. I couldn't look away as his face, almost frozen in time, unfolded out of itself, jaw pushing forward, nose elongating, teeth piercing through gum and skin until there was nothing left of him but the beast.

It wasn't cinematic or elegant. It was downright awful. Beautiful, in a way, but absolutely brutal, like watching a man die and something else crawl out of his remains.

And when it was done, when the last sound died, the wolf that used to be him looked at me.

I didn't realize I wasn't breathing, that cold sweat covered my skin, that my whole body was shaking while somehow my spine remained stiff in terror, until the wolf padded toward me, butting his head against my hand, as if nothing had happened.

As if he wasn't human just a few moments before.

But when I glanced at the discarded robe on the couch, I knew I wasn't imagining things, and the understanding that what I'd witnessed wasn't just my theories and daydreams, but *real*, was so exhilarating, I found it hard to breathe.

After all this time of fighting a losing battle against everyone, after years of writing about supernatural phenomena and insisting I knew the truth, trying to convince not just my few readers but my family, too, that I was in the right . . . Finally, the universe had sent me a solid acknowledgment that all this wasn't for naught.

That I hadn't imagined that monster eight years ago.

That unlike what everyone else thought, I was of sound mind, and I had a werewolf before me to fucking prove it.

"Lucien," I whispered, cupping the wolf's head as I stared at him like it was the first time I was seeing him, full of wonder and ecstasy, vindication and conviction. "Oh, Lucien . . . Thank you. *Thank you.*"

His fur was warm under my hands yet coarse around the ears, softer between them, like thick velvet over muscle. His chest rose and fell in heavy, rhythmic breaths, and his arctic eyes, normally so sharp, were softened with gentleness I'd never seen there before.

I didn't move, just kept one hand curled around the side of his face, fingers buried in the fur. My pulse was hammering against my chest. I was far more hyperaware of him than before, when I didn't know for sure whether he had a human form or not. Now I knew what he looked like as a human, and while I couldn't quite take the leap connecting the Adonis with the wolf yet, I could feel the truth humming in my blood, heating me up from deep inside.

Then I felt it.

A tremor under his skin, like something winding up deep inside his chest, vibrated under my touch. The fur twitched beneath my palm before it sank, vanishing into flesh like dust pulled into a vacuum. I flinched but didn't let go.

His bones started shifting beneath the surface—grinding, stretching, reshaping. His snout began to collapse, lips pulling back as the structure of his face folded in, jaw cracking and shrinking until it wasn't a muzzle anymore.

Suddenly I was cradling a human's face. An exquisitely handsome man's face. And cupping his face like that, his skin instead of fur, felt so overwhelmingly intimate, I jerked back, my hand dropping to my side.

Lucien's piercing gaze followed my movement before he rose from his hunched pose and turned his back to me. He reached for the bathrobe on the couch, exposing his broad shoulders, the toned curves of his shoulder blades, and the hardened yet round butt cheeks I could easily imagine my nails digging into . . .

But the wound was there—still raw, still bleeding—and any sort of desire was snuffed out at the sight.

I closed my eyes and turned away, my cheeks burning. I mean, yes, he was scorchingly hot, but come *on*. I shouldn't make a spectacle out of myself, especially when he was obviously still injured.

"I'm decent now." Lucien's silky voice echoed with blatant amusement in the room, and I peeked at him, seeing that his chiseled, sun-kissed body was wrapped in the white bathrobe.

My mouth dried, but I refused to turn into a bumbling buffoon, so I cleared my throat and headed to the kitchen again, focusing my attention on the spilled shadow mark.

Before I could take another step, though, large, warm hands wrapped around my upper arms and pulled me back—hard. "Don't get too close." Lucien's voice was lower than before, the previous amusement gone, replaced by graveness that made me go still.

His palms were so hot, his touch seared through the sleeves of my shirt. It made an involuntary shudder run through my spine. But I refused to fall into *that* rabbit hole, and so I refocused my gaze on the shadow mark. "You called it a portal," I recalled in a clear voice, and tugged at my arms, trying to break free.

But Lucien did not let me go. Instead, he stepped closer until his robe-clad, hard chest aligned against my back. "Let me pick it up," he said instead of answering my obviously burning question. "Go sit in the living room and wait until I'm done. We need to talk."

His authoritative tone pissed me off, and I welcomed the anger. It was a far less dangerous emotion than everything else I'd been feeling since Lucien's human form appeared out of the blue. "Don't order me around in my own home," I said, tugging hard against his hold this time.

He froze for a moment before he finally let me go. I whipped around once I was free and planned to glare at him, but when I saw his hypnotizing eyes locked on the shadow mark, I was momentarily distracted, transfixed by the dark look on his beautiful face.

In all fairness, it had been . . . well . . . a *very* long time since I'd last had sex. This onslaught of gorgeousness without warning, out of nowhere, was far too overwhelming for my very weak, very thirsty heart.

But Adonis or not, Lucien was the key to a number of matters at hand that required my attention. I had so many questions, so many mysteries that Lucien could solve for me. It was the first time I'd *really* met someone from the supernatural community. This was a moment I'd been waiting for, for *years*.

So I swallowed my absurd, obviously one-sided attraction and folded my arms over my chest. I was about to speak when Lucien walked toward the shadow mark and paused a few inches away from the murky liquid. "Do you have a scoop?" he asked suddenly.

I did, in fact, have a scoop. I fished it out of the kitchen cabinet and handed it over to him, careful not to get close to the shadow mark. Lucien nodded in thanks, his auburn curls bouncing around his head.

I was mesmerized by the movement of his hair as he crouched down and started scooping the mark back into the bottle. I'd never seen such a deep, rich auburn hair color before. There was even a glint of gold in between strands, which gave his hair the illusion of a faint halo.

In short, his hair was beautiful. Everything about the physique of this man was beautiful. So beautiful I had to actively tear my eyes away, lest I be in danger of drowning in his unfathomable, *supernatural* gorgeousness.

Lucien was quick, and the shadow mark was fully scooped into the bottle within less than a minute. He stood and turned to me with the bottle in his hands. "I need a lighter," he informed me, brilliant blue eyes finding mine.

I swallowed hard and forced myself to ignore the heat unfurling in my gut at his intense stare. "Why?" I asked, jutting my chin out in defiance stemming from basic survival needs.

Because despite his beauty, this man was dangerous. He was a *werewolf,* for God's sake. He was supernatural, not fully human, if at all. Even though he was still wounded, he was more than capable of tearing my throat out if he so wanted.

Sure, a deep instinct tried to assure me he wouldn't hurt me. Normally, I counted on my instincts to be correct. But I'd already learned my lesson a long time ago; those instincts were absolutely useless in the face of a hot man.

And this hot man now looked at me, his gaze as searing as his touch had been, or perhaps even more so. "You don't trust me," he stated suddenly.

"Of course I don't," I replied immediately, because attraction or no, this was the truth. I did *not* trust this stranger.

He cocked his head, narrowing his eyes. "But you trusted the wolf."

I opened my mouth, ready to deny that, but paused, because memories of the past few days went through my head one after another.

From the moment I had found him in his wolf form, thinking him to be a dog, bleeding and dying outside the back door of my building, the same instinct that told me Lucien wouldn't hurt me had guided me then as well. As if my gut knew something I didn't know about the dog, or rather, *werewolf*.

It wasn't just that I trusted the wolf.

"Yes, I did," I agreed now, my heart pounding faster. "But I knew the wolf. I don't know *you*."

Lucien put the bottle on the counter and stepped toward me, pausing so close I had to tilt my head back to meet his gaze. He was so much taller than I was, at five-eight, that it now made perfect sense why his wolf form was absurdly large. "The wolf and I, we are one and the same," he informed me, eyes searching mine. "And both parts of me are forever grateful to you for saving me that night."

My eyes widened.

"With that in mind," he continued, raising his hand until his fingers reached for a strand of hair that fell over my shoulder, "at least believe me when I say that I owe you my life, and thus will never, ever cause you harm."

He tucked the hair behind my ear, his knuckles brushing against the lobe, and a shiver that had everything to do with not just his touch, but also his words, coursed its way through my body, leaving a hot, confusing flush in its wake.

CHAPTER 7
THE SORCERER'S SECRET

Anticipation made me feel restless and jittery as I watched Lucien light up an old, dusty unused candle I had put on the kitchen counter. His face was set in concentration as he lifted the shadow mark–filled bottle and, very carefully, tipped its opening over the small flame.

I'd tensed, bracing myself for whatever was to come, when I saw the oddest thing happening. The shadow mark liquid, once poured from the bottle onto the flickering flame, dissolved into thin air, leaving tiny, dark particles in its place that floated aimlessly until they disappeared.

Wonder filled me as I looked on while the liquid slowly vanished, not taking my eyes off the oddly beautiful sight until the last drop made it out to the fire.

Lucien was the first to break the silence. "This type of portal leads to the Underearth," he said quietly, and I snapped my eyes up to meet his. "I don't know what it's doing in a human neighborhood, but no human should come into contact with it."

My lips parted in surprise as I searched his gaze. A gold glimmer entered his eyes from the flame. "I don't understand," I confessed now, so many questions running through my head. "Portal? Underearth?"

Lucien blew air over the candle, and the flame disappeared. The stench of smoke filled the air in the kitchen as he made his way back to the living room and settled down on the couch. "It's time we talk."

I followed him, feeling a little unsettled. Not by him, though; for whatever reason, I felt oddly at ease with his presence, be it human or wolf. But rather by the impending talk.

Taking a seat on the sofa, my ass had barely touched the cushion when he asked, "How much do you know about my kind?"

Spine stiff, I found his gaze, which now was cool and calm, the complete opposite to what I was feeling. "*Your* kind specifically, nothing," I told him, fidgeting with the seam of my shirt. "But I have been researching the supernatural for a few years now, so I found some stuff out."

He eased onto the couch, careful not to lean on his injured back, and put one long, strong leg over the other while spreading his arms over the back of the couch. The movement caused the robe to slide loose a bit in the chest area, revealing a glimpse of hard abs dusted with hair only a few shades darker than his skin. The sight made something tug deep in my gut, and I felt my cheeks heat up. Before I drooled and panted like a starved animal, I tore my gaze away.

His voice, when he spoke, helped me focus back on the subject at hand. Especially when his words rang with an ominous tone. "First of all, where did you find the portal?"

Since I now knew he meant the shadow mark, I could at least answer that. "Right where I found you."

Chancing a look up at his face, refusing to let my eyes roam back to the tantalizing chest, I saw his face take on a dark expression. "This is bad news," he said, his arms falling to his sides as he leaned forward. "Actually, it's the worst news."

My heart pounded in sudden alarm. "What do you mean?"

Lucien didn't reply immediately. Instead, he rose to his feet and began pacing back and forth, grabbing his chin as his face set in grim, deep thought. "This type of portal appears only when the Syndicate is involved." He paused, glanced at me, and added, "The Sable Syndicate," as if I was supposed to know what that meant.

"When I mentioned I knew some stuff," I said, drawing his full gaze, "it means that I studied the supernatural world on my own."

He cocked his head, pretty curls falling to the side. "How do you mean?"

Swallowing hard, I jumped to my feet and strode to my desk. Grabbing my notebooks—the sigils I copied and named and theories I gathered from all the research I'd done—I handed them to Lucien and sat back down, watching as he carefully read through them.

Silence stretched in the room, and the more he read, the wider his eyes became. His face slacked further and further in shock with every page he flipped until, long minutes later, he finally looked back at me. "You've done all this?" he asked, stunned. "On your own?"

I nodded, ignoring the uncertainty I began to feel. He probably thought I was a joke. He might be a part of the very thing I'd been studying for years, but that warranted even more disdain. Because I was merely a human woman trying to delve into a world that wasn't hers. If I were him, I would think I was either presumptuous or stupid.

But to my surprise, Lucien said, "While all terms and definitions are entirely off, especially when it comes to Spellscripts, this is outstanding work." He studied me as if he saw me for the first time. He turned so he faced me fully, his gaze serious. "Drew," he suddenly said, and the way his lips shaped my name made heat flare up between my legs. "Why have you been doing so much research?"

My heartbeat picked up. This was a loaded question. A very loaded one. One I didn't want to answer.

So I deflected. "How do you know my name?"

Lucien frowned. "I heard Chase calling you that." He paused for less than a second before he added, "Like I heard you calling him by his name."

"Huh," I murmured in response, looking away, trying not to think back to what he'd asked.

But Lucien obviously did, because he said, "Why are you avoiding the question?"

Panic made my heart flutter, and my eyes returned to find his, which were now filled with both confusion and curiosity.

Telling him the real reason wasn't an option, so instead, I redirected the question into something less personal. "I'm a columnist for *The Hallowing Hour*," I replied quietly. "It's a magazine that studies the supernatural and reports incidences of potential paranormal activity."

He narrowed his eyes and opened his mouth to speak before he closed it and took a deep breath, seeming to have changed his mind. After a few more silent moments, he finally said, "I didn't know such a magazine existed."

That wasn't surprising. "It's not particularly famous," I told him. "It's very niche." That's to put it mildly; we had barely reached five thousand subscribers last month, and that was after the magazine had been running for ten years.

Lucien seemed to mull it over before he spoke again. "This changes things."

I had no idea what he was talking about. "Changes *what* things?"

His face grew serious, grave even, as he stared at me.

But before he could answer, a knock on the door interjected.

For a few long moments, both Lucien and I froze, staring at one another with wide eyes, like deer caught in the headlights and waiting for the danger to go away. But the knocking didn't stop, and soon we could hear Chase calling through the door, "I know you're home! Open up!"

"What should we do?" I whispered, feeling my face grow pale. In the last three days, Chase had visited a few times to check in on me and the wolf. But now the wolf was gone, and instead there was Lucien, fully fledged walking eye candy.

Lucien seemed to compose himself quickly and rose to his feet, roping the robe around himself. "Open it," he said grimly, luminous eyes on the door.

Swallowing hard, I stood up as well, wondering what he was thinking of doing. But since Chase continued knocking, I could hardly think myself, and simply went to the door and pulled it open.

Chase strode inside without even looking at me, his dark eyes fixing on Lucien. He kicked the door shut and folded his arms, his muscles bulging as he gave him a once-over. "You know the protocol" was the first thing he said.

I glanced between the two of them. Lucien didn't seem surprised. If anything, he seemed to brace himself for something. "I know," he said slowly, "but I need you to answer a few questions first."

My neighbor did not like hearing this. I could tell by how his face turned into a deep scowl. I wanted to speak just then, to ask what the hell was going on, but the words got stuck in my throat as the tension rose in the room, making it hard to breathe. My instincts told me to keep quiet.

"I'm willing to answer," Chase now said, though his tight voice and expression seemed to indicate anything but, "but first, I need to erase her memories, so I need your blood."

My heartbeat quickened as I watched Lucien's face darken in anger. "Answer me first. Why is a sorcerer living in this dump?"

His words caught me so off guard, I whipped my head toward Chase, eyes widening, as shock rippled through my body, making it hard to stand on my two feet. Chase was a sorcerer? An actual, honest-to-God supernatural being?

It made no sense!

Chase's face didn't change, but his eyes flashed. "Why is it any of your business, wolf?"

I jumped again, though now with far less shock. Because if he was a sorcerer, then it wasn't surprising he knew Lucien was a werewolf . . . but then again, I had so many questions . . .

"It might not be, but if you want to draw my blood for your creepy spells, then you have to answer." Lucien's voice cut through my whirring mind.

A short, loaded silence spread through the room as Chase stared at Lucien with barely contained fury, before, to my shock, he motioned with his hand toward me. "I'm here to keep an eye on dear Drew here."

This time, the shock was so big, I couldn't keep silent anymore. "I beg your finest pardon?" I spluttered, staring at Chase. "What the hell does that mean?"

But the one who answered wasn't Chase. "Because of the occult-focused pieces you write for your magazine," Lucien said, drawing my gaze to him. He looked at me with a grim, almost pitying gaze. "Even if your magazine isn't popular, it makes sense the American Supernatural Society keeps track of your, and your colleagues', movements."

My jaw fell down, and I turned to look at Chase. "So you're a supernatural being," I said slowly as I tried to digest the information, and the indignity I was starting to feel made my face heat up with rage. "And yet you kept mocking me, telling me I'm delusional, that the supernatural isn't real, when you *are* one?! What the fucking hell, Chase?!"

Chase did not seem apologetic whatsoever. "It is for your own safety, Drew," he said quietly now, taking a step toward me. "Knowing about our kind would bring you nothing but trouble. I tried to dissuade you. You've been poking too much into stuff that is way out of your league; you're bound to find yourself in real danger."

I closed the distance between us and pushed him with all the frustration and anger that were boiling inside me now. Or tried to push him, since he didn't budge. "You're a liar and a fraud!" I snarled at him, glaring at his infuriatingly calm face. "Didn't it ever occur to you that I was writing for that magazine in the first place to actually *draw* that danger towards me?!"

His calm disappeared, replaced by confusion. "What?"

I pushed at him again, and this time he took a step back just to humor me, though it angered me further. "Fuck you, Chase," I spat, and turned toward Lucien, who glanced between Chase and me with a narrow-eyed look and a ticking jaw.

For some reason, seeing the wolf's face, ticked off as it was, made me feel a little better, and I walked to stand next to him, grabbing his hand in mine, before I turned to Chase again, whose eyes were now on our linked hands, and hissed, "Get out of my apartment."

Chase didn't move, instead folding his arms again.

Before I could erupt again, Lucien squeezed my hand and walked toward him. "I have always hated how righteous you and the rest of those who work for the Council are," he said, face serious. "Everything you just revealed now makes my hatred grow even more."

Chase's lips curled. "Whatever you feel about me or the Council doesn't really matter, Delterre," he said coolly. "So now that I answered your question, it's time I take your blood."

Lucien smiled. It was a very sinister smile. "I have more questions, though."

Impatience entered his face as Chase said, irritated, "The time for questions is over."

The werewolf shrugged. "Then you leave me no choice."

For a moment, the two men were simply staring at one another.

Then, between one blink and the next, Lucien grabbed Chase's head and hurled him into the floor so hard, a crack appeared in the lamination.

I gasped as Lucien flattened the rest of Chase's body to the floor with his own strong muscles, restraining Chase as he tried to thrash against his hold, while smashing Chase's head against the floor over and over again until his body turned limp and blood pooled under his head.

Staring at the blood, I could barely get my thoughts together as Lucien jumped to his feet and started taking Chase's clothes off. "Pack a bag, Drew," he said, voice terse with hurry. "We need to leave. Now."

My brain did not compute his words. "Why?" I asked, lips dry, as I saw him dressing up in Chase's clothes. His build was similar, though Lucien was taller, so he stretched Chase's dark tee and jeans a little.

Lucien pulled Chase's sneakers off and put them on. "I think it's pretty self-explanatory," he said hastily, "considering he wants to wipe your memories of not just me, but probably anything you have to do with the supernatural."

My heartbeat picked up again, and I moved just then, grabbing my notebooks and bandages for emergencies, packing my laptop, and every charger I needed, in a duffel bag.

The moment I told Lucien "I'm done," he grabbed me by the waist and pulled me over his shoulder like a fireman before I could protest.

I gasped, wincing in pain as his shoulder dug into my stomach, while I saw the back of his shirt growing soaked with his own blood from the still-raw wound. "Lucien, you're bleeding! Put me down—"

"No time" was the only thing he said before we fled my apartment.

CHAPTER 8
OFF TO AN ADVENTURE

Lucien ran like the fucking wind.

With me draped over his shoulder as though I weighed nothing, and him bleeding through the shirt so much that the fabric was quickly soaked, Lucien passed through the streets of North Hollywood as though his life depended on it.

And, considering the way he'd knocked Chase unconscious, his life did seem to depend on it.

While he ran without taking a break, it took everything in me to simply breathe, what with his shoulder digging into my stomach. But I didn't dare complain, so I bit my lip hard to stifle any grunt of pain I might've uttered. Lucien needed to get us to safety.

After what felt like hours later, Lucien finally came to a stop somewhere in Glendale, which was a city in the LA area southeast of North Hollywood. I only knew it was Glendale because I could see the Museum of Neon Art from the playground he'd stopped at.

He gently slid me down to the ground, his hands on my hips until I was steady on my feet. I ignored the way his touch made me tense and instead looked up at his face. He was wearing a grim expression as he stared back.

"I have questions," I told him matter-of-factly.

"I imagined you would," he drawled back.

"But before then, I need to bandage your wound again," I said, motioning for him to sit down on the nearby bench.

Lucien's lips quirked as he followed my silent order and sat down, back to me. I settled next to him and pushed up his shirt, revealing the injury that refused to heal.

After I'd unwrapped the wound and cleaned the excesses of dead tissues and dry blood, I took out the bandages I'd packed in my duffel bag. Then, as gently as I could, I wrapped the bandage roll around his torso before tying it together so it would hold.

"Done," I said, moving back.

Lucien turned to face me, his beautiful eyes almost luminous in the night. "Why do you take so much interest in the supernatural?" he asked suddenly, repeating his question from before.

I wanted to look away and avoid the question. But after everything that happened with Chase—his threat to wipe my memories of the supernatural and the fact he was an agent for some supernatural organization assigned to keep an eye on me, if I understood everything correctly—I knew I had to tell him. "Eight years ago," I said softly, staring down at my hands, "I witnessed an event involving the supernatural. That event changed my life."

This much was true. I just couldn't bring myself to tell him that the result of that event was my two sisters being killed.

When Lucien didn't speak, I raised my gaze to meet his. He studied me with a contemplative look on his face. Flushing, I couldn't stand his silence any longer and said, "Now it's your turn to explain."

He nodded slowly, thoughtfully. "As you probably guessed, my kind—not just werewolves, but other races as well—live in secret and in hiding from the human world."

I jerked my head in affirmation.

Lucien's expression grew dark. "There are people in our society, however, who do not believe living in secret is right. Who think that we need to step into the spotlight and reveal ourselves to humans."

His words made my heart skip a beat. "Why do you even hide yourselves in the first place, then?"

Lucien smiled humorlessly. "There are many theories as to why that is," he said. "According to our history books, a few thousand years ago, we lived alongside humans peacefully. Humans had worshipped us, turned us into gods. Until the Mycenaeans rose to power."

"Are you talking about that Greek civilization from almost two thousand years BCE?" I inquired, brows arched.

He nodded. "The Mycenaeans liked us the most of all others. They recorded in writing the initial scripts detailing our escapades and powers, in what would become the Greek mythology. But the Mycenaeans had many enemies due to their rise in power and territorial disputes, and those enemies saw us as the key to the Mycenaeans' destruction."

Lucien let out a sigh. "Long story short, from being adored and worshipped, we turned into pawns in the wars between the Mycenaeans and their enemies. We were manipulated and used, brainwashed into sacrificing ourselves for the humans' sake, until our numbers dwindled and our leaders back then refused to remain pawns in wars that had nothing to do with them."

"And so they went into hiding," I summed it up, scowling. "How very human it is to take your object of worship and turn it into a weapon to be used and discarded like trash right after."

He smirked, though his eyes were bleak. "You would be surprised that humans aren't the only ones who use those kinds of tactics for their own gain. My kind had learned from the best, and perfected those strategies to a fault."

That made me feel heavy. "So why do some of you want to expose yourselves to humans again, after thousands of years of successfully hiding in plain sight?" I couldn't imagine a reason for them to want such a thing.

Lucien looked away. "Times have changed," he replied quietly.

His voice was a little off, bitter almost. I watched him, pondering his words, and going back to his conversation with Chase.

"I have always hated how righteous you and the rest of those who work for the Council are," Lucien had said.

While I didn't know what exactly the Council was, I deduced it was some sort of a ruling body for the supernatural and that Chase was working for it. And if Chase, who worked for this Council Lucien hated so much, needed to erase my memories to keep his kind a secret . . .

That, along with the fact Lucien had seemed extremely unfazed about revealing his true nature to me—even willing to do so, to some extent . . .

"You want to expose the supernatural," I concluded, eyes wide.

Lucien grinned a little, though it was tinged with bitterness. "Yeah," he said, glancing at me. "And I'm not the only one. There are many of us out there who believe it's high time we stopped hiding."

I wanted to ask him why. But before I could, he turned fully to me and said, "Can you bring me your phone? I need to make a few calls."

I dug out my phone from my bag and handed it over to him. He rose to his feet as he dialed a number and pressed the phone to his ear, turning his back to me as he headed to the playground's swings.

As he talked on the phone, far enough away so I could barely hear the rumble of his murmurs, I watched him, feeling my curiosity, and also fear, boiling under my skin.

It wasn't a lie when I told Chase I kept writing for *The Hallowing Hour* to grab the attention of the supernatural and draw them out. I wanted to find answers about what happened to my sisters all those years ago. To understand what kind of monster I had encountered. Why there was a shadow mark at that scene.

And why only I was spared.

Chase wanted to take this away from me. To erase my memories of the supernatural and turn me back into the clueless seventeen-year-old Drew. And he would've succeeded if Lucien hadn't been against it.

It was only now that everything began to sink in, after this long, hectic day of finding out the wolf I'd saved and bandaged was actually a gorgeous werewolf; that my neighbor, whom I'd considered a friend, was actually a sorcerer secret agent sent to keep an eye on me; and that I was suddenly involved in some sort of a supernatural power struggle.

A lot had happened, and I was suddenly exhausted.

After ten minutes or so, Lucien came back and handed me my phone. "Thanks," he said, grabbing my duffel bag before I could protest. "Let's head to the road. The car should be there soon."

"Car?" I asked, following him, debating whether I should tell him he didn't have to carry my bag for me, especially with his injury.

He swung the bag over his shoulder, where I'd been not long ago, and said, "Yeah, we need to go. We can't stay in the city now that I attacked a Council agent."

Startled, I snapped my gaze to him. "Me too?"

We stopped at the side of the road, and he frowned at me. "Of course you too. Unless you want to have your memories erased?" He arched a brow.

I shook my head immediately as my heart kicked into overdrive. I wanted to ask where we were going, but then I remembered my bag was heavy and pressing against his shirt-clad, recently opened wound. "I can carry my bag, you know," I said, worried he would start bleeding again.

He shot me a confused look. "I know you can."

I scowled. "I meant, give me my bag."

He cocked his head, the same way his wolf form did, as though he didn't understand what I was saying. "Your bag weighs nothing."

Folding my arms, I gritted my teeth and said, "For you, it might not feel heavy, but it's still fully packed, and it presses against your wound."

To my surprise, he suddenly grinned, a twinkle entering his eyes. "You're quite the worrywart, aren't you?"

My cheeks heated under his gaze, which did things to me I refused to acknowledge. "Your wound is refusing to heal," I insisted, ignoring my far-too-visceral reaction to him. "You can barely lean against a seat without it opening, and yet you're willingly pressing a heavy bag against it. Are you *trying* to kill yourself?"

His grin disappeared, and he looked away. "I'm fine," he said flatly.

It felt like he'd suddenly erected a wall between us, and it made my heart sink. "Lucien," I said softly, letting my arms fall and taking a step toward him, "I *am* worried. I always thought the supernatural had better healing abilities than humans, but it seems to be a lie, and your adamant refusal to admit it is going to make you bleed to death."

His face darkened, and he turned to me, opening his mouth. But before Lucien could reply, a car horn cut through the air like an annoyingly loud trumpet. Cursing internally at the interruption, I would've attempted to ignore it if Lucien hadn't turned toward the road, where a car came to a screeching stop right next to us.

And for the thousandth time today, I was absolutely dumbstruck.

I had never seen a Rolls-Royce up close before.

Out of the Rolls-Royce emerged a man. He was almost as tall as Lucien at over six feet, with the body of a swimmer—broad shoulders and a narrow waist. His hair was light brown with just as many curls as Lucien's, and his eyes were almost as blue, too, though a few shades darker and far less piercing.

He was gorgeous, and there was no way in hell the two men weren't related.

When the man saw Lucien, he smiled, and two dimples appeared in his cheeks. "*Bonsoir, cousin blessé,*" the man said in French.

Lucien smiled back, shoulders relaxing in evident relief. "*Petit gars,*" he said in French, too, and the way his voice lowered when he spoke his native tongue made me want to lick my lips like a pervert.

The two men did the handshake with half a hug men always did, and at that moment, it was hard to remember that Lucien was a werewolf. He acted like every human did, and so did the other man. As if they weren't actually mythological creatures.

The discrepancy was a little disorienting at times.

"Drew." Lucien's voice pulled me out of my thoughts, and I fought a blush as he looked at me with certain fondness, the darkness in his expression from before completely gone now. "This is my cousin, Rémi. Rémi, this is the woman who saved my life."

Well, now I had no choice but to blush profusely. "Nice to meet you," I told his cousin with a stiff nod.

Remi smiled in return. "Thank you for saving my dear cousin's life," he said with no French accent in his voice, as if he was born and raised in the US, before returning his gaze to Lucien. "The key's inside. And I printed the files you asked for."

Lucien's eyes, which had been lit up when he saw his cousin, dimmed a little now. "Thank you," he said, adjusting the duffel bag on his shoulder. "Have you told them?"

Glancing briefly at me, Remi nonetheless nodded. "Most of them seemed to believe it."

"That's good enough." Lucien sighed. "Let's just hope the ones I need will take the bait."

Remi snorted. "They probably will. But, Lucien . . ." He grew serious. "Are you sure you don't need my help?" He hesitantly glanced at me again. "I mean, taking a *human* is risky, and the ASS won't be happy once they find out . . ."

"Drew is under my care now," Lucien replied with resolution that made my chest expand a little with a sense of importance. It also made me wonder whether his cousin knew Lucien advocated the exposure of his kind to the human world. "Also," he added, "the ASS could go fuck themselves."

This didn't seem to sit well with Remi, which made my suspicion grow, but to my surprise, he let it go. "All right, then. Good luck. It was nice meeting you, Drew," he told me.

I gave him a strained smile and said, "It was nice meeting you too. And don't worry," I added, pulling my baggy shirt aside to reveal the holster attached to my jeans. "I can take care of myself."

Both Lucien and Remi seemed stunned by the sight. Lucien especially, since his eyes snapped to mine, wide with shock. "You didn't tell me you owned a gun," he said somewhat accusingly.

Hottest man alive or not, I didn't like his tone. Letting my shirt go, I folded my arms and arched a brow. "You really thought I would leave my place without my pistol?"

Remi barked out a laugh. "I like her already," he told Lucien, grabbing his shoulder and squeezing it.

"By the way," I said without heat, "I also don't like when I'm being talked about as if I'm not in the room, so don't do that ever again."

Remi laughed again, but Lucien remained quiet. In fact, his face turned inscrutable as his eyes searched mine, as if trying to figure something out.

Then he said—or rather, stated—"You don't trust me."

This was the really confusing part. The logical part of my mind knew I shouldn't trust him. In fact, I rarely trusted anyone, so trusting a man, a supernatural creature, after a few days of knowing him, mostly in his wolf form? Yeah, not happening.

And yet the other part of my brain, the emotional part, the gut feeling, told me he was safe. That he wouldn't hurt me. That I should give my trust to him, because unlike everyone else in my life, he wouldn't break it. Wouldn't throw it away. Wouldn't dismiss it as a given, and would respect it, cherish it, instead.

He'd also proven he at least cared about my wishes when he didn't leave me with Chase to get my memories erased. He knew I wouldn't stand for it, and he cared enough to take me away from that danger.

But I feared leaning on that part of me that seemed to be led by the visceral attraction I was feeling toward the man. I wasn't completely sure what his true motives were, and so I couldn't trust him.

"Not yet," I replied now. "But I do trust that you're not a bad person."

It wasn't a lie. Despite everything else, an understanding, or even a certain kind of knowledge deep in the core of my being, knew that he was a good person. A good man.

That didn't change the fact that even the best of men could abuse my trust or harm me unintentionally.

He said he wouldn't, and I believed him. It didn't mean he wasn't capable of it. Besides, I had yet to know how he was in his wolf form when he wasn't bleeding to death. What if his wolf form was dangerous?

Lucien seemed to understand what I did and didn't say, and nodded with a somewhat sad look on his face. "Right," he said quietly, before shifting his attention to Remi. "You have a way to go back?"

"Got my ride waiting a few blocks away," Remi replied and stepped back. "I hope you have a fruitful hunt, cousin, and that you'll come back home quickly."

A few moments later, he was gone, leaving me alone with Lucien and the Rolls-Royce.

Lucien now opened the back seat door and put my bag inside. He then grabbed the neat folder Remi had left him and handed it to me. "Please hold on to this," he told me.

He shut the door and was about to round the car for the driver's seat when I asked, "Do you even have your driver's license on you?"

Lucien paused, grinned, and said, "You want to drive the car, don't you?"

I flushed. *Busted.* But still—"If the police stop us and you don't have a license on you, it could hinder us."

He chuckled, amused. "I promise to let you drive it later," he said, pulling the driver's seat door open. "And to ease your mind, look in the glove box."

Frowning, I slid into the passenger seat and pulled open the glove box. There, on top of all the car files, rested a shiny new license, with an unfairly hot picture of Lucien's head—how could he look so good in a damned ID picture?!—under the name *Lucien Delterre.*

I deflated. There went my excuse. "Damn."

Lucien chuckled again. "I told you, I'll let you drive later." His amusement died down now as he pulled away from the park. "Now, it's time I tell you what's really going on."

CHAPTER 9
ON WOLVES AND FAMILY

The moment we hit the road, Lucien said, "The first thing we need to do is find who tried to kill me."

That was one way to start the conversation. "When I found you, I wondered who hurt you," I told him, frowning. I'd been so busy caring for him, I had put that thought in the back of my mind. "It also begs the question why you were outside my apartment building in the first place."

"Yeah," Lucien said in a somewhat strained voice, and I looked up. He was facing the road, one hand leaning on the gearshift and the other grabbing the wheel. There was something so sexy about men driving. "That's a long story, though, and for now, I'd rather we focus on the most pressing matters."

My curiosity wasn't curbed, but I let it go for now. "So we need to find the perpetrator of your attempted murder," I said, studying him. "But why do you need me for that?"

I didn't ask that out of malice or not wanting to help him find the culprit. It was just that helping me escape the fate of having my memories erased was one thing, but involving me in his affairs was a completely different matter.

Lucien grimaced, hand tightening on the wheel, flexing his biceps and making my thighs jerk involuntarily. "Because, if what I think is true, you might be in danger now too."

I tensed. I didn't even consider that as an option. "Do you mean because I helped you out?"

"Not only that," he said, glancing at me, and there was something remorseful on his face. "But because there is a big chance someone saw us together when we ran through the streets. That puts you in danger by far more than mere association."

"Oh," I murmured, seeing him return his gaze to the road, his jaw set in a hard line.

He opened his mouth to say something before he seemed to think twice about it and closed it, clutching the wheel and gearshift instead.

Clearing my throat, I returned to the subject at hand, if only to alleviate what I believed was his guilt—even though he had nothing to be guilty about. "And where do you suggest we start?"

"I already have a few suspects in mind," he replied, motioning with his chin toward the folder in my hands, visibly relieved that we had moved back to our most dire topic. "While I drive, can you read through the files for me?"

"Sure," I said, pulling the envelope open with a little smile. "You know, I haven't met many people like me who prefer using hard copies rather than digital files."

Lucien's chuckle made my belly flutter. "I'm old fashioned in a way, I guess," he said, and his light voice drew my gaze back to him. I couldn't help myself. The small smile on his face made my chest squeeze. "Besides, a manual paper trail is far harder to follow than digital."

I couldn't help but smile back. "That's right," I said, before I returned my attention to the files and flipped through the pages.

"So, werewolves live in packs," I said as I read through the files. They mostly consisted of pack members' profiles, logs of the comings and goings of the members from the pack territory, and handwritten notes about any suspicious activity Remi had found.

"Most supernatural species live in close-knit communities," Lucien replied. "We're not very different from humans in that aspect."

"A community," I murmured, thinking this through. "Does it work like in the wild, though? I know there's an alpha wolf that leads the pack, the omega who's the weak link, and so forth." I paused. "It works like that in pop-culture books as well."

To my surprise, his face lit up, and his lips twitched. "You know quite a lot about wolves."

I arched my brow. "I didn't realize this was niche knowledge."

"It isn't," he said, "though it was disproved long ago. In the wild, there are no alphas or omegas. Instead, there are family units."

Intrigued, I leaned toward him. "Family units?"

He nodded. "These units consist of the breeding pair and their children, mainly," he explained. "There are no battles for dominance or any of those things. One thing is true, though." He paused, glancing at me briefly before returning his stunning eyes to the road. "Wolves do mate for life."

His last words made me even more intrigued, but first things first. "So for werewolves like you, does the pack symbolize more of a family, rather than a community?"

Lucien visibly tensed. His knuckles on both hands turned white, he was clutching the wheel and gearshift so hard. I wondered what it was about my question that triggered this reaction, but while curiosity urged me to nag, I kept my mouth shut.

Eventually, he replied. "In most cases, it's a community, a safe place for werewolves to live their lives. Within that community, there are family units, of course, like with wild wolves."

He spoke as though he were reading a sentence out of a textbook, his voice was so emotionless. But I didn't pry and ask him what was wrong. I had some tact. So, I simply scribbled down what he'd said. "So you belong to a pack, then?" I asked once I was done.

He was still tense, and yet his face, which had been lined with tension, was now cleared of any and all expression. As if he'd sucked it out to keep his face carefully, unnaturally blank. "Yes," he answered plainly, his voice giving nothing away.

I frowned, wondering if I should change the subject, despite the fact I had so many more questions. As I mulled it over, I returned my gaze to the files and saw that at the top of every page, there were three small words written: *Pack of Montrévère.*

But before I could ask anything, Lucien interjected. "Let's get to the point. Will you read the profiles for me?"

Hearing the finality in his tone, I didn't argue. "All right," I said, my shoulders relaxing. I hadn't even realized his tension brought mine out.

Grabbing the first profile, I began. "Mack Page, twenty-seven years old. Works as a . . ." I squinted. "Um, a Beta?"

Lucien chuckled, and the sound made any remaining tension in the air lift. I looked up, saw the lopsided smile on his face, and did *not* feel flutters in my stomach again. "Unlike wolves in the wild," he answered my implied question, "werewolf packs have hierarchy. Starting with an Alpha, his Betas, and so forth. Mack is one of those Betas."

"Oh," I murmured, and a memory suddenly hit me out of nowhere.

Seventeen-year-old me was sitting in my parents' home in Seattle, in the backyard. There was a hammock there I was always afraid to climb into for fear of it toppling over, but my younger sister, Willow, who was fifteen at the time, had no such qualms. She was reading a book, leisurely resting in the hammock, and ignoring the giggling and yelping sounds of our youngest sister, Jules, who was twelve, playing with Thayer, our elder brother.

It was summer vacation, and I was already done with my summer homework, so I was utterly bored. I tried tanning on the beach chair, but Seattle didn't provide such good sun for that, so I gave up and went to annoy Willow.

"*What are you reading?*" I asked, trying to peek at the words on the page.

Willow jolted and closed the book with a thud. "*None of your business,*" she replied with flushed cheeks, irritation and guilt written all over her face.

Curious, I pretended to be nonchalant and shrugged. *"Gee, Wills, I was just asking. No need to get all worked up about it."*

She glared at me and was about to reopen the book, but in her moment of distraction, I stole the book from her hand and stepped back, grinning smugly.

"What the hell, Drew?!" she yelled, struggling to get off the hammock. *"Give it back!"*

It was amusing, seeing her try to get off the hammock without it throwing her down on the muddy ground, but I was more interested in her book. Its title, *The Alpha's Bride*, was especially intriguing.

Prying it open, I landed on a random page and read. It was a scene between a woman, whom I realized was abducted from the context, and the love interest who'd rescued her. The perfect damsel-in-distress situation to show the heroic fits of the male lead.

The words *werewolf* and *Alpha* jumped to my eyes, but before I could read any further, Willow finally reached me and tore the book from my hands. *"Don't ever touch my books again!"* she said angrily, her gray eyes glaring daggers at me.

"Then don't act so suspicious when I ask what you're reading," I said, sticking my tongue out at her. I might've been the older one between the two of us, but sometimes I acted far more childish than my mature sister.

"I'm not joking, Drew," she said, and I could finally see she was dead serious. *"If you touch my books one more time without permission, I will never forgive you."*

After that, I remembered I'd apologized to appease her but didn't really take her threat seriously. Because a few months later, I had stolen a book from her room, a book she refused to let me borrow—a book I needed for a book report too—and when she found out, she was true to her word.

Until the day she cried for me to help her, which I failed to do. Before we could make up, she was already gone.

A touch on my cheek made me tense as I returned to the present. I blinked, realized a warm, large hand was cupping my cheek, and turned my head to see Lucien leaning forward, his arctic-blue eyes concerned. The car had stopped moving too.

"Hey," he said softly when his gaze met mine. "Are you okay? You seemed . . ."

He let his voice trail off, but I knew what I seemed like. I probably had the same look on my face, reflecting the same feelings, as I always did when I was triggered into remembering a memory I'd tucked away for far too long.

Despair. Misery. Helplessness.

I sucked in a deep breath, my chest heavy, before I spoke. "I'm okay now."

He searched my eyes, and his thumb caressed my cheek, which made a bolt of electricity shoot down from his touch to places it had no business reaching. "All right," he said slowly, not entirely convinced, as he withdrew his hand. The moment his touch was gone, my body instinctually leaned forward, following it, missing it already, and I had to force it back so I didn't look so desperate for his warmth.

Our gazes were still locked, and something passed in his eyes, an inexplicable glint I couldn't quite decipher. But then, his eyes lowered a little, and if he wasn't a gorgeous man way out of my league, I would've thought they lingered on my lips before he turned to face the road, taking off from the shoulder where he'd stopped.

My heart, which had stopped throughout the whole interaction, too, began beating again.

CHAPTER 10
A WOLF'S PHILOSOPHY

There were ten profiles in total. The logs were also about these pack members' movements during the past two months.

Throughout the entire ride, I read everything out loud to Lucien as he kept on driving south on I-5. He hadn't said yet where we were headed, but I was far too preoccupied by the new information I procured to ask.

According to Lucien, werewolf packs operated as a mix of feudal and capitalistic systems. There was the Alpha, who was the leader of the pack and who called the shots, and the Betas, who were like his private council of advisors. The rest of the pack members held jobs that had to contribute to either the pack's finances, like taxes, or the pack members' well-being in general.

In all the profiles I read, Mack Page was the only Beta, while the others had different jobs. It piqued my curiosity, and when I finished reading everything out loud for Lucien, I said, "This is the list of suspects, right?"

"Yes," Lucien replied as he suddenly took an exit from the interstate onto a highway bound for San Diego. "All ten are suspected of trying to kill me."

I nodded. "Right. So, how come there's a Beta, who's part of the pack leadership, on the list?" I asked, frowning. "Are you on bad terms with your pack's Alpha? Which reminds me . . ." I turned to stare at him. "What *is* your job in the pack?"

Lucien's lips stretched into a thin smile. "Will you believe me if I tell you I am the Alpha?"

My frown deepened. "I mean, when we speak of a werewolf Alpha, I imagine them looking like the Rock," I said, thinking of the bald-headed wrestler, "only probably hairier." Looking at Lucien, with his otherworldly beauty, he didn't strike me as the archetype I imagined in my head.

He chuckled and pushed his auburn curls back, which looked far too sexy for such a mundane act. "So that's a no?"

"That's an *I don't know*," I corrected, shrugging while trying to distract myself from any dirty thoughts by focusing on the subject at hand. "Is Remi part of the pack?"

Lucien's face softened. "Yes, he is. Why?"

"I mean, he treated you like the cousin you are to him," I said, my heart tugging a little at the true affection I could tell he felt toward his cousin. "I would assume an Alpha requires more . . ." I bit my lip and looked away. "Respect, I guess."

"You're not wrong, Drew," Lucien said, and when I hesitantly returned my eyes to him, I saw his smile was gone, the amusement on his face replaced by grim seriousness. "An Alpha demands—or rather, *commands*—respect from his pack members. He is the absolute ruler of the pack. His word goes, and those who do not follow his lead meet an unfortunate end. It's similar to a dictatorship, in a way.

"However, not every Alpha is the same." He narrowed his eyes as he made a sharp turn at a corner. "Each Alpha leads their pack as they see fit. Some ignore the Betas completely and go on to become a *true* dictator. Others listen to the Betas and take their advice into account when making a decision. Very few, though, consider their pack as more than a company to manage or a mere power trip, and those few see their whole pack as one big family, and treat them as such."

For some reason, my heart ached at his words. Perhaps because I could hear a slight pain in his voice. "Seeing a pack as a family sounds lovely," I said quietly.

"Yes, it does," Lucien murmured. "Or rather, it *is*. But each leadership path the Alpha takes has its flaws. Even this one."

I nodded, following his trail of thoughts. "A dictator Alpha is doomed to fall one way or another because of a member who's had enough," I said, thinking about modern human history. "But the other way around, an Alpha who sees his pack as family might not be taken seriously, or could be seen as weak."

"You got the gist of it," Lucien agreed. "But you forgot one: an Alpha who takes the advice of his Betas. Can you see the flaw in this one?"

Frowning, I thought about it for a few moments but came up empty. "It actually sounds like the most solid way of leadership out of the three you presented."

"On paper, it does," he said, and his voice tightened, "but that, too, has its flaws. That kind of Alpha could unintentionally trust their Betas to the point of blindness, and the wrong Beta could take advantage of that and manipulate the Alpha in return, thus risking the pack as a whole."

He sounded bitter, I noticed, and his face was both grim and disgusted. And I had a hunch why. "You think this is the worst outcome of the three."

There was no hesitation when he said, "Yes."

When I realized he wasn't going to elaborate on his reasoning, I let that go and asked instead, "So if every leadership way has its flaws, what is the correct way to lead a pack as an Alpha?"

Lucien smiled, but it was humorless. "A perfectly balanced blend of all three."

I couldn't help but be skeptical. "Is it even possible?"

"I can only hope that if I believe it enough, it will be true," he said somewhat ominously before he suddenly tensed and said, "We're being followed."

Tense now as well, I glanced at the side mirror to try and see who was following us. But though it was nighttime, there were still a few cars on the highway, and I couldn't tell which one it was.

Lucien seemed to sense my confusion because he supplied, "The silver Jeep in the leftmost lane."

I turned to look through the driver's side window at the Jeep in question. Its windows were tinted, and even if they weren't, in the dim streetlights of the highway, it would be kind of hard to see who was inside.

"Are you sure they're following us?" I asked, trying not to sound skeptical.

"Yes, I'm sure," he said quietly. "They've been following us ever since we exited I-5. I wasn't sure, either, but I felt a brush of fluxion coming from that direction."

"Fluxion?" I asked, staring at the silver Jeep.

"Magic," Lucien said. "There are Otherborne in that car."

I wanted to ask what "Otherborne" were, but I felt like a broken record, asking him all these questions while we were apparently being followed.

So I swallowed that question and filed it for later before I asked, more to the point, "What are we going to do?"

"We'll have to take a detour," he replied, putting both his hands on the wheel. "It's time to drive this expensive fucker to its full potential."

My heart hammered in my chest when he suddenly pressed the pedal and the Rolls-Royce shot forward like a fucking bullet.

Clutching the upper handle, all I could do was stare, wide eyed and full of adrenaline, as Lucien cut through the light traffic, passing the cars like a maniac behind the wheel, all the while looking as calm as a cucumber, entirely unfazed.

Through the mirror, I could see the silver Jeep was also accelerating, trying to catch up to us, but the Rolls-Royce was much faster.

When Lucien took the exit toward San Diego, I glanced at him. "Where are we going?"

Lucien's eyes were trained ahead as he maneuvered the car expertly toward the main road. In the side mirror, I could see the silvery glint of the Jeep far behind, still racing after us. Then he said, "Hospital," and didn't elaborate.

It wasn't until we arrived at a spacious parking lot, where Lucien parked as close to the building as possible, that I let out the breath I was holding.

He threw the door open, and I followed suit, grabbing my duffel bag. I could barely see the sign on the building reading LANE MEDICAL CENTER before we entered through the automatic doors.

I expected him to go to the front desk, but to my shock, he strode hurriedly past the desk with me in tow, and I saw a couple of giggling nurses waving at him excitedly with bright blushes on their faces, as if they knew him.

"Are you a doctor or something?" I asked him in a quiet murmur.

Lucien's lips twitched, but he didn't have time to reply before a door opened at the end of the hallway, out of which a man wearing a doctor's coat emerged. He was about as tall as I was, but the authoritative air about him made him seem a few inches taller. He was in his late thirties, with dark hair, a deep set of velvet brown eyes, and olive skin. He had laughter wrinkles near his eyes that gave him an approachable and friendly look.

He smiled widely when he saw Lucien and me. "Ah, *the* Lucien Delterre," he said in a fond yet loud voice that echoed through the busy hallway, bringing almost everyone's attention to us. Especially when the man grabbed Lucien's hand in both of his like a father would his son.

Lucien didn't seem to mind, though. In fact, his face relaxed, and a genuine smile spread across his lips. "Enoch," he said softly. "It's been a while." But then he grew serious. "We've been followed here by Council agents. Can you—"

The man, Enoch, raised his hand and said, "Say no more," before he pulled out his phone and called someone. Then he said to whoever he was speaking to, without preamble, "If they ask for a redheaded man, tell them visitation time is over."

He hung up and simply smiled before he returned that dark gaze to me. "And who might you be?" he asked kindly, but before I could reply, he gasped, and his eyes widened, practically popping out of his sockets, as he whipped his head back to Lucien. "Is that—"

"Not now," Lucien immediately cut him off, an underlying warning in his voice.

Enoch clamped his mouth shut, seeming sheepish. Feeling an awkward silence coming, I decided to chime in. "I'm Drew Colter," I said now in a clear, pointed voice, drawing both men's attention. I put out my hand for him to shake. "I'm a columnist for the online magazine *The Hallowing Hour.*"

Enoch seemed shocked. "*The Hallowing Hour?*" he repeated, something akin to wonder in his tone. "The occult magazine?"

I was so surprised a man of his station knew about the obscure magazine, all I could do was stare at him and nod. Defensiveness rose inside me instinctually, urging me to tell him the magazine was legitimate, that my work was real, but I bit my tongue. Since Lucien had told him about the Council agents after us, I assumed Enoch must also be a supernatural.

A sudden touch on my back made me stiffen in surprise, cutting my trail of thoughts, and I glanced at Lucien just as he told Enoch, "Let's talk more in your office, Enoch. Too many ears out here."

Enoch agreed, and he led us down the hallway toward the room he'd emerged from earlier. All the way there, Lucien kept his hand gently pressed against my back while looking straight ahead, and I wondered why.

Especially since it made me feel a certain way I didn't like to acknowledge.

Nonetheless, I let him keep his hand there and refused to think about it any further.

CHAPTER 11
THE HOSPITAL DIRECTOR

His full name was **Dr. Enoch Lane, MD, FACC, Hospital Director**, according to the gold nameplate on his desk in the surprisingly cramped office that reminded me of my own living room, with piles of papers covering every little space of floor, cabinet, and the desk too.

It was quite surprising, really, that such a relatively young man had risen up enough in the ranks to become a hospital director.

"Want something to drink?" Enoch now said as he settled behind the desk. "My secretary, Jamie, makes one mean coffee . . ."

"It's all right," Lucien replied as we sat down on the two available chairs. "Instead, we have a few things to discuss first."

Enoch nodded. "I suspect I know what it's about."

Lucien's lips curled. "I had a feeling you do," he said darkly. "Tell me everything."

Hesitantly, Enoch glanced at me. "All right."

"She's the one who saved my life," Lucien stated, as though reading Enoch's mind, which made Enoch's brows rise. "And I believe she will be a great asset for our cause."

Enoch looked at me fully now, a furrow between his brows. "I read *The Hallowing Hour* once, a few days ago," he said. "A colleague sent me an article from there. It was about something you titled the shadow mark." He paused, smiling slightly. "It was a fascinating read, seeing things from the viewpoint of those who speculate. I also rather like the fact you named the portals shadow marks. It's an apt term."

It was the first time someone had ever complimented me in person about an article I wrote for *The Hallowing Hour*. In all the years I had written for the magazine, not once was I thrown a good word beyond my editor's "good work" comments when I submitted an article.

Embarrassingly, Enoch's words brought tears to my eyes, and I looked down, trying to hide how emotional I was over what he'd said. "Thank you."

Lucien grabbed my fisted hand and gently pried it open before pressing his palm against mine. It was a gesture of comfort, and it only made me even more choked up than before.

"You're welcome," Enoch responded now, and I took a deep breath and glanced up at him. He was smiling kindly at me.

I looked away, cleared my throat, and changed the subject. "So. Are you a werewolf as well?"

The hospital director chuckled. "No, I'm a different kind of Otherborne." He paused momentarily before he added, "A Luminar, in fact."

I was both confused and intrigued. Returning my gaze to the hospital director, while squeezing Lucien's hand, I leaned forward, my inner journalist coming out as I asked a little too eagerly, "What's an Otherborne? Is it a term for a supernatural race? What about *Luminar*?"

Enoch opened his mouth to speak, but Lucien responded instead. "I promise to explain later," he said gently, drawing my attention to him. He gave me a serious look and squeezed my hand back. "We're really short on time right now." He paused when I deflated, unable to hide my disappointment, and smiled a little. "What's really important right now is that, no, Enoch is not a werewolf."

I sighed. "Fine."

"Now back to the topic," Lucien said without further ado, his smile replaced by a grave expression. "Who came looking for me here?"

Enoch glanced at me briefly before he returned his gaze to Lucien and leaned back. "It was two days ago," he said, rummaging through the piles of papers on his desk. "I wrote down their names after they left . . ."

After a minute or so of searching, Enoch plucked out a piece of paper with a satisfied "Aha!" before he handed it over to Lucien. "Do those names ring a bell?"

For the first time since I met him, Lucien's face took on a stormy expression that made him appear more dangerous than beautiful. In fact, his entire demeanor changed as his eyes lingered on the paper; it was as if he flipped a switch, and gone was Lucien the sexy, grinning Greek god.

In his stead was a man who oozed not just danger but also something akin to brutality. I felt it so viscerally, goose bumps rose on my arms and trailed down my spine. He looked more like a wolf than a human, especially with his arctic-blue eyes shining bright with unbridled rage.

The shift in the air was so drastic, my breath caught, and I leaned back from him, releasing his hand, watching him with wide eyes as if I hadn't really seen him before.

Because apparently, beyond the beautiful exterior was a terror-instilling creature waiting to come out. And that knowledge shook me to my core, because so far, I hadn't felt anything but safe when I was with Lucien, and now I wasn't so sure anymore.

I suddenly remembered his earlier question. "*Will you believe me if I tell you I am the Alpha?*" he'd asked half jokingly. Self-deprecatingly, even.

When Lucien spoke, his voice was guttural, a growl reverberating in his chest. "I suspected, but I didn't want to believe it was him."

Enoch's eyes were sad. "I'm sorry, Lucien," he said quietly. "I know you promised never again, and yet . . ."

Lucien shook his head, raising his eyes to look at Enoch with an expression so full of bloodthirsty wrath, not a shred of his former beauty remained, replaced by the callous look of an avenging demon. It was eerie how completely his face contorted and changed in the space of a minute.

"You can say it, Enoch," Lucien now said in that inherently threatening low voice, so unlike the smooth baritone I was starting to get used to. "You can tell me I was being naive again."

Enoch flinched. "I will never say such a thing, Lucien, because I don't believe you were naive. I think . . ." He hesitated. "I think you were desperate to find someone to trust again, and you unwittingly chose wrong."

Lucien laughed, but it was a dark, scraping sound, like chalk scratching against a board. "Which means that I didn't learn my lesson, and acted like a fucking fool."

I wasn't entirely sure what they were talking about, but I had a hunch I knew which name appeared on that piece of paper. To confirm, I softly asked, "May I see?"

Lucien's head whipped toward me, and his eyes widened in sudden realization. Then, like he flipped that same switch again, his terrifying fury and agitation, the contorted, tortured, enraged look on his face, and the entire air about him . . . all of it disappeared between one blink and the next, and he was back to the Lucien from before this sudden change, the Lucien with the face blessed by the gods and the relaxed vibe.

The sudden whiplash made me feel a little lightheaded to the point I was wondering if maybe I'd imagined everything.

Lucien sucked in a deep breath and gave me a small smile that didn't reach his eyes. "Sorry about that," he said, handing me the piece of paper. "Here's our suspected culprits."

I looked down at the paper and read.

There were three names in total. Alby Dawson and Dianna Rook were the names of two pack members who worked as historians, which surprised me, but what made everything make sense was the third name.

Mack Page.

The Beta.

And suddenly, our whole conversation about Alphas and leadership types, and Lucien's little telling actions, made sense.

First, Lucien was the Alpha. Of that, I had no doubt.

Second, Mack Page, being his Beta, betrayed him by trying to kill him some way or another, and might've succeeded if I hadn't found him in time.

And third, and probably most important of all, it was not the first time Lucien had been betrayed by a Beta.

I turned to look at Lucien again, now that light had been shed on the situation. "What are we going to do?" I asked quietly, filling in the silence that had stretched thin in the office.

Lucien grimaced. "Well, we need to hunt them down." He looked at Enoch. "Rémi said he's certain they must still be in San Diego, snooping around the hospital to see whether I'll show up or not, considering my body is missing from the crime scene."

Enoch nodded. "Perhaps. It is the only hospital on the West Coast that accepts Otherborne, after all. But we have talked enough." He rose from his seat suddenly and demanded, "I can smell blood. Werewolf blood. Why didn't you tell me you're wounded?"

With a grimace, Lucien stripped. I swallowed my drool before I got up to stand next to Enoch, staring at Lucien's back.

When Enoch saw the sigil, he cursed. "I don't recognize this Spellscript," he said, touching the sigil—or rather, Spellscript, apparently—with the tips of his gloved fingers, causing Lucien to tense. "There are very few Spellscripts I cannot recognize, Lucien. Do you know what that means?"

"Yes." Lucien's voice was strained. "It means it's really, really bad."

"Yeah." Enoch let his hand fall from Lucien's back. "It really is. But while I can't identify the Spellscript, I can still treat the rest of your wound. Did you treat it before?" he asked me.

I nodded. "I didn't really know what to do," I told him frankly. "I just bandaged it over and over again while Lucien was in his wolf form until it stopped bleeding."

This information made Enoch's eyes narrow. "First things first, how long has he been bleeding?"

"Four days," I replied at once. "Every time I thought the wound had finally stabilized, it started bleeding again."

The hospital director's hands curled into fists, and his lips thinned as he snapped his head toward Lucien, who turned around to look at us. "Why did you remain in your wolf form instead of shifting?" he demanded. "You know better than anyone that werewolves heal faster and better in your human form!"

Lucien's lips curled down, his eyes filling with that same rage from before. "I was unable to shift until earlier today."

Guilt crawled inside me, and I found myself blurting, "I'm sorry. I tried to do my best. I even called a vet since I didn't know for sure what Lucien was and thought initially he was a stray dog, and maybe I made things worse . . ."

"It's not your fault," Lucien said resolutely, his eyes finding mine. "You did your best. If anything, I'm the one who needs to apologize for all the inconvenience I caused you. Both with the vet, and in general."

I shook my head, still feeling guilty nonetheless. "You were hurt and vulnerable. None of it is your fault."

Enoch turned to look at me now, drawing my gaze to his. "It really is not your fault at all, Miss Colter," he said, face still angry, as he motioned toward the wound. "This Spellscript must've done this, since normally, werewolves can shift between human and wolf form at will, no matter their condition, and they also heal much faster than most Otherborne. If it weren't for this Spellscript, Lucien here would've healed in less than a day."

Lucien nodded. "If it weren't for the Spellscript, I wouldn't have been mortally wounded like that in the first place."

Enoch let out a deep breath. "I'm going to have to patch up some of the tissue that didn't heal well," he announced, and out of the piles of papers he pulled a briefcase. It was a far better first aid kit than the one I had in my place, since it had antiseptics, needles, and whatnot.

Lucien didn't say a word, didn't even flinch or move one muscle of his face, while Enoch patched him up. He'd done it without anesthesia, but Lucien acted as if his flesh weren't being sewn together.

When the doctor was done, he gave Lucien a clean white shirt and disposed of the blood-soaked tee Lucien stole from Chase. Once he was completely dressed, Lucien looked at the doctor and said, "It's time I face the culprits."

Enoch didn't seem happy to hear that. "You should rest for at least a couple of hours, Lucien—"

"There is no time," Lucien cut him off, folding his arms. "Not with the agents determined to catch Drew and me. They'll probably receive a police waiver to enter the hospital sooner rather than later."

This didn't seem to sit well with the doctor either. "I'll take care of the agents," he said resolutely. "They know better than anyone that the hospital is a neutral zone. You can rest—"

"Enoch." Lucien put his hand on the doctor's shoulder, interjecting, much to Enoch's evident frustration. "Rest comes after retribution."

The hospital director seemed extremely tired all of a sudden, as his shoulders slumped with obvious defeat. "I'll talk to the Imperative, ask for their help to keep the agents at bay." He paused and caught Lucien's gaze with a grim one of his own. "Keep me updated, Lucien. I need to know you're safe."

"Will do," Lucien promised.

I gave Enoch a nod of my own, curbing my curiosity as to what the Imperative was, and said, "It was nice meeting you."

Enoch's smile returned as he responded, "The same goes for you. Take care of him, yeah?"

Lucien sighed. "You're aware I'm six foot four of pure muscle, right?" he drawled, shooting a mock-annoyed look at Enoch.

The hospital director arched a brow. "And we all saw how that worked out for you," he said quietly, motioning at Lucien's back.

I was half afraid the mood would sour again at the joke, but Lucien surprised me again when he chuckled. "Touché, old man, touché," he said, his French accent slipping heavily on *touché*, and causing me slight confusion, since Enoch was far from an old man.

In any case, there was no more time for ruminations, and soon after, we left the hospital, and the real hunt finally began.

CHAPTER 12
THE PRICE OF BETRAYAL

Once upon a time, when I was really young, my father used to watch the Discovery Channel every Sunday. Even back then, when we were on good terms, he wasn't the warm type, more absent than present, and being a small girl, all I wanted was to get his attention in some way.

So even though I was bored out of my mind, I watched shows about nature with him.

Many times during those shows, when a leopard, for instance, was on the hunt, it lay in wait in the grand savanna a couple of miles away, watching its prey—usually a zebra, for some reason—like a hawk as it waited for the right moment.

In these shows, the narrator always said predators can be very patient when it comes to hunting their prey. A stakeout like this could sometimes take hours, and sometimes less than ten minutes. It depended on the prey's movement, whether it was alone or with a herd, and even unforeseen natural elements.

I hardly ever listened to the narrator when they said those things, though, because the edit made it seem like only three minutes or so passed before the predator jumped into action.

Now, as I sat alone in a café near the hospital, I finally felt the clock ticking, and it was excruciating, since I could not let my guard down even for a moment and had to stay tense and alert for any possible openings. Staying in that kind of state was absolutely exhausting.

After we left the hospital, Lucien had explained his plan very briefly. "We have to wait for the right timing," he had informed me as he led me to the café. "That's a good vantage point to watch over the hospital entrance area. Be sharp, and tell me if you notice two tall men and one woman arriving together."

"Aren't you coming with me?" I'd asked, perplexed.

He'd shaken his head. "No, I'll be someplace else. But here, take this." He handed me an old, heavy Nokia that made me frown in confusion. "It's a burner phone, very hard to trace. Text me the moment you see them. I'll be around here."

He was gone soon after, leaving me in the café all by myself.

I felt awkward, sitting alone in a café full of friend groups and families, especially without anything to do. If I wanted to be fully on guard, I had to be focused.

What I did bring with me was each traitor's profile, since it included their headshot as well.

Readjusting my glasses over my nose, I scanned the parking lot outside and the hospital entrance on the other side of the road, feeling excited and agitated despite my exhaustion. It was four o'clock in the morning now, still utterly dark, and it was hard to see anything in the dim streetlights. I squinted my eyes, too, as if it would help.

Still tense and alert, I nonetheless took breaks to commit the three images to memory. The two historians, Alby and Dianna, looked as average as any other person, both with dark hair and eyes, Dianna's hair longer and pulled into a tight bun. They could pass as everyone's next-door neighbors in a nice suburban neighborhood.

Mack Page, the Beta, on the other hand, looked like what I imagined a werewolf would look like.

He had a bodybuilder physique, thick neck, and hair to his waist. In the image, his face was almost deadly, contorted in that same chilling way Lucien's face had been back in Enoch's office. He still looked human, but everything about his expression seemed inhuman. As though the wolf inside him was brought to the surface in all ways but his true form.

I wondered why Mack Page wanted his headshot to have this expression. It made him seem like an absolute vile menace, which he apparently was, considering the fact he tried to kill Lucien. But I thought he wanted Lucien fooled, for Lucien to trust him? That face screamed anything but trustworthy.

Or perhaps that's how I saw it. Maybe there was a different reason for this that I, a mere human, didn't know about. I wrote down a reminder in my pocket pad to ask Lucien later.

Sipping my strong Americano, I returned my gaze to the outside and almost spilled the drink all over my clothes. Because three people had just rounded the corner of the street and approached the hospital. Two men and a woman, one of those men long haired.

I took out the burner phone and immediately texted Lucien. His response was Stay put.

I frowned. Why? I texted back.

Because it's dangerous and I can take care of them myself was his reply.

Yes, I knew it was going to be dangerous. It was kind of obvious, considering Lucien was going after the trio who attempted to murder him, and if there was one thing I knew without a shadow of a doubt, it was that anything related to the supernatural—people, locations, objects, and incidents—was far more dangerous than anything humankind could possibly come up with.

But Lucien said that those who were after him might be after me too. So it wasn't just *his* fight.

And if that wasn't reason enough for me to participate, my gut was telling me that getting involved with Lucien in the first place might finally lead me to the answers I'd been looking for, for eight long, lonely years.

So, no, I wasn't going to sit back while Lucien confronted the traitors who stabbed him—literally—in the back. My own life was at stake here too. I was in this for the long haul, and that meant getting my hands dirty if need be.

Don't worry, I texted Lucien now, slapping some cash over the bill the waiter had just served me. *I won't get in your way.*

I put the phone in the back pocket of my jeans and exited the café, full of determination, excitement, and, yes, some fear—but all it did was make me feel the most alive I had felt in a very long time.

Mack, Alby, and Dianna were inside the hospital, talking to the front desk. I could see that through the glass doors, from where I hid behind a nearby car. I had no idea where Lucien was, but I assumed he was somewhere around here.

He didn't text me back after I shot him that message, and I took it as a green light to do what I could to help.

I watched as the three werewolves left the hospital, their faces grim. Mack's face, unlike the other two's, didn't resemble his picture at all; his expression was far more laid back, even friendly and kind, which was at odds with his tank of a body and long, unruly hair.

With light washing over him, though, I could see his dark eyes. And nothing about those eyes was either friendly or kind.

A chill crept down my spine as my gut twisted. This was one of the werewolves who went after Lucien. Who tried to kill him and were now trying to figure out if he was dead or not.

That made me wonder about a few things that didn't line up, though. First of all, how did Mack and the others attack Lucien in the first place? I mean, Lucien was an Alpha werewolf. He was supposed to be stronger than a Beta. And why hadn't they made sure they finished the job before they left Lucien to die? If I were in their position—which made me sick to even consider—I would've made sure my target was dead. This was too sloppy to make sense. Why was Lucien left there, then, with that Spellscript on his back? Was it so he would die slowly, painfully?

But *why*?

The three werewolves' murmurs as they spoke to one another grew louder, snapping my attention back to them, when, to my horror, they walked close to where I hid. I pulled back from my peeping position and clamped my hands over my mouth, trying to muffle any noise I might make as I listened to their approach—and their chat.

"It's getting ridiculous, Mack," one of the men, apparently Alby, said in a whiny voice. "I'm telling you, there's no way he could've survived that. The Syndicate said that their weapon's death rates were ninety-nine point nine percent—"

A low growl made the tiny hairs on my arms stand on end, and Alby shut up. "Then tell me where his body is if you know better," another man's voice snapped.

What followed was the sound of a doggish whimper.

To my dismay, Dianna's voice, when it came, was far too close, to the point where I thought they must've been on the other side of the car, near the driver's seat. "We can go visit the Underearth again," she suggested placatingly. "Ask to see the owner of the Mathenio, whatever that is, and demand answers."

Someone pulled the driver's seat door open so hard, the entire car shook against my back. The back door was opened, too, as Mack's irritated voice said, "Alby, contact Zairos and arrange for an emergency portal."

I heard a single person's footsteps heading in my direction as one of the trio was rounding the car to get into the passenger seat. *Of course the one car I chose to hide behind would be theirs,* I couldn't help but think in annoyance as tension and fear rose within me.

There wasn't enough time to flee, and besides, I was neither fast enough nor quiet enough. So, my only option was to get caught.

Thankfully, I *was* good at acting.

Quickly, I lay down on the ground in an unnatural position and pretended to be passed out cold.

A moment later, the footsteps came to a screeching stop. "Guys!" I heard Dianna call, caution in her voice. "Somebody's dead here!!"

She wasn't the smartest cookie in the basket, was she?

I heard both men getting out of the car. "Now what?" Mack snarled, and I heard two sets of footsteps rounding the car to where Dianna and I were. Then all sounds stopped and Mack cursed. "She's not dead," Mack sniped. "Don't you see her chest heaving?"

It was heaving indeed—and slowly, too, since I was currently regulating my breaths to slow down my erratic heartbeat and try to get rid of the tension that threatened to overtake my purposely relaxed body.

"Oh," Dianna said, embarrassed. "I'm sorry, she just looked so . . . serene."

"That's because she's knocked out," Alby said, and I realized the whiny tone was actually his voice and not a form of expression. "The hospital's right here, though, so maybe we can carry her inside?"

With a growl that made me almost yelp, Mack snapped, "Why should we concern ourselves with a fucking *human*?" He spat the word as if it was the most derogatory insult he could think of. "Leave her, and *let's fucking go.*"

Unfortunately for Mack, I had a different plan for the three of them; I refused to let them disappear before Lucien could make his strike and complete the hunt.

So I mumbled unintelligibly and moved slowly, stretching leisurely, as I opened my eyes. "What . . . ," I then mumbled, attempting to sit up and falling back on the ground with a grunt, my hands going to hold my head.

"Shit," Dianna murmured, and suddenly she was crouching next to me, her hand waving over my face. "Hey, you. Are you okay?"

I blinked slowly at her. "Where . . . am . . . I?" I asked, slurring my words.

She made a face but answered nonetheless. "The parking lot outside Lane Medical Center. I recommend you go inside and get checked."

"Or at least get off the road so we won't run you over," Alby added.

After a few more grunts and pretending to be incapacitated, I finally "managed" to sit up, with the kind help of Dianna and Alby, who supported me. Mack, on the other hand, remained standing, looming over me like a huge shadow, tree-trunk arms folded and face twisted into that sinister, bloodcurdling expression from his image.

Suddenly, I felt like I was the prey, and they—or rather, he—the predator.

But I refused to give in to my fight-or-flight instinct—which told me to run away, by the way—and, through the dread I was feeling, I croaked, "Please help me inside." *Anything to stall you until Lucien arrives.*

Mack didn't seem to want to, but Dianna and Alby complied, helping me up to my feet.

Unfortunately, the movement caused the contents of the back pockets of my jeans to fall out.

I couldn't help but tense just then when I saw the burner phone falling to the ground.

Shit.

Unaware of any change, Dianna picked up the burner phone and scrunched her nose. "Who uses this crap anymore in today's day and age?"

Panicked, I was about to come up with an excuse when Alby scowled. "Don't pry, Di," he admonished Dianna. "Just give her the damn phone and let's get this over with."

But before I could breathe a sigh of relief, Mack's quiet voice said suddenly, "No."

I whipped my head up to see, to my utter horror, Mack snatching the phone away from Dianna's hands. "This is not a regular phone," he said, his dark eyes filling with rage as they met mine and saw the hysteria I wasn't able to hide. "This is a burner—"

Before he could complete the sentence, however, a huge beast appeared seemingly out of thin air and, in one quick blur, latched its giant teeth onto Mack's jugular, forcing the big man to fall down on the ground with a yell.

Then Mack suddenly screamed, *"Run!"* and Alby and Dianna, who'd just been beside me, took off at a sprint without a second glance.

But I wasn't going to let them run. So I let the beast, with its pretty bronze fur and furious arctic-blue eyes, take care of Mack, trusting him to get done what he needed done.

A few thoughts raced through my head in the span of a second. First, I thanked God that the parking lot was empty of other living beings. Second, I hoped Enoch would get rid of any video evidence, since I was sure there must've been security cameras around.

And third, but most importantly, I couldn't let Alby and Dianna get away.

So for the first time in my life outside the shooting range, I took out my pistol, turned around, aimed, imagined the target dummies instead of the actual living, breathing people who were running, and pulled the trigger.

I released six shots one after the other without pause, my heart drumming in my chest with every shot that vibrated through my arm and the noise tearing my ears. My mind was reeling with a cluster of contrasting emotions—a horrible coldness, along with a rising hysteria, fear, and looming anxiety.

Only two out of the six bullets hit their targets. One hit Dianna right in the back of her knee, making her scream and fall down. The other pierced Alby's shoulder. Unfortunately, that wasn't enough to bring him down, too, and he continued to run like a man possessed.

So, with a hand that was now shaking as it held on to the pistol, I let out a few more shots that cut through the air, my body jerking at the loud noise over and over again, until finally a bullet hit his back and he crumpled to the ground, unable to keep standing and bear the pain, if his grunts and curses were anything to go by.

"What deal did you strike with the Syndicate?"

The inhuman growled words made me jump and whirl around to see Lucien, now in his human form and naked, holding down Mack entirely with a single hand pressed against his neck. The sight of him pinning the big Beta down so strongly with little to no effort made me gasp, especially since Mack was trying to thrash against his hold and failed.

And Lucien's face . . . It was the same as earlier, in the hospital. The same kind of face I saw on Mack. The sinister, twisted one that spelled trouble. That seemed like the wolf part was in charge under his sun-kissed human skin.

Mack tried to growl, but Lucien put pressure on his vocal cords, so the growl turned into merely a hiss. "Fuck you, French mutt," he managed to spit, though, in a strangled whisper.

Lucien raised his free hand, and the sight of his extended claws made me subconsciously take a step back, because those were lethal. I could see the tips glint with how sharp they were. "Last chance, Mack."

Mack's only response was to spit in Lucien's face.

And Lucien responded by disemboweling him with one savage, bloody sweep of his claws.

Mack screamed, and I felt myself almost screaming, too, because I watched as Mack's guts literally spilled out in a mass of tissue and distorted organs. I felt sick to my stomach, as if Lucien had just impaled *my* gut, and my head grew light, as if I were really going to pass out this time.

But like watching a horror movie, I couldn't look away from the gory sight. Not even when Lucien climbed off Mack, grabbed the hem of his former Beta's shirt, and wiped his bloodied claws—now a mere human hand—clean.

And despite my stunned state, I couldn't help but conclude there was no fucking way Mack was actually the one who had physically attacked Lucien. The power imbalance seemed far too great for that to even be an option.

Lucien then turned to me, and his face was no longer twisted with the wolf but no less intimidating with his anger. "What the hell were you thinking?" he asked, stepping toward me slowly.

Against my will, my legs forced me to step away from him.

He stopped, and something flashed in his eyes. He seemed . . . hurt. Grimly, he shook his head and strode past me, toward Alby and Dianna.

I didn't follow him, though, since my eyes were now latched on to Mack's face, which was staring blankly into the sky, slack with eternal serenity.

CHAPTER 13
ONE ROOM, TWO BEDS

Apparently, regular bullets weren't fatal to werewolves, so while they were in pain, Alby and Dianna wouldn't die from blood loss.

"Werewolves' blood clots faster," Lucien explained while the paramedics carried the wounded werewolves inside the hospital, ignoring the gory scene as if it was nothing to write home about. "The real scare here is from contamination, which is why they still need to be treated."

I looked on as Alby and Dianna succumbed to their fates quietly, faces pale not just from pain but also from sheer terror. They couldn't even look directly at Lucien, they were so terrified. That helped the paramedics usher them inside quickly, leaving Lucien and me alone in the parking lot only mere minutes later.

Before I could ask him anything, Enoch exited the hospital and headed toward us, glancing briefly at Mack's lifeless body, his white coat billowing behind him dramatically. "You have no idea how many favors I had to call in to sweep this whole thing under the rug," he said, glaring at Lucien. "It's also time you rest."

Lucien grinned humorlessly. "There is no time to rest, Enoch," he said quietly. "If what we think is right, time is of the essence."

Enoch folded his arms. "You need to rest," he repeated with a soft growl, eyes flashing.

The two glared at one another, and I glanced between the two of them, concerned and also burning with a need for answers, before, to my surprise, Lucien sighed and pushed his hair back. "Fine," he growled lowly. "We'll get to the hotel."

The hospital director's face lit up with triumphant satisfaction. "Good. Call me tomorrow morning."

Lucien gave him a single nod, and without goodbyes, grabbed my hand and dragged me toward the Rolls-Royce.

His touch made me stiffen. I was still trying to reconcile the monster who killed Mack without so much as breaking a sweat and the man who'd been nothing but kind to me. The disparity was so wide, I was left in utter confusion, and even fear.

Lucien must have noticed that because he immediately released me as if my skin was on fire once we arrived at the car. Wordlessly, he pulled open the passenger seat door for me.

This gentlemanly gesture only added to my overwhelming emotions, and my throat closed up as tears threatened to well in my eyes. "Thanks," I barely whispered as I slid into the car.

I expected him to close the door, but to my shock, he kept it open, grabbing the top of the car as he leaned toward me, blue eyes stormy. Yet his voice, when he spoke, was overwhelmingly gentle. "I'm not going to hurt you," he said softly, his gaze ensnaring my own in an unbreakable hold. "I will *never* hurt you. If you can't believe anything else, at least believe that you have no need to fear me on that level."

My body began shaking, not just because of his words and the real hurt I could feel emanating from him at my sudden mistrust and distance, but also because the events of the last twenty-four hours—hell, the last few days since I found him, even—were finally catching up to me, as though my mind was only now processing it all.

It was far too much for me to bear.

Yet seeing Lucien staring at me with those guarded, beautiful eyes, his body strained with tension, his gaze searching my own, I knew this, right now, wasn't about me.

Lucien had just had to kill a man who'd betrayed his trust.

He was also still injured because of that man's actions.

Yet here I was, fearing him for simply exacting his rightful revenge.

I recalled the wolf who slept with me in bed, offering me his warmth. The wolf who trusted me, despite being in his most vulnerable position. The wolf who pretended to be a mere animal as he offered me a comfort no one else had in a very long time.

Then I thought about the human shape of this wolf, the one who was now in front of me, the man I'd spent the last day with. He'd said he wasn't able to shift back to his human form until earlier today, when he did shift to stop me from touching the shadow mark.

I also thought about the man who grabbed me and ran out of my apartment, ignoring his own bleeding wound, just so I wouldn't have to have an eye kept on me and my memories erased by Chase and the Council.

It was the same man who showed remorse when he told me the people who were after him were probably now after me, too, due to his supernatural run through the streets with me draped over his shoulder.

The man who grabbed my hand back in the hospital director's office and didn't let go.

I might've only known him for four whole days, spending most of those with him in his wolf form, yet I couldn't lie to myself.

I cared about Lucien Delterre.

I didn't want to fear a man who had done nothing but be kind, and helpful, toward me.

Who cared enough to give a shit when I was in danger.

Who kept looking at me with endless gratitude for saving his life.

But I didn't know what to make of any of this.

So all I could do was whisper, "I know you won't hurt me, Lucien."

Liar, a little voice murmured in my head. *You think he will hurt you like anyone else.*

My heart beat fast as he leaned his head against my forehead, his eyelids hooding his eyes, his long, pretty lashes fanning his cheeks. "Thank you, Drew."

A guilty, painful feeling twisted my gut, but I ignored it.

We stayed like that for a few long moments, before Lucien let out a breath and gently pulled away. "I think it's time we retire for the night," he said now, and I looked up to find him watching me with eyes so brilliant, they were vivid even in the darkness of night.

"Yeah," I agreed, watching him as he stepped back and closed the door, my forehead tingling, burning, despite my heart fearing, too, to touch him again.

Once Lucien was driving deeper into San Diego, he said, "So you're good with your pistol."

Up until then, there had been a heaviness weighing on me following the events of the night, but his words, and the lightness of his tone, alleviated it almost at once. Relieved, I matched his tone and said, "I told you, I won't get in your way."

"Yeah," he drawled, and I glanced briefly at him before quickly returning my gaze to the road. "But I took it as in, you're going to stay put."

I snorted, putting one leg over the other and leaning my elbow against the door. "Yeah, staying put wasn't an option when I saw they were about to leave, and you were out of contact."

His lips curled downward. "You risked yourself unnecessarily," he countered, eyes on the road, but I could feel his whole attention fixated on me. "I was a couple of minutes away from making my move when you decided to play detective and hid behind their car. I had to readjust my entire plan."

Opening my mouth, I was about to speak, but he cut me off before I could. "I would've knocked them out, taken them somewhere far more quiet and secluded, and interrogated them to my heart's content," he explained in a still-light yet strained voice, as though he was trying to keep his composure and not lash out. "But I had to be quick before they could raise a ruckus and alert nearby humans and hospital workers, which would've put me, or rather, Enoch, in a lot of trouble. So I had to be quick and decisive, meaning I killed Mack in a rush, trying to protect both you and myself, and thus I'm now out of any and all leads."

He paused his rant and sucked in a deep breath before falling silent, focusing on the road determinedly.

Feeling a little less helpful and more guilty now, I winced. "I'm sorry," I said quietly. "I didn't know. Maybe . . ." I hesitated and braced myself. "Maybe you should share your full plans with me next time, so I won't make such mistakes again."

Lucien nodded curtly. "Agreed. And apology accepted."

We fell silent then, which made endless thoughts run through my head. I wanted to ask him about his powers. How strong he was. I also wanted to ask about the Imperative he and Enoch had mentioned, since it sounded important. I also wanted to inquire about Otherborne, Luminar, and all the other terms that had been thrown around in Enoch's office and I had yet to get the definitions of.

It also made me wonder one thing in particular. "You and Enoch want to expose the supernatural, right?" I clarified, breaking the silence.

If Lucien thought my question was oddly timed, he didn't show it. "Yes."

Thoughtfully, I continued. "Then why would it have mattered if you got caught in action back in the hospital parking lot? I mean, that would sure help with the exposure both you and Enoch want."

He glanced at me briefly, face unreadable, before, to my surprise, a small, somewhat sardonic smile stretched his lips. "Imagine seeing what you've just witnessed on the news. Imagine that being humans' first impression of the supernatural. What do you think would happen?"

I immediately saw where he was going with it and couldn't help but feel like an idiot. "That was a stupid question."

"No, it wasn't," Lucien countered, making me latch my gaze onto his profile. "If I were you, a human who isn't aware of supernatural politics and the powers in play, I might've thought the same. Alas," he added with a brief glance in my direction, "the situation is a tad bit more complicated than simply going out and announcing to the world we exist. We might want to expose our existence, but there is a way to go about it too."

Everything he said made sense. I still felt foolish, but mostly because I'd pretended to know anything about the supernatural world, while I was merely a human. An outsider. Someone who didn't belong in that world to begin with.

Not that I *wanted* to belong to that world. The image of the monstrous being who killed my sisters floated in my mind. The shadow marks appearing in murder crime scenes. The supernatural creatures preying on unsuspecting humans under the guise of mere homicide.

I glanced at Lucien now and, not for the first time, found it almost fantastical to believe he was a werewolf. He was so human, even in his wolf form, that comparing him to the mythological beast was almost laughable. But at the same time, I remembered how his face twisted and contorted into that monstrous inhuman expression. The sight of him disemboweling another person with a sharp wave of his clawed hand was also still very vivid in my mind.

The deep contrast was staggering, so much so that my fascinated fixation on the supernatural, which had been stronger than my fear, was now overtaken by a sense of terror that hadn't been there before.

It wasn't just Lucien either. I thought back to Chase. How he pretended to be my friend. How he acted as if I was crazy for writing about the supernatural, pretending he wasn't one of them. We'd been neighbors for three years now. I even still remembered the way he'd approached me first when he moved in next door. How he brought a chocolate cake he claimed to have baked as a greeting. How wary I was of him, closed off as I was from the world due to my chosen path.

But Chase hadn't given up. He came every morning with baked goods, making his way into my life, until at one point, I couldn't take it anymore and invited him in for coffee.

After that, from time to time, we drank coffee together. I even told him about myself, about my estranged relationship with my family, even the fight I had with Thayer, my older brother, a year ago. I told him about my feelings. My life. And he shared his own story, too, about his abusive family and how he'd escaped their clutches when he was seventeen.

Thinking about all of it now, it suddenly hit me that everything he'd done, all the things he'd said, the stories he'd told, must've been lies to get me to like and trust him as a friend. All so he could keep an eye on me, because I was sticking my nose into the supernatural business.

Had any of it been true?

Something wet and salty hit my lips, and I realized tears had escaped my eyes. Up until now, I hadn't had the leisure to think about it all too deeply. Yet once everything calmed down somewhat, the realization that Chase, the only person in my life I regarded as a friend, was actually manipulating me to get what he needed broke my heart.

The car suddenly came to a stop in an underground parking lot, and before I could ask where we were, a hand suddenly cupped my cheek, a thumb wiping my tears away. "Hey," Lucien said softly, gently pulling my head to face him. He searched my gaze. "What's wrong?"

His sincere worry made me cry harder. "He was my friend," I whispered, the tears falling freely. "Or at least I thought he was. A friend wouldn't want to erase your memories, memories he knows are extremely important to you, just to protect his own fucking ass."

Lucien grabbed the back of my head with his free hand and pulled me close, leaning my head against his shoulder. "You couldn't have known, Drew," he said quietly. "Secret agents who work for the supernatural global governing body, the Council, are fickle and cunning. People like him are the kind they always hire: magically powerful, heartless, emotional manipulators. Their mission is to keep the supernatural society a secret from humans. That is the only driving force behind any action they take.

"I'm so sorry you had that happen to you," he said, squeezing me tightly to him. "But please believe me when I say it wasn't your fault. You're not stupid for falling for his lies. Anyone in your shoes would have—and a lot already did, and will do too. He's the one who got you to trust him, and betrayed that very trust."

I knew he was right. Of course I did. Yet I couldn't help but mourn the loss of the one friend I had. Mourn my broken trust. Beat myself up over my gullibility.

Distracted by my own overwhelming pain, I barely even registered that his touch brought me only comfort, even though his hands, while clean now, were still covered in blood in my head.

Hotel Reveria was a five-star establishment with the largest lobby known to man. Its posh exterior and interior made me feel as if I'd stepped into a movie scene about high society.

In my faded jeans and baggy band tee, I felt like a fish out of water, but Lucien strolled inside, barefoot and shirtless, as if he owned the place, striding with a confidence and authority that made him, once again, seem like the Alpha I now knew he was.

When two female guests did a literal double take when they saw Lucien approach the front desk, I didn't blame them. The luster of him in his shirtless glory was a sight to behold. So much so I had to look anywhere but at him, lest I start drooling like the thirsty woman I was.

Now that I was all cried out, especially after him offering me his comfort, I was all too aware of him again.

The man at the front desk welcomed us with a bright smile, his eyes full of awe as he looked at Lucien, to the point he even made a little bowing movement with his head. "Good morning, Mr. Delterre," the man said.

I glanced at Lucien in confusion, wondering how the man knew him. But Lucien was focused on the man as he said, "Morning to you, too, Finn."

Finn beamed at him. "Thank you. Would you like the regular?"

Lucien gave Finn a small smile. "The regular is taken, isn't it?"

Frowning, Finn checked on the computer, and when a hot blush colored his cheeks, I felt bad for him. "Y-You're right, sir, it is," he said, clearing his throat. "But there is one of the largest rooms available—"

"We'll take that," Lucien said, impatience in his voice. I could see the exhaustion in his eyes, on his face. It seemed he had truly reached his wits' end.

I could relate. I was just as exhausted.

Finn mumbled something as he handed him the key cards, and soon after, we were in the elevator, traveling up to the fortieth floor.

"Do you own the hotel or something?" I asked once we were alone, rubbing my tired, bloodshot, puffy eyes.

Lucien leaned against the elevator wall, watching me closely. "I'm a shareholder."

"Oh," I murmured. "Okay, then couldn't you take two rooms? One for each of us?"

He peered at me with a strange look in his eyes. "Why waste the hotel's resources when we're perfectly capable of sharing a room?"

I couldn't help the blush coloring my face. "I can think of a few reasons," I said, shifting from foot to foot in both discomfort and . . . anticipation. Which was exactly the problem. "I mean, we're still a man and a woman, and it's not like we're in a rom-com, forced to share the only available room in the hotel . . ."

I was rambling, I knew, but I couldn't help it. I felt extremely vulnerable after everything that had happened in the last twenty-four hours. I also felt about as sexy as though I had been run over by a truck. The thought of sharing a room with the hottest, sexiest man I'd ever met—yet the same man who was also a werewolf, who could disembowel another person like nothing—made me feel both self-conscious and uneasy.

When Lucien didn't respond, I chanced a look at his face and saw he'd turned his head, hiding his eyes from me. The elevator didn't have mirrors, so I couldn't really see his expression.

I tensed momentarily, then deflated. *Right, Drew,* I thought bitterly, *putting the fact he's a dangerous man aside, he's way out of your league. Have you learned nothing from Matteo?*

No, it appeared I hadn't. Punching above my station when it came to men was something I'd always done, but it had gotten worse after Matteo, ironically enough.

Any sort of heat I might've felt disappeared, and only nerves remained. Nerves about sharing a room with a half man, half beast I was attracted to and somehow inherently trusted, yet was also wary of. The mix of contradicting emotions both tired and confused me.

Silence lingered between us until we reached our floor and continued to linger as we walked through the spacious, expensive-looking hallway toward our room. Once we entered, however, and I saw that there were two double beds, I realized why Lucien had said nothing before.

"Oh" was all I said as Lucien put my duffel bag on the bed closer to the wall. "So, it's this kind of room."

Lucien shot me a wry smile. "Disappointed?"

I fought another blush, because this was getting ridiculous, and glared at him. "No, I'm just relieved I don't have to share a bed with a man I barely know."

That wasn't a complete lie, especially considering everything I was feeling toward the man. But if there *had* been only one bed . . . and Lucien was someone who could be attracted to *me* . . . in my current state, I would've jumped his bones easily.

If only to distract myself from my own emotional turmoil.

But Lucien wasn't the type to want someone like me, and it wasn't about me lacking confidence. I knew what I was worth, but I was also realistic, and this world—both human and supernatural,

I assumed—ran on beauty standards. Within those standards, I was scraping for six out of ten, while Lucien was, like, a hundred or something. The gap was far too big.

Pretty people were attracted to pretty people. That was the unofficial law. And people who looked like Lucien would never find someone like me worthy to look at. That was me being self-aware rather than anything else.

There was also the fact he was a werewolf and I was human, which might also play a part. I couldn't imagine being attracted to a human when the beautiful succubi existed.

The reality check made my shoulders slump. "Want to shower first?" I asked now, not wanting to think any more about any of this.

Unaware of my trail of thoughts, Lucien shook his head and said, "Ladies first."

Folding my arms, I arched a brow and insisted, "You're obviously far more exhausted than I am. Go shower."

Lucien turned to face me with a slow grin. "You know, as an Alpha, I don't usually take orders very well."

It was the first time he'd outright admitted to being the Alpha, yet neither of us was surprised—not me at the so-called revelation, and not him at me already figuring it out.

"That has nothing to do with this," I commented now, narrowing my eyes. "You're still injured, so go take a shower first."

He chuckled and stepped toward me, his arctic-blue eyes sparkling. "If you wanted me to do so first, why ask?"

As a five-eight woman, I wasn't used to tilting my head back when trying to keep eye contact, but Lucien drew so close, I was forced to, since I refused to look away. "I was trying to be polite."

He leaned forward, the grin still flirting with his lips. "There's no need to be polite with me," he murmured, and when his hand rose to tuck my hair behind my ear, I froze, feeling like a deer caught in the headlights. "You're not a subject under my command. You're the woman who saved my life."

His grin dissipated, replaced by an expression I couldn't read. His fingers lingered behind my ear, barely touching my skin but still causing my belly to flip-flop. "I have never met someone as selfless as you are."

My lips parted, and I blurted, "I thought you were a dog. I mean," I added hastily, "a wolf."

For some reason, that made him lean even closer until his nose was a breath away from mine. "And I still am that wolf," he said with a soft, sad smile. "The same wolf you slept next to for the last three days." He paused, his gaze suddenly inexplicable. "*Your* wolf."

I tried to look away, but his hand left my ear and grabbed my chin, bringing my face up so I was forced yet again to look into his beautiful eyes. "I promised I wouldn't harm you," he said, repeating the words, the promises from earlier. Yet this time, something about his voice was so hauntingly sad, I realized he was looking at me with grief that, I was sure, had nothing to do with me. "I intend to keep that promise. So will you let me in?"

An emotion I couldn't name expanded through my chest, almost bringing tears to my eyes, again, as I watched him watching me with eyes full of grave sincerity. "Earlier tonight, I saw what you're capable of doing," I whispered, trying to put into words what I really felt. "If you want, you can simply wrap your hand around my neck and tear my head off. You have the power to do that."

His face grew dark. "Yes, I do have this power," he agreed, "but I won't use it on you. I will *never* use it on you."

That emotion in my chest made my throat clog. His voice had an edge of desperation that hadn't been there before. His eyes, too, stared at me as if this was a crucial moment. As if whatever I said would decide our relationship going forward.

It was a turning point, I realized, and I had to choose which way I wanted to go.

I could keep on seeing him as that beast who killed another man with a flick of his hand.

Or I could see him as the man he appeared to be now, and had been for the last almost twenty-four hours. A man who was kind to me, protected me from the shadow mark and Chase, but also held deep resentment and dark hunger for retribution against those who wronged him, and who might be a threat to me too. A man who taught me things about his world with patience and dedication, as though he enjoyed sharing his knowledge.

This man was also the injured dog, *wolf*, I had found. The wolf that somehow trusted me enough to take care of him, even though he probably saw me as a foolish human woman who was in way over her head.

I might've only known him for a short amount of time, but I felt as if I'd seen so many sides to him, so many facets, most people don't get to see with their friends and partners in a whole lifetime.

Perhaps it was time I let go of this fear.

But what if he hurts you? asked the wounded part of me that had been betrayed by far too many people, and most recently by a man I thought was a friend. *What if he leaves you like everyone else?*

I wasn't a clairvoyant. I couldn't tell the future. It would have to be a leap of faith.

"How?" I asked him after a long silence, feeling as lost as he seemed desperate. "How do two people build this kind of trust?"

Lucien's face was suddenly split by a smile, all traces of desperation and grief disappearing the wider his smile got. I was truly, genuinely relieved by that and by seeing the mirthful glint entering his eyes too. "How about we get to know one another?" he suggested in a lighter voice, leaning back and letting his hand fall from my chin. "I think that would be a good place to start."

Ignoring the sense of longing following the loss of his close proximity and touch, I simply nodded, feeling utterly drained, yet lighter, somehow. "All right."

He nodded. "Then it's settled," he said, determination entering his gaze. "I will not let you down, Drew. I promise."

My lips quirked. "You make a lot of promises," I noted.

He grinned, but a shadow of the former grief briefly flashed in his eyes. "I don't make promises I don't mean to keep."

CHAPTER 14
A SPOON FOR YOUR THOUGHTS

While I appreciated the view of Lucien emerging from the shower with a towel covering his lower half a short time later, I was far too tired to process the sight. It appeared I was just as exhausted as he was, because the moment I stepped out of my own shower, I crawled into the bed and fell asleep in less than a minute, Lucien already deep in slumber, tucked under his own blankets.

I woke up a couple of hours later, however, to the sounds of pained grunts and heavy breathing.

At first, I was disoriented, wondering where I was and what the hell I was hearing. When my eyes adjusted to the darkness and I saw the hotel room, I recalled we were in San Diego, after one hell of an eventful day, and that Lucien—the wolf who was now a werewolf who was a man before all that—was sleeping in the bed next to mine.

Or not, since the grunts grew louder, closer to yells now.

I pushed the fluffy duvet off me and stepped toward his bed. He was lying on his stomach, probably to avoid putting pressure on his wounded back, and I could see the sweat trickling down his spine where the duvet had slipped down.

"Lucien," I said, and when he still grunted and began to shudder as well, I said louder, "*Lucien!*"

But Lucien was apparently deep in sleep, in what seemed to be a panic-inducing nightmare. I recognized it for what it was, since I'd had those before too. The uncontrollable trembling and sweat, the grunts and the pain, feeling as if you were frozen, unable to move, forced to relive your worst memories.

I put my bare knee on the bed—I was sleeping in a baggy white shirt I often used as pajamas—and tapped his shoulder, feeling his skin was unnaturally hot. "Lucien, you're having a nightmare," I said in a strong, loud voice, trying to be heard over his pained cries.

It seemed my voice wasn't enough, though, so with a deep breath, I climbed fully on the bed and grabbed his hard, hot shoulders firmly, digging my nails into his skin. "Wake up, Lucien!" I yelled now, trying to shake him, but he was like an unmovable rock. "Come on, *wake up!*"

One moment, I was trying to shake him awake, and the next, in a disorienting blur, he was out of the bed and on his feet on the other side of it, staring at me with arctic-blue eyes that seemed to glow in the darkness of the room, his chest heaving rapidly, his dark sweatpants sticking to his sweaty skin. His chest, in full sight, was perspiring as well.

I simply watched as he slowly registered what was happening and started regulating his breathing. He took a few deep breaths, wiping his sweaty forehead, and pushed his auburn curls back. After a few silent minutes, he finally breathed out a barely audible "*Fuck.*"

Seeing that he was better now, I asked, "Are you okay?"

He looked at me with a bewildered gaze and nodded. "Yes," he said, voice rough from his grunts and yells. "Thank you for waking me up."

"No worries," I replied, frowning. "You should go take another shower before you return to bed. It'll help you calm down."

He nodded again, and without another glance, he walked to the bathroom and closed the door. I heard the shower start running, and I returned to my bed, heart still pounding from what had just happened.

I wondered what he'd dreamed about that made him go batshit crazy like this in his sleep. If it was a nightmare about a memory, like I assumed it was, I wondered what that memory could be.

Because ordinary sporadic nightmares normally didn't cause such a reaction. This was something different. Trauma induced, I would even say.

Pulling the duvet over me, I closed my eyes and sighed. Whatever it was, it was none of my business, and I didn't want to pry. If he wanted to share, he was more than welcome to, but I wasn't going to be the one to bring it up. Besides, I knew men were touchy about being vulnerable in front of others.

Or at least the men I knew were.

I tried to go back to sleep and give him space.

I heard the shower turning off, and a minute later, he walked out. I expected him to go back to his bed, but to my surprise he paused near mine and said quietly, in a now-clear voice, "Are you still awake?"

Tensing at the sudden question, I slowly sat up and said, "Yes."

He was standing near the end of my bed, his gaze, even in the darkness, piercing mine. "Is it okay if I sleep in your bed tonight?" he suddenly asked.

I blinked a few times, trying to process the question.

Seeing I wasn't responding, Lucien walked toward the side I was lying on and sat on my bed, much closer to me now. "When I slept next to you in my wolf form," he said quietly, "it helped the nightmares go away."

My heartbeat quickened as I remembered the night he spooned me in his wolf form. I'd had one of the best sleeps I'd ever had then, and it seemed he had liked it too.

But back then, I didn't know he was a full-blooded, gorgeous Alpha male werewolf. This changed things.

"Please," he croaked all of a sudden, his face obscured by the darkness but his eyes completely shattered. "Just tonight."

The grief I'd seen earlier had returned to those eyes. Grief and even fear, as if he was terrified of dealing with whatever he was currently going through.

And when he looked at me like that, I could still see the *wolf* that he was. The wounded wolf who'd put his trust in me, a stranger, to make him better.

So I found myself nodding, murmuring softly, "All right."

He let out a breath. "Thank you," he said just as softly and rounded the bed to climb in on the other side.

Once we were both under the duvet, I debated with myself whether I should ask or not until I finally caved and said, "Do you need me to touch you?"

I could tell he was surprised by my question without even looking at him. He was quiet for a few long seconds, during which my heartbeat escalated exponentially, until he finally said, "I appreciate it, Drew, but being close to another person is good enough."

A rush of disappointment and humiliation made me feel stupid. "A-All right, then," I mumbled, rolling so my back was to him and he wouldn't be able to see the hurt on my face.

But it seemed I couldn't really hide it because I felt him shifting closer. "Hey," he said, voice right behind me, "I didn't mean . . . I . . ." He hesitated before he took a deep breath and said, "I thought you were asking out of pity."

I shrugged, refusing to roll over. "Whatever, Lucien." *Shit, I sound too pissy.*

When I felt his arm suddenly wrapping itself around my waist, I gasped. I was about to tell him to go sleep on his side and so be it, but before I could, he slithered his other arm under my head and pressed his hard, naked chest against my back. "I'm really happy you asked," he whispered in my ear, causing involuntary shivers to run through my body. "Thank you for letting me have this tonight."

A sudden flare of panic made my heart race, and I found myself saying, "Only for tonight."

His responding chuckle reverberated from his chest to my body, filling my belly with uncontrollable flutters. "As you wish."

That night, as we lay curled against one another, I thought I wouldn't be able to sleep. I thought having a man spooning me would leave me awake until morning. But when I heard and felt his breaths evening out, it was as if I was put under a spell, because my eyes fluttered shut, and any tension I had felt left my body.

And just like when we slept together in his wolf form, it was the best sleep of my life.

Hotel Reveria's breakfast was ridiculously delicious. It was so delicious, in fact, that I was tempted to buy bento boxes and pack some for later but stopped just short of making a spectacle out of myself.

"This is so effing tasty," I told Lucien with a mouthful of hash browns.

He grinned. "I was really nitpicky about the food when the hotel was first picked. We shape-shifters are very particular when it comes to food."

Swallowing the bite, I couldn't help but smile back. "I would've thought wolves should have a wide palate." I paused as a thought occurred to me. "You promised to answer some of my questions today."

Lucien's grin widened. "And I will," he said, before his eyes glanced behind me and he frowned. "Later."

I turned around and saw two men walking into the dining room.

One was sporting a three-piece suit that made him seem slick. His dark hair was smoothed back as meticulously as his mustache and beard were trimmed. His eyes, a pair of startling ruby orbs, stared straight at us.

Next to him, wearing more casual attire in trousers and a simple tee, was Chase.

I grew stiff and watched as the two stopped next to our table and, before Lucien or I could speak, sat down right next to us.

Lucien kept on eating as though he couldn't be bothered, but I could tell he was tense. There was a tightness to his eyes, his jaw locked, and his whole body was rigid. I, too, was alert, though I didn't hide it as well as him. I shifted my chair farther from my former friend.

Chase noted that, but his face remained in its impassive expression.

"Well," the ruby-eyed stranger said, glancing leisurely between Lucien and me, his voice as crisp as his suit. "I must admit, Delterre, your hotel is quite comfortable."

"This is precisely why Dr. Lane recommended this hotel to you," Lucien said lightly, though his eyes were hard. He put down his fork and knife and leaned back. "I thought he told you I would call on you later today."

Chase leaned forward, menace oozing out of him. "After you knocked me out, you do not get a say about anything, wolf," he hissed, eyes flashing with rage. "You're lucky it's only us here and not the entire Bureau of Unregulated Movements' elite unit coming after you."

I had no idea what this bureau was, but from its title, I could safely assume this was some sort of law enforcement entity. And if it worked like the human police, with the elite unit being something like the FBI or CIA, only supernatural, that made shivers run down my spine.

Looking at Lucien, I saw him staring at Chase with a deep distaste he couldn't quite hide. "You wanted to draw my blood by force for a spell," he said, voice deep and quiet but carrying across the table clearly. "I believe that's a far worse crime than what I've allegedly committed."

Chase glowered, but the other man interrupted before he could. "This is why we're here alone, Alpha Delterre," he said, looking at Lucien with a somewhat condescending expression. "My colleague here was in the wrong for his momentary malpractice, just like you were by exposing your true nature to a *human*." He glanced at me when he said *human*, scrunching his nose a little as if it was a degrading term. "This does not excuse assaulting an ASS agent and leading us on a car chase all the way to San Diego."

I couldn't help the snort that escaped me. All three men whipped their heads toward me with confused frowns. I choked down a swell of laughter and pretended to cough. "I'm sorry," I murmured, trying not to think about the *ass agent* sitting next to me. "Please continue."

The prim man, whose name I had yet to learn, stared at me for one more moment, a look of disapproval on his face, before he returned his gaze to Lucien, who stared at me still, his eyes somewhat unfocused. "What I would like to know, Alpha Delterre," the man resumed, his high-and-mighty voice rising a notch, "is why did you go to such lengths to keep us at bay? We've been having such a good relationship for the past six months, after all . . ."

Lucien kept on staring at me, and I found myself unable to look away from him when he replied. "This has nothing to do with our working relationship, Avenor. I was merely waiting until I had the opportunity to speak to Drew here before I inevitably had to tell you."

I couldn't read Lucien's expression. Something about his tone of voice had shifted. He was even tenser than before. It was as though he was trying to contain some emotion while also, evidently, overcome by it.

What this emotion was, however, I didn't know.

Until Lucien spoke again, his voice tight, his face both angry and grim, and said, "Drew Colter is my Eteria."

CHAPTER 15
SUPERNATURAL WEAKNESS

I had no idea what the hell *Eteria* meant.

What I did know, however, was that the way he spoke that word made a chill crawl up my spine, causing an ominous, foreboding feeling to pool in my gut along with a confusing, expectant thrill.

"Eteria," I murmured, tasting the term before I made the mistake of looking at Lucien.

He was so stiff, a vein threatened to burst in his temple.

Chase and his companion—Avenor, apparently, as Lucien called him—were staring at Lucien, just as stiff as he was, before they slowly, simultaneously, turned to look at me, shock slackening their faces. Especially Chase's; he looked at me as if it were the first time he was truly seeing me.

Whatever this Eteria was, it was obviously significant.

The first one to break the stunned silence was Avenor. "I see," he said in a low rumble, pushing back his chair and rising to his feet before clearing his throat and adding in a sincerely apologetic tone, "Thank you for letting us know."

Confounded, I glanced at Chase as he rose slowly to his feet, too, seeming somewhat defeated.

"You will keep it to yourself," Lucien suddenly said, and I whipped my head toward him, seeing him shoot a warning look at the two men. It wasn't a request. It sounded like an order.

That seemed to snap Chase out of his stupor. "We're not stupid," he barked in an indignant voice, though why he reacted this way, I had no idea.

Lucien stood up and stared at Chase flatly. "Make a vow, then."

The color ran out of Chase's face before Avenor put a hand on his shoulder and stared at Lucien. "How about we do you one better?" he said, putting on a harmless, amicable smile that was so at odds with his earlier condescension, I was taken aback. "Chase and I are going to erase everything that happened in the last twenty-four hours from the systems and effectively sweep this whole ordeal under the rug. Think of it as a gesture of good faith, so you could trust us to keep this crucial information to ourselves."

Lucien folded his arms. "Make a vow," he repeated unyieldingly.

Avenor's smile quivered while Chase looked like a deer caught in the headlights. "A sorcerer's vow is a little overkill, don't you think?" Chase said quietly, attempting a friendly smile, too, though it looked more like a grimace.

Lucien's face remained determinedly resolute, and he said nothing, simply staring at the two men.

Avenor sighed. "Fine. We'll make a vow." He paused, adding under his breath, "*Goddamn Alphas.*"

"Now," Lucien added.

Both Avenor and Chase scowled.

I was still confused by the whole thing, but nonetheless, I followed along when we exited the dining hall and Lucien led us to one of the rooms in the hotel's convention center.

Once there, Lucien locked the door and turned to me. "They will need to draw your blood," he told me, scowling a little, as Chase produced a dagger seemingly out of nowhere and Avenor used an antiseptic wipe over his inner arm.

"I don't understand anything," I informed him with a scowl of my own, folding my arms. "I want to know what this is all about before I let even a drop of my blood touch Chase's dagger."

Lucien visibly stiffened, and the impassiveness in his eyes suddenly disappeared, replaced by an odd shine filled with so many layers of emotions, it made my chest tighten. "*Eteria* is a word in old Myrrenic, the dead language of the Otherborne, or as you call us, the supernatural," he said quietly, hesitantly. "In general terms, it means that your soul is bound to me."

I froze, frowning, trying to process what he was saying. What did it mean, my soul was bound to him? What did this entail?

He must've seen the questions running through my mind because he added softly, "For now, all you need to understand is that you are my greatest vulnerability, and because of that, if anyone who wishes me ill learns what you are to me, they will do everything in their power to hunt you down and kill you."

My lips parted slightly as I repeated his words in my head over and over again. But before I had any more time, Chase's voice cut our conversation short. "We're ready."

The emotions on Lucien's face disappeared as if by magic, replaced by a flat expression. "I'll explain the rest later," he told me in a quick murmur before he straightened and headed to Chase and Avenor with me following him, still confused but now genuinely scared too.

While I had yet to learn what *Eteria* meant, I at least understood why this whole making-a-vow thing was necessary.

Lucien didn't trust Avenor and Chase to keep their word after informing them of his biggest weakness out of pure necessity. So he wanted to magically zip their mouths closed on the matter.

"Before we start," Chase said, glancing at me briefly, "please show me your arms."

Lucien, Avenor, and I showed our arms.

Chase then lifted his own arm and, with one swift cut, let a few drops of his blood into a small stone bowl he'd placed on the table.

He hovered his palm over the bowl, blood still flowing out of his fresh wound, as he muttered words in a language I didn't understand.

It resulted in a soft glow surrounding the blood at the bottom of the bowl.

Grimly, Chase turned to me and said, "First, I need the blood of the subject matter."

I pressed my lips together, bracing myself, as I nodded.

To his credit, Chase made the cut so quickly, the pain didn't register until after he squeezed a few drops into the bowl. Only when I lowered my arm did I wince, feeling a little lightheaded and unsteady on my own two feet.

Lucien's free arm wrapped around my waist, causing my heart to stutter, as he nudged me to lean against his side. "I didn't take you for a wimp when it comes to blood," he murmured softly while Chase held his palm over the bowl and mumbled gibberish again. "You tended to my injury with a cool head, after all."

A thin layer of cold perspiration crawled over my skin. "When it's others' blood, I don't mind," I murmured as my vision started to turn blurry at the edges.

"Hey, sorcerer," Lucien said, loud now, "you don't need Drew anymore, right?"

Chase, who'd just finished his mumblings, turned to look at Lucien with a frown. "No, but . . ." He trailed off when he saw me. "Shit, she's pale. Lay her down on the floor and bring a chair to put her legs over."

"Yeah, that's what I thought," Lucien murmured as he placed me gently on the floor.

The next few minutes, I was fighting not to pass out, not wanting to feel more humiliated than I already did. Tending to deep, bleeding wounds was no problem. Shooting other people wasn't any trouble, apparently, either. But a little slice to my arm, and I was done.

It wasn't like I was afraid of pain or anything—at least not any more than the average person. But my blood pressure was naturally so low, the slightest injury could make me lose consciousness, as if my body couldn't handle that.

With everything that was going on, I had completely forgotten about this quirk of mine. And now I'd made a spectacle out of myself.

And after Lucien told you you're his weakness, too, a little voice whispered in my head, making me feel a pang of guilt. I wasn't weak, not by a long shot. But this current display might make Lucien lose any faith he had in me, if he even had any to begin with.

As the ritual of the vow continued, all I could do was close my eyes and focus on my breaths. Chase's quiet murmurs sounded like they were coming from far away. They were also monotonous enough that they were almost calming, in a way.

I was still trying to calm myself down when I heard more murmurs, this time from all three men, and tried to understand what they were saying. They were speaking so quietly I could only hear certain bits and pieces, like *the Society won't let it go* or *the Underearth* without actual context.

Some time later, a hand cupped my face, swiping my sweat with gentle fingers, and I opened my eyes to see Lucien crouching next to me, concern in his expression. "They're gone," he told me, searching my face. "Are you all right?"

"Yeah," I croaked and, with his help, took my legs off the chair and slowly sat up. "Is the vow done?"

Lucien nodded silently, his hand lingering on my cheek. I stared at him. His auburn tousles were a mess around his head, and his arctic-blue eyes were filled with emotion I couldn't describe. The sight of his concern did things to my body that made me force my gaze away and swallow hard in sudden nervousness.

He let me go and stood up. He offered me his hand, and I took it, climbing to my feet as well. He didn't let my hand go, though, even though I was no longer bleeding or feeling like I was about to faint. "I need to wipe your wound," he said quietly. "Can you handle that?"

Pursing my lips, I nodded. "Just be gentle."

Chase must've left some antiseptic wipes for him, because Lucien plucked one out, held my arm, and cleaned the wound.

My eyes went over to his own arm. It was still bleeding.

Suddenly alert, I said, "Lucien, your arm—"

"I know," he said with a dark tone that made me clamp my mouth shut. He finished cleaning me up and threw the wipe away. "It seems that whatever antihealing Spellscript my attacker carved on my back is not restricted to *just* my back."

"That's bad," I said, finding his gaze with my own concerned one. "We need to find a way to deactivate the Spellscript or something, if possible."

"It is possible," he confirmed, but his face was grim. "However, it can only happen if we know what it means. For that, I need to go back to the pack."

The fact he said *I* and not *we* made me stiffen. "What about Chase and Avenor?"

Lucien gave me a tired, sad smile. "The vow is bound to their life. It forbids them from telling anyone about you, and if they break the vow, they will die. I also made them vow they would let the last twenty-four hours go. That means the American Supernatural Society is no longer after us." He paused, hesitated, and said, "With you being my Eteria, they are not allowed to erase your memories anymore either."

I heard what he was saying, and I knew I should've felt relief, but I could read between the lines. His face, sad as it was, and the squeeze of his hand on mine told me what he wasn't saying. "So you're going back to your pack," I said quietly, heart fluttering in my chest like a caged hummingbird, "and I'm not coming with you."

He grimaced, stepping closer to me. "That's for the best, Drew," he said quietly, stopping an inch away, and with his free hand, he gently took hold of my chin and lifted my head up so he could lock my gaze with his. "If others find out I'm keeping a human by my side, it would be like I was showing the world that you're my Eteria. It will put a target on your back.

"I have many enemies, Drew. They won't hesitate to hurt you, since they know it's very unlikely for them to be able to hurt me."

I opened my mouth to speak, but he cut me off before I could. "It's for your own safety that you go back to your own life and forget about me," he said, and I saw a flash of something akin to desperation passing in his eyes. "I can't promise I will see you again, but you'd be safe and sound, and that's all that matters."

There were so many things I wanted to say. For starters, would I really be safe and sound if I went back to my life and continued writing for *The Hallowing Hour*? Chase had been stationed as my neighbor to keep an eye on me due to this very job, after all. So going back to how I was before I found a bleeding wolf outside my building couldn't exactly work. If it was all about keeping a low profile, that wouldn't be entirely possible, at least not on that front.

And what about me being his Eteria? I wasn't quite sure how that worked. Had he picked me as his Eteria? And if so, why did he want to get rid of me? Was he, in some way, rejecting me?

As for his enemies not wanting to hurt him since they couldn't, that was a blatant lie. He would've been dead had I not found him in time. He'd admitted himself that I saved his life. And not only that, but his own Beta betrayed him. He even had enemies within his very own pack.

But looking at Lucien now, seeing that lingering desperation, the worry, it made me swallow my words. The thought of arguing with him and making my points when he was staring at me, stripped bare, practically begging me with his own brilliant eyes to agree, was enough to do me in.

Besides, what could a mere human like me do for an Alpha werewolf like him?

Logically, there was no reason for me to remain involved with him.

Even if every fiber of my being begged to differ.

So I dropped my shoulders, defeated, and simply said, "All right."

CHAPTER 16
THE REAL DANGER

Silence stretched between Lucien and me as we headed to the hotel parking lot after checking out and climbed into the Rolls-Royce. Some part of me wanted to light up the air by mentioning that perhaps it was now my turn to drive, but the mood was far too somber for me to feel even a little humorous.

I couldn't help but think over all the conversations I'd had with Lucien since he'd shifted into his human form the day before. It felt like a lifetime had passed since he stopped me from touching the shadow mark.

All this time until now, he'd spoken as if we were in this thing together. That it was a given I join him on this adventure. That I was a part of whatever this was.

But now that Chase's threat to wipe my memories was gone, and that he'd been forced to tell the agents that I was his Eteria, it was as though a switch had been flipped, and suddenly he couldn't get rid of me fast enough.

At least that's how it felt when he drove out of San Diego like a demon out of hell.

It also didn't help that watching Lucien driving had become a perverted habit of mine. Sure, the California landscape was quite monotone, and Lucien was much more of a feast to the eye, but staring at his striking profile set in a dark, contemplative expression as he leaned an arm against the window, which made his shirt ride a little too high and expose a little of the V leading underneath his pants, made me feel both hot and bitter.

Told you he was way out of your league. A traitorous mocking voice slithered into my head. *How sure is he even that you're his Eteria? This sounds like a title that belongs to someone far more deserving.*

I didn't want to believe that him taking me back home had anything to do with him not being attracted to me or something like that. My heart wished to think that it was all due to very valid reasons—valid for him only, though—and his own sense of righteousness about not putting an innocent human in danger.

But some part of me couldn't help but take it this way too.

His reasoning might've been somewhat sound, but it only sounded like excuses to me.

Matteo had used such excuses, after all. Sure, they weren't on a life-danger level, but they were about potential financial ruin. His wealthy parents, who disapproved of me, had threatened to close down *The Hallowing Hour* and spread rumors that would prevent me from finding another job if I continued dating him. They said this to my face.

I'd thought that Matteo had broken up with me to protect me from that.

Later, I learned he'd been cheating on me.

So two truths could exist at once. He did protect me from his parents. He just also hurt me irrevocably when I discovered his affair and that his love was nothing but a fucking farce.

Who was to say that Lucien wasn't doing something similar now?

Perhaps he wanted to get rid of me with or without the danger aimed at me because of him. Maybe, like Matteo, he realized I was attracted to him when he'd totally lost interest.

Maybe, like Matteo, he weaponized the truth as an elaborate excuse.

I had over ten new messages and about twenty missed phone calls.

About half an hour into the drive, when the silence started to become unbearable, yet neither of us seemed willing to break it, I took out my phone from my bag, wanting to play some online game to pass the time.

It hadn't occurred to me until then that I hadn't been on my phone since the morning, when I woke up, due to everything that was happening. Apparently, in the few hours since, people had started looking for me. Since I wasn't exactly popular, I hadn't really expected it. Aside from the occasional nasty nagging by my parents or requests from my editor, my phone was more often than not as silent as a graveyard.

I checked the call log first. One was from my editor at *The Hallowing Hour*, Andra, and another one was from Ellie, a very distant friend from high school who insisted on keeping in touch with just about everyone from our former friend group.

The other eighteen calls were from Thayer.

My older brother.

Who hadn't been speaking to me for a year.

My chest tightened when I saw his name and the number of times he tried to reach me.

It felt like a heavy weight landed on my shoulders when I opened the message app and began reading. I wanted to read Thayer's first, but Andra's text caught my eye.

The first was from a couple of hours ago. A few sponsors pulled out. We might not be able to publish this month. Will let you know what's happening when I have more info.

My heart stopped. The sponsors she was talking about were the only things keeping our magazine afloat. Without them, there would be no magazine.

I swallowed hard, my hand tightening on the phone. My job was in danger. The job I poured my blood, sweat, and tears into. The job I had taken on to find out what exactly killed my sisters that awful day eight years ago, through access to crime logs, and my attempt to draw the well-hidden supernatural to me.

Losing this job wouldn't be just about losing my livelihood. It would mean I had spent the last few years wasting my fucking time.

Especially since Lucien wanted me "safe and sound" and far away from him.

I could feel the answers slipping through my fingers, as though I were trying to hold water. My frustration was growing, and along with it, a deep, never-ending grief that whispered in my mind that perhaps I would always be left hanging as to what really happened eight years ago.

With a trembling finger, I returned to the messages log, and since I only had one text from Ellie, I opened it, hoping it would bring me some levity.

Hey, Drew! I'm moving to LA next month (can you believe it?!) and I would LOVE hanging out with you and catching up! I'll let you know once I'm settled and we can meet for coffee or something! SO EXCITED!

The tightness in my gut relaxed slightly. At least one thing never changed, and this was Ellie. She was the brightest, most charming person I'd ever known. Charming enough to keep in touch with me, the outcast of our former friend group, from time to time.

Her moving to my city actually made my chest tighten.

Ellie had been the only one who hadn't abandoned me after everything that happened to my sisters. She'd been the only one to sit with me during lunchtime in our senior year of high school; she'd often stood up for me when classmates called me crazy and stupid and far worse things.

She'd been the only one who hadn't entirely dismissed me when I insisted that what I saw happen to my sisters couldn't possibly be human.

However, when I moved to LA after high school, I wanted to start anew, and I'd cut her off. It wasn't her fault she was a reminder that I had become an outcast, but knowing she was still in touch with the other people I had once upon a time thought of as friends, that she refused to change her people-pleasing ways, made it easier for me to let go.

Especially since my sole priority in life was to find out what really happened to my sisters eight years ago.

Because I knew what I saw. There had been a shadow mark and also a sigil, or rather, a Spellscript, at the crime scene.

And while Ellie never told me that I was wrong, she always had that doubtful look in her eyes.

Feeling the sudden gloom falling on me, adding to the weight on my shoulders, I took a deep breath and moved on to the messages from Thayer.

But I hesitated before I opened the first one.

What if my parents told him about our recent call a few days ago, and he decided to send me a rant about upsetting them? Sure, it wasn't like him to do that, especially since we weren't on speaking terms, but Thayer could have a short fuse sometimes, and my parents were experts at knowing which of his buttons to push, manipulative as they were.

Still, while I didn't want to read the messages, I knew I had to get it over with.

We need to talk was the first one he texted me a few hours ago. Then, soon after, he texted Why aren't you answering the phone?

He had given up for about an hour before he sent the next message. Are you ignoring me because you're still mad?

And then, a flurry of texts.

I know I fucked up, Drew, he wrote. The way I went about the whole fight was wrong. I insulted you and looked down on you and I want to apologize for it when I arrive in LA.

I paused, heart freezing over. Arrive in LA? What the hell was going on? He couldn't possibly be coming here for me. He had a whole-ass life back in our hometown of Seattle. Last I heard, he even had a girlfriend who'd moved in with him.

But I really want to meet you because something happened, I read, my confusion growing, replacing my gloom with a sudden sense of tension. I received a letter—an actual letter—from an unknown sender. I really need to talk to you, and it better be in person. Can you send me your new address so we can meet face to face? I booked a flight and should arrive later this afternoon. Please call me.

The last text he sent was from an hour ago. Please at least text me so I know you're alive and well, Drew. You don't have to call. I just need to know that you're safe. Please.

Thayer hardly ever pleaded for anything.

I'd never seen him say *please* so many times.

Something was wrong.

I dialed his number and called, but it went straight to voicemail.

Now multiple things were wrong.

Was he already on a flight to LA? Why?

Why did Thayer think I was in danger?

He couldn't possibly know about what had been going on the past few days. He had no ties to the American Supernatural Society or anything—I mean, he was the most avid denier of the truth, out of everyone in my life, even my parents.

Maybe he's like Chase, that awful, traitorous voice murmured in my ear. *Maybe all this time, he knew everything and pretended not to. Maybe he's a supernatural himself. Don't trust him.*

The car suddenly screeched to a stop. I jerked in surprise and froze when Lucien's hand suddenly pried mine from my phone and held it in his.

I whipped my head toward him and saw he was staring at me, searching my face. "You're shaking," he said softly when he saw my confused frown.

He was right. I was trembling all over, and I hadn't even noticed. "It's n-nothing," I murmured, cursing inwardly at my stutter.

"Obviously, it's not nothing," Lucien said a little dryly, but the worry in his eyes was apparent. "You've been looking at your phone like you just saw a ghost."

Seeing those texts from Thayer was certainly the equivalent of that. I opened my mouth and almost blurted the truth before I caught myself and clamped it shut, averting my gaze. Thayer wrote about some sort of danger, and my brother wasn't one to exaggerate, so telling Lucien about it was probably the smart thing, the *right* thing, considering a danger to me meant a danger to him . . .

Sliding my hand out of his hold, I folded my arms and stared ahead, refusing to return his gaze. "You said that being your Eteria meant my soul was bound to yours," I said quietly. "But other than that, and the fact that hurting me means hurting you, you didn't explain how this whole thing came to be, and what else it means for me, other than the fact that this title puts me in danger."

He was silent for so long that I reluctantly returned my gaze to him. He was staring straight ahead, jaw ticking, his elbow leaning against the window and his other hand clutching the wheel tight enough to turn his knuckles white.

My heartbeat quickened now that he was practically screaming without opening his mouth that he did not tell me everything. "Since you plan to leave me behind," I said, bitterness entering my tone, "I deserve to at least know the whole truth, don't you think?"

He snapped his head toward me, eyes filled with sudden anger, before he inhaled slowly and pushed his hair back, staring at the wheel as if it held all the answers to the universe. "It's not about leaving you behind," he said quietly. "It's about protecting you."

"Don't avoid the real question here," I said, growing angry myself. "What is it that you aren't telling me?"

Lucien's face grew dark before he looked at me again and said, "You understood one thing wrong. Your soul isn't bound to *mine*, but rather to *me*."

And he lost me. "Isn't that the same thing?"

"No, Drew, it's not," he said, sucking in a breath, and his shoulders slumped. "I didn't plan on telling you, since I didn't plan to remain in your life for it to be an issue."

His words were like a knife to my heart, and I winced, hugging myself. "Well, you have to now," I hissed, looking away. "Since you might have to stay in my life for a little longer, even if you hate it."

"I don't—" Lucien began, his tone snappy with anger, before he paused and asked, "What do you mean by that?"

I swiped my phone open and looked at the still-open messages from Thayer. "My older brother is flying in from Seattle today to visit me at my apartment," I said, angry at how perplexed he sounded. "We haven't spoken in a year since we had a huge fight. No texts. No calls. And yet he tried to reach out to me earlier today and insists he needs to talk to me in person about some letters he received. His messages allude to the fact he thinks I'm in danger."

I turned to glare at Lucien, who in return seemed to become as still as a statue. "He can't possibly know about you or the agents," I said with a scowl, "so this must mean there is something else."

Lucien sat back, a horrified kind of realization settling on his face. "Yes, there is something else," he murmured, and before I could ask what the hell he meant by that, he put the car into gear and raced down the road. "We need to meet your brother. Together."

My eyes widened. "What?"

"I thought there might still be time," Lucien said, and there was fury in his voice now. "Time for me to make it seem like you're not involved in anything. But it looks like my calculations were wrong. They must be onto you."

"Who are you talking about?" I asked persistently, before I paused and realized it myself.

With Chase and Avenor chasing us down, and our ambush on Mack, Alby, and Dianna, the most pressing matter had completely escaped my mind.

The matter of who physically tried to kill Lucien.

Lucien himself said yesterday that his attacker might be after me, too, by mere association. That whoever they were might've also seen Lucien and me when we fled from my apartment and Chase.

Slowly, I turned to look at him. "You were resolute yesterday," I said, trying to wrap my head around this whole thing, "about the fact I might be in danger from your attacker. And yet you said I was no longer in danger and asked me to go back home and be 'safe and sound.'"

He must've heard the sarcasm in my last three words because he visibly flinched.

My suspicion grew. "It has something to do with me being your Eteria."

He didn't even bother hiding it, judging by the way his lips curled down. "I intended to station guards near you, just out of sight, so they would protect you."

That infuriated me, but I forced myself to focus. "Lucien," I hissed, hands curling into fists, "what the fuck aren't you telling me?"

He drove faster, so much faster that I had to hold on to the upper handle for support. He didn't seem to notice his foot was pressing the gas pedal for long periods. In fact, there was an odd look on his face that made him seem cornered.

And then he let out an unnatural, animalistic growl that made me stiffen and the short hairs on my body stand on end. "I'm the real danger, Drew," he said in a guttural voice. "I'm trying to protect you from me."

CHAPTER 17
A COURT OF GLASS AND THREATS

I was still reeling from what he'd just said, still trying to understand what the fuck he meant by all that, when my phone went off.

Angered by the interruption, I looked at the screen and saw it was a number registered to *Remi*. I didn't know a Remi.

But then I remembered the man who brought us the car. Lucien's cousin. Lucien must've saved his number in my phone.

I showed him the screen, scowling. "Your cousin's calling."

Lucien stopped growling, and his entire body visibly relaxed as he took the phone from me, put it to his ear, and answered with a calm and irritatingly relieved voice, *"Je te dois ton putain de milkshake préféré. Quoi de neuf?"*

Without any idea what he was saying, or continued to say, as he spoke to Remi, I looked through the window at the view, feeling my fury refusing to abate.

I might not know Lucien that well yet, but he hadn't struck me as the type to avoid uncomfortable topics. With him being an Alpha, it made no sense he would be.

But something about my being his Eteria set him off and made him squirm in a way that seemed uncharacteristic.

His mere reaction to the word *Eteria*—a tightening to his eyes and lips, a steely gaze, and rippling tension—was enough to make me fear whatever it actually meant, beyond the dry details he'd provided.

My fear drove me to impatience, though. I needed to know what he was unwilling to share.

But Lucien continued speaking in French to Remi on the phone until we eventually arrived at my apartment building.

Once we parked, Lucien abruptly hung up, leading me to suspect he'd purposely spoken to Remi for the duration of the drive to avoid talking about the whole Eteria thing. Then, without looking at me, he said, "Let's go."

I exited the car and followed him toward the entrance of my apartment building, my anger and frustration growing to serious proportions, before everything I felt came to a screeching halt.

First, I couldn't see our resident homeless men. Caveat and Johnny usually loitered by the front steps, making themselves at home with their worn-out sleeping bags and patched blankets. They'd always been here in the last three years I'd lived in this building.

And yet when Lucien and I entered through the gate, they were nowhere to be found. Neither were their belongings. Their absence was rather noticeable.

Second, and more importantly, my brother was waiting with a backpack near the building entrance door.

I immediately came to a stop, staring at him as if it were the first time I'd ever seen my brother. And it certainly felt that way. The man standing before me was tall and lanky, thinner than I remembered. He was far too pale, with a bleak expression on his drawn face and dark bags under his bloodshot gray eyes behind thick-framed round glasses. His hair, the same shade of brown as mine, was much longer than I remembered, too, reaching down to the middle of his back in haphazard, knotted wavy strands.

If I didn't recognize him, I would've thought he was a new homeless man visiting our place.

My brother's gaze, still razor sharp despite his current messy, exhausted state, found me immediately. His lips thinned, and he walked toward me with a straining line of worry marring his forehead. "Drew."

His voice was raspy, as if he hadn't used it in a long while.

Its sound was also so nostalgic, a sense of melancholy settled deep within me.

"Thayer," I blurted in a mumble, so out of my depth, I didn't know how to act around my older brother, the person I had once believed would always be on my side and yet who'd caused me so much pain.

A year ago, it had felt like I lost my only remaining sibling.

Seeing him now, hearing his voice, felt surreal.

Thayer raised his eyes when Lucien settled next to me, but before he could inquire about him, Lucien raised his hand and said with a friendly expression, "Nice to meet you, Mr. Colter. I'm Lucien Delterre, Drew's friend."

I tried not to show how tense I was as Thayer shook his hand with understandable confusion. I saw my brother take in Lucien from head to toe and back, noting his corded arms, the abs he couldn't hide under the tight tee, and the pair of arctic-blues that could pierce one's soul.

"Call me Thayer," my brother now said in a slow, contemplative voice I recognized. It was the tone he always used with me and my sisters—Willow in particular. A tone that meant he was assessing the situation carefully and meticulously before he chose how to react. While my sisters and I had been close in age—with only two years between Willow and me, and three years between Willow and Julianna, the youngest—Thayer was our parents' "accident" from when they were seventeen. He was five years older than me.

He had always been patient and caring with me and my sisters when we were young. He'd been like a third parent to us, helping us with homework, sometimes going to parents' day at school when our parents were too busy or didn't care to make time for it, making us lunch boxes to take to school, cleaning up after us, and everything else a parent should do, basically.

Our parents always saw him as the responsible golden child of the family. He was the smartest out of all four siblings, starting college when he was sixteen and finishing up his bachelor's in physics before he turned twenty. He'd gone on and completed his master's and PhD by the time he was twenty-five—my current age—and started working for an elite biotech company based in Seattle, which, as far as I was aware, he was still at.

That same genius golden-child brother of mine watched Lucien like a hawk as the Alpha released his hand.

Sucking in a deep breath to calm my erratic heart, I shakily dug the keys out from the duffel bag and murmured, "Let's head inside."

Lucien and Thayer turned to look at me. Both of them seemed to want to say something, but with almost comic timing, they both thought better of it and closed their mouths.

Tense and uncomfortable with this whole situation, I entered the building with the two following close behind.

A nagging feeling told me something was wrong. For instance, the light switch in the corridor didn't work, and the entire building was shrouded in darkness. There was no buzzing noise of the air-conditioning motors, or the murmurs of electricity in general. It was quiet.

Too quiet.

Lucien must've realized that something was wrong, too, because when we reached the door to my apartment, his hand suddenly folded over mine. "I will lead," he murmured, and I ignored the little jolt of heat that I felt when he gently pried the keys from my hold, his palm brushing against mine.

The heat was gone a second later, and my heartbeat quickened for drastically different reasons. An ominous feeling crawled into my stomach, making me feel a little ill, and my anxiety caused my entire body to shake like a leaf.

Wordlessly, Lucien stepped forward, slid the key into the lock, and pushed the door open.

The moment he did, however, my nerves multiplied and my blood rushed out of my head, making me feel dizzy.

My apartment was trashed.

Completely, utterly trashed.

Sheets of paper were scattered all over the place. The couch and sofa had been aggressively torn, the cushion stuffing spilling out of them not unlike Mack Page's guts had when Lucien disemboweled him. Glasses and plates were shattered all over the kitchen floor, spices spilled all over the counter, as if someone had pushed them away too hard.

Then there was my workstation. My wooden desk was no more; its legs were folded into splinters, as if something huge had sat on top of it, and the surface, along with the drawers, was carved out, as if whoever broke into my apartment was trying to find some hidden things *inside* the wood.

The deeper I walked into the apartment, the more my shakiness grew. Pictures I'd hung on the walls were completely torn and defiled. The bedroom seemed as though a hurricane had passed through, with all my clothes spilling out of the open closet, most of them completely messed with, as if someone had taken a knife and sliced everything in their way. The same went for my bed; the mattress was half on the floor, half on the bed frame, completely torn just like everything else, while the wooden bed frame itself suffered the same fate as my wooden desk: crumbled to the floor, jagged splinters causing it to look like a spike trap.

The only place that seemed to be untouched was the restroom. Though *untouched* might be stretching it; the cabinet doors were open, with the towels and my toiletries spilled and despoiled. But the toilet seat itself was intact, and so were the sink and the shower. Though to be fair, breaking marble was much tougher than ruining wooden furniture.

"Drew."

As though in a dream, I turned around to look at Lucien, who watched me with open worry. He searched my gaze before he said, "We need to see if something was taken."

I opened my mouth to speak, but no words came out. My vocal cords defied my silent commands.

Seeing my struggle, Lucien put a hand on my shoulder and squeezed for a short moment before he turned around and headed back to the trashed living room.

It felt as though I were gliding through a bad, disastrous dream, as I walked back into the living room, too, and took in the damage to my place. Sure, this apartment hadn't been perfect. It had always felt temporary. A temporary home, without feeling like home at all.

But it didn't deserve this. Not at all.

And it was still *my* place. The one place that belonged to me. Seeing it abused like this made me feel sickly violated, so much so that I stumbled over the mess back to the toilet and retched.

Lucien and Thayer were suddenly behind me. Thayer held my hair back while I puked over and over, while Lucien crouched by me, his hand rubbing my back as he continually whispered the same words: "You're safe. You're okay. Your wolf is here . . ."

Whether it was his words, or the fact I had nothing left in my stomach to empty, I slowly stopped retching and leaned back from the toilet, cold sweat covering my skin. Lucien held me, his arm wrapped around me, and I felt so tired, my head lolled on its own and rested on his chest, eyes closed.

It felt like everything that'd been happening since I saved Lucien a few days ago finally caught up to me, with the violation of my apartment being the last fucking straw.

An arm slid under my knees, and suddenly I was lifted up by Lucien, princess-style. I opened my eyes as he walked back to the living room and set me down against the wall. "I'll look everything over," he told me quietly, his gaze colliding with my own. "Just rest here for now."

When Lucien straightened up, he turned to Thayer, who'd been silent this whole time. But his gray eyes were on me, filled with evident worry, even as Lucien spoke to him, saying, "Drew mentioned you think she's in danger."

"She is," Thayer confirmed, before he reluctantly turned his gaze to meet Lucien's. "I received a letter."

He fished out an envelope from his backpack and handed it to me. I took it with still-shaky hands. "Read it now, Drew," he said. "I'm afraid this can't wait."

I turned to look at Lucien and he nodded, face grim with fury. "Read the letter," he said quietly.

Feeling depleted, I gave him a single nod, having no energy to even speak, before I unfolded the envelope and pulled the letter out. To my faint surprise, neat cursive handwritten words greeted me from the high-quality paper.

Then I cleared my throat and started reading out loud.

> To Thayer Colter,
>
> We are not strangers to your bloodline, though our names need not be spoken. Suffice it to say, we have long been near when you presumed none lingered. It is for this reason that our hand is turned to you, for your sister has proven . . . difficult to reach by ordinary means.
>
> Know that she is not unseen. Her steps are followed, her company observed. She strays where she ought not. You may not ken the peril in such binding, but we do. Her course, if unaltered, hastens to ruin.
>
> If her life be of worth to you, then take her away. Bear her back to Seattle, where watchful eyes may grant her safety. Delay, and the hefty cost shall be hers to pay.
>
> Think not that we are ignorant of what has befallen your line. Others before her were lost when heed was not given. Will you now forbear, and let another be sundered likewise?
>
> This is the final courtesy we extend. Comply, and she breathes. Withhold, and she does not. It is as simple as that.
>
> —Those Who Collect in Kind

I read the letter over and over again silently, a chill climbing up my spine. It was written vaguely, in language that no one in their right mind spoke nowadays. Some of it I wasn't even remotely close to understanding.

But one thing was clear: It was a threat.

They came to Thayer to threaten him about me. Because whoever they were knew I was with Lucien—this part was the least obscure one—and so were probably too cautious to approach me, either out of fear of Lucien or simply out of a healthy dose of caution.

So they went to Thayer for "help."

"Something doesn't add up," Lucien said, making me snap my eyes back to him. He seemed confused as he glanced between Thayer and me. "Why did they mention your family?"

Both Thayer and I looked at one another simultaneously. His face was grave, and fear filled his eyes.

But I wasn't afraid. If anything, my exhaustion was suddenly gone, and I sat up straight, my mind reeling. "Lucien," I said, looking at the wolf, whose eyes were now narrowed in suspicion. "Do you know who wrote the letter?"

Lucien grimaced, obviously dissatisfied, but he nonetheless said, "Yes."

From the corner of my eye, Thayer whipped his head toward him. "You do?" he asked, incredulous. "How?"

Lucien didn't reply. Instead, he walked toward me and crouched so his face was at my level. "Those who collect in kind," he said quietly as Thayer approached us as well. "This is one of the pseudonyms the Sable Syndicate love to refer to themselves as."

"The Sable Syndicate?" Thayer and I spoke together, our tones so eerily similar, we both glanced at each other in surprise before quickly looking away. But then I realized the term wasn't unfamiliar and returned my gaze to Lucien, who studied me with such a focused look, I found it hard to look him straight in the eyes. "You mentioned them before," I said, trying not to stumble over my words despite having Lucien's undivided attention on me. "What are they?"

He stared at me for a moment too long before he plucked the letter out of my hands and rose to his feet. He then stretched his hand toward me, and after a slight hesitation, I took it, and he helped me up. I immediately let him go afterward, the searing touch of his palm against mine still lingering.

Lucien glanced at Thayer then. "Drew mentioned you flew in from Seattle while you could've just as easily taken a picture of the letter and sent it to her," he said, and his words sent a jolt down my spine as I turned to look at Thayer, who was now watching Lucien with open suspicion. But Lucien ignored it as he said, "That means you believe your phones are rigged."

My heart pounded loudly as I fumbled to take out my phone. "Rigged?" I repeated, staring at the innocent-looking phone.

"That's right," Thayer murmured, folding his arms. "Who are you?" he suddenly asked, eyes narrowed on Lucien, before he paused, lips thinning, and tweaked his question. "*What* are you?"

Before Lucien could respond or I could comprehend what Thayer was saying—Thayer, the person who was so avidly convinced I was a delusional crackpot for believing, or rather, *knowing*, that what killed our sisters wasn't of human origin—the living room window exploded.

In a split second, I was flat on the floor next to Thayer with Lucien's arms over both our chests, protecting us from the sharp glass shards.

Pain hit me from the impact, and I sucked in a breath while Thayer groaned and said, "What the—"

But his words were cut short when Lucien suddenly pulled back, and as he did, his skin began to ripple.

I gasped as I realized what he was doing, and Enoch's words were suddenly ringing in my head in warning. "*You know better than anyone that werewolves heal faster and better in your human form!*" he had scolded Lucien just yesterday.

And yet Lucien was transforming before my eyes into his wolf form, his skin replaced by auburn fur, his back hunching as his limbs curved and changed, the ends turning from fingers to claws and from palms to paws. His ears grew sharp and filled with tufts, and his nose and mouth elongated into a canine snout.

He was on all fours a moment later, a gorgeous, humongous wolf stepping over sharp shards of glass that were bound to cut him open. "Lucien!" I called after him, pulling myself up, "you have to remain in your human form—"

A shadow entered the room through the now-nonexistent window. It was so swift and quick, I couldn't even make out what the shadow was until it lifted two daggers and threw them at Lucien.

Lucien was nimble; he sidestepped the daggers at an astonishing speed while drawing closer to the attacker, who was on the move once again. The attacker, which I realized now had a supple, lean human form covered by a low-hanging hooded cloak, jumped into the air, pulling their knees to their chest and successfully avoiding Lucien's sharp teeth as he tried to bite down.

The next few seconds were a blur of darkness and shimmering red fur as the two attacked and missed one another. Lucien was growling loudly enough to make the entire building rumble with the vibration, and the attacker was silent. If I'd closed my eyes, I would've thought Lucien was fighting air.

When the attacker pulled out two more daggers from their boots, I belatedly realized this wasn't merely an attacker but an assassin.

They came here for Lucien.

To finish the job they started?

But why now? Why here?

The questions disappeared from my head, however, the moment the attacker launched one of the daggers into the wolf's side.

Lucien howled.

I heard a scream.

I didn't realize it was mine until Thayer grabbed my shoulders and shook me.

But I couldn't stop screaming until something hard hit my head and darkness swallowed me whole.

CHAPTER 18
THE PRECIPICE OF ETERNITY

I woke up in an unfamiliar room.

Terribly confused by where I was, and how I got here, I sat up, wincing when I felt dull pain in my right side. I went to lift up my shirt and investigate the source, but I realized my clothes had been changed. Gone were my jeans and band tee, replaced instead by a simple gray nightgown.

Finding my glasses resting on the nightstand, I slid them up my nose and pulled the nightgown up.

My skin was clean. No wound—not even a scratch. I frowned, still feeling that dull pain, but seeing as I was utterly healthy, I lowered the fabric back down, my confusion growing.

I looked up and studied the room. It was a simple bedroom with a cottage feel to it: wooden dresser and TV stand, wooden nightstands next to the wooden-framed double bed I was currently sitting upon. The door to my right, wooden as well, was closed, and the window to the left showed nothing but a mass of glaringly green bushes and an assortment of lanky trees, seemingly leading to a forest beyond.

Considering there was no forest within the city of Los Angeles, I concluded I was far away from any sort of urban area.

And that made me wonder *why*.

The last thing I remembered was seeing Lucien being stabbed in his wolf form . . .

I froze.

Lucien.

Panic set in, and I pushed the heavy duvet away and stumbled off the far-too-tall bed. Someone had placed a pair of slippers nearby. I put them on before I opened the door and exited to find a short corridor outside.

The corridor was short, leading to a couple of other doors, while opening at its other end to a surprisingly spacious living room, a kitchen, and a modular desk that was probably a makeshift study.

The common areas were empty, though. Voices came from behind one of the doors to my right.

I pulled the first door open and saw another bedroom, a mirror to the one I'd just woken up in, but it was empty. The next door led to a stunningly luxurious bathroom that seemed out of place in the general cottage design of this house. Finally, I tore open the last door.

Lucien was there. He was still in his wolf form, awake, and lying on his front on top of a king-size bed, with Enoch, no longer wearing his doctor's coat and dressed casually, spreading some sort of creamy liquid over Lucien's back—and raging red wound. He was assisted by a petite, pretty woman with slanted dark eyes and brown skin, who was continually murmuring something, reading out from the huge, thick open book she was holding.

Next to the bed sat Thayer, whose face was as white as a sheet.

The moment I opened the door, though, Enoch and the woman paused and turned to look at me. Thayer immediately jumped to his feet and strode toward me, lifting his arms as if to hug me.

I flinched.

It was an instinctual response. I didn't mean to. But the thought of hugging my older brother after a year of him refusing to acknowledge my existence as if I were carrying a contagious disease was too much for me at the moment. Him flying over and telling me about the threat to my life might've been enough for other people, but it wasn't enough for me.

Him worrying about my living or dying wasn't enough to make me forget all the ways he'd hurt me.

When he saw my stiffness, Thayer froze a few feet away and slowly let his hands fall, pain crossing his still-pale face. He then said in a hasty tone, "I was just about to come check up on you."

I folded my arms. "How long have I been out?"

"Three hours," he replied, gray eyes scanning my face before he swallowed and shifted from side to side. "Drew, I . . . I mean . . ."

Realizing he was about to talk about *that*, I put up my hand to stop him. "This is neither the time nor the place," I hissed at him, scowling, before I walked past him and approached Enoch, his assistant, and Lucien, who turned his head to watch me with exhausted arctic-blue wolf eyes. My gaze traveled to Enoch, though, and from the pitying look in his and his assistant's eyes, I could tell Lucien had told them I was his Eteria.

Wordlessly, I looked at the wound. It was as raw as if it had been pried open, fresh blood pouring out of it too fast.

I returned my gaze to Lucien. "You're dying," I whispered, tears welling in my eyes, raising a hand to softly touch his shimmering auburn coat. "Why are you still in your wolf form? Enoch." I turned to the hospital director, whose face was starkly bleak. "You said werewolves heal better in their human form—"

"He can't shift right now," Enoch answered quietly, as he resumed pouring whatever liquid he was using over the wolf's back. "Much like when you first met him, it seems that the holder of the Mathenio renewed the Spellscript effects, causing him to be unable to shift, meaning that the attacker was definitely Fae, and definitely from the Sable Syndicate."

Enoch dropped all those terms as if I could understand and offered no explanation even though I stared at him, frustrated and desperate for answers.

The assistant then closed the heavy book in her hands and dropped it with a satisfying thud on top of the dresser before she came over to face me. I was taller than her by at least a head, but that didn't seem to deter her from looking at me with a disapproving scowl. "You need rest," she said, eyes dropping to my side. "You must still feel the pain."

My heart stopped. "How do you know I feel pain here?" A dull pain, but pain nonetheless.

She arched a brow. "Because when I checked up on you an hour ago, you were still bleeding?"

I blinked rapidly, uncomprehending. "There is no wound," I blurted, eyes wide. "I feel *some* pain, very faintly, yet there is nothing there."

Both the woman and Enoch froze. The two immediately exchanged glances before Enoch's face twisted in true anger, startling me. I'd only seen him being kind, calm, and collected; this bout of anger was far too drastic a change. "You fucking fool," he snarled at Lucien, whose unblinking eyes were still on me. "Do you *want* to die?"

Lucien remained unmoving and unflinching as his gaze lingered on my face, as though he wasn't even bothering to listen to Enoch.

And that seemed to enrage the doctor further. "Anais," he snapped, and the assistant turned to him. "Help Drew lift the dam on her end so this idiot can finally stop killing himself."

Anais narrowed her eyes. "She's human, without a drop of fluxion within her," she argued, scrunching her nose, though I could see the deep worry that flashed in her eyes. "A fluxionless human is merely a vessel, not a conduit."

"I don't care." Enoch glared at Lucien. "Infuse her with Inverna for a temporary solution." Whatever Enoch meant seemed to cause Anais to freeze and widen her eyes with incredulity, but Enoch didn't stop. "One liter should do it, straight to the brain to create a pathway. That should help move things up—"

Before he could finish the sentence, and before I could process the fact Enoch wanted to inject something into my brain, the wolf's fur rippled and hissed. I jumped, watching as the fur withdrew into golden skin, the body elongated, paws and claws turning to hands, and the wolfish face turned into an infuriated, beautiful human one.

Lucien was no longer lying on the bed. Instead, his arms were suddenly wrapped around me from behind as he pulled me close to his mouthwateringly naked body, a low growl reverberating from his chest to my back.

Enoch was on his feet now, too, with Anais right by his side, looking beyond me at Lucien, with alarm and worsening worry. "Lucien," Enoch said, his anger turning into fury too. "We are not trying to harm her—"

"Leave."

The baritone voice behind me that until now had only sounded like music to my ears, it was so smooth and melodious, was now guttural, as though ripped out of his vocal cords, mingling with his ceaseless growling.

Enoch seemed to want to argue, but Anais, whose pretty face was now taking on a grayish undertone as she suddenly seemed sick, grabbed Enoch's arm. "Let's get out of here," she said softly, almost fearfully. "Staying here will only provoke him further."

Before Enoch could argue, Thayer, who'd been silent until now, suddenly piped up. "What about my sister?" he snapped, glaring at Anais. "Don't you see his claws? He's going to kill her!"

My eyes dropped to Lucien's hands, and sure enough, his nails were long and sharp, his wolf claws apparent in his human form. But they weren't aimed at me. In fact, if anything, Lucien was cocooning me protectively.

"She's going to be fine," Anais barked back and took my brother's arm. "Let's get out of here, human, before you're ripped to shreds."

Thayer protested, but Anais was surprisingly strong despite her head barely reaching Thayer's chest, and she quite literally dragged him outside.

Now it was only Enoch here. And he looked at me. "His side is also injured," he said quietly now, reluctantly resigned. "Force him to put this cream on all wounds, no matter what."

I opened my mouth, wanting to say something, but Lucien squeezed me tight, almost too hard, to his chest, cutting off my train of thought.

Enoch grimaced, shook his head, and murmured, "I hope you know what you're doing," before he strode out of the room and closed the door behind him, leaving Lucien and me alone.

But Lucien did not let me go. He was still stiff, his claws still out, still caging me in his arms as if he was prepared for any threat.

It wasn't until I glanced down to his side and saw the wound there bleeding incessantly, in addition to the one on his back, that I finally snapped out of it.

Angry myself, I tried to turn in his arms, but he didn't let me. "Lucien," I said warningly, "I refuse to watch you die, so you'd better lie back down on this damned bed and let me apply this damned cream."

Lucien growled again, though far less threateningly. Instead, it was a growl that sounded almost like a tantrum of sorts. And I realized then that I wasn't talking to the normal Lucien, or the Lucien I'd come to know. Instead, it was as if I was talking to a cornered animal.

Sucking in a deep breath, I forced myself to relax in his arms, though nothing about him bleeding to death behind me was relaxing. Then, I said in a calm voice, "You said I'm your Eteria."

The low growl that had still been vibrating in his chest up until then came to a sudden stop. Taking it as an encouraging sign, I continued in a more confident tone. "You said being your Eteria meant my soul belongs to you. You said before that hurting me would hurt you, so that must mean it goes the other way around, doesn't it?"

I saw his claws slowly return to normal nails.

Heartbeat quick, I took in another deep breath and said, "I don't know what's going on, Lucien, but I do know I feel pain exactly where you're wounded on the side." I paused when I felt him stiffen. "I might not feel pain on my back, but I have a feeling that this is still related to me being your Eteria, is it not?"

It seemed my deduction was right because Lucien's arms dropped from around me, and he stepped back. Slowly, I turned to look at him.

His beautiful face was set in cold, inhuman fury.

But I knew that this fury had nothing to do with me. So I ignored it and, catching his eyes, I said, "That means if you die, I might die as well. Doesn't it?"

It seemed that, at last, my words finally penetrated whatever supernatural wall he'd put up because his expression shattered, replaced by a pained look that cut me as deep as his wound did. "Drew," he whispered, voice hoarse.

I cupped his face, searching his gaze. He seemed so defeated, it made my chest tighten. "Lie down on your front," I said softly, "and let me take care of you again."

He closed his eyes, putting his hands over mine and pressing them tight to his face. My palms tickled at the brush of his bristles.

We stood like that for a few long moments before he finally released me and said with a tired, soulful gaze, "All right."

The moment he lay down and I leaned over him with a pair of gloves and the cream, Lucien spoke.

"Are you familiar with the concept of mates?"

I tensed as I gently applied the mysterious cream over the still-bleeding Spellscript wound. "Since you're not talking about what Australians call one another, I assume you're talking about animal pairing?" I tried to joke, but my voice was off. Because *I felt* off.

Willow, who used to read romantasy books, had once told me how she wished mates were a real thing. Since I wasn't as versed in the genre, I had asked her to explain. She had then told me about how, in this kind of book, *mates* was short for "soulmates," and that it was a magical occurrence that happened between two people, binding them together.

Those words now raced in my mind as Lucien continued, his voice cautious. "Like mating in the wild, werewolves mate too. Any Otherborne could find a mate, really."

I had yet to find out what an Otherborne was, but I wasn't an idiot. From the few times I'd heard this term, and the context in which it was said, I believed it referred to supernatural creatures in general.

But more important was what he'd just said. And I could no longer wait to get a concrete answer. "Does *Eteria* mean 'mate'?"

He froze, and I slowly traced the straight lines that made the Spellscript on his back, applying extra cream directly on the tissue gaps. "Every Otherborne can find a mate," he said quietly. "It is by *choice*."

Before I could protest, he suddenly pulled away and rolled to his unwounded side to sit up and face me, his expression stormy. But I was furious with him now too. "I'm not done," I snapped.

"Yes, you are," he said in a low growl, snatching the cream from my hands and putting it away. "Take off the gloves."

I glared at him. "You are still bleeding!"

"Fine, then," he said flatly and grabbed my hands, rolling the gloves off me.

"Lucien!" I protested. "You told me you'd let me take care of you—"

"And I did let you." He cut me off with an angry look. "But now you need to understand why you care so much about a stranger, man and wolf, when you barely even know me."

His words shut me up, and I stared at him, stunned. A rebellious part of me wanted to yell at him that *of course* I would worry about him, just like I would worry about anyone else in his position . . .

But that was not true, was it?

"Having a mate means the Otherborne chose that person," he now said, eyes filled with frustration. "Eteria, on the other hand, isn't a choice."

I didn't know what to think. My mind drew a blank. So I simply stared at him as he sat down on the far end of the bed, as far away from me as he could. "*Eteria* is a term for a very rare phenomenon," he said softly, though his entire body was tense. I could see the veins down his corded arms popping, he was fisting his hands so hard. "That phenomenon is triggered when an Otherborne encounters a human they feel an instant, inexplicable connection to."

My heart stopped.

"It is a connection beyond friend, lovers, family, or mates," he said, voice lowering to a whisper. "It is an eternal tie between an Otherborne and a human that transcends time and space."

My breath caught as a sudden, shocking thrill made my gut clench in anticipation. It was as though he was explaining what Willow had once mooned over all those years ago. As if the concept of mates from her books was actually *real*.

He opened his mouth, but no words came out. He clamped it shut, scowling, and looked away. At that moment, as if by perfect timing, the dusk sunlight speared through the window, covering him, making it seem as if he was glowing gold. He seemed so otherworldly just then, it made my breath catch again.

The sight made my heart stutter, and that stutter turned into a full-blown cardiac arrest when he finally spoke again. "Back in that alley behind your building, the moment I opened my eyes and saw you, a deep, unavoidable knowing settled inside me, and I knew. I just *knew* you were that for me. An Eteria—a human mate whose soul is bound to the Otherborne for eternity."

My heart was so loud, I swore he could hear it. And the tightening in my gut, caused by a sudden sense of excitement, made me search for his arctic-blue gaze.

But it almost seemed like he refused to look at me. As if he were *ashamed*.

Why?

"It may sound like a blessing," he said hoarsely, "but it's a fuck-ing curse."

That caused me to stiffen further, and I blurted in a barely audible whisper, "I don't understand."

I understood that being his Eteria had put me in danger. But it didn't seem like a curse to me. To him, though, perhaps it was. He didn't really want me to be his Eteria, after all. Maybe he hated that we were tied on such a deep level like that.

And yet, I knew there was something more to this than just that. The thing he was avoiding telling me every time I asked him about my being his Eteria.

His shoulders slumped and he dropped his head, the auburn curls casting a shadow over his face as the sun set behind him. "One of the main reasons why Otherborne are not allowed to associate with humans beyond what's necessary is the possibility of finding their Eteria," he said in a somewhat emotionless voice. "I always thought that this reason made no sense, since you have the same odds of finding an Eteria as winning the lottery. But the law was still put in place under the pretense that it's to protect us Otherborne from having an unnecessary weakness that the humans could use against us."

He turned to look at the window, showing me the back of his head and his hard shoulder blades, his gleaming golden skin pale around the raw wound.

"The reality is, however," he murmured, "that it protects humans from us. And for a good fucking reason."

Still not looking at me, he said, "Because once a human manifests as an Otherborne's Eteria, they can never love another."

His words felt like a punch. Him dropping the l-word was even more gut wrenching. I had always thought Lucien was drop-dead gorgeous, but I viewed him like an unblemished Greek statue in a museum. I hadn't allowed myself to think anything else about him, if only because I still believed he was way out of my league.

But now, what he was saying . . .

"The Otherborne, however, can make a choice, unlike the Eteria," he said, and suddenly he turned to face me, catching my gaze with his own grave one. "They can decide whether to consummate their bond, thus tying their Eteria to them until the end of days and even beyond, or let the Eteria go, never knowing about that bond, and have them recoil from anyone else, being unable to love or have sex with another person, until they die."

My head bobbed back and forth, nodding automatically as if I understood what he was saying. But I didn't.

I didn't love Lucien. Hopelessly attracted to him, sure, but not in love with him whatsoever.

Did I feel some sort of instant connection to him from the moment I saved his life? Yes, I did. But I would've felt it with any other injured animal for sure.

And yet it was one thing to find a dying wolf, think he was a dog, and try to save him.

It was quite another to insist on having the dog, now wolf, stay with you instead of calling animal control.

"But that's not even the worst of it all," he said now, his eyes seeming almost dead now, as if he was done with everything. "The same cosmic magic that turns the human into an Otherborne's Eteria would also force them to love the Otherborne unconditionally."

I shook my head, refusing to believe that.

He gave me a smile so humorless, it sent a chill down my back. "Basically, you are magically wired to not just lust after me, and only me, but to love only me too."

CHAPTER 19
WHO'S WHOSE?

I studied Lucien now as he silently watched me. From the moment I first saw his human form, I was a goner for his looks. No one could be this good looking, after all. And yet to be able to want only him for the rest of my life? Knowing that the chances of him returning these feelings were zero?

It sounded like a fucking nightmare.

But what about everything that happened? a little nagging voice whispered in my head. *What about going with him to San Diego and helping him confront his Beta?*

My own memories, and possibly life, were at stake by then, though, I replied to that voice.

So why were you angry with him when he told you he would return you home safe and sound? the voice insisted.

Because that sounded like an excuse! I snapped back. *Besides, the danger from the Sable Syndicate, whatever they are, was still unresolved, so that must've meant I was still in danger too.*

I could swear my own inner voice was laughing at me, taunting me. *He said he would put security on you to ensure your safety, though. But there is no being safe from* him. *He said he's a bigger danger, after all.*

He's a werewolf, a creature from storybooks. Why did you so readily trust him? Why did you believe with your entire heart that he wouldn't hurt you, body and soul?

I'm his Eteria, I cried back. *He couldn't hurt me, or he would risk hurting himself!*

But is that even the truth? the voice whispered. *He said your soul is bound to* him, *after all, not that your souls are bound to each other . . .*

"I feel pain where you were wounded on your side," I said now, my voice distorted somehow, as I felt suddenly lightheaded. "That's because I'm your Eteria."

It wasn't a question, since now, I knew the answer.

This wasn't just about brainwashing and being able to love only him.

It was also about much more than simply my soul being connected to his—or rather, to *him.*

"Yes," he replied in a lower voice.

"Because my soul is bound to you," I murmured, and saying the words out loud now, after what he'd just revealed, sounded utterly unbelievable all of a sudden. On the surface, it sounded like I was his soulmate or something—but this couldn't be. It was *me* we were talking about.

And my position was always to look up to men like him, not to get involved with them.

"Yes," he said again, gritting his teeth this time.

Pain spread across my chest at his obvious disgust at the situation. Of course he would be disgusted. Why would someone like him want *me* as an Eteria?

The thought caused my breath to catch and the pain to turn sharper, deeper, and so I swerved my thoughts in a different direction. Returning to focus on the matter at hand.

Recalling what Enoch and his assistant, Anais, had talked about before Lucien shifted into his human form and kicked them out, I had a feeling I finally got it. "You're doing something to prevent me from feeling the wound on your back," I deduced, watching him closely.

His lifeless expression suddenly twisted into obvious displeasure. "I wish you didn't realize that," he growled, angry, but obviously not at me.

I folded my arms. "This is why it takes you so long to heal," I said, glaring at him now. "You're trying to protect me from the pain."

He rose to his feet suddenly, and I did everything I could to keep my eyes on his face. Because now that I knew what it meant to be his Eteria, he suddenly no longer seemed like a statue in a museum.

He seemed far too real. Tangible.

And I was terrified I would forget myself.

Yet my heartbeat quickened when he grabbed a pair of sweatpants and put them on before he drew closer to me. "This is not the only reason," he said, stopping when he was before me, forcing me to tilt my head back. "So don't worry about it."

I jumped to my feet and closed the gap between us, folding my arms as I scowled. "If I'm injured, would you feel the injury?"

He scowled back, eyes flashing as he saw where I was going with it. "Yes," he gritted out.

"And I would not be able to block you from feeling the pain, right?" I pushed, glowering at him now.

He almost bared his teeth. "I can take the pain," he growled, eyes narrowed. "You're a human. Pain like what I feel on my back will make you feel like you're dying."

"Fuck that," I spat, shaking with fury, yet I didn't know what else I could say to convince him. He seemed resolute. Set in his own decision.

And that drove me mad even more for some reason.

Perhaps it's the brainwashing. That treacherous voice returned with a vengeance. *Perhaps you're mad with worry because, as he said, you are wired to be . . .*

I wanted to refute this. To argue with it. But the doubt had been planted from the moment Lucien said that me being his Eteria meant I was bound to him forever and beyond. That without meaning to, he could easily manipulate me into feeling love and care for him.

So the fact he refused to let me feel his full pain, even at the cost of slowing his healing, made me feel ironically defeated.

My arms dropped back to my sides, and I stared at him with wonder, almost. The last few days ran through my head. Every conversation we had. Everything he'd shown me about himself. Even the fact he wanted to put distance between us by bringing me back to the apartment once Chase and Avenor were no longer a threat now made sense too.

If nothing else, one thing I was sure about, and it was that Lucien was a good man. He didn't want me to be magically forced to love him. He preferred to let me go, never understanding the extent of our bond, unable to love anyone else, and never knowing why. He saw it as the kinder option of the two.

Yet now he was telling me about it all . . .

"Why?" I asked in a whisper. "Why did you tell me all this now?"

His face shattered, and I saw his desperation just then. "There is no turning back for you to any sort of normalcy," he told me quietly. "The Sable Syndicate have made a move, warning me by threatening you that they know you are involved. They might've written in that letter that you won't be harmed, but the Syndicate is fickle and cunning. Their words cannot be trusted."

"So you'd rather keep me close and protect me from them instead of putting a security detail on me," I concluded, searching his gaze.

He nodded, opened his mouth, then seemed to think better of it and closed it, looking away from me. "Your brother, too, will now be under my protection," he said almost matter-of-factly. "He's also on the Syndicate's radar, after all."

I realized then he was steering the conversation away from what we'd been talking about. And while some part of me insisted I should get back to that subject—of him protecting me from pain and the whole Eteria thing, that it was important—I also felt emotionally exhausted.

"Enoch mentioned something about the Fae," I recalled now, feeling a sudden desperation to talk about anything but me being brainwashed to love him or him refusing to share his physical pain. It was all too much for me to process right now.

Lucien seemed visibly relieved as he gave me a faint smile that didn't reach his eyes. "The Sable Syndicate is a mob of supernatural creatures—Otherborne—known as Fae," he said now, his voice taking on a lecturing tone almost. "They reside in the Underearth, a place accessible only by the portals."

That was what he called the shadow marks, I remembered.

Our conversation was forced to a stop just then, when Enoch opened the door with a now-calm expression. "You've had an hour," he said, pointing at Lucien. "I need to reapply the stitches, so lie down, and don't argue with me, Lucien."

Lucien growled at him. "You wanted to inject *my Eteria* with faux fluxion," he snapped, and his hand immediately caught mine as if by instinct. "Inverna can cause Overflow in humans!"

Anais and Thayer, who entered the room behind Enoch, wore looks of fear as they avoided looking at Lucien. He did seem quite scary right now. But oddly enough, or maybe understandably now, I didn't find him scary at all.

"That only happens with humans who have a lick of fluxion," Enoch sniped back, pointing at me. "Drew here has not a single drop of fluxion in her. We checked!"

"Doesn't matter," Lucien growled, pulling me behind him protectively. "You are not injecting anything into her without her or my approval. Ever."

Enoch groaned in frustration, throwing his arms into the air. "Fine!" he said somewhat dramatically. "Don't come running to me when this wound never heals properly!"

Terms like *fluxion* and *Overflow* meant nothing to me, but I gathered the general issue here, and it forced us back to what we had discussed. Or rather, argued about. "Lucien," I said quietly, tugging at his hand, which still clutched mine in an unbreakable hold.

He whipped his head toward me, arctic-blue eyes filled with anger. "I'm not going to let you feel the pain, Drew, and that's final."

I heard a squeak, and from the corner of my eye I saw Anais retreating with a wince on her face. Frowning, I focused back on Lucien and hesitantly raised my free hand to cup his face. "Let's make a deal, then."

He arched an eyebrow, and when he spoke, the sarcasm dripped bitterly from his words. "What part of *that's final* do you not understand?"

"The part where I believe that as your Eteria, I should at least have a say about this, if I'm to be stripped of any autonomous thought before long," I hissed back. "So shut the fuck up and listen to me, you stupid wolf."

He stared at me, eyes wide with shock and disbelief. I used his momentary silence to launch straight ahead, grabbing his chin now so he would not look away from me. "The deal goes as follows. You let me feel your pain and finally heal properly." He was about to open his mouth, but I covered his lips with my palm, narrowing my eyes. "And if you're heavily injured again in the future and you don't want me to feel your pain, I will let you have your way."

His shock was replaced by fury as he took my wrist and pushed my hand away from his mouth. "Drew—" he started, but I wasn't having it.

"I'm trying to meet you halfway here, Lucien," I cut him off, searching his gaze, letting him see my determination—and my worry. "This is the least you could do to make up for the fact I'm now bound to you for eternity whether I want to be or not. That I will never be able to love another person. That I am going to worry about you till the end of days."

His face fell, and suddenly I was in his arms as he hugged me tightly. "I'm sorry," he whispered into my hair. "I'm so sorry, Drew."

I hugged him back, and from behind him, I saw Anais, Enoch, and Thayer looking anywhere but at us. I realized then that they had witnessed our little spat, and that made me feel somewhat embarrassed.

But not embarrassed enough to deter me or make me feel any less relieved when finally, Lucien, still holding me, said, "Just this time, Drew. And never again."

Lucien and I were lying on the bed together, both of us on our fronts. Enoch was ready next to Lucien with gloves on and some sort of an injection, while Anais, seemingly alert and ready, was holding open that thick book from before.

Thayer, bless him, seemed utterly lost as to what was happening. He simply sat in that room and pretended to be a houseplant. To be fair, he seemed to be in shock from everything he'd witnessed in the past few hours. It didn't look like he had processed it all, and I knew that when Thayer encountered information he had no context for, or that defied his own firm beliefs, he could go hours without speaking while his head was spinning.

That seemed to be the case now.

"On the count of ten, let the barrier go," Enoch now instructed, drawing my attention to the task at hand.

Lucien and I looked at one another. His dissatisfaction was obvious. His face was set in a scowl I feared would become permanent.

Enoch counted, and as he did, I mouthed to Lucien silently, *I'll be okay.*

That only made his scowl deepen.

"Ten!" Enoch called, and Lucien sucked in a deep breath and, without taking his eyes away from me, grew stiff.

The next moment, unfathomably excruciating pain exploded within me, so much so that I couldn't even scream; my vocal cords were locked tight as the pain spread through my veins and all the way to my back like wildfire.

It was pain like nothing I had ever felt before. I held on to the pillow under my head and bit into it, too, to try and ride wave after wave of endless, horrible pain. It was like someone was trying to peel the skin off my back.

Tears burned my eyes as I attempted to hold on for dear life, but the pain was far too much to bear. Through a ceaseless ringing in my ears, I could faintly hear shouts. But opening my eyes wasn't an option. Paying attention to anything else, really, was impossible.

All I knew was pain, and pain was all I was becoming.

There was also a pain in my side, where Lucien had been stabbed earlier, but it was nothing like what was going on in my back. In comparison, it felt like a faint throbbing.

Whereas it felt like lava was pouring over my back. I felt like I had been injected with acid straight into my veins. My muscles were locked, and I couldn't even move.

Fear mixed with the never-ending pain. What if this went on forever? What if I would feel like I was being skinned alive for the rest of my life?

Then, what felt like hours—maybe even days—later, as suddenly as the pain had assaulted me, it suddenly stopped.

My throat constricted as if trying to take a deep breath of air, yet the muscles were still stretched taut. I couldn't move my body at all, with my hands still clutching the pillow and my teeth tearing its case apart. Everything felt stiff and still, as if the pain were still there, still in effect, even though it wasn't anymore.

"Drew."

Lucien's voice was hoarse and soft. I couldn't respond to it. I could hardly even breathe.

"Drew, give me a nod if you can hear me."

Could I nod? I tried, and a spasm cascaded through my spine, making me jitter as my head jerked, causing my teeth to release the pillow. The fact I still had no control over my faculties even though the pain was gone made a deep sense of terror spread all over me, and I began shuddering uncontrollably.

"I'm going to touch you now." Lucien's voice cut through my fear. "If you can't handle it, move your fingers."

He must've seen me trying to nod and failing. But I didn't move my fingers now, even if I could've. I wanted him to make it better if he could. To relieve my body from the trauma it had just endured.

Gentle hands hesitantly grabbed my shoulders from behind. Involuntarily, I jerked at the touch over my still-sensitive skin, but I swallowed my whimper and tried to remain still, despite my shudders.

Then, slowly, those hands began kneading.

Lucien was giving me a massage.

The tears fell down my eyes, wetting the pillow that was already damp from when I'd bitten it in a silent scream. It wasn't because his touch hurt me, or that I felt any pain now; the tears were for him.

How could he have endured this kind of pain the whole time?

He'd mostly acted as if he wasn't injured, to the point I had to tell him when he was bleeding, because he didn't seem to notice.

How *couldn't* he notice?

Lucien's kneading grew more intense as he lowered his hands, massaging my upper arms, then my lower arms, before intertwining my fingers and clutching them to release the tension that still had them curled into fists around the pillowcase. Ever so slowly, I began feeling my muscles finally relax.

My fingers left the pillow then, and he warmed them up before moving back up to my shoulders. Then he started kneading my back.

I expected to feel pain, but instead, all I felt were his soft yet rough palms as they worked on my skin and muscle expertly. Faintly, I wondered how come a werewolf Alpha knew how to massage, but whatever the reason, I was utterly grateful he did.

When his hands reached my waist, he grabbed it and kneaded the little dimples in my lower back with his thumbs. I felt myself tense, though this time, it wasn't entirely uncontrollable. In fact, the lower his hands roamed, the more a different kind of feeling rose to the surface.

A feeling that had no business being here right now.

The moment his hands grabbed my thighs, heat—a very different kind of heat from the pain before—lit up within me, causing a soft, needy pounding in a very specific spot between them.

At once, all I could think about was how I wished he would push my thighs apart and touch that aching spot with his nimble hands.

The moan that escaped me then was very much involuntary.

Lucien paused. "Does it hurt?" he asked, and was it my imagination, or was his voice a little lower than before?

I found that I had regained agency over my head, so I managed to shake it.

He resumed his movements, and I had to bite my lip not to moan again when he drew closer to my ass but didn't touch it.

My heartbeat was now on overdrive.

However, the logical part of me suddenly whispered in my ear, *Did you forget what he said about you being his Eteria? That you will be magically manipulated to lust after him? Love him? Isn't that what's going on here?*

Was it? Because this felt real. I didn't feel manipulated. The heat pooling between my legs was definitely of my body's own doing, caused by Lucien's innocent touch.

Is it really innocent, though? that voice questioned, obviously skeptical.

But I knew that it was. It had to be. That I was his Eteria wasn't of his choosing; he'd said so himself. I doubted he would've chosen me given the option.

I mean, the man was earth-shatteringly gorgeous. And I was . . . average.

As Lucien went lower to massage my knees and then my calves, the desire slowly dissipated. My thoughts had poured much-needed icy water over any heat I might've felt.

A few minutes later, Lucien took his hands away from me and asked, "Can you move?"

My muscles were still stiff and aching but not as much as before. Slowly, I pulled myself up into a sitting position, wincing slightly at the groaning of my limbs, before I turned to look at Lucien.

He seemed completely haggard. His face was etched with rage, and his eyes were no longer arctic blue but almost an electric shade, practically spitting fire when he caught my gaze.

He growled, and the sound made my heartbeat quicken again, especially when he snarled, "Never again."

CHAPTER 20
PROVOCATIONS

Anais had given me a pair of fresh jeans and a tee that somehow fit me perfectly. She then ushered me to the fancy bathroom I'd seen before to take a much-needed shower.

Once I was clean and dressed, my muscles slowly loosening up and returning to their natural state, with the memories of the pain still sharp in my mind, I exited the bathroom and saw Lucien and Thayer standing outside, apparently waiting for me.

"It's time we discuss a few things," Lucien said in a business-like voice.

I frowned at him, seeing he was freshly showered and dressed as well. "What about your injuries?"

He clearly didn't like this question, because he scowled—again. "After I shared the pain with you," he said, a growling edge to his tone, "Enoch and Anaïs managed to heal the wound."

I wanted to be angry at him for refusing to share his pain with me all this time, knowing that he could've been healed when we visited Enoch in the hospital, but the memory of the pain, how it wasn't just bad but the worst thing I had ever felt, shut me up. If anything, I felt gratitude, in a way, that he wanted to protect me from this absolute misery.

It also made me worry that he'd had to endure it this whole time.

But seeing as this was neither the time nor the place for this conversation, all I did was nod and give him a small, hesitant smile. "That's good. I'm relieved."

"Well, I'm not," Thayer chimed in now, folding his arms. "You've done whatever that was for hours. It's now midnight." He glowered at me. "On the bright side, Lucien here gave me a rundown of everything that happened."

The sarcasm wasn't lost on me, and I decided to return as good as I got. "I thought you didn't believe in the supernatural," I said with a saccharine smile. "I thought that Willow and Julianna simply drowned in that river, that I was a delusional crackpot with a victim mentality who didn't get over her teenage emo era."

Thayer visibly flinched, his glower replaced by guilt. "Look, Drew, I've been meaning to apologize—"

"Would you have if you hadn't gotten that letter from the Syndicate?" I cut him off bitterly, and he tensed. "Your care for me only extends to your selfish need for me to stay alive because you can't tolerate having another sibling die out of your reach. That doesn't make you a good person, or a good brother. So save it."

His gaze turned sharp with hurt, but he didn't reply. Or rather, he couldn't, because Enoch entered the corridor from the living area and, looking at Lucien, said, "Your Betas are here."

Lucien groaned and pinched the bridge of his nose. "Of course they are."

With a tight jaw, he turned to look at Thayer and me. "My Betas must know by now that I've brought back two humans to the pack," he said, "so you're going to have to sit in on this meeting."

I was stunned. "We're at your pack?"

"Yeah," Lucien said, giving me a tired smile. "When you passed out, I brought you and Thayer here to my house, deep within the pack territory. It's the only safe place for you two right now."

"Oh," I murmured. That made sense. But then I realized I had yet to learn what happened after I'd passed out back in my apartment. What happened to the attacker?

Before I could ask, Lucien led us to the living area, a large space with a nonetheless cozy vibe and a surprisingly lavish, professionally equipped kitchen with all the high-end appliances, next to which was a large round dining table.

Lucien, his face troubled as his mind seemed to be elsewhere, motioned for us to sit at the table next to him. Anais was in the kitchen, drinking what looked like tea, and seemed hesitant and confused. Lucien noticed and said, "You will sit with us."

Anais frowned. "I'm a mere healer, Alpha."

Lucien gave her a cryptic smile. "I want you to sit in on this discussion."

She stared down at her teacup. "I'll make some coffee and tea for everyone, then."

Lucien seemed to want to protest, but Anais was already working her way through the kitchen as if it wasn't her first time there.

He must've noticed my surprise, because Lucien said, "My house serves as a reserve meeting place, as well as a rest stop for werewolves for any sort of reason."

To my surprise, Thayer chimed in with "What kind of resting stop do werewolves need?"

It was a good question, and Lucien answered it with "My house is deep within the forests of the Montrévère pack. Many pack members—old and young—use these forests for all kinds of things. Training, playtime, any-thing, really." He smiled genuinely now, fondly almost. "Since it's a long way from the main pack area, the members sometimes stop by my place to grab a drink, shower and dress, take a nap, this kind of thing. This is why I stored clothes for all ages in all sizes all over the house, and why there are guest rooms."

Something about that sounded so serene and beautiful. As if the pack were a family, with Lucien as the main caretaker. That made my chest tighten somewhat.

Thayer was silent, too, as he thought it through.

Just then, Enoch opened the entrance door, and into the room walked five people—two women and three men.

Wordlessly, the Betas sat around the table, along with Enoch and Anais, who now brought a tray with coffee, a teapot, and mugs for everyone.

Once everyone was seated, I realized that all five Betas were glancing between Thayer and me—which wasn't a surprise, considering we were the outsiders here. But still, the attention made me shift uncomfortably in my seat and look at a certain point on the wall.

"Before we start," Lucien said as a greeting, "let me introduce you to Drew Colter and her brother, Thayer. Drew, Thayer," he said, making my brother and me focus our gazes on him, "meet my Betas—Callista, Blaise, Oz, Teya, and Ren."

The three male Betas—Blaise, Oz, and Ren—were very good looking, but the women, Callista and Teya, were exceptionally beautiful, especially since their beauty seemed natural and effortless. Callista was a gorgeous woman, with a pair of startling green eyes that seemed even brighter in contrast with her smooth black skin. Her ebony hair was tied in a plait that was so long, it reached the floor when she sat down. She reminded me of a painting of Artemis, the Greek goddess of hunting, I'd once seen. Something about her upright posture and resting bitch face, perhaps.

Teya, the other female Beta, was tall—even taller than I was, I thought, which put her somewhere over six feet. She had silky-smooth natural platinum hair, something I could tell since her brows were almost the same shade. Her eyes were the color of molten gold, which, combined with her pearly-white skin and slightly pointed ears, made her look like an elf. She also held herself with an air of dignity that seemed to add to the overall effect.

Seeing these two ethereally beautiful women made me feel so self-conscious, I shifted uncomfortably in my seat as I sneaked a glance at Lucien.

He was smiling, his eyes on one of the Betas before him. The two female Betas were sitting right where his gaze was aimed.

And that gutted me, even though I already knew he was way out of my league. That if he could've had a choice, he would've never chosen me as his Eteria.

Because why would Lucien go for me, with my plain brown hair and eyes, glasses, and mousy appearance, when women like Callista and Teya existed?

"Where is Mack?"

The words snapped me out of my depressing thought back to the present, where one of the male Betas, Oz, had just spoken. His slanted dark eyes glared at Lucien, and the tips of his lips curled down, showing obvious disapproval and displeasure.

Lucien, however, didn't get angry like I somewhat expected him to. Instead, he said in an even tone, "He's dead."

All five Betas stared at Lucien with stunned expressions that almost seemed comical. But not even a second later, Oz's face twisted, and he growled. "Dead?"

Lucien looked at his Beta with something akin to pity. But when he spoke, his voice was authoritative and cold. "He conspired with the Sable Syndicate to kill me. When his plan failed, he suffered the consequences of his actions."

Oz stopped growling, but he was obviously still furious. As if his fellow Beta trying to kill their Alpha wasn't a good enough reason to have him die.

But Lucien ignored Oz's blatant disrespect and looked at the others, who were watching him quietly.

"Five days ago, I received an anonymous report about a few werewolves who wished to go rogue," Lucien said now, leaning forward to meet each Beta's eyes. His biceps bulged when he rested his elbows on the table, and I tried not to let my eyes linger too much, especially since I didn't want to be distracted. Not now.

Lucien's eyes finally landed on Oz, who glared back for a moment before looking away, his lips curled downward. Lucien's eyes remained on him as he continued. "I tracked those rogues from downtown LA to North Hollywood. I was also aware I was being followed."

He paused, his gaze still fixed on Oz, whose jaw clenched, before he resumed. "At first, I ignored the follower, since I wanted to find the rogues first. But then it occurred to me: The follower might be after the rogues. Perhaps it was a Society agent using me as a compass. So I led them to a dark alleyway and confronted them."

His face darkened. "In retrospect, I know the assassin was already enveloping me in their magic. There is no other reason for why my reaction time was suddenly slower, and why the assassin was able to pin me down and carve a Spellscript over my back."

Callista and Teya seemed shaken by this information. Ren, another male Beta, had a disturbed look in his bright gaze. Oz's seemed to freeze in shock, while the fifth Beta, Blaise, watched Lucien with an impassive face, though his eyes betrayed him, practically spitting fire with worried rage.

"I would've died," Lucien said simply now, as though he were talking about the weather, "had Drew not found me in time."

He turned to me with a heavy look. "The assassin who attacked us this afternoon is the same one who almost killed me," he informed me suddenly, and my eyes widened as shock stiffened my spine. "I recognized their smell. It's very . . . particular."

My heart lurched in my chest. "Did you kill them?" I asked in a whisper, searching his gaze.

He grimaced. "After they stabbed me and you . . . fainted"—I winced—"they fled the premises." He paused, and frowned. "I'm not sure why, though. I'm certain they knew I had two humans with me, though I didn't feel like I was being followed this time, and that you wouldn't be a threat. They injured me too. Everything was perfectly set up for them to try and take me out. Yet the moment they realized you fainted, they suddenly froze and left."

He seemed to be thinking out loud, as if realizing something was amiss for the first time since the recent attack. And now I felt on edge, too, especially since the assassin was still out there.

"So why do you think Mack was involved in all this?" Oz suddenly snapped, glowering at Lucien. "What proof do you have to show for your suspicions?"

Oz seemed to be itching for a fight. His voice was dripping with skepticism, and his face showed his apparent distaste.

But Lucien wasn't having it. He said in a low, emphatic voice, "Are you doubting my judgment, Oz?"

Oz bared his teeth. "Why would I believe a French mutt?"

Tension immediately spread through the room. Lucien stood up, eyes freezing, as his whole body seemed ready to beat the life out of Oz. Oz, on the other hand, was grinning, goading him, as if he'd been waiting for this.

The other four Betas also rose from their seats. Teya, Callista, and Ren were glancing frantically between Oz and Lucien, while Blaise walked toward Lucien and put his hand on his taut shoulder. He murmured quietly, "*Il est en deuil, Lucien. Mack était comme un frère pour lui.*"

I wished I could know what he said, because Lucien seemed to slightly relax as he replied with a bitter voice, "*Il me provoque depuis des mois, Blaise.*"

Despite the tense situation we were in, I couldn't help but be mesmerized by the way Lucien's beautiful baritone voice rolled in flawless French. I could listen to him speak in French all day long without understanding a thing, and I would still die a happy woman.

Stop it, Drew, I chastised myself, and thankfully, I was provided with a distraction when Oz snapped, "You're in America, fuckers. Talk in fucking English!"

Lucien stiffened again, and Blaise's hand tightened on his shoulder before he turned his head to Oz. "I'm trying to save your hide, *imbécile,*" he said, and unlike Lucien, who had a mild accent, Blaise's was rather thick. "Or you'd rather die?"

Oz laughed out loud in bitter humor as he returned his glare to Lucien. "As if this poor excuse for an Alpha would *dare*—"

He didn't get to finish the sentence because in less than a second, Lucien broke away from Blaise's hold and was on the other side of the round table, pinning Oz to the floor with a long sharp claw at his throat, his arctic-blue eyes cold enough to cause frostbite.

I was on my feet, heart booming in my ears, as I strode toward Lucien. But I stopped in my place when I saw Lucien was merely grazing Oz's throat with his sharp claw, just enough to draw blood but not to cause serious damage.

Then I looked at Oz's face and saw his eyes were wide with triumph, and I was suddenly angry on Lucien's behalf.

I had no idea about Lucien and Oz's history, but evidently, it was nothing good. Maybe there was a good reason for Oz's hatred—I didn't know, like I was still learning to understand Lucien—but one thing I was sure about.

A person who truly believed they were in the right wouldn't stoop to personal insults.

"Why wouldn't I dare, Oz?" Lucien now said, his voice venomous as he stared at Oz. "Killing you would be as easy as swatting a fly. I already plan on replacing Mack, so it's not going to be that difficult to find another wolf to replace you."

Even though he was obviously facing death, Oz laughed. "The pack won't stand for it, you fucking moron," he spat out. "You can't kill me for merely talking shit."

I was reminded just then of my conversation with Lucien about what type of leadership an Alpha should enforce in their pack. He'd said he was trying his best to find a balance. That treating a pack as only a family, for instance, was bound to fail. He said the same thing was true for being an absolute ruler—a dictator.

When Lucien cut into Oz's throat, I realized which type he believed was right to deal with the current situation.

Oz's eyes bulged as he screamed, but suddenly his voice cut off, his screams silent, as Lucien tore something in his throat—his vocal cords, perhaps.

Silence spread through the room as Oz, who thrashed and tried to scream, suddenly turned still, blood spilling down from the wound into a pool on the floor.

Once Oz was down for the count, Lucien rose to his feet, grabbed a napkin from the table, and cleaned his razor-sharp claw. "Anaïs," he commanded in a curt tone, and Anais, who'd been silent the entire meeting, simply observing everything, came to stand next to him at once. Surprisingly, her face was blank, unfazed.

"Yes, Alpha," she said, staring down at Oz.

"Call Rémi and take him to the Ward," Lucien instructed, turning to look at her with eyes still bright with anger. "I want him fully healed—but for his vocal cords. He'd better remain silent."

The fact Lucien thought Oz could be healed was astounding to me. This kind of injury would've killed any normal person.

But werewolves must be built differently, because Anais gave a jerky nod and made a call before she leaned down next to Oz and grabbed his hand, closing her eyes.

Lucien then turned to the remaining four Betas. "I hope none of you have any more criticism to share," he said dryly.

Callista, Teya, and Ren all shook their heads, faces grim. Blaise merely sighed.

"Good." Lucien nodded and turned to look at me. His face softened somewhat. "I'm sorry you had to see this," he told me quietly, and turned to look behind me. "You too."

Frowning, I turned around to see he had spoken to Thayer. My brother had been so quiet, I forgot he was even here. Seeing him now, with his face pale, his lips pressed together, and his fingers twitching in agitation, I realized Thayer was having a hard time processing this.

An idea occurred to me just then. "Lucien," I said quietly, "it's already late. Maybe we can continue this meeting tomorrow? When everyone is much calmer?"

I caught Lucien's gaze. Behind his resolute anger, he was exhausted. I could tell. It had been a long day, after a long week, and he needed rest. Thayer and I, too, and I was sure Enoch did as well, since he'd been practically snoozing in his seat the entire meeting.

Lucien seemed to realize the same thing, and he let out a breath before turning to his Betas. "Callista, Teya," he said, addressing the female Betas, "you take the first guest room. Blaise, Ren, and Enoch—you can use sofas in the living room. They open into beds. Thayer"—he turned to my brother—"you can take the second guest room." He paused, returned his gaze to his Betas, and said, "We'll continue this tomorrow morning before the pack meeting."

I had no idea what the pack meeting was, but I had far more pressing matters to attend to. As everyone left the room—including Enoch, who moved unsteadily on his two feet, and Thayer, who seemed so lost, I kinda pitied him—I grabbed Lucien's arm to draw his attention to me. "Where do I sleep?" I asked in a soft murmur.

It shouldn't have come as a surprise when he replied matter-of-factly, "In my room, of course."

My heart raced now. "Are you sure?" I asked, letting him go in favor of fiddling with the hem of my shirt. "I can sleep with Thayer, if you want—"

"Drew," he said, making me freeze. "It's been a long day, and I spent most of it worried about you."

His words made me snap my eyes up to meet his. He looked at me with stark sincerity. "I don't want to let you out of my sight even for a moment," he admitted with sudden vulnerability that caught me off guard.

I couldn't help the flush that crawled up my cheeks. "Oh."

He let out a sigh and took my hand in his as he pulled me toward the corridor. Once we were in his room, he let me go and pulled his shirt off.

Trying not to stare, I simply stood there as he got into bed. When he realized I was still standing, unable to move, feeling out of my depth, he turned to look at me. "Would it be better if I turned into your wolf?"

It wasn't the first time he'd said he was *my* wolf, but it was definitely the first time I felt a little sense of possessiveness. But I had no right to be possessive. Lucien wasn't mine. I might be his Eteria, but that was all there was to us . . .

And suddenly, my flush, the heat, the fuzzy feelings I got from him telling me we would sleep together in his room disappeared.

He said he didn't want to let me out of his sight not because he *cared* about me as Drew, but rather because I was his Eteria. His weakness.

His vulnerability from before was about me being his Achilles' heel, and nothing more.

I'd seen the way he cut Oz's throat. Lucien refused to show weakness to anyone. And I was a walking, talking, sentient weakness.

Of course he wanted to keep an eye on me.

It had nothing to do with the fact I was a woman and he was attracted to me. Because that was all my stupid, hopeless hopes in my head talking.

Lips thin, I quickly changed into pajamas in the bathroom before getting into the bed, pulling the duvet over me. Then I flatly said, "You don't have to shift," before I turned to my side, showing him my back.

That night, there was no spooning.

CHAPTER 21
WHAT THE FAE?

"We should go back to Seattle."

Thayer's words barely registered as I sipped my coffee the next morning, tired and dejected. I'd barely slept a wink, and when I woke up, Lucien was gone.

According to Enoch, who was sitting in the living room with us for the morning coffee, he'd gone out with the Betas earlier to bring them up to speed before they came back for the continuation of the meeting from the night before.

Now, I looked at Thayer, pushed back my glasses, and sighed. "I can't go back to Seattle."

My brother's gray eyes sparked. "When you were out yesterday, Lucien told me about how you came to know him," he said through gritted teeth, his own coffee mug forgotten in his hand. "I know you don't care what I think, you think I only care about you for selfish reasons, but that's not true. You're in way over your head, and you know it."

I shot him a foul look. He was right. I *was* in way over my head. But the truth was, I was already involved in this whole clusterfuck. Until the threat to Lucien, and therefore to me, was resolved, I couldn't go anywhere.

Lucien himself said that it was not an option to believe what was written in that letter Thayer received. That the authors, the Syndicate, were fickle and cunning.

That meant Thayer was in danger too.

"We can't go back," I told him now, giving him a pointed look. "And to be honest, even if we could, I still wouldn't."

Thayer grunted. "Why the fuck would you stay around these . . ." He glanced at Enoch, who was reading a medical book next to us, and added in a whisper, "*Monsters?*"

It hadn't occurred to me until then, but all Thayer had seen ever since his arrival yesterday was pain and violence—especially from Lucien. A part of me understood why he seemed to think of the supernatural creatures, the Otherborne as Lucien called them, as monsters.

But that didn't mean it sat well with me.

"They aren't monsters," I said, downing the rest of my coffee before slapping the mug against the coffee table a tad too hard. "They might be different from us in essence, but they are still as human as one could be."

Thayer did not like my response. "If I am to believe everything I've witnessed in the last twenty-four hours," he murmured darkly, "and believe everything you shared about what happened eight years ago, then they *are* monsters, no matter what you say."

I froze, not believing my ears as I stared at him with wide eyes. "What did you just say?"

His face suddenly relaxed, and he offered me a tentative smile. "After I received the letter, I started to suspect I might've been wrong," he explained in a soft, sheepish voice. "Now, after everything, I'm sure that you've been right all along about what really happened eight years ago."

The words—words I'd been waiting to hear all this time from someone, *anyone*—should've soothed the hurt, lonely part of me that felt like I was fighting alone in search of the truth.

Instead, they stoked a cold flame within me that iced my blood.

It was far too little, too late.

"Do you think it makes it all okay, then?" I asked in a drawl, masking my cold rage with pure sarcasm. "Did you think I would be thankful that you believe me after all this time, after all the accusations you threw my way a year ago?"

That wiped the smile off Thayer's face, and I found savage satisfaction at seeing him shift uncomfortably in his place. "I wasn't there, Drew," he murmured, looking away with a grimace. "I didn't see what you saw."

"So you chose to alienate me and take Mom and Dad's side to show me just how much you didn't believe your only surviving sister," I hissed bitterly. "Got it."

He reached for me, taking my hands in his, gray eyes frantic. "I'm sorry," he said hoarsely, and to my astonishment, I saw tears rise to his eyes. "I'm really sorry, Drew. I should've never called you all those names. I should've never dismissed you outright. I'm sorry I didn't listen. That I *refused* to listen."

Seeing his tears brought mine to the surface as well, slicing through the coldness I was feeling. "It angers me that you had to be in danger yourself to believe it," I barked at him, tightening my hold on his hands. "It angers me that the only reason you came looking for me was out of fear for my physical safety rather than my mental well-being."

His tears fell, and suddenly I was enfolded in his tight arms. "I'm sorry," he whispered. "I'm so sorry, Drew, I'm sorry . . ."

I cried now, too, as I found all the fight I'd felt leaving my body, defeated in the face of my brother, my strong, resilient brother, actually crying in front of me.

Even when our sisters died, I hadn't seen him cry.

And for some reason, that broke me further.

I pulled my arms around him and hugged him back, burying my head in his shoulder. "You hurt me," I muttered, whimpering. "You really hurt me. But I'm sorry, too, for the things I said."

He shook his head, tightening his hold on me. "Don't be," he said, sniffing. "I deserved every word you threw my way, because you were right. I had always promised you, Will, and Jules that I would protect you. Be there for you. Love you unconditionally. And I failed at each and every promise I made."

My throat constricted as the memories of that day eight years ago hovered in my mind. "Even if you had been there with us," I whispered, "you wouldn't have been able to do anything, even if you tried."

That's rich, a voice murmured in my head as Thayer's soft sobs filled my ears. *Considering you didn't even try.*

I pushed the thoughts away. It was neither the time nor the place to deal with them anyway.

So I held on to Thayer and hugged him tightly, unable to hold on to any grudge anymore. Not now, now that he'd apologized, that he was crying in my arms, that he'd admitted I'd been right, even if it was far too late.

Life was too short to keep on hating the only sibling I had left.

And with the danger still lurking behind the corner, I refused to lose him too.

I could feel Enoch's eyes on me as Lucien and his Betas returned to the house and settled around the table.

Ignoring his looks, which made me feel like he was trying to peer into my soul, I stared at Lucien, who motioned for me and Thayer to join them. Enoch sat at the table too.

When I sat next to Lucien, I could see the Betas were staring at me strangely. Yesterday, they had barely spared me a look, and now it seemed as if they couldn't take their eyes off me.

I had a hunch as to why that was, and I knew I was right when Lucien leaned down and murmured in my ear, "They know."

Goose bumps rose all over my skin, though not from his confirmation of my suspicions, but rather because his voice made me shiver. His lips had brushed accidentally against my earlobe, and that made me feel all kinds of things I really didn't want to feel right now.

Giving him a jerky nod, I leaned back from him, hoping for some personal space.

However, while he leaned back, he spread his arm on the back of my chair in a way that made me feel as if he was making a claim of some sort.

That movement wasn't lost on the Betas, nor on Thayer, who, with bloodshot eyes, stared at Lucien's arm as if he had a personal vendetta against it.

When the minutes ticked by and no one was talking, I couldn't help but break the silence and ask, "What are we waiting for?"

Before anyone could respond, the door opened again, and Anais walked in. Behind her was Oz, with a thick bandage wrapped around his throat.

He glared at Lucien, who stared patiently back, as he took his seat. Anais hesitated for a moment before Lucien gave her a nod, and she slid into the last free seat, next to Enoch.

"Let's start," Lucien finally said, and turned to look at Blaise, whose eyes were still on me. "Now that everyone is up to speed, it's time that you, Blaise, head to the Underearth."

Blaise glanced at Lucien and nodded silently while my brother asked, "What the hell is the Underearth?"

It was Anais who responded, to my surprise. "It's a place under the earth," she said curtly, and when I looked at her, I saw her staring at Thayer with open distaste.

Thayer seemed to share her dislike because he snapped, "I got that part, thanks."

Anais jutted out her chin condescendingly as she replied, "Your question is quite redundant, then, isn't it?"

I stilled as Thayer glared at her. Thayer was a scholar. He prided himself on asking the right questions, which, he always claimed, was quite the achievement in his field. With his bachelor's in physics, then master's and PhD in comparative literature, it didn't seem far fetched. My brother was smart.

Yet Anais, for whatever reason, had found the right button to push.

Why was she needling him?

"Anaïs, stop," Lucien now interjected, frowning at Anais, too, who nodded and sat back—though she still shot a smug smirk at Thayer that practically made smoke come out of his ears.

"The Underearth is the place where the Fae dwell," Enoch now explained, drawing everyone's attention to him. He was into his third cup of coffee for the morning, and he sipped it as if it were his first before he resumed. "Not all Fae, of course, but a very specific subrace of Fae. We refer to them as Underearth Fae."

He paused and glanced at me momentarily before he looked at Thayer, who still seemed pissed off from Anais's obvious provocation. "The Underearth Fae are governed by an organization called the Sable Syndicate. While they dabble in all kinds of illegal businesses, and many of their actions warrant a healthy dose of suspicion, they care deeply for their kin and rule the Underearth fairly."

"The irony of the Syndicate," Blaise chimed in, his thick accent making his voice drawl, "is that their ruler, the Syndarch, is a part of the Council."

"The Council for Regulation of Arcane Phenomena," Lucien explained when Thayer seemed confused, and I remembered Lucien mentioning them, though only as the Council. "They are the global organization that oversees the world's entire Otherborne population."

Anais suddenly jumped in, staring wickedly at Thayer. "*Otherborne* is an umbrella term for all supernatural races," she told him in the maddeningly slow voice that people often used on kids.

My brother had never been quick to anger—Willow had always been the hotheaded one among us siblings, which made Thayer reprimand her more often than not—but Anais was deliberately poking at him, and he bit into it almost willingly. "I know that already," he snarled at her.

That surprised me. "Do you?" I asked, sincerely confused.

A sudden tug on my hair made me grow still. Slowly, I turned to look at Lucien, who gave me a soft smile as he murmured, "When you were passed out, Thayer and I talked."

Right. "I see."

He curled a few strands of my hair around his finger, making me stiffen further, as he returned his gaze to the rest of the table. "That means that the Syndicate, and thus the Underearth as a whole, can bend the law however they want."

Lucien and Enoch exchanged glances then, and I realized there was more to what he was saying. I remembered then what Lucien's main objective was: to expose the supernatural world to humans.

But what did it have to do with the Syndicate? The same Syndicate that had conspired with Mack Page to kill Lucien—and almost succeeded in doing so?

"So even the *Otherborne* government is corrupt," Thayer murmured, throwing a filthy look at Anais, who rolled her eyes as if she hadn't been the one to taunt him.

It was Blaise who spoke next. "I've set a meeting with one of my contacts in the Underearth for later today," he said matter-of-factly, and seeing that no one but Thayer and I was surprised, it seemed to be old news. "They might know what kind of . . ." He frowned a little. "What's the word . . . *cost? Price?*" He shook his head. "Whatever Mack offered the Syndicate."

His fumble would've been cute if he hadn't been a huge muscular werewolf whose face was set in a permanent flat expression.

"You mean *favor.*" Teya, for the first time, joined the conversation. Her gold eyes shot a heavy look at Lucien. "The Fae, and especially the Syndicate, don't deal in money."

"Yes, *favor*'s the word." Blaise nodded solemnly.

Lucien grimaced. "Whatever Mack offered them, I still believe the Syndicate have their own personal reasons to get rid of me." He looked at Blaise. *"Vous devez vous renseigner pour savoir s'ils seraient disposés à conclure un accord avec moi en tant que représentant de l'Impératif."*

The sudden transition to French made me blink, and the others seemed confused as well.

Oddly enough, Enoch seemed to understand, if his sharp look at Lucien was any indication, while Blaise responded with a determined *"Oui, Alpha."*

Seeing the confusion—and frustration—of his other Betas, Lucien, still twirling my hair, explained, "As nonnative English speakers, Blaise and I sometimes have days where we need to hear our native tongue to understand anything."

I glanced at Lucien, suspicious. His face didn't give anything away, and when I glanced at the Betas, it seemed like they bought it. But to me, it sounded like a load of bull.

Especially since I understood one word from what Lucien had just said.

L'Impératif.

The Imperative.

Enoch had mentioned the Imperative before. I remembered it was when he spoke to Lucien in the hospital. It didn't seem like it had anything to do with the pack, or werewolves in general.

So what the hell had Lucien just ordered Blaise to do?

"Now that we cleared that up," Lucien said, "let's return to the subject at hand. The Syndicate—"

A hand suddenly slammed on the table. My eyes snapped to Oz, who was on his feet, face red with fury. He tried to talk, to mouth whatever he wanted to say, and growled deep in his chest when he couldn't.

Lucien stared at him lazily and said, "Anaïs, bring him a pen and paper."

"Yes, Alpha," Anais said at once, shooting to her feet.

When she passed by Thayer, he murmured quietly to her, "To think you'd give me attitude when you're a mere lapdog."

This time, it was she who glared at him, and my brother who shot her a satisfied smirk.

I wondered what the hell was going on between these two. They had only met yesterday, after all. When did they have the time to grow such a deep dislike of each other?

Maybe, like love at first sight, there was also hate?

When Anais approached Oz with the pen and paper, he snatched it out of her hands and wrote in thick, big letters that he lifted the paper to show us: **If the Syndicate itself wants you dead, then it wasn't Mack's fault!**

Lucien pinched the bridge of his nose. "As Mack's childhood best friend, you knew him better than anyone else, Oz," he said now, giving his Beta a pitying look. "You know how he felt about me from the moment I set foot in this pack six months ago."

That was news to me, and I couldn't hide my shock. Lucien had only been an Alpha for six months? But he acted, and sounded, as if he'd been at it much longer. In fact, with all his talk about the different leadership options for an Alpha to rule their pack, he sounded far more experienced.

Oz wrote another thing on the paper and showed it to us. **Fae can use mind control. I know Mack betrayed you, and the pack, but I refuse to believe he actively sought out the Syndicate on his own. That's not who he was!**

"Oz." Lucien's voice lowered, a warning undertone to his words. "The Fae might be able to control the mind, but you forgot a crucial detail." Anger colored his voice. "Under section 2(b), clause 9, in the Otherborne Enmity Agreement, the Sable Syndicate would never actively look for, or initiate interaction with, werewolves."

Whatever that meant, it didn't seem to appease Oz.

And Lucien's patience seemed to have reached its limits, as his face filled with rage. "It seems you have a short memory, Oz, so let me refresh it."

Oz bared his teeth, but Lucien ignored it and continued. "Remember how I was given an anonymous tip about the rogue werewolves?"

When Oz didn't respond, Lucien suddenly snapped, "Yes, or no?"

With bared teeth, Oz reluctantly nodded.

"Good," Lucien growled, his hand fisting in my hair suddenly, making my heartbeat grow loud enough I feared everyone could hear it. "Now, you know the mailbox near my office, right? The one where pack members can send their complaints and requests anonymously, right?"

Despite his remaining reluctance, Oz knew better than to argue and gave a single sharp nod.

"Good, so you're not completely clueless, then," Lucien mocked as his hand slowly released my hair. I would've sighed in relief had his hand not moved to the nape of my neck in a hold that felt confusingly possessive. "I found that note there. The only ones who can put a note in the box are pack members."

A growl filled the room, coming from Oz, who wrote with an angry flourish of his arm, STOP TREATING ME LIKE A FUCKING TODDLER.

"When you stop acting like one, I will," Lucien promised in a threatening, silky voice, his thumb rubbing the side of my neck, forcing me to suppress a shiver as I desperately tried to ignore the very inappropriate heat pooling in my gut. "Now let us proceed. Once I found the note, I was immediately on alert. After all, it wouldn't be the first time some young pack member decided to push my limits. However, since I take such notes seriously, I still went looking for the rogues."

Oz didn't move as he listened intently, his eyes burning.

Lucien pointed at Teya all of a sudden. "Out of all of you, and the rest of the pack, Teya is the only one who has enough physical strength to take me on," he declared, "and while she still loses to me when we spar, she always manages to get in a few hits, and wears me down."

Teya seemed surprised at that because her eyes widened, her lips parting in shock.

"Since I'm the only Alpha in the western part of the States, there is no Alpha nearby who could challenge me either," Lucien stated matter-of-factly, as if talking about his unparalleled power was a mundane part of his routine. "If someone attacked me, whether in broad daylight or in the middle of the night, I would be able to sense them, even without switching on my senses in my human form. But that night, the attack came from nowhere. Or so it felt."

He pointed at the table, and when I looked, I saw nothing there, other than . . . well, his shadow. "That's right," Lucien said with a bitter smile, "certain Underearth Fae have the unique ability to blend into one's shadow. It took me a couple of days after the attack to think about it, about *how* I couldn't sense my attacker, when it occurred to me that if the Syndicate was involved, then obviously, this was an option."

Callista raised her hand hesitantly, and when Lucien simply glared at her, she winced and said in a soft voice, "But for the Fae to enter your shadow, they need to have at least followed you to target it."

"Not necessarily," Blaise said in that solemn voice of his. "Umbral Fae can shadow hop, moving from one shadow to another without being noticed. That Fae could've hopped between shadows of nearby humans until they found our Alpha."

"That's exactly it." Lucien's angry voice was now sarcastic. "That Fae must've belonged to the Syndicate's Covert Umbral Neutralization Taskforce—the assassin division."

Something occurred to me just then, and I had to cough to hide a snort. Thankfully, no one noticed.

Lucien, glaring at Oz, whose face was now white, resumed. "That Umbral Fae couldn't have known which neighborhood I was in without an informant on the inside," Lucien said now, furiously, but I could see beyond that. His arctic-blue eyes might have been sparking with anger, but I could see the pain he was trying to hide. The pain of the betrayal. That wiped away any sort of humor I might've felt. "Since I don't exactly advertise my whereabouts, I had a few suspects. Blaise and Rémi compiled a definite list, according to everything I told them."

Oz slowly sat down, his hands clenched into fists so tightly, his knuckles turned white.

"Mack Page's involvement was definitively proven when Drew and I visited Enoch's hospital in San Diego," Lucien continued, pulling his anger back under a mask of coldness, as he nodded to Enoch. "Mack had gone there to inquire about someone bringing in a werewolf, after he failed to find a body where his Umbral Fae assassin hire told him I should be. He thought then that the plan must've failed somehow, and I got help. The most likely conclusion would be that another werewolf, or Otherborne, found me and brought me to the only hospital on the West Coast that accepted Otherborne patients. He probably wanted to finish the job when I was at my most vulnerable, but he was continually being told there was no werewolf patient in the hospital, which confused the hell out of him.

"And that's when I finally showed up and showed him what exactly is the price of betrayal."

Dead silence spread through the room, and I watched Lucien with concern. He seemed to have his emotions under control now, but my gut told me it was all a facade. That he was far more stripped down than the Betas at the table could ever know. He might've looked to them like a pissed-off Alpha who had taken revenge on his traitor subordinate, but in reality, I could tell he was hurting.

When Lucien killed Mack Page, he did not take pleasure in it. He did not seem elated to have taken his revenge. He seemed lost. So utterly, completely lost. Like a man who didn't know where he belonged.

And I could relate to that. I'd felt it myself, too, more often than not.

Even now, as he stood in this room full of his Betas, he looked so sad and alone, it made me hurt too.

Now that I knew the whole truth about what happened that night I found him, things started making a lot of sense. I finally understood now how everything connected.

Or almost everything.

Because there was one thing that still didn't make sense.

If Lucien was all-powerful, so much so that only another Alpha, or maybe Teya, could take him out, then how had a Fae nearly managed to kill him? Sure, they had the element of surprise, but after seeing Lucien in action, I doubted that was all there was to it.

Especially since there was this specific Spellscript on his back that seemed to prevent him from healing properly. That affected his ability to shift to his wolf form and back.

But seeing as, soon after, Lucien ended the meeting with the promise of reconvening after Blaise did some investigating, I didn't bring any of that up.

If Lucien didn't tell, it was certainly not my place to tell either.

CHAPTER 22
AN ALPHA'S TRUE POWER

When the meeting was over, the Betas left, while Anais, Enoch, and Thayer stayed behind.

Lucien, who seemed weary already from the whole ordeal, turned to look at the two. "The Spellscript on my back," he said quietly, looking at Anais specifically. "I need you to crack it."

She pursed her lips and nodded. Enoch nodded, too, and said quietly, "I'll do whatever I can to help, though Spellscripts are not my main area of specialty."

"That's all right," Anais told Enoch. "All you need to do is study some old writings with me to try and figure out what the Spellscript's effects are."

A light switched on in my head, and I jumped to my feet. "Lucien," I said, looking at the gorgeous, tired man. "Where is my duffel bag?"

Lucien frowned. "I think it's still in the car—"

"Give me the keys," I said, stretching my hand forward expectantly as I looked up at Anais. "Please wait."

Confused, Lucien handed them to me. "It's right outside."

"Thanks," I said, and left the house. Or rather, the cabin.

I headed to the shiny Rolls-Royce, which stuck out like a sore thumb in the midst of an endless spreading wilderness that surrounded Lucien's house—cabin—and clicked it open. I grabbed my duffel bag and returned inside, dropping the keys on the table as I rummaged through my things.

It occurred to me then that the contents of this duffel bag were all I had left to my name. My entire apartment had been trashed, my furniture, clothes, everything I owned damaged beyond repair, after all.

The memory of the apartment haunted me as I pulled out my notebook and handed it to Anais. Trying to ignore the sudden suffocating feeling that squeezed my throat, I answered Anais's silent question when she looked at the notebook. "For the past eight years, I've compiled a list of all sigils I encountered."

"Sigils?" Lucien, Enoch, and Anais echoed simultaneously, turning to look at me with confusion.

My cheeks flushed at my little slip of the tongue. "I mean, Spellscripts," I mumbled, embarrassed. "Before, I named them sigils. But they're Spellscripts. Obviously."

Enoch took the notebook from Anais and studied it, his eyes widening. "You encountered a lot of different Spellscripts," he noted, flipping through the pages, stunned. "I know you write for *The Hallowing Hour,* but I didn't expect that you would've done such extensive research."

Anais peered at the notebook as well, with a narrow-eyed expression, but she didn't say anything.

A moment later, Lucien rounded the table toward us, heading to Enoch and staring down at my notes with a heavy contemplative look. Thayer, too, approached us, or rather, me, with a confused yet curious look. "What's all this?" he asked me in a low murmur.

Still flushed with embarrassment, I stared down at my feet. The response to my notebook, which indeed contained years of dedicated research, made me shift from foot to foot uncomfortably. I felt like an obsessive, die-hard fan of the supernatural rather than a journalist.

But I wasn't a fan. All I had ever wanted was to meet the supernatural—the Otherborne—and find out what really happened to Willow and Julianna.

"You know why I took the job at *The Hallowing Hour*," I said now, folding my arms. "You know what my end goal is—and has been since that day."

Thayer didn't reply. Instead, he merely put his arm around my shoulder, which made me automatically stiffen before I slowly relaxed. "Can you tell me again?" my brother asked. "About what happened?"

I stiffened again, this time in surprise—and dread. I hadn't retold everything that happened then in detail after that one time, when I tried to convince our parents and Thayer that what I saw was real. It was hard enough that the memory didn't seem to vanish with the years but only embedded itself harder into my psyche. The thought of speaking about it, reliving it, made a chill crawl down my spine.

"You already know what happened," I evaded, shrugging off his arm.

His gray eyes were full of emotion. "Back then, I didn't believe you," he said, regret coloring his voice. "Because I didn't believe you, I hardly listened to anything you had to say. I'm ashamed of it, but it's the truth."

I scowled but let out a long sigh. "I don't . . ." I started, before dropping my gaze to my fingers, which fiddled with the hem of my shirt. "It's not . . . easy to talk about."

"Talk about what?" Lucien's voice suddenly interrupted, and Thayer and I raised our gazes to him. Anais was now holding the notebook in her hands, and the three were staring at us with identical suspicious gazes.

Thayer and I exchanged glances, as if we could read each other's minds. And at that moment, peering into his gray gaze, I knew our thoughts, for the first time since God knows how long, were aligned.

They should hear that too, Thayer's eyes said, echoing my own thoughts. *They must be able to help.*

But I hesitated. There was a reason I hadn't said anything to Lucien so far—though, admittedly, a part of it was the fact we hadn't had a dull moment or a right time to sit down and talk things through.

Yet I couldn't help but fear what Lucien's reaction would be.

So I stalled as I turned to him. "I thought you have another meeting?"

Lucien didn't seem satisfied by that, yet he looked at the clock on the wall and grunted. "Yeah, it's almost time."

"I'll go to the Ward and start looking into this until the gathering's over," Enoch said, shooting me a momentary glance before looking at Lucien. "I need Anais for that, though."

Lucien nodded and looked at Anais. "You're exempt from the gathering—and from any other work you have for the rest of the day. If anyone asks, tell them you're under direct orders from me. If they have issues with that, tell them to book an appointment with my secretary."

Anais's spine straightened, and she said determinedly, "Yes, Alpha."

Next to me, Thayer snorted mockingly, and Anais shot him a fiery glare that would've flayed him alive if it could.

The exchange wasn't lost on Lucien, who glanced between my brother and Anais with a little furrow between his brows before he rested his gaze on Thayer. "You can stay here and rest. We'll be back later." He paused. "There's food and drinks in the fridge."

"We?" Thayer and I asked together, and we glanced at each other with a frown.

Lucien smiled. It was a genuine smile I didn't think I'd seen from him before. It made his eyes sparkle with warmth, and in return, my heart skipped a beat and butterflies fluttered in my stomach. "Drew's coming with me."

Blushing for a whole different reason now, I glanced at Thayer again and saw him frowning. "Can't I come, too, then?"

"I'm afraid that's not possible," Lucien replied apologetically, his smile disappearing as his gaze turned thoughtful. He glanced at Anais for a moment before he seemed to reach a decision. "If staying here isn't what you want, you can accompany Enoch and Anaïs to the Ward."

Anais whipped her head toward Lucien and snapped, "No!"

Lucien's lips twitched, his eyes almost wicked, while Enoch frowned, looking at Anais disapprovingly. "This is not very hospitable of you, Anais."

She glowered at Thayer. "He's only going to slow us down."

And again, she knew exactly which buttons to push, because Thayer suddenly straightened and shot her a strained smile as he retaliated. "You know what? I would *love* joining you. Maybe I'll even learn a thing or two. Unlike *some* people, I'm not afraid of a little intellectual challenge."

The provocation was obvious. The gauntlet was thrown. And Anais, whose face reddened with fury, couldn't help but pick it right up. "Fine," she spat venomously. "I would *love* seeing you eat your words." She paused, glaring. "You have no idea what you're getting yourself into, *Colter*."

Thayer put his hands in the pockets of his jeans, gray eyes flashing silver as he stared at her, grinning wickedly, and drawled, "It's *Dr. Colter* to you."

She was so livid, her curly hair seemed to slither around her head like Medusa's snakes. But Lucien put an end to the best show I'd seen in a while, especially from my normally cool-as-a-cucumber big brother. "We have to go. Thayer, go with them. Anaïs, be nice."

Anais growled deep in her chest, the sound rumbling like thunder. "Yes, Alpha," she grated out almost too menacingly.

As the three left the cabin, with Enoch standing between my brother and Anais like a human shield, I wondered how and why the hell these two hated each other so much.

The site of the Montrevere werewolf pack was absolutely, heart-wrenchingly beautiful.

From the narrow river trickling through the residential wooden cabins to the majestic vines covering the sole brick building of the pack's library, everywhere I looked, nature flourished.

I was so used to the Californian dry colors that the vivid green grass and healthy brown earth were like feasts to the eye.

Whipping my head from side to side, I took it all in as Lucien drove us deeper into the pack territory. Other than the residential cabins, there were a bunch of others that belonged to certain pack establishments: the school classroom, restaurants, and even local designer clothing shops. They were all surrounded by tall, bushy trees that gave the place a fairy-tale feel and made my heart ache with strange nostalgia.

But none of it compared to when Lucien came to a stop, with me right next to him, in front of a round plaza surrounded by five large wooden cabins. The trees around the plaza curved inward, toward the circle created by the cabin entrances, and cast shade over everything, with only hints of sunlight in between the leaves. But there was one beacon of sunlight that cut through the circular space between the tops of the trees, and it hit right smack in the middle of the plaza, over a flower garden.

It was hands down the most beautiful sight I'd ever seen.

Lucien's chuckle snapped me out of my temporary daze, and I slowly turned to look at him. He watched me, his lips curved into a warm smile that made my heart flutter. "Like what you see?"

I couldn't help but smile back. "Yes," I said softly, "a lot."

Our gazes caught and held as he said, "This is the pack's Heart, the middle of the territory, where all the official offices that run the pack are placed." His smile disappeared. "Since the pack has lost one of its Betas, I now have to address the members. It's my job as an Alpha."

The loaded tone of his voice made me want to reach out to him, but his face, which turned darkly grim, seemed to be telling me any sort of consolation or encouragement right now would be ill-timed.

So instead, I looked at the plaza, the Heart, and asked, "Is it okay for me to be here?" before I returned my gaze to him.

He stared at me with an inscrutable glimmer in his eyes before he suddenly confessed, "I find it hard to leave you out of my sight."

I blinked rapidly, trying to process his words and failing. "You had no problem planning to send me back home with bodyguards," I said slowly, scowling at the memory. "What the hell has changed?"

Lucien clenched his jaw and looked away. "With Mack's betrayal, and the break-in and attack in your apartment," he said quietly, "I can no longer trust anyone, not even my pack members, not to hurt you."

A chill went down my spine. "You think there are others here who work with the Syndicate like Mack did?"

"I don't know," he said, and the frustration coloring his voice was apparent. "So I'd rather not take any chances."

His words scared me a little. That he couldn't trust his own pack members saddened me too. And also reminded me of something. "It was mentioned this morning that you've been the Alpha here for a short while," I remarked.

Arctic-blue eyes found mine, filling with emotions I couldn't decipher. "I used to be the Alpha of a werewolf pack in Paris," he told me, and there was a hollow undertone to his voice. "This pack's former Alpha died unexpectedly seven months ago, and since this pack lacked an Alpha, and I lacked a pack, the ASS—the American Supernatural Society—offered me the opportunity to become the Alpha here."

There was gravity to his words, and also a tone of finality, as if he didn't want to talk about it any longer—though his story made no sense to me. He said he led a pack in Paris, so how come he lacked a pack?

But seeing that his face was set in hard lines, I let it drop, and, to alleviate the heaviness, I mentioned something I'd been thinking for some time now. "Are they aware their name spells *ass*?"

To my utter relief, Lucien's lips twitched in response, the distraught emotion receding from his eyes. "Well, in all fairness, everyone refers to them as A-S-S rather than the word itself."

"It still begs the question, who came up with this name, and if they did it on purpose," I noted with a wry grin and then stared when he let out a chuckle that seemed to surprise both him and me.

"Yes," Lucien murmured, grinning now as he looked at me with dancing eyes. "You know, every country inhabited by Otherborne—which, you may be surprised, is not all countries—has an official organization like the ASS. For instance, France has the Fédération Française du Surnaturel."

His French popped up as he mentioned the organization name, and I was fascinated by that for a few moments before it occurred to me why he'd mentioned it, and I snorted. "So the initialism for that would be FFS."

Lucien's cheeky grin made me chuckle. "Perhaps the same person who coined ASS is at fault here too," he said, gaze softening.

That reminded me of one other. "I think that person is at fault for more than just these two," I said, giggling. "You mentioned the Syndicate's Covert Umbral Neutralization Taskforce, otherwise known as CUNT."

He laughed out loud now, and I watched, mesmerized, as I imprinted the sound and the visual of him laughing so hard into my brain. My heartbeat was loud and quick as pride filled me because *I* was the one who made him laugh.

Stepping closer to me now, Lucien leaned forward, making me gasp quietly and freeze as he found my ear. "Remember the Council's full title?" he murmured in a sexy, amused voice that made me shudder. "The Council for Regulation of Arcane Phenomena?"

I giggled again. "CRAP? Seriously?"

Lucien leaned back a little so his face was close to mine. Too close. That made me giggle once more, even before he murmured in that sexy voice of his, "There is also the organization Enoch and I belong to. The one that shares our objective of exposing . . . you know."

I definitely knew. "Okay, this organization name can't be worse."

He grinned wickedly. "The Imperative for Transparency and Symbiosis would beg to differ."

"TITS." I snorted and burst out laughing. He joined me, too, laughing at the silliness of the pseudodeliberate unfortunately initialized names.

After a few moments, our laughter subsided and we stared at one another, grinning.

And suddenly, his close proximity, his beautiful eyes, the soft wind blowing his auburn curls, and his ethereal beauty hit me like a truck. My grin disappeared, and I watched his follow suit as I stared at him, searching his gaze. "I like seeing you laugh," I blurted in a whisper, throat clogged with emotion.

Before I could drown in those beautiful eyes of his that bored into mine as though he were looking straight into my soul, he murmured, "I like seeing you laugh too."

My lips parted, my eyes widening at his mirroring confession. "Oh."

His gaze hooded as it dipped to my lips, causing me to shudder uncontrollably. "Drew," he murmured in a raspy voice, a hand suddenly cupping my cheek while the other arm curled around my waist. His palm pressed against the small of my back and pulled me toward him until my front was pasted against his. His fingers stretched over the small of my back, while his thumb traced my lower lip.

His touch felt like an electric shock to my nerves, and I shivered again as my hands instinctually grabbed the front of his shirt to keep me steady on my utterly weak knees. When my knuckles brushed against his exposed collarbone, his expression suddenly shifted, gaze flashing with something akin to hunger.

And in the daze I was in, all I could think was *Kiss me. Please.*

"Alpha?"

Both of us jumped, releasing one another as if we were on fire, and stepped back, putting much-needed distance between us. We snapped our heads toward the intruder and saw Callista, one of the Betas, standing there, glancing between us with a little furrow between her brows.

Lucien cleared his throat and straightened, squaring his shoulders. "Head in," he said, now in an authoritative, flat voice, without a hint of the former moment of carefree humor. "We'll be right there."

With a slow nod, Callista threw me another look before she walked toward one of the cabins in the plaza and entered.

Silently, Lucien began walking toward the same cabin. It was the largest one in the Heart, with tall walls, a grand double door, and windows shaped like those in churches. A sign hung on the wall near the door, reading **Montrévère Pack Hall.**

We stopped before the door, and Lucien turned to me. He gave me a serious look, empty of whatever the hell had almost happened between us, and instructed in a soft, barely audible voice, "Stand behind the door when I walk in, then count to twenty and enter as quietly as possible. Stay in the back, near the door, as out of sight as you can."

Swallowing hard at the clash of emotions boiling inside me, I forced myself to ignore the many questions I had for him and instead whispered back, "All right."

With a heavy nod, Lucien straightened, turned to face the door, and took a deep breath.

Right before my eyes, I saw him transform.

Not into a wolf, but into the chilly, threatening, deadly version of him I'd seen once before, in San Diego.

Gone were the smiles or seriousness from his face. Gone was the spark in his eyes that had filled with amusement just a few minutes ago. Instead, his face was drawn into a flat yet somehow murderous expression, and his eyes were cold.

I felt a chill run down my spine at the sight and had to jump back when he suddenly threw the door open and walked inside menacingly.

As I hid behind the door and counted to twenty, I heard murmurs from inside, which slowly grew silent while Lucien's footsteps echoed deeper into the building.

Once I reached twenty, I slipped into the cabin and stood near the door, as Lucien asked.

Then I had to wrap my head around what the hell I was seeing.

Because the inside of the cabin wasn't, well, what an inside of a cabin would look like, no matter how large. In fact, it didn't look like the inside of *any* building I'd ever visited before.

From the entrance door, a wide staircase led down to the biggest auditorium I'd ever seen—it looked closer to a semicircular stadium than anything else. A few hundred people were perched in the stands, not an empty place in sight, while at the front was a stage with six seats, split into three and three, and right in the middle, a large, throne-like chair.

Five of the six seats were occupied by Lucien's Betas.

Lucien himself sat on the would-be throne.

And the silence that reigned was so thick, it could be cut with a knife.

Adjusting my glasses, I watched Lucien as he was silently given some papers by Callista, who was sitting next to him, and started to read through them with that same menacing expression. As he did, my eyes latched on to Callista, who didn't move away; instead, she leaned over the pseudothrone's armrest with her deep neckline, pointing things out on the papers Lucien was reading in a voice not audible from where I was standing.

I had noticed before that she was beautiful, but I hadn't fully realized the extent of it until now. It was as if a screen had been removed from my eyes, and I *really* saw her.

She was beyond beautiful.

She was gorgeous.

Almost as gorgeous as Lucien.

I was suddenly irritated. Beyond irritated; I was downright angry. *Take your hands off him,* I thought, folding my arms, seething, when she rested her elegant hand on his arm. When I saw her lips curve a little at something Lucien murmured in return, my anger multiplied. *Stay away from him! He's—*

My mind screeched to a stop. He's *what*, exactly?

And who was I to tell Callista to stay away?

This behavior was so unlike me, and yet I couldn't contain the sudden hatred I felt toward the woman. This wasn't rational. It pressed down on me like a force beyond my control.

I just wanted her to get away from Lucien before I went down there and ripped her hands off—

The fuck, Drew? I forced that last thought to stop, especially when I realized my entire body was trembling with rage. *What the hell is wrong with me?*

The longer Callista remained physically close to Lucien, the more jealous I became. Murderous thoughts circled in my head like a bunch of sharks ready for an attack. My breaths came out short and uneven, as if I could hardly *breathe* unless she pulled away. My body kept on trembling, no matter how much I hugged myself and tried to calm myself down. The anger simply would not let go, boiling my blood and putting me on a fucking edge.

When the woman finally leaned back, taking the papers back from Lucien, and put some distance between them, only then could I finally *breathe.* The trembling slowly stopped, and the blinding rage retreated, finally giving back the space to a clear head.

But even with my head clear, logic and rationality escaped me. I couldn't explain what had just happened, other than the obvious, but this was far beyond mere jealousy.

I had never felt anything like this before.

I was so at a loss, confused by my own mind, that I was grateful when Lucien started speaking, drawing my attention to what was going on in front of me.

He put one leg over the other, hooking his heel on the knee, while leaning his arms on the armrests. "I don't believe in coincidences," he began in a clear, low voice that sounded unnaturally loud, since it echoed in the room as though he were speaking into an invisible microphone. "I also don't believe any of you in the pack can take me down if you wish to."

There was movement in the audience. It seemed his words made the pack members uncomfortable. I could understand; it was the way Lucien spoke, with a somehow dramatic matter-of-factness and a threatening undertone laced in the words he wasn't saying.

"Some of you may have wondered where I disappeared to in the last week or so," he continued now, and I could see his right index finger tapping steadily, rhythmically, on the armrest—the only movement he made, thus so emphatic. "Last week was the twentieth of April, a date that officially marked the end of my first six months as the Alpha of this pack."

Silence still reigned, but it felt suffocating now, especially when Lucien's voice transitioned from indifferent and flat to threatening and even cruel. His finger froze too. "On that very same day, I was attacked."

The tension was so thick, I had to hug myself tight, as if to protect myself from violence that could erupt at any given second. Especially when Lucien stared at the audience with a savage look on his twisted face. "The attacker was neither a wolf nor a mere human. And they came prepared to kill an Alpha."

He suddenly smiled, but it was so sinister, I felt a chill run down my spine, and I shuddered, wishing he would return to the Lucien I knew. Because this Lucien was even worse than the monster who spilled Mack Page's guts or severed Oz's vocal cords.

This Lucien felt ten times more dangerous, and he was barely even moving.

Charisma, I suddenly realized. *An overwhelming amount of it.*

"As you can see," Lucien said with a chilling smirk, "I'm alive and well, so the attack failed. But many questions arose following the event." He paused, straightening in his would-be throne. "Ambushing an Alpha werewolf requires very specific information that the majority of Otherborne are not privy to. I am not built like the rest of you, after all."

His smirk fell, replaced by a deadly expression. "The only conclusion I could've reached was that someone in the pack colluded with said Otherborne attacker," he said in a soft murmur that was still somehow loud enough to be heard throughout the entire hall. "Thus the main question I had was, which pack member assisted the attacker?"

Leaning back, Lucien let his words ring in the room for a few beats before he resumed. "As I told you, I don't believe in coincidences," he said quietly. "That on the same day that marked the end of my first six months I would be attacked like that *cannot* be a coincidence, after all.

"The pack member was a fool to think they could take me to begin with," Lucien continued, back to his matter-of-fact voice. "But they were far more naive than I would've believed to think they could get away with it if I survived. They underestimated an Alpha's true power, and they paid for that mistake with their life."

His face, serious as it was, cooled over. "The perpetrator was Beta Mack Page."

Despite everything, this time the audience couldn't stay quiet. Yells, chatters, and gasps reverberated in the hall. I saw two women in the last row, right before me, break down in tears.

The moment Lucien raised his hand, though, silence spread across the room once more, though it wasn't as deadly as before. Instead, I could hear barely muffled sobs from all corners of the hall. "I understand your sorrow," he said, to my shock, and when I caught the look on his face, I saw it didn't soften. He said the words, but I could tell he cared little for the pack's collective grief. After he was betrayed by his *Beta*, of all people, and his two assistants, who were seemingly regular pack members, I got it completely.

"But Beta Page chose that path, and unfortunately for him, it led to his demise," he continued. He paused dramatically before adding in a snarl, "I strongly suggest you not be like Beta Page."

Even the sobs hushed following that unveiled threat. It wasn't an empty threat either; everyone, me included, could tell he was dead serious.

He would kill anyone who came after him.

CHAPTER 23
TO KILL A MOCKING MAN

The rest of Lucien's speech was about seemingly mundane pack matters, and the shift from his savage and intimidating beginning to a more civilized and indifferent rhetoric was so staggering, it took me a few minutes to snap out of my shock.

He then proceeded to talk about a lot of stuff I didn't understand. Something about pack guilds and something called Velunor that I didn't have the context to understand the meaning of.

At one point, tension rose when he said, "This week's hearing will be postponed to next week, due to the upcoming full moon."

That had caused many pack members to murmur among themselves.

I was a bundle of curiosity, especially about the full moon, by the time Lucien stood up and said, "Montrévère pack meeting is now adjourned," in a tone that sounded far too formal, even for this formal setting. He added in a low growl, "Go back to work. I sincerely hope this is the last pack meeting I'll have to hold for a while. Am I clear?"

The audience as one chanted tersely, "Yes, Alpha!"

With barely a nod to acknowledge their response, Lucien easily hopped off the stage and walked up the stairs. I realized everyone else was remaining seated, waiting for him to leave first before they would follow.

As he drew closer to the doors, his arctic-blue eyes snapped to me and lingered. My heart beat a little too fast as he held my gaze with such intensity, all kinds of butterflies came to life in the pit of my stomach.

He reached the doors, and before I could say or do anything, he pulled me into his arms and whisked us out the door so fast, within one blink we were back outside at the beautiful meadow-like Heart of the Pack.

I gasped when he suddenly lifted me princess-style and ran to the large cabin on the Pack Hall's right. Only when we were inside with the door closed did he put me down.

But his arms remained around me.

And his twisted monstrous face shattered, revealing his beautiful one once more, only gravely exhausted. I opened my mouth to speak, but before I could, he said, "Let me hold you for a few more moments." He swallowed hard, eyes searching mine. "Please."

He looked so tired, and so broken, too, that I felt my heart wrench. Slowly, hesitantly, I raised my hand to his face to cup his cheek, like he'd done to me earlier. An unnamed emotion unfolded deep within me at seeing him so vulnerable all of a sudden, leaning into my touch. The feel of his faint bristles tickled my palm, and I traced my thumb over his cheekbone, watching his eyes flutter closed as he let out a deep breath.

His arms squeezed around me, causing my gut to tighten, and something inside me made a circus-worthy flip-flop. Wordlessly, I raised my left hand, more assured this time, to cup his other cheek, holding his face between my palms.

When he let out another sigh, an uneven, stuttering one, I felt like I was in a trance, holding this outrageously gorgeous and dangerous man's face.

After his display of power in the Pack Hall, the realization that this man was truly an *Alpha* of a *werewolf pack* completely settled deep in my gut. Seeing him so vulnerable now, it seemed almost foreign for someone in his position to show such emotions.

I was suddenly sent back almost a week, to when I'd petted his soft, beautiful coat as he lay, bleeding, in his wolf form, on my sofa. He had leaned into my touch then, too, just like that. He had let me soothe his pain as much as I could.

Until now, I realized, he hadn't had any time to truly breathe. He'd been constantly on guard—against Chase and Avenor, his pack members, and of course, the Syndicate—and he hadn't let himself simply *be*.

And that applied to me too.

So we stood there for a few long moments, taking in the much-needed albeit short break, and simply breathed.

Lucien was quiet, saying nothing, as I looked around me. I noticed that pack members watched us when we passed by on our way back to Lucien's car. Mostly, they stared at Lucien—some of them in awe, others with fear, and a few with displeasure evident on their faces.

There was also more than one woman and man who sneaked him appreciative looks.

That made me extremely, irrationally irritated. I wanted to grab Lucien's arm and dig my nails into his skin to show them who he belonged to.

But I stifled the urge to do so, since Lucien belonged to no one. Least of all to me.

And that thought, for some reason, was too devastating for me to acknowledge.

What irritated me even more was the fact no one seemed to notice me, or rather, everyone simply ignored my existence. It was as if Lucien sucked all the attention to himself without meaning to, just because that's who he was. And I understood; while all the werewolves I saw were attractive, Lucien was in a league of his own.

But it chafed, too, to have people look past me, as if I were invisible.

It was a feeling I was familiar with. With my plain girl-next-door looks and baggy band shirts, I was nothing to look at. Usually, I couldn't care less; as long as I was living the life I chose, wearing what I wanted and avoiding makeup at all costs, I was content.

Now, however . . .

I shook my head. Whatever I looked like to these werewolves didn't matter. Not when there were far more pressing matters to attend to. Like investigating Alby and Dianna, Mack's associates I had shot.

A chill made me shiver. Right. I *shot* people. I'd actually shot two people for the first time in my life, and with everything turning into pure chaos, I'd barely had the time to even think back to it.

And now the memories of the deafening noise of bullets shooting forward, the click of the trigger as I pulled it, the sight of the bullets hitting real flesh . . .

Lucien suddenly stopped, and I snapped out of my dark thoughts. We'd arrived at the car.

The drive passed in silence. My mind was running in circles, bringing to the forefront the memories of shooting Alby and Dianna, memories I hadn't realized I was suppressing. Now, though, they repeated over and over in my head.

I told myself I'd done the right thing. I'd reacted when I should've. If I hadn't, Alby and Dianna would've gotten away without punishment for conspiring to kill Lucien.

If there was one thing I refused to do, it was to have more regrets.

After some time, Lucien parked the car near a warehouse-like cabin. There were two casually clothed werewolves standing guard at the door, where a sign read **Pack Penitentiary**. When they saw Lucien and me get out of the car and approach the entrance, they straightened their backs and gave a curt bow of their heads simultaneously.

Lucien nodded back, and the two let us in.

The lobby was surprisingly bright and colorful. There were plants all over, and little sculptures of mushrooms and beetles, and whatnot. The man who sat behind the front desk was also wearing bright neon colors.

When he saw us coming in, he immediately jumped to his feet and saluted. "Good afternoon, Mr. Alpha, sir."

To my surprise, Lucien's lips twitched. "I told you calling me Alpha is enough, Miguel."

Miguel didn't reply but kept saluting.

Lucien seemed half amused, half tortured, as he sighed and gave a quick salute back to release him.

Once he wasn't saluting anymore, Miguel smiled, eyes twinkling, and asked, "How can I help you today?"

"We're here for Alby and Dianna," Lucien said, face growing serious.

Miguel nodded quickly and motioned toward the door next to his desk. "They're at cell twenty-six, sir."

"Thank you," Lucien said quietly, nodded, and headed to the door, but before he opened it, he turned to Miguel and said, "I know you're new, and you're still getting the hang of things, but remember, this is not the military."

The bright man nodded so fast, his hair flew everywhere. "I know, sir, Alpha," he said, smiling a little. "I'm working on it."

Lucien, to my surprise, smiled back. "All right, then."

Once we walked through the door, I looked around me as the surroundings took on the opposite feel from the front desk's. Here it was bleak and moist, gray walls and floors, an aisle of prison cells greeting us. To my surprise, most cells were empty, but the few that weren't were inhabited by werewolves in their wolf form, who seemed to be avoiding looking at Lucien altogether as we passed by.

The silence, though, was heavy, broken only by our footsteps—and my curiosity, which thankfully pushed my dreadful thoughts from before to the back of my mind. "So Miguel is new?"

Lucien heard the question in my voice and glanced at me with a somewhat cryptic look. "Yeah. He hasn't been a werewolf for long."

My heart came to a screeching stop as my throat grew dry. "What do you mean—"

"We're here," he cut me off as he stopped by cell twenty-six.

Biting my tongue and swallowing the rest of my questions, I looked into the cell through the thick metal bars. There were two wolves there, both with dark fur and gold eyes, though they weren't identical in the slightest. One had a sharper face, and a shorter tail that had a pretty silver ring around its edge, while the other had thicker fur and a longer tail.

"Alby, Dianna," Lucien now said, looking at the wolves. "Shift."

The wolves stared at Lucien as they immediately shifted. While I'd witnessed Lucien shift before, the sight still startled yet fascinated me as I watched their fur being sucked into their skin, followed by a hissing sound. Their limbs grew longer, and a faint sound, almost like a paper being folded into origami shapes, filled the silence.

When they were finally in their human form, both were naked, but they didn't seem to care about it. It made me wonder about the nudity culture in the werewolf society. Lucien had been comfortable in his nudity, too, every time I'd seen him without his clothes on.

Which, granted, were a few very precious moments.

I also did my best to keep my eyes on their faces rather than on their other body parts. And both their faces were surprisingly freshened up, if a little pale.

Lucien stared at the two of them for a quiet moment before he spoke again. "Tell me everything you know about Mack Page's dealings with the Sable Syndicate."

Some part of me expected the two of them to be surprised Lucien knew about the Syndicate's involvement in his attack, but instead, they kept blank expressions, seemingly impassive about this turn of events.

Dianna was the first one who spoke. "If I tell you, will you let me see her?"

Alby's head whipped toward her, glaring in warning, but Dianna kept her eyes on Lucien, determined.

Without missing a beat, Lucien said, "I will."

Alby bared his teeth as he turned his glare to Lucien. "What will I get, then?"

"A more merciful death," Lucien said in a darker voice. "Considering this is not your first crime."

That seemed to shut Alby up.

Dianna rose to her feet, her dark hair gliding over her shoulders as she did. "Mack has always hated you," she said without preamble, glancing briefly at me before returning to Lucien. "Though it was a mere distaste in the beginning, when you first arrived."

Lucien's face remained devoid of emotion, but I saw his eyes glint. There was pain there from Mack's betrayal still. It made me want to hold his hand, but I had a feeling he needed to keep his hard-ass Alpha mask on.

"When you declared your first order would be to change the pack's name, Mack was livid," she continued, her hands curled into fists as she seemed to tremble. "He, and others, too, felt like you were trying to erase Jericho's memory from existence. Even worse when the name you chose was not of American origins, but French. It felt like you were pissing on our territory, not to mark it—but to spite us all."

She shook her head and stared at the ground. "At first, Mack felt he should protect the pack from you." Her voice grew tight. "He pretended to be civil around you and was elated when you appointed him Beta. It was his ticket to have as much influence as a werewolf can have without being the Alpha."

Pausing, Dianna's lip trembled as she glanced up at Lucien, hesitant. Lucien, who was now as still as a statue, prompted with a low voice, "What changed?"

Wincing, she sucked in a breath and looked away, hugging herself. "Mack kept tabs on you. He knew you had frequent visits to San Diego, to the Lane Medical Center. At first he didn't think much of it, since he knew part of the Alpha's duty was to be in continual contact with the regional Otherborne medical facility. Until Dr. Lane came to visit for the first time two months ago.

"That's when he started digging into you."

Lucien's lips curled, but he didn't say anything. Dianna was shaking like a leaf now, as though speaking was too hard on her, yet she seemed to force herself to continue. "Mack has . . . friends within the ASS. He asked those friends to obtain certain classified files. I'm not sure exactly which, but he told us that they contained sensitive information. Information like the fact that Dr. Enoch Lane is being closely monitored not just by the ASS but by the global Council as well, as a potential threat to the Treaty. The math was simple after that, and Mack realized what your true objective is."

She stilled, then, and raised her gaze to meet Lucien's cold one. "Both you and Dr. Lane are part of a terrorist organization known as the Imperative for Transparency and Symbiosis."

I froze and glanced at Lucien. There was no sign on his face that he was surprised. If anything, a dark realization seemed to settle on him, clouding over his face.

Alby interjected then, and his voice made me jump. "We know what happened to your pack in France," he growled deep in his chest, and I could feel Lucien go still. "Mack, and us, too, know you're the weakest, most waste-of-space Alpha that's ever existed." He spat on the floor.

Anger built up inside me, and before Lucien could talk, I snapped, no longer feeling so guilty about shooting them—or at least Alby. "The only waste of space here is you, now that Mack is gone, and thank fuck for that." Venom dripped from my voice. "You can only wish to be half the man, the werewolf, Lucien is!"

Lucien grabbed my arm and murmured in a low, grim voice, "Don't."

But I was too angry, as if something had cut my fuse short, especially when Alby smiled in both delight and viciousness and snarled, "At least I'm not a fucking coward who used his own pack as a shield." Then, he practically crooned, "And I know for sure that, Alpha Marker or not, Mack would've been ten times the Alpha this terrorist could ever be!"

I hardly understood what he was saying, and yet I couldn't help but laugh. He thought *Mack* could've been a better Alpha? "Then why did your precious Mack send some Fae asshole to kill Lucien and didn't do it himself, if he's oh so capable?"

Alby was suddenly at the bars, grabbing them with dirty hands and pressing his face against them so I could smell his disgusting breath. "I don't need to answer to *you*," he growled, eyes bright. "You're just a fucking human slut—"

The cell door was suddenly wrenched open, and Lucien strode inside, oozing fury as he grabbed Alby by the neck and pressed him against the wall, jamming his arm against Alby's air pipes. "Forget about merciful death," Lucien growled, and the sound was far stronger than Alby's, and far more terrifying, as it echoed through the entire prison. "I'm going to watch as the air leaves your lungs and you silently scream and beg me to let you breathe."

Alby couldn't speak. He moved his mouth, grabbed at Lucien's arms, as his face started to turn purple.

I instinctually barricaded the cell entrance at that time so Dianna wouldn't take the chance to run—though, rationally, I knew I stood no chance against a werewolf—but to my surprise, Dianna merely stared at Lucien and Alby, her expression dark and weary. She didn't seem like she wanted to push me aside and flee—which she definitely could have. If anything, she seemed utterly defeated.

The choking sounds of Alby, though, drew my attention from Dianna back to Lucien. His murderous gaze remained on Alby's face. "Don't you dare," he snarled. Tears escaped Alby's eyes as he tried, weakly, to struggle against Lucien's unbreakable hold. "Not after you plotted and aided Mack to get rid of me, and the countless occasions where you couldn't contain your anger and assaulted other pack members. As far as I'm concerned"—he squeezed his throat—"you don't deserve a trial."

My heartbeat was so loud as I watched Alby grow weaker by the minute. "Lucien," I whispered, but clamped my mouth shut, doubt ringing in my head. It wasn't my place to tell Lucien what to do. He was the Alpha here. I was merely a human. An Eteria. Effectively a slave.

And yet some part of me wished he wouldn't kill him. His death wouldn't solve anything.

Most terrifyingly, however, a deeper, meaner, and far more sinister voice inside my head thought, *He dared to call Lucien a waste of space. He dared insult* my man *right in front of my face after he wanted to kill him. He deserves everything coming his way.*

That voice won, and I kept my mouth shut until Alby stopped writhing, the choking noise faded away, and his body became limp and eerily still.

CHAPTER 24
WILDLIGHT

Lucien drove us back to the plaza, the Heart, with another car containing Dianna and a couple of werewolf guards following us. Once everyone was parked, he led our entourage to one of five large cabins, this one stationed to the left of the Pack Hall. The sign near the entrance door read **Concordian Ward**.

When we entered, I couldn't help but feel confused. During the drive, Lucien had told me we were going to the pack hospital, and I asked him why he wanted me to come along. He had given me a loaded look I couldn't quite read as he said cryptically, "You'll see soon."

The place, however, looked nothing like what a hospital should look like. If anything, it looked like I imagined a mystical apothecary would: shelves and cabinets full of herbs and mysterious powders, a front desk showcasing flasks in its vitrine, another table with a few boiling pots—or rather, cauldrons—along with a wide selection of tea and a huge Persian carpet covering the entire place from wall to wall in different shades of red.

Along with all those things were hospital beds that seemed far more cushy and comfortable than regular ones, along with separating curtains with the same patterns and color scheme as the carpet, and all the medical equipment stored in glass cabinets.

The smell, though, was unlike the smell of any hospital I'd ever visited. Normally, there was the distinctive smell of disinfectants, but here, the main scent was of the brewing tea and a number of herbs I couldn't possibly identify.

Behind the front desk stood a familiar figure, who looked up the moment Lucien and I entered with a big, welcoming smile on his handsome face, putting his dimples on display.

"*Cousin!*" Remi, Lucien's cousin, said as a greeting in French, rounding the desk to give Lucien a one-armed hug, which Lucien returned. *"J'ai l'impression de ne pas t'avoir vu depuis une éternité."*

"It's only been a few days, Rémi." Lucien responded to the rapid French chatter with a weary smile, and I could see him visibly relax. He'd been tense the entire drive here.

Remi grinned as he released Lucien. "I heard you went full Alpha mode today."

And just like that, the tension returned, straining Lucien's face. "There was no other way," he said quietly, resolutely, but his eyes betrayed him. I could see the heavy gravity he felt that he didn't allow himself to show. "I needed to remind them who their Alpha is."

Feeling the tension, Remi's grin disappeared. "From the way the members talk about it, it seemed the message was well received."

The two exchanged loaded glances, and I could see they were sharing thoughts I wasn't privy to. I wondered if it had anything to do with what Alby had said. About Lucien and his pack back in France.

Lucien then took a deep breath and asked, "Is Anaïs still here?"

Remi shook his head, a frown on his face. "An hour ago, she headed to the library with Enoch and a human man."

That reminded me that Thayer had joined Anais and Enoch on their research of Lucien's Spellscript. With everything that had been happening, it hadn't crossed my mind since that morning.

With a curt nod, Lucien said, "Don't forget to tell Anaïs when she comes back that we visited, okay?"

Remi's bright eyes flicked behind me, toward where Dianna stood, waiting, with the guards on each side, as he nodded absentmindedly. "All right."

Lucien then led us past the front desk, leaving Remi behind, and deeper into the Ward. He came to a stop before one of the beds, which was fully hidden behind the thick curtains. Through it, however, I could see a shadow. Someone was lying there.

He then turned to Dianna, who was now fully dressed, and said, "You have fifteen minutes."

She barely gave a nod. In fact, she was so stiff, one of the guards gave her a gentle nudge forward to get her going. She finally did, disappearing behind the curtains.

After Lucien told the guards to wait outside, he turned to look at me, gaze heavy. "Werewolves don't easily get hurt," he suddenly said.

I frowned, thinking back to Alby and Dianna and how they were still somewhat fine even after being shot, and wondered why he was telling me that.

"This is true in the physical sense," he continued, face grave. "When it comes to our mental health, however, we are far weaker than humans."

Feeling the gravity in his words, I could only nod as he slowly pulled the curtain away, revealing Dianna sitting next to the hospital bed, her hand holding the old man's who rested there.

Though *resting* wasn't the right word for his state.

The man's glassy eyes were staring unblinkingly at the ceiling. His face was full of wrinkles and completely pale, which made him appear to be in his eighties or nineties, and his skin was paper thin, with spots and blemishes. His thin, wispy layer of hair was entirely white. What I could see of his body under the blanket was thin and frail.

He seemed like a wraith, really. All skin and bones. As if with one slight shove, he would fall apart and turn to ash.

We paused at the foot of the bed, and Lucien leaned toward me so he could murmur in a barely audible voice, "This is Kate."

"*Kate?*" I repeated in a small whisper. Well, shame on me for assuming the patient's gender.

"Kate," Lucien confirmed, and took a deep breath. "She's eight years old."

"Eight," I mumbled, unable to process what he was saying. "Don't you mean eighty?"

"No, eight." Lucien's voice was now low, and the grim pain I could hear in it made me look up at him. There was evident darkness in his eyes. And guilt.

So much guilt that it made my own heart ache for him. I reached out to hold his hand, squeezing it.

He squeezed back, though he kept his eyes on Kate. "Every full moon," he said in a soft murmur, "werewolves go through a forced transition. Our humanity is pushed to the back, and the animal takes control. Before the full moon fully rises, we shift into our wolf form so we won't cause any damage, because if we stay in our human form while our humanity is wiped out for a whole night . . ."

His shoulders slumped, his head hanging low. "Depending on the werewolf's age and inherent temperament, if we stay in our human form during the full moon, our actions may vary, but none of it is good. For instance, more aggressive werewolves in their young adulthood could attack and kill each other, or do something far more vile." The disgust in his voice was apparent, and I didn't want to imagine what those vile things could be. "Those who are more levelheaded, whether young or old, could potentially be harmless—unless provoked, and no one knows what the trigger for that could be."

Lucien's eyes returned to Kate, full of despair. "And sometimes, no matter the age or temperament of the werewolf, they can catch a fatal mental disease called Wildlight."

I stared at Kate now, too, as I started to realize where he was going with this, holding on to his hand now for my own sanity too.

And the blow came when he explained in a barely there whisper. "When a werewolf spends the full moon in their human skin, the animal within goes completely wild. The infected wolf can lose their humanity completely, and not just for the duration of the full moon—but for life."

He squeezed my hand again, and I could feel him tremble with barely contained rage. "That loss of humanity causes the werewolf to go berserk. Young or old, they turn into horrendously strong killing machines that could physically tear anyone apart. Only an Alpha can restrain them without getting fatally hurt in the process."

Horror filled me as I listened to him when he added, "I had to immobilize an eight-year-old girl suffering from Wildlight after she killed her own parents."

My throat was closed up. I couldn't speak. All I could do was hold Lucien's hand and stare at the half-dead person lying in the hospital bed, and Dianna, holding on to her with empty eyes and a hopeless face.

"Two months ago, Kate was infected with Wildlight," Lucien said, his voice even, but the tone broken. "She didn't shift into a wolf in time. Very early in the night, she killed her parents, then ran to the woods in search of prey—any prey. She was so small, Drew." He sucked in a breath, and I slowly turned to look at him. "A small little wolf who could kill an adult. It's the most absurd sight you could ever see."

He trembled, turning to look at me with unbearable pain in his gaze. "And while her humanity was gone, she was still only a baby. I had to fight a *baby*, hit a *baby*, and knock a *baby* unconscious so she wouldn't kill anyone else."

I choked, tears escaping my eyes.

"I had never encountered someone so young being affected by Wildlight," he whispered, and I could see tears in his eyes too. That sight broke me. "In France, the youngest I had to subdue was fifteen, which, while not an adult, is still not a baby either. This little girl was *a baby*."

"Lucien," I breathed, feeling suffocated, as I shook my head, holding on to his hand almost as tightly as Dianna held Kate's.

A tear fell down his face too. "When she regained consciousness, she was already shackled and caged," he said in a hoarse voice. "Seeing a tiny girl struggling against her shackles is a sight I don't wish on anyone."

He gave me a faint, bitter smile. "Wildlight doesn't just affect the line between our human and animal sides," he said, "but it also affects our very soul."

He took a deep breath and let go of my hand as he averted his gaze, staring at Kate, though his eyes seemed far away. "She fell into a Concordian Stasis. This state occurs when the balance between body and mind of the werewolf is broken beyond repair. It's the inevitable, incurable result of Wildlight." He dropped his gaze. "With the horrible side effects of accelerated aging and remaining in the realm between life and death, unable to be killed, Wildlight victims have no choice but to wait until their body rots away, and their soul fades into nothing."

My knees gave out as I fell to the floor, shaking, stifling my sobs with a fist in my mouth.

Because as he told me the story about Kate, and Wildlight, all I could do was look at Dianna. Seeing her face was like staring into a mirror.

No one needed to tell me Dianna was Kate's older sister. It was obvious.

It was also obvious that Dianna would never forgive herself for what befell her sister—and, consequently, her parents.

The guilt and grief over losing a younger sister was something that would never go away. Especially when you were helpless.

Because just like Dianna, who couldn't do a thing to help her sister, I, too, had only been able to stare in absolute horror as a monster took my sisters away from me.

It wasn't Wildlight that killed my sisters.

And yet, just like Dianna, all I could've done back then was watch Willow's and Julianna's dead bodies disappearing right before my eyes.

Arms wrapped around me, and I leaned into them heavily, crying into the shirt that smelled like Lucien. His arms locked behind me, and he cradled me close, rocking back and forth on the floor, murmuring unintelligibly into my hair in a soothing, comforting tone that was still broken, still shaky, as if he was trying to calm himself down too.

I held on to him for a long time as I let my anguish pour out of me. Distantly, I was aware of the guards taking Dianna out of the Ward, and my sobs grew louder as I couldn't help but feel a suffocating empathy for the woman.

"Drew." Lucien's voice was clear all of a sudden, his hands grabbing my shoulders as he pushed me back a little so I could see his face. His was just as distraught as I felt mine was. "I'm sorry," he said now when he caught my eyes. "I'm so sorry for dumping this on you. I'm sorry for bringing you here, but I . . ." He swallowed hard and looked away. "I couldn't . . . visiting Kate is . . ."

I cut him off with a sharp shake of my head. "N-No, Lucien," I said, sniffling, looking at him as the tears still came out. "Y-You have nothing to apologize for." Because I understood now why he brought me here, and under any other circumstance, it would've warmed my heart to know he wanted me here for support.

But now . . .

His hands cupped my face as he brought it close, leaning his forehead against mine. "But you're crying, Drew," he hissed in what sounded like self-deprecation. "I hate seeing you cry."

My breath stuttered. "It's not your fault," I said in a whimper. "It's just . . ."

Gently, he leaned back a little so he could search my gaze with bright electric-blue eyes. "What is it?"

As my heart froze, I couldn't help but think somewhat bitterly that I was far too partial to his eyes. It felt like these eyes could stare into my soul. They tempted me to spill all my secrets to him.

I had seen him kill not once, but twice. I had seen him at his scariest. Yet what truly made me fear Lucien Delterre was the fact he could disarm me with a single glance.

And it almost felt like compulsion when the words spilled out of my mouth.

"Eight years ago, I watched my sisters die."

Eight Years Ago
Seattle, Washington

"I wanna go back home."

Willow scoffed, and I tried not to roll my eyes as we climbed up the hiking trail. For the last ten minutes, Julianna had decided to throw a tantrum. Even though she was already twelve years old.

"I'm serious," Julianna insisted in her whiny annoying-little-sister voice. "I'm *tired*, and hungry, and my thermos is almost out of water."

I stopped, turned around, and folded my arms, staring as Julianna, her face red and sweaty from the excursion, was startled into pausing too. "We *told* you not to join," I said, irritated. "So suck it up."

Julianna's pretty little face scowled. "I'm going to tell Mom on you."

It now seemed Willow lost it—though to be fair, Willow had always been the hotheaded one among us—and she walked down to stand right before Julianna. The latter flinched, her gray eyes wide, and I knew why.

When Willow lost it, she *lost it*.

"All Drew and I wanted was to take a nice Saturday hike like we always do," Willow now snapped, and with her wild chestnut brown tousles springing around her face and down her back, she looked like a dragon about to spit fire. "We would've had no problem with you joining if we thought you could handle a simple hike, but since you're a *princess little brat*, we refused."

Julianna's lower lip trembled, and tears welled in her eyes, but Willow wasn't done. "We don't plan on turning around anytime soon.

You can tell on us to Mom if you want to, but that would just make Drew and me never take you anywhere together ever again."

That seemed to seal the deal for Jules, who sniffled, wiped her eyes, and nodded, cheeks flushed.

Without another look, my scary, younger, fifteen-year-old sister whirled around and resumed the hike.

I couldn't help but feel a little warm inside at Willow's words. Our relationship had taken a dive in the last few months. It started when I stole a book from her room without her permission—for an important book report—and she hadn't spoken to me for what felt like forever. Our weekly Saturday hikes had come to a stop. She ignored me during meals. She acted like I didn't exist, as if I had a contagious disease.

While I was hurt and frustrated with her, I knew that, as the older sister, it was my duty to be the bigger person. And I loved Willow; I wanted my best friend back.

So I kept on asking her to join me on hiking trips every Saturday to no avail. She either ignored me or snapped at me to leave her alone. I didn't give up, though, and this morning, for the first time in five months, Willow had shocked the hell out of me by saying yes.

I'd wanted this hiking trip to be an opportunity for Willow and me to make up and reconnect. Alone.

But if I hadn't taken Julianna, Thayer would've scolded me until my ears bled.

Thankfully, Julianna didn't speak again until we reached the end of the hiking trail, where a beautiful river awaited. When she saw the sight, Jules, who'd never been here before, was no longer pouting and fighting tears but staring in wonder at the stunning view.

Willow and I spread out the blanket we brought and sat down on it, facing the river and the view of the mountains beyond. Julianna sat down on my other side, hesitant, sneaking wary glances at me while she tried to nudge closer.

My chest tightened as I felt a little guilty about being angry that she'd forced us to include her, so I put my arm around her shoulders and squeezed her to my side. She melted into my hug and hugged me back with her small, dainty arms.

"It's pretty, isn't it?" I asked Jules in a soft murmur, kissing her forehead.

She nodded silently.

Willow took out sandwiches we'd prepared beforehand from the satchel I'd carried and handed one to Julianna, who hesitated before taking it. A peace offering. Willow noticed our youngest sister's remorseful mood, and since she wasn't heartless, despite her temper, she grinned and said, "You see why we come here every week? It's worth the hike."

My mouth automatically opened with the impulse to snap at her, *You mean came here every week before you decided to turn into a jerk,* but before I could endanger my frail truce with Willow, Julianna smiled a little and nodded, her shoulders slumping in relief, and I swallowed the words back.

The three of us were quiet as we munched on our sandwiches, but once we were done, I decided to broach the subject I'd been curious about. So I asked Julianna, "Why did you want to join us, knowing you don't like hiking?"

She didn't expect the question, I could tell, because she began shifting uneasily in her place. "Just because," she murmured, shrugging, feigning indifference.

Since she was obviously lying, I prodded. "I highly doubt this is the reason, Jules."

Flushing, she looked away. "I was bored," she said, as she attempted half-heartedly to find another excuse.

But neither Willow nor I bought it. "You've been binging that show lately," Willow said with a slight snort, "and I know for a fact you aren't done with it. So obviously, that isn't it."

Jules frowned and released me from the hug, pulling her knees to her chest and hugging them instead. "Fine," she murmured. "I just . . . I wanted to spend time with you, okay?"

Willow and I exchanged brief glances, surprised. Julianna had never shown much interest in what either Willow or I liked to do. She was extremely self-centered, which made sense, considering her age and maturity level, and often kept to herself, much like Thayer, our older brother, in that regard.

But unlike Thayer, who'd refused to join our hike when Jules begged him to tag along, Julianna was still young and still craved affection.

And perhaps she had also noticed the distance between Willow and me and wanted to do something about it. Jules was a sweetheart like that.

When neither Willow nor I knew what to say, Julianna rocked back and forth, uncomfortable, as she blurted, "You two are so busy all the time. You don't join Mom, Dad, and me for dinner. You barely leave your room, and when you do, it's to get a snack from the kitchen or fight each other. Even during summer vacation, it felt like I saw less of you than during the school year."

Guilt clawed at my conscience. Jules felt neglected. That explained her abnormal behavior today.

Willow suddenly rose to her feet and stretched her hand out to Jules. "Come with me," she said, gray eyes determined.

Julianna's own gray eyes, softer and far less steely than Willow's, flickered, and she grabbed Willow's hand.

Willow dragged Jules into the river and splashed water on her, laughing when Julianna's small body became soaked immediately.

But Jules retaliated and splashed Willow too.

The two of them splashed each other, laughing, smiling brightly in the setting afternoon sun.

I watched the two, feeling warm and fuzzy. I loved my sisters—and my brother, of course—more than anything in this world. Even if they were annoying. Even when they hurt me. Seeing Jules upset made me sad, and seeing her hiccupy laughter now made me feel absolute joy.

Seeing Willow acting so carefree, too, for once, made me also feel lighter than I'd felt in a long while.

So I stared at the two playing in the water, smiled, and even dozed off feeling so content—and tired from the hike too.

That's probably why I didn't see what came next.

A shrilling scream made me jump to my feet before I even opened my eyes, and when I did open my eyes, what I saw made me freeze in place, because for a moment, I thought I was dreaming, and this was an extremely vivid nightmare.

What I saw couldn't be of this world, after all.

The *thing* that came out of the water was a monstrosity almost as tall as the trees in the woods. It had the vague shape of a human body, but there were black flames instead of limbs. Its head was narrow, and it didn't even have a face—only two diagonal slits glowing white. The monster had a mane of long hair, too, but the hair seemed like a mirage almost, as it blew unnaturally in the nonexistent wind.

Before I could even process what I was seeing, a scene out of a horror movie played right before my eyes, and I watched it as though I was staring through a telescope rather than being there too.

Because the monster's arms of flames curled around my sisters, lifting them up from the river as they screamed, crying, thrashing in the hold of the unmovable monster.

"DREW!"

Willow's scream was what made me snap out of my terrified haze, and I tried to take a step forward as I stammered, shaking all over, "Let them go . . . Let my sisters go . . ."

My legs didn't respond to my wishes, though. It was as if I was rooted in place, either by some sort of external force or by my own terror.

Helplessly, I watched as the monster began to sink into the river with my sisters in his arms, and I tried to stretch out my shaking hand, to try and walk and reach them, to do something, *anything*, rather than just stand there and watch like a fucking idiot as my sisters were being kidnapped.

Before the monster disappeared, I suddenly realized their screams had stopped. My sisters were immobile in the monster's hold, their heads turned at unnatural angles.

My heart dropped just as the monster disappeared under the water with my sisters, and I fell to my knees, shuddering, tears falling down my face, lips parted, and a terrible sense of shock spreading all over my body.

They are dead, a small voice whispered in my head, shaking too. *You saw their heads. They cannot be alive.*

The river, which had undulated with the monster's appearance, and now disappearance, suddenly washed over its banks, like an ocean wave, before returning to its serene, tranquil state, as if nothing had happened.

As if my sisters weren't dead, their bodies taken underwater by a monster.

Still shaking, still unable to comprehend what I'd just seen, I somehow climbed back to my feet and took step after step toward the river.

Then I paused, seeing a sign carved on the muddy ground, as if by a knife. It was neither big nor small, just close to the water, and I wouldn't have noticed it if something else didn't catch my eyes.

The small puddles of water near that sign weren't really water. It was some sort of liquid with a murky color that, despite the last rays of sun, didn't shine like water, but remained muted.

And it surrounded the odd sign, which consisted of a mishmash of lines and dots that looked like an ancient sigil from another realm.

Present Day

"Later, after I checked the river's water, diving in and out in a desperate attempt to find my sisters, and the monster, I took a photo of the sign—the Spellscript—with my phone and returned home, still in shock, still shivering, still filled with terror at everything I'd seen, and also full of a different kind of fear. As in, how would I break the news to my family?"

I was shaking, unable to look at Lucien's eyes anymore. "No one believed me when I explained about the monster. Everyone thought it must've been some sort of an accident in the river, that I'd been irresponsible in taking care of my sisters and that their bodies must've been washed into the Pacific Ocean, which was the so-called reason why they were never found."

Something salty touched my lip. Fresh tears burned my eyes. "That's why I started researching the supernatural. Why I'm writing for *The Hallowing Hour*. Why I hoped someone like you would appear and help me find answers."

I couldn't help but glance at Kate's bed, feeling drained, exhausted, and utterly helpless. "I couldn't help them," I whispered, thinking about Dianna. "I wanted to so much, but I couldn't move, like a fucking coward. But even if I could move, I know I would've simply died too. And that, more than anything else, kills me inside."

I covered my face with my hands, trying to get ahold of myself as I sobbed, "Julianna was close to Kate's age too."

Wordlessly, Lucien pulled me to him again, holding me close. He didn't offer empty encouraging words; he seemed to understand there was nothing he could say that would make it any better.

This kind of pain and grief would never go away, and a deep feeling in my gut told me he knew that. That he understood.

And faintly, I wondered why.

CHAPTER 25
NOT HER WOLF

I felt completely empty by the time Lucien pulled into the gravel driveway near his cabin. It had been a silent trip from the Concordian Ward back home, with me stuck in my own thoughts and Lucien remaining silent, as though he understood I needed space after my emotional breakdown.

Once inside, Lucien grabbed my wrist and pulled me toward him. His arms enfolded me, and his lips brushed against my forehead in a soft, comforting kiss.

My heart rebelled against my rib cage at the sudden act, and the emptiness within me filled with so much warmth, I had to close my eyes and instinctually lean into him, needing his heat.

His soft kiss, his strong muscular arms around me, holding me close as though I mattered, as if he cared, spoke more than any words could, and I was a little scared I would burst out crying again at the almost painful feelings he brought up inside me.

Thankfully, though, before that happened, Lucien abruptly let me go, giving me a loaded look that made me freeze.

Before he could say or do anything else, a door opened from the corridor's direction, and Thayer appeared. He was freshly showered, his too-long hair damp, and he came to a stop when he saw us, glancing between Lucien and me with narrowed eyes and open suspicion. "Good evening," he said in a slow, assessing voice.

Lucien stepped back from me and nodded curtly. "Evening. How was your time with Anaïs and Enoch?"

His eye twitched slightly as his jaw ticked, but his voice was calm when he replied, "Enlightening, and very informative." He paused and looked at me. Something lit up in his gaze that I couldn't quite decipher—pride?—when he added, "Your notes were extremely helpful. More than you could ever realize."

I flushed at the unexpected compliment. "Really?" I asked in a small voice.

"Yeah," he murmured, glancing hesitantly at Lucien before returning his eyes to me. "Especially a certain Spellscript you recorded from . . . eight years ago."

I stilled, and my eyes snapped to Lucien. He sensed my gaze and returned it, his own somewhat inscrutable. "I've been meaning to ask Blaise," he told me in a murmur. "He's the most well-versed and widely contacted pack member when it comes to the Underearth. What you described . . ."

Swallowing the sudden log in my throat, I merely nodded and gave him a wobbly smile. "Thanks."

His eyes caught mine in an almost unbreakable hold, and they were filled with so much warmth and other emotions I couldn't decipher, all I could do was stare, wishing I could get into his head and peel back the layers to reveal what he was really thinking.

The sound of a clearing throat made me jolt, and I looked away to see Thayer glancing between us again, that earlier suspicion still there.

Ignoring his look, Lucien headed toward Thayer. "I'll go shower," he murmured, glancing briefly at me before looking at my brother again. "There's leftovers in the fridge if you're hungry."

He disappeared into the bathroom a moment later.

Now Thayer and I were alone.

I stared as Thayer walked toward me.

"You told him."

It was a no-brainer what he was referring to. "Yes," I said hoarsely.

He paused before me and let out a heavy sigh. "Figures. He's your boyfriend now, isn't he?"

My head whipped toward him so fast, it was a wonder my neck didn't twist. "He's my *what*?" I said in a little panicked voice, because I was sure he didn't just say what I thought he said.

But Thayer folded his arms and arched a brow in disbelief. "Boyfriend," he repeated, jerking his head back to motion toward where Lucien had just disappeared to. "I'm not blind. I saw the way he looked at you."

I mouthed his words on repeat, confused, as the panic rose. "You're wrong," I said, hugging myself as I dropped my gaze to the floor. "He's just . . . protective of me."

"Ah, yes," he murmured, and his bitter tone made me glance back up at him. He was scowling. "You're his Eteria, after all."

My heart rate picked up. "How—"

"They told me earlier today," he answered, making me clamp my mouth shut. "They said it was something like a binding of souls. That the basis of it is that you were born for him."

There was doubt but also a certain amount of grimness in his voice that told me everything I needed to know. Whatever Anais and Enoch told him, they hadn't mentioned the other part. The fact that I would never be able to love, or want, another man. That I quite literally belonged to Lucien. Otherwise, Thayer wouldn't have remained so calm and collected.

You're way too calm about it yourself, too, Drew, a little voice murmured in my head.

And for the first time, I acknowledged it. Because it was right.

I *was* too calm about having my soul enslaved by Lucien for the rest of my life.

Was it because I trusted Lucien to never use that against me?

Or was it because some part of me suspected everything I felt for Lucien, all the emotions I was desperately trying to suppress, existed in the first place because I was magically forced to feel them?

That thought made a chill go down my spine.

"Drew?"

Thayer's voice snapped me out of my spiraling thoughts, and if I'd had any sort of appetite before, it all disappeared then and there. So had my appetite for talking to him about anything.

Instead, I felt the urgent need to talk to Lucien.

"No, Lucien isn't my boyfriend," I said hastily, "and yet, I'm his Eteria. It's been a long day, Thayer. I'm going to sleep. Good night."

Thayer opened his mouth, but I was already striding toward Lucien's room and, a second later, latching the door shut behind me.

But I never got to speak to Lucien that evening, because the moment I sat down on the bed, exhaustion poured all over me. I knew I was mentally drained, but I hadn't realized just how much until I found myself crawling into bed and under the warm duvet, sleep pulling me under before I could even form another thought.

Something fuzzy and fluffy surrounded me. It felt like a cozy, warm cloud, and I snuggled closer to it, shuddering at the embracing heat.

It took me a few more seconds to realize this wasn't a cloud, and I was no longer dreaming.

Instead, I was wrapped like a pretzel around a giant bronze wolf.

Growing still, I tilted my head back. The wolf was sleeping deeply, wrapped around me like I was around him.

My heart skipped a beat as I stared at the wolf. He was such a majestic creature, so gorgeous and soft, but I knew how deadly he was. That his teeth could rip apart my jugular if he so wanted.

Yet I wasn't scared of him. Not anymore, at least. Seeing him kill Mack Page had been a shock, and it had taken me a moment to get myself together. But seeing him ripping into Oz, or attacking the assassin with murderous intent, I'd felt nothing but a sense of just retribution.

I couldn't help but wonder, however, if I could trust my feelings. What if my being his Eteria influenced the way I viewed him and his actions? He'd said I would be manipulated into having feelings for him by the Eteria magic, or something like that. He'd told me I would never feel that way for anyone else. That I was bound to love him only.

Maybe, for that to happen, I needed to have the fear manipulated out of me?

Fisting my hands in his fur, I closed my eyes and rested my head against his neck. I didn't want to believe that. It didn't even *feel* like that. The way I felt toward him couldn't possibly be influenced by some so-called magic, right?

But could I say that with full confidence? I didn't think so. Not when being his Eteria effectively meant being forced to love him for the rest of my days.

Did I love him, though? What was it exactly that I was feeling for him, aside from obvious attraction?

And what did he feel about me? Did he even feel anything for me, other than pity and guilt over my Eteria status? If so, why did he sleep in bed with me? Why had he almost kissed me yesterday?

He'd said the Eteria magic only worked on me, but what if he was wrong? What if it worked on him in some way, too, and magically influenced him to be attracted to me?

Because in what universe would someone of Lucien's caliber find me, a plain woman by all accounts, worthy of his attention?

The wolf shifted slightly, making me raise my gaze to his face again. Arctic-blue eyes pierced mine when they met.

I swallowed hard as my heart stuttered, and slowly, hesitantly, I lifted my hand to caress his head. He closed his eyes and leaned into my touch almost like a cat.

Then I felt it.

The fur got sucked into his skin.

His limbs grew longer, firmer.

His snout pulled back, turning into a strong, masculine nose, and lips I longed to taste.

Then, under the duvet covering us both, Lucien shifted into his human form. His *naked* human form, covered by mouthwatering gold skin.

With his auburn curls spread on the pillow like a bright red halo around his head, his strong, corded arms wrapped around my waist, and his eyes gone soft in the morning light, he looked so otherworldly, my breath caught.

I was about to pull my hand away from his face when he grabbed my wrist and made it stay. "Don't," he murmured in a raspy voice, gaze languid as he leaned his bristled cheek into my palm.

Every fiber of my being was attuned to him then, as awe and wonder clouded my brain. Lucien looked like a Greek god straight from Mount Olympus. Untouchable, yet tangible. Far beyond the realm of mere humans, yet still present right here.

And like someone had flipped a switch, a burst of need coiled through my veins, shooting electricity from where he still held my wrist straight to my loins, and heat pooled in my gut.

I wanted him.

So much so that I gasped, snatched my hand away from him, and scooted back, removing myself from his embrace.

Lucien's gaze hardened as he watched me retreat, but I ignored it as I rolled out of bed, heart beating like a war drum, as I blindly looked for my glasses, which someone, probably Lucien, had placed on the nightstand.

Sliding my glasses up my nose, I cleared my throat, and without looking at him, I announced, "I'm going to make some coffee."

My hand was on the handle of the door when a pair of arms wrapped around me from behind, pulling me closer, hard, against a muscular chest. "What's wrong?" Lucien asked in a sexy murmur that made me shiver uncontrollably.

"Nothing," I said, my voice strained. "Just thirsty." *For more than just coffee.*

He tightened his hold on me. "Are you mad?" he suddenly asked, and I felt his lips at my ear, which made me shudder again, goose bumps rising all over my skin.

"Mad?" I squeaked, tense, as I tried to fight my body's reaction.

"That I got into bed with you without your permission," he murmured, and his lips suddenly pressed a kiss to my neck. I gasped again and felt my nipples pebble. "I thought that if you saw your wolf, you would find it easier . . ."

For a long moment, I couldn't speak. Especially as his lips trailed faint maddening kisses down my throat toward my shoulder. He called himself my wolf. *Mine.*

But he wasn't mine.

If anything, I was his. My soul was his. I was *his* Eteria.

Lucien didn't belong to me. No matter how much my body wanted him to.

Or my mind.

I knew my place, though. I knew exactly what I was worth, both physically and mentally. I'd been full of confidence once upon a time, thinking I could get anyone I wanted if I just tried hard enough.

That kind of overinflated sense of self-importance had eventually bitten me in the rear.

I was better, smarter, than to fall for someone I had no chance with. I had done that once already—without being magically induced.

But now . . .

"I can't trust myself around you," I blurted out, hand tightening on the door handle, turning my knuckles white.

He froze.

Sucking in a deep breath, I closed my eyes and said, "You make me *feel* things, Lucien, and I can't handle that."

As if those words were a bucket full of ice, Lucien abruptly let go of me and stepped back, as if I were on fire. "Oh" was all he said, voice dark.

I didn't turn around. I felt so vulnerable, exposing myself to him with my words, that I wanted to flee the room. But I had to address one last thing before I did, so I forced my feet to stay rooted in place as I gritted out, "You're not my wolf. I'm your Eteria slave. That's all there is to it."

"*Slave?*" he repeated, and I could imagine his eyes were wide with shock. "Drew—"

But I'd already pulled the door open and gotten out without looking back.

I would be damned if he saw just how desperately I wished my emotions were truly my own.

CHAPTER 26
UNCONTROLLED

Lucien was gone.

After I left the room and made coffee, he came out, fully clothed, and said, "The full moon is tonight. I have a lot of work to do in preparation. Anaïs should come here later to give you a full rundown of what to expect."

He said all this without looking at me and was out the door before I could open my mouth to ask him a question. A moment later, I heard the Rolls-Royce engine come to life, and then he was gone.

And I felt like absolute shit, because in all my self-centeredness, I'd forgotten tonight was the full moon. And after seeing Kate yesterday, I had an idea as to what Lucien had to prepare for, as the Alpha of his pack. He was probably worried sick about having another Wildlight case.

Yet here I was, stuck in my own head and selfishly taking it out on him.

With the day off to such a great start, I wasn't prepared for Thayer to come out of the guest room he was staying in looking like he'd had the best sleep of his life.

"Good morning, sister," he said with a small smile when he saw me, before that smile faltered at my irritated expression. "What's up?"

"Nothing," I mumbled, glaring at my coffee cup.

He murmured something unintelligible before he grabbed a cup of coffee himself and came to sit next to me. "Does it have anything to do with"—he started in a soft whisper, looking pointedly at the corridor—"him?"

I scowled and sipped my coffee without a reply.

Thayer sighed and leaned back against the sofa. "You don't have to talk about it if you don't want to," he said quietly, and I turned to look at him. His gray eyes were piercing, as if he could read my mind. "But know that I'm here for you."

There was a deeper meaning to his words, I could tell. It was like he was apologizing again for not being there for me when I needed him the most. Like he wanted to make up for it.

And that made my throat constrict and my chest squeeze. "Thank you."

For a few minutes, we drank in silence—until the cabin door opened and Anais walked in.

She gave me a nod before her eyes snapped to Thayer and narrowed. "Good. You're both here."

Thayer seemed tense all of a sudden, narrowing his eyes in the same manner. "What is it?" he asked, voice lower than before.

Anais sat down on the couch across from our sofa and glanced between us with a little furrow between her brows. "You have the same nose."

Both Thayer and I snorted at the same time at her comment and immediately looked at one another with a frown. We did have the same pointy nose. Though why Anais felt the need to remark on that, I had no idea.

Thayer's gaze returned to her, and as if he couldn't help himself, he sipped his coffee and smirked. "Get to the point, Ana," he drawled in a taunting manner that made me, not for the first time, question what the hell his problem was with her—and vice versa.

Because she snarled back, "I told you not to call me that, *Colter*."

Looking far too smug for his own good, Thayer said, "We don't have all day, you know."

Anais seemed ready to kill my brother as she growled deep in her chest, her hands clenched in fists. But then she took a deep breath, and another, before she relaxed and folded her arms. "Tonight is the full moon," she said flatly. "We werewolves are stripped of our humanity for the entire night, and so we shift into our wolf form before the night comes. Once the full moon rises, we don't have anything remotely close to a human thought for a few hours.

"That means you two must stay in this cabin." She gave us a serious look bordering on a warning glare. "If we smell humans in our vicinity when we are mindless animals, we *will* kill you."

Thayer sighed and gave her a lazy look. "Is that all?"

Anais seemed more than ready to kill my brother *now*. "You are not allowed to leave the cabin starting at five o'clock." She paused, then shot a saccharine-sweet smile to Thayer. "Though you are more than welcome to try your luck."

My brother's corresponding grin was just as venomous. "I bet I can take a little she-wolf, *Ana*."

Her eyes flashed, and she leaned forward, baring her teeth. "Try it."

"Stop it," I scolded my brother, who was about to come up with another clever retort, I could tell.

Rolling his eyes, Thayer downed the rest of his coffee and put the cup on the table. "Anything else?" he said, arching a brow at Anais.

She jumped to her feet with one more glare at Thayer. "That's all."

But she didn't leave. In fact, I could see her shift from foot to foot, keeping her glare on Thayer as if she didn't want to show him her hesitation, despite it being clear.

And my brother, the asshat, didn't miss the opportunity to needle her. "You want my help again at the Ward, don't you?" he said in a low, intimate murmur that made me cringe and Anais's glower intensify.

Yet Thayer's gaze was suddenly hooded, his lips curled into a flirty smile, and I felt a little ill. There were some things a sister should not see her brother do. Especially a brother who'd never behaved so recklessly and wildly before.

Anais growled again, and she said in a spiteful tone, "Enoch asked for you."

Thayer chuckled as he rose to his feet. "That's an obvious lie," he drawled, smirking, as he walked toward her, towering over her by more than a head, and stopped just an inch away from her. Her body was rigid, her arms folded tightly, and her head tilted back as she continued to growl. But Thayer didn't seem to care; instead, his gray eyes were alight with some sort of mischief when he leaned down and whispered something in her ear.

I could see her eyes widen, a splash of color marring her cheeks, before he stepped back, grinned devilishly down at her, and gave her a mock bow. "Your favorite human, at your service."

Her growl was so loud now, it practically vibrated through her body to the parquet floor. "Go fuck yourself," she bit out, glaring daggers at my brother.

He winked at her, making me gag, before he turned around and walked out the door.

She started to follow him out but paused and turned to look at me. "I hate your brother," she informed me, as if I hadn't noticed. "I sure hope you are nothing like him."

I couldn't help but snort at the mere thought of being anything like Thayer. "Don't worry," I told her, finishing my own coffee. "Thayer is one of a kind."

That seemed to aggravate her even more, and she sputtered a curse before she left, slamming the door shut behind her.

With the rough morning I'd had, I felt the need to take a long, warm bath to cleanse myself.

For a few minutes after I wiped myself dry and put on a fresh pair of jeans and a simple black V-neck tee, I truly felt cleansed. I had let my mind roam aimlessly when I lay in the bathtub, and changed its direction when it tried to bring up all the thoughts I was desperate to put at the back of my head for now.

Once I was dressed, with my hair blown dry and my teeth brushed, I made myself a simple peanut butter and jelly sandwich before I grabbed my laptop and settled down on the sofa.

I had neglected my job, and everything else, really, due to everything that had happened in the last week. But now that I had some time for myself, I needed to get back to things. Perhaps write a new column for the magazine.

However, my hopes were crushed the moment I saw an official email from Andra, my editor and boss at *The Hallowing Hour*. It read:

> Dear Drew Colter,
> This letter serves as formal notice that your position as a columnist with *The Hallowing Hour* is terminated effective immediately.
>
> As you are aware, the magazine's operations rely on a small group of key sponsors. Recently, these sponsors have expressed concern regarding the direction and tone of your published columns. Despite internal discussions and our attempts to mediate in the past few days, the pressure placed upon us has become untenable.
>
> While the official reasoning provided to us speaks only of "brand alignment" and "public positioning," it has been made clear—both directly and indirectly— that continuing your employment would place the magazine at risk in ways not fully disclosed to us. Certain decisions arrive from levels to which we are not privy, and we have been instructed to comply accordingly.

We want to emphasize that this outcome does not reflect the quality of your work or your dedication to the publication. We appreciate your contributions and regret that circumstances beyond the editorial team's control have forced this conclusion.

Your final paycheck, including any outstanding compensation owed to you, will be processed immediately. Please return any company materials in your possession at your earliest convenience.

We wish you the best in your future endeavors and sincerely hope you find a platform where your voice can continue to be heard without interference.

Sincerely,

Andra M. Stewart,

Editor

The Hallowing Hour

My heart fell as the blood rushed out of my face.

The job I'd had since I turned eighteen was now gone.

I was fired.

Lips trembling, I slowly closed the laptop and pushed it away from me. *The Hallowing Hour* had been my everything, the center of my world, for so long. It had been more than a mere paycheck for me; it was my only hope of one day reaching the supernatural world and having resources and backing to research what happened to my sisters.

But now . . .

It was gone.

Sure, the supernatural world had found me instead when Lucien appeared at my door, yet the only constant in my life—the only thing that stayed firm, consistent, and always there for me, the magazine—was now gone.

The timing seemed odd, and the wording of the termination letter made me think this couldn't have been a coincidence. Never before had

Andra said anything about firing me. Hell, for the last seven years I'd been there, *The Hallowing Hour* had never fired anyone; if anything, people quit on their own. The magazine couldn't really afford to let go of employees.

My heartbeat quickened as I lifted my laptop screen back up and read the letter again.

It spoke of the sponsors—of which there were so few I could count them on one hand—and since I knew those companies, had met with their investment divisions, I knew there was no way they were really behind this.

Certain decisions arrive from levels to which we are not privy, the letter said. And that told me everything I needed to know.

Because this couldn't have been a decision from my direct superiors or even sponsors. This meant someone else got involved. Someone with power who really didn't want me to continue writing for *The Hallowing Hour.*

I couldn't help but think of Chase and Avenor from the ASS, and the letter from the Sable Syndicate that Thayer received. I had a strong feeling either one of the two could be responsible.

Either way, I had no proof other than my own account and my involvement with Lucien.

An image of my apartment after the break-in came to mind. The ruined sheets upon sheets of paper on which I'd dedicated all my adult life to recording everything supernatural I had encountered. The torn world map with the colored pins on the floor. All I had left was my laptop and my Spellscript notebook.

But being the technophobe that I was, I hadn't bothered to document anything online, preferring to use good old pen and paper. So all I had were the articles I wrote, without any of my research in existence.

I also no longer had access to the magazine's resources.

But you're not going to start from scratch, a little voice reminded me. *You have Lucien now. He mentioned talking to Blaise, with his connections to the Underearth . . .*

That gave me pause. Right—yesterday evening Lucien had said something that alluded to the Underearth being in some way connected to what happened to Willow and Julianna.

I glanced at the entrance door and grimaced. In my bout of utterly selfish thoughts, I'd also forgotten about what really mattered. Willow and Julianna were what really mattered. My job, my apartment, my feelings for Lucien . . . These things wouldn't bring justice to my sisters.

So the question that remained was, what would?

Thayer and I were eating dinner when the howling started.

My brother seemed a little ill at ease from the sounds, shifting uncomfortably in his chair as he barely touched the pasta on his plate.

I had to admit, I wasn't feeling much better. The howls were eerie, like a bad omen, and with the image of Kate in my mind, and what Lucien might need to be put through, I couldn't help but feel a chill crawling up my spine.

Neither Thayer nor I talked as we attempted to eat the takeout Thayer had brought over when he returned from a whole day in the Concordian Ward with Anais and Enoch, and when the howling didn't stop, we both gave up trying.

As Thayer washed the dishes and I rinsed, he broke the terse silence and said, "I wonder what it feels like to lose yourself for a whole night."

Thinking of Kate, I felt sick. I didn't want to tell him about Wildlight.

"I imagine it feels both terrifying yet freeing," I responded, rinsing the plate, trying not to jump when some howls echoed ominously close. "Though what would I know?"

Thayer nodded slowly, rigidly, as he handed me the last plate. "It's surreal," he murmured, "to think that this kind of creature has been living under our noses all this time."

His words made me freeze as I put the plate I rinsed in the rack, and I turned to him, letting my anxious curiosity get the better of me. "You've been adapting exceptionally well to the whole idea of the supernatural ever since you landed here, all things considered," I stated cautiously.

His gray eyes were filled with grief when he turned to stare at me. "A lot of things have happened in the last few days," he said quietly. "Your apartment was trashed. You were hurt through Lucien. The threatening letter I got. It would be more surprising if I kept denying what I saw with my own eyes—let alone stupid."

I couldn't help but smile a little. "God forbid a person acts stupid."

Shooting me a somewhat filthy look, he stepped back from the sink and folded his arms. "All these years, I didn't want to believe you, Drew," he suddenly said, face serious. "I didn't want your words to be the truth, even though the moment you told me what happened eight years ago, a deep part of me knew you had no reason to lie. Not about something like this."

Catching my gaze, his expression was full of regret when he said, "Out of all of us four, you were always the most sensible one. You hardly ever lied, unless it was for Will's or Jules's sake. You were always the most reliable. If I didn't believe *you* of all people, then who should I have believed?" He paused, sucked in a deep breath, and looked away when he softly added, "I just . . . I needed an explanation I could process. A concrete logic I could follow. That our sisters were gone because of some supernatural creature appearing out of nowhere wasn't enough to ease my own guilt."

My heart broke a little at his admission. To think that some part of him believed me all this time yet was forced down in denial . . . it hurt. It fucking hurt.

But at the same time, I couldn't erase the fact he was feeling guilty about that day too. After all, I wasn't the only one who lost two sisters.

Thayer did too.

There was nothing left to say after that, and Thayer excused himself and retired for the night.

I, on the other hand, couldn't sleep.

It wasn't just the never-ending sound of wolves howling to the moon that prevented me from falling asleep, but rather the conversation with Thayer that kept circling in my mind.

So after hours of trying, I got out of bed and went to the living room to make myself a cup of coffee. It was already four o'clock in the morning at that point, after all, and it seemed sleeping was not in the cards for me tonight.

With a hot mug of latte, I sat on the couch and stared out the window at the darkness of the forest. Even though it was pitch black, I caught the leaves' rustle as wolves, most likely, passed by.

I wondered how Lucien was faring. He didn't tell me how he, as an Alpha, endured the full moon, aside from being the only one capable of restraining a wolf afflicted with Wildlight.

His face when he stared at Kate's body, so full of despair, wasn't a sight I wanted to see again. I hoped no one would suffer from Wildlight tonight.

I couldn't help but think about what it would be like to be a werewolf. With the ability to shift forms between human and wolf—did it feel liberating in a way? Being a human, even if only in shape, had constraints an animal didn't, be they cultural, physical, or mental.

Hearing the animalistic howls outside, I wondered what it would be like to lose my humanity for one night every month. I mean, I already had something similar—my PMS hormones caused my behavior to be as close to that of an animal as I would ever be able to feel—yet this, obviously, was different.

From the howling sounds, I could tell the werewolves weren't running around alone. There was something melodic, like a question-and-answer cadence, to their howls. Despite it being somewhat terrifying, there was also something musical and magical about those sounds.

Werewolves lived in packs, after all, and while Lucien viewed it through the lens of the leader, the Alpha, the rest of the pack probably acted like some sort of community. It had to be the only way for all these supernatural creatures, Otherborne, to coexist without ripping each other's heads off.

To be part of such a community, even if built on the mere common ground of being the same race, to *belong* somewhere like that . . . Those things made me feel a deep, longing ache in my heart.

The supernatural world took your sisters, Drew, the voice of reason reminded me bitterly. *Why would you yearn to become an Otherborne?*

It was a good question, but I also knew the answer.

Because I'm lonely, and at least if I were a werewolf, or even another type of Otherborne, I would belong somewhere. Anywhere.

I wouldn't be thought of as some sort of a cuckoo. A crackpot. A delusional grief-stricken sister.

I wouldn't have to convince my parents of anything for the sake of some hopeless approval.

And, I knew, all that was selfish of me. It was like joining the enemy who killed my sisters.

But was it really the enemy, though?

Lucien wasn't an enemy . . .

Shaking my head, I forced my thoughts away and distracted myself by looking at my phone. There were a couple of missed calls from my parents. I'd been in the cabin alone the entire day, with Lucien gone and Thayer only returning in the evening. I could have answered them if I wanted to.

But I didn't.

Thayer and I had already changed the SIM cards in our phones to avoid any possible tracking by the Syndicate, and we also changed our numbers in the process. Thayer must've given our parents his new number and mine, too, because otherwise, they couldn't have reached out to me.

Which would've been better, though I didn't fault Thayer for doing that.

Either way, I couldn't bring myself to care about my parents right now. Besides, I knew why they called: to tell me about another job opening one of their rich friends' son's friends had in their wealthy conglomerate company. They would try to force my hand, to make me move back to Seattle and take that job, as they always did. They wanted me under their control, after all, so I would stop ruining their oh-so-precious reputation.

My resentment toward them was so integrated into my very being, I couldn't imagine ever going back to Seattle, even just to visit.

They would never change. They would always put everything else first over their own kids, as they had always done. And I was sick and tired of playing their game.

I was sipping my coffee, tired yet wide awake, when the entrance door burst open. I jumped to my feet, spilling coffee on the carpet as I put the mug on the table. The door had been locked before we went to bed. Thayer and I made sure of it.

Yet now the door barely hung on its hinges after the wolf walking inside literally broke into the cabin.

A feeling I couldn't quite name expanded in my chest as I watched the wolf, with his silky, glistening bronze fur and bright arctic-blue eyes, padding toward me, his eyes set on my face like a hawk's.

Footsteps announced Thayer coming into the living room. The wolf's eyes remained solely on me as Thayer asked, voice sleepy, "What the hell just happened?"

I didn't look at him, didn't move, didn't break eye contact with the wolf as I spoke softly. "Thayer, close and lock the entrance door, please, and go back to your room."

In truth, I had no idea if that was what to do. Anais hadn't prepared us for a wolf breaking into the cabin—especially the Alpha of the pack.

Thayer, to my utter relief, didn't argue or question my command, and did as I said. Tomorrow, I knew he would demand answers, but for now, I focused on the wolf.

"Lucien," I murmured, trying to make my voice as soothing as possible, like I'd done when I first brought him into my apartment what felt like a lifetime ago. "What are you doing here?"

The beautiful wolf didn't respond. There was nothing in his eyes but pure fixation as he stared at me, as still as a statue. I could barely see him breathe.

I was completely at a loss, but I couldn't give up. Swallowing hard, I slowly took a step forward, trying not to make any sharp movements. "Lucien," I whispered now, "what do I need to do?"

Because why would he be here if he wasn't in some sort of trouble? Lack of humanity or not, Lucien should spend the night roaming the forest like the others, shouldn't he?

The wolf stared at me for a few more moments in complete, still silence before, to my utter shock, I saw his fur being sucked into his skin, followed by the paper-folding noise of him starting to shift.

"Lucien, no!" I hissed, eyes wide with fear, images of Kate in my head. "The full moon is still out! You should stay in your wolf form—"

My words cut off, my throat dry, when the gorgeous man appeared before me—his face so inhumanly beautiful, his sun-kissed body rippling with strong, taut muscles, easily towering over me as he got in my face, his eyes glowing an impossible bright blue.

I gasped. His gaze was so sharp and piercing, it rendered me immobile. It felt as though he was a predator on the hunt and I was his prey.

Which was exactly what we were. Werewolf and human.

At the full moon.

"Lucien," I whispered, shuddering when he raised his hand to cup my face so gently, so in contrast to the almost beastly expression on his face, I almost whimpered. "Lucien, what's happening?"

He opened his mouth, and a guttural voice came out, saying one word.

"Drew."

Those beautiful eyes roamed over my face as though he was studying every nook and curve of my features, until they landed on my lips. Lips that I now parted when his gaze shifted, turning absolutely feral.

And for a moment, I forgot this Lucien wasn't completely human, and a strong emotion rose inside me. Something mindless with desperation. "I'm the Eteria here," I murmured, searching his eyes, watching his gaze sharpen. "You shouldn't be controlled by the Eteria magic, should you?"

If his muscles were rigid before, he was now as hard as the wall he suddenly pressed my back against. His knee pushed my legs apart, settling between them, making me almost sit on his lap, while his hand lowered from my cheek to my throat in a gentle yet unmovable hold. His other hand settled on my thigh.

Heat flared up deep within me, almost bringing tears to my eyes with how much I wanted him there and then. I wanted his knee to move up, to brush against me. I wanted the hand on my thigh to slide to my butt and squeeze it roughly, possessively. Those lips I'd been avoiding looking at out of fear I would long for them too much I now desperately wanted, *needed*, anywhere on my skin.

This abrupt, absurd, almost compulsive need for his touch broke me. "Let me go," I said, my voice barely audible as I was too weak, too submissive under his strong touch, to put any conviction in my tone. "Let me go, Lucien."

"It's not your fault you're my Eteria."

I would've jumped if he hadn't held me so strongly. His voice was like gravel. Barely human. Yet I understood him. I also saw the vehemence that entered his gaze.

But I focused on his words, because a different kind of heat flared up inside me. "Yet I'm subjected to loving you, and wanting you only, whether it's my fault or not," I hissed, glaring at him now. "So why are *you* here? Why now, when it's the full moon and you should be out there? Why did you come here when you barely have any hold on your humanity? When you're the Alpha of this pack? When you have other responsibilities? When you avoided me the whole day to take care of those responsibilities?"

The fury in his eyes should've scared me; it almost twisted the lines of his face into the monstrous expression I'd only seen twice before. But instead of being scared, I felt my own anger rise.

I sucked in a breath and snapped, voice louder now, "You're toying with me, Lucien. I have no say when it comes to my emotions, but you do. You can leave me alone. You can put distance between us so my emotions would remain my own!"

"I would never subject you to such a fate."

The gravelly words were followed by a deep, ominous growl that I could feel rising from his naked chest and reverberating through my own body. He was so close now I could see the little streaks of silver in his irises. I could see the deep wine-colored shade of his thick lashes.

With him so close, any kind of strength I'd mustered was now gone, and I deflated in his arms. "What fate?" I whispered, frustrated.

That frustration turned into desire as his knee rubbed against my clothed center. My eyes rolled as my head fell back against the wall, and I had to bite my lip not to moan.

"You will never love another," he suddenly said, mouth at my ear. *"You are* my *Eteria. Mine."*

His words made me grab his shoulders as my own knees grew weak and I could barely hold myself up, even though his words drove me mad. "So if you don't want me to die alone, then there is only one other option, isn't there?" I bit out, and almost moaned when I felt his lips brushing against my throat.

But then he lifted his head up, and his stunning eyes found mine again. He seemed even more furious than before, so much so that his hold on my throat and my thigh tightened, making me gasp. *"You'd rather be mind controlled?"* he snarled, the growling in his chest growing stronger.

I shuddered as I tried to rub myself against his knee, but his hand on my thigh tightened its hold so much it forced me to stop. I wanted to cry in frustration. I wanted release. And I wanted this release from *him*.

Through the needful haze in my head, I managed to grit out, "It's not your fault I'm your Eteria either."

As if I'd said the magic words—the wrong kind, that is—Lucien suddenly released me and stepped back, putting distance between us, his face set in a fury more human than before. From behind him, the first signs of dawn cast a soft, golden halo around him that made him seem like a fallen angel.

Without him holding me, I fell to the floor, staring at him from below, like the peasant I was to his ethereal existence. The strong pull within me, though, ignored that notion. It wanted me to grab him and hold him tight, to ravish him, and have him ravish me, until there was nothing of me left.

"I should've let you go," he said now in a rough voice, no longer so guttural, though he was still growling in evident anger, and he kept stepping back from me as though *I* was the danger here. "I shouldn't have let you take care of me, mortally wounded or not. That would've been kinder than the alternative."

Putting my hands on the wall, I slowly pulled myself back up to my feet, though I was shaking all over from everything that was happening here. "So why didn't you?" I asked hoarsely, something salty on my lips.

Tears. I was crying.

Shit.

His back hit the window as he shook his head. His expression shattered, revealing shame and desperation that hadn't been there before, as if the wolf was receding completely, letting the human part of him out. "I was being selfish," he hissed, his gaze still holding mine. Neither of us could look away. "I was . . . I was *elated* when I realized *you* were my Eteria . . ."

"*Why?*" I pressed, confusion mixed with anger making me stride toward him as my knees regained their strength. His eyes widened, and he looked almost cornered when I reached him and grabbed his shoulders. Sparks flew from his skin straight to my palm. "*Why, Lucien?*"

For the first time, I saw in his eyes what I had never seen, or had refused to see, before.

I could see the heat.

The want.

The *need.*

His hands wrapped around my wrists, and I didn't know if he wanted to push me away or pull me closer. I wasn't sure he knew what he wanted to do either.

"Answer me," I pleaded with him, unable to take his silence, as I gave in to my body and pressed my front against his, causing an electric current to course throughout my entire being.

His face suddenly twisted in pain, in guilt. Shame. Defeat. "Because the moment I opened my eyes," he said in a rasp, his hands suddenly on my hips, making my breath catch, "I wanted you like I'd never wanted another woman."

I froze, staring at him with shock.

He gave me a bitter smile as he grabbed my hair in his fist and forced my head back, his lips hovering over mine. "And the truly sick thing is," he hissed, "I can force you to want me too."

Before I could process his words, or even say anything, his lips crashed against mine.

CHAPTER 27
CONSEQUENCES OF NAIVETY

It felt like coming home.

The warmth of his lips, the rough feel of his dark-red bristles under my palms, the pressing of his hands against my hips . . . It felt as though I'd returned to a place I had never even visited.

A place to finally call *home*.

And when he immediately opened his mouth and flicked his tongue against mine, making every part of my body fill with unbidden desire, as if he couldn't hold himself back anymore, it was everything.

His hands left my hips, and he enveloped me in his arms, crushing me to him, taking me over, controlling me like a marionette and leaving me breathless, unable to do anything but succumb to his passionate touch.

And when he suddenly flipped us so my back pressed against the window, and his thigh nudged my legs apart, causing me to half sit on his lap as he devoured my mouth with hunger that left me dizzy, all I could do was hold on to him and kiss him back with everything I had.

I drowned in the madness of his touch, of his kiss, of everything *Lucien*.

And it almost felt like he was drowning, too, and I was his breath of air.

I clung on to his shoulders, desperately kissing him back, entangling my tongue with his, pressing so hard against him, moving my fingers through his soft auburn curls, wishing I could touch him everywhere. That he would touch me too.

At that moment, I couldn't give a flying fuck if it was mind control or not.

I just knew I wanted him with every fiber of my being.

And for the first time, I could *feel* him wanting me too.

A slamming noise caused Lucien to break the kiss and release me, stepping away as he turned to look at the entrance door.

The same entrance door Thayer had readjusted before he retreated to his room was now barely holding on to its hinges, thanks to a large, stunning inky-black wolf who was now padding toward Lucien. Light spilled into the room, indicating the arrival of the sun. The wolf shifted, the sound hissing, and faintly, I realized Thayer had exited his bedroom due to the noise again.

The wolf shifted into Blaise, eyes on Lucien. "Anaïs," the Beta now said, face stricken. "Wildlight."

Lucien stared at Blaise for a moment as he processed the words.

And the next moment he was a blur of bronze and auburn as he shifted into his wolf form midway through running out the door.

Disoriented from the kiss with Lucien, and trying to process myself what Blaise had just said, I had to lean back against the wall and watch as Thayer strode toward the Beta. "Take me to her," he said, face dark.

Blaise's eyes studied Thayer for a short moment before he nodded curtly. "I'll take you by car," he said in his heavy accent.

"I'm coming with you," I hastily said, heart beating loud in my chest now that understanding finally settled inside me.

Minutes later, Blaise was racing through the forest in his Jeep, with Thayer and me in the back seat, until we reached the beautiful plaza that was the pack's Heart. Then Blaise led us at almost a run inside the Concordian Ward.

The first bed in the row was occupied by a petite human woman with curly dark hair and eyes that had gone completely black, until not even the whites were present. She was growling loud enough to wake the dead, her teeth unnaturally sharp as she tried to bite the people surrounding the bed the rest of her body was shackled to.

Next to her bed, Remi and Enoch were staring at Anais with dark expressions.

Lucien, in his human form and dressed this time, had blood around his mouth.

"You got her in time," Blaise murmured as he came to stand next to Lucien.

Lucien nodded shortly. "I managed to restrain her before she killed Layla."

Blaise nodded, wiping sweat from his forehead.

Thayer walked to the other side of Anais's bed, his face devoid of emotion. He might've disliked Anais for whatever reason, but seeing her in this state, her humanity gone from her human body, wasn't an easy sight for anyone.

My chest ached as I watched her. She was such a composed woman. Seeing her like this was absolutely devastating.

"What should we do now, Alpha?" Remi now asked, his voice soft, as he stared at Anais with unhidden sadness.

Lucien didn't reply. Instead, he kept on staring at Anais, looking almost haunted.

Remi tugged at Lucien's hands. "Alpha?"

Lucien whipped his head at Remi and snapped in a menacing growl, "*Don't touch me!*"

Immediately, Remi let him go and raised his hands in surrender, eyes wide in shock, his lips clamped shut.

Blaise murmured something in French I didn't quite hear, and Remi paled as he nodded and walked away toward another occupied bed, hidden by the curtains.

"You have to find a cure."

I whipped my head toward my brother, whose voice was strained. His face was as white as a sheet, and his eyes were staring at Anais unblinkingly.

Enoch, who'd been watching Anais silently, said quietly, "There is no cure for Wildlight, Thayer."

"There has to be," Thayer snapped, lips trembling, as he grabbed Anais's shackled hand. Her nails had curled into claws, and she dug them into Thayer's palm deep enough to draw blood, but Thayer didn't seem to notice. Or care. "You have to do *something*!"

Lucien stepped back from the bed, his face so haunted, gaze far away, and said nothing.

I didn't know what to do. My heart was hammering in my chest, especially from the constant inhuman growls coming from Anais. But also because Lucien seemed as if he had just seen his worst nightmare come to life.

Thinking of Kate, I shivered.

When no one responded to Thayer's plea, he suddenly turned to glare at Lucien. "Right before the full moon rose," he now said, trying to catch Lucien's gaze, "we found a solution for the thing on your back. The Spellscript."

At once, Lucien's gaze became focused and landed on Thayer, eyes wide. "What?"

Thayer pursed his lips and nodded. "She said she now knew how to neutralize the Spellscript's effects," he said, both urgent and cajoling. "She's the only one who knows how."

Despair filled Lucien's face. "It doesn't matter now," he said hollowly. "Wildlight is incurable, Thayer."

A cleared throat made us all turn to Enoch. He seemed paler than before. "I . . . ," he started, swallowed hard, and turned to look at Lucien. "There might be a way . . . temporarily . . ."

Lucien looked back at him, and they seemed to have a silent conversation, which caused Lucien to tense and Enoch to become distraught, yet determined, too, at the same time.

I held my breath as I watched the wordless exchange until Lucien, face grave, bitterly said, "Fine." Without another word, he turned and walked out of the cabin.

I glanced, confused, at Enoch, who seemed just as grim faced, and Thayer, whose face lit up with hope, before I followed Lucien outside.

He was almost at one of the other cabins in the plaza when I grabbed his arm and made him stop. "Lucien," I said, heartbeat so loud, I wondered if he could hear it. "What just happened?"

Lucien whirled around to face me, his face stormy. "Enoch is going to do something he shouldn't," he snapped harshly, but I knew his anger wasn't aimed at me. "Something that will do far more harm than good."

I searched his gaze. "What is he going to do?"

He laughed humorlessly, the sound scraping my ears like sandpaper. "He's going to use forbidden magic. The kind that comes at a cost. All so he can neutralize the Spellscript on my back."

Lucien's eyes were filled with misery, begging me to understand, almost, when he hissed, "I'm sick and tired of people sacrificing themselves to protect me as if I'm not an Alpha who's naturally, genetically capable of enduring far more than the average werewolf, or any other Otherborne."

Belatedly, I realized he was talking about something else. Something about Anais catching Wildlight brought something else to the surface, something Lucien was obviously struggling with.

"Lucien," I murmured as calmly as I could, before I wrapped my arms around him, hugging him close. "Talk to me." I closed my eyes. "Please."

For a moment, I thought Lucien would push me away. He was so tense, his body was like a hard mass of skin and muscles. But to my utter relief, he put his arms around me and pulled me close, burying his head in my throat. "Do you know why I joined the Imperative for Transparency and Symbiosis? The organization that believes in revealing our existence to the human world?"

While I knew it was a rhetorical question, I still shook my head. I'd never really questioned his motive behind why he wanted the supernatural to be exposed. I'd simply accepted it as it was.

But nothing was ever so simple.

"I used to be an Alpha of a werewolf pack in Paris," he suddenly said, voice hoarse, as he tightened his hold on me. "The Montvoilé werewolf pack, it was called. 'The veiled mountain.' It was named that way to put an emphasis on our secrecy. Our hidden existence."

I felt his hands fisting on my shirt. "I was born with the Alpha Marker. It's a genetic marker that makes me different from regular werewolves. It makes me stronger, faster, and deadlier than any werewolf. It also gives me a strategic mindset, and an analytical one. All for the sake of protecting my pack to the fullest." He almost spat the last words.

"I was appointed Alpha officially at fifteen," he continued, voice growing darker, and impossibly, even more bitter. "Too young an age for this position, especially in a pack that had been one of the top largest packs in Europe. But only a werewolf bearing the Alpha Marker can become an Alpha, and the Alpha before me was already old, and so he passed away. Thus I became the next Alpha, as the only Alpha Marked werewolf in the pack."

I took it all in silently, listening closely, smoothing my hands over his back, trying to calm him down. Because I could feel his distress. I could feel him recalling the memories. And I knew the ending was not going to be good.

"As the years passed, I settled into my role as an Alpha," he continued, derision dripping from his voice. "I appointed a few Betas and ran the pack as I saw fit, believing in the political philosophy of treating the pack as one big happy family." He laughed, but it was so brittle and humorless, I felt myself shiver. "And that was my mistake."

He suddenly leaned back so he could face me, and his eyes were bright with despair. "Because I insisted my pack was my family, I didn't realize one of my Betas was aiming to overthrow me and bring another Alpha from another pack in my place."

His auburn curls fell down over his face like a curtain. "That Beta, Jacques, was my closest friend. A man I considered a brother."

Hearing the little break in his tone at the word *brother*, my chest squeezed, and I hugged him tighter, trying to merge our bodies and offer him warmth and comfort. Telling him I was here.

He sucked in a breath and looked away, lips thin. "Before the rebellion erupted, I was striking deals with human companies to bring profit to our pack. It's not unheard of for Otherborne to do business with humans, as long as they kept their true nature under wraps, but werewolves hardly ever did such things. We're very homogenous. We don't mix with other Otherborne races, let alone humans. I was the odd one out; I insisted we couldn't continue living among ourselves without spreading out to other races. Jacques, along with other conservative pack members, did not like that at all."

Slowly, his arms fell from around me, and he took a step back, staring at me without really seeing me. "I was an idealist. Still am, for better and for worse. But back then, I turned a deaf ear to others' opinions. Instead of listening, I preached. And Jacques and the others simply stopped complaining when they realized they were talking to a wall."

The self-deprecation, and self-loathing, in his voice made my heart break. I stepped forward, wanting to reach out to him again, to hold him, but he shook his head and put up his hand. "No, Drew. I don't deserve your sympathy. The fall of the Montvoilé pack was of my own making."

"Lucien—"

"Yet I could've prevented it," he cut me off with a bitter smile, "if only I could have told the human companies and their representatives, who became my friends along the way, about what was happening."

Pushing his auburn curls back, he gave me a desperate look. "You must understand, Drew. I wasn't entirely unaware of my pack members' building resentment. I saw things from a different perspective, my own perspective, really, and wouldn't bother to try and look at everything from theirs. For so long, Otherborne and werewolves, too, thought humans to be weak, meek, and useless. But when I dealt with them myself and interacted with them on a daily basis, I realized just how wrong this state of mind was." His voice turned somewhat choked. "Humans had their own strength. They had the power of curiosity, the endless need to better themselves, unlike most Otherborne, especially werewolves, who believed that they could only use the cards life had dealt them at birth."

He suddenly looked as if all energy evaporated from his body as he sat down on a bench, burying his head in his hands. "But just like I didn't listen to them, my pack members didn't listen to me. And so one fateful night, while I was away, in Marseille for a meeting with a human company, a rebellion broke out inside my pack and started a civil war."

Tears welled in my eyes as I slowly, hesitantly, came to sit next to him. I was scared of what he was going to tell me next.

"Jacques led the rebellion," Lucien said hoarsely, and I saw him tremble. "He brought half of the pack over to his side, and they went around the pack territory, threatening the members with death if they didn't join them. A few did, but most didn't, and the forests of Paris turned into battlefields."

He stopped, and I could hear him trying to catch his breath before he said, "I received the call too late, and ran in wolf form all the way from Marseille to Paris without pause for a full day at full speed. But by the time I arrived, I was already too late.

"They were all dead."

I sucked in a breath as he slowly raised his head and turned to look at me with that haunted gaze from before. "When werewolves turn against each other, the odds of survival of either side are close to zero. The entire pack territory was filled with bodies of werewolves in both human and wolf form. My family . . ." He swallowed hard and looked away. "I had a mother and two younger sisters, just like you did, Drew. And I failed to protect them. I arrived too late. The rebellion killed them."

He was trembling so hard, I couldn't help but hug him again. I didn't care if he didn't want to; he needed to be held. And I needed to hold him, too, because I'd never seen him like this before, never heard him as broken.

"Lucien," I whispered, tears escaping my eyes as I cradled his head close to my chest, "you don't have to . . . you don't have to c-continue—"

"I was an *imbécile*," he hissed as he let me hug him, though his arms remained at his sides. "For trusting that my pack was like family to me. That they would never dare cross that line. I had put faith and trust in them, in *Jacques*, and now I will have to suffer the consequences of my naivety for the rest of my life."

I was about to object, to deny all that, to tell him he was not an *imbécile* for trusting the wrong people, but before I could, he suddenly raised his head and met my gaze, his own tears wetting his bristles. "Before then, I had never killed," he whispered, his tears falling freely. "I hadn't had any reason to. But when I saw the bodies of my mother and sisters, I felt rage like I had never felt before. I saw red. And I, along with my sole surviving Beta, who was on my side, who was a true brother to me, unlike Jacques, went hunting."

He shook his head, looking away. "I killed and killed until all I could smell was that metallic stench of blood. But no matter how many disloyal pack members I killed, no matter the dark retribution I felt by ending Jacques's life, my slaughtered pack members would never come back."

The betrayal he'd described, the gravity of the situation, of everything he was telling me, made me sob. I realized, now, why he killed Mack Page, almost emotionlessly. Why he thought himself an idiot for trusting another Beta after Jacques's betrayal.

"Only two members of the pack survived," Lucien said now in a hollow voice, leaning back from me and staring at the ground, unseeing. "Rémi, my cousin, though he was no longer a part of the pack ever since he moved to the States as a child, and Blaise, the only Beta who survived the attack and never left my side.

"After the Montvoilé pack's demise, Blaise and I stayed with a human family," he continued, and his tears dried as his face grew fierce with a frustrated kind of affection. "It was the family of a man I met during my business with humans, and who became a true friend. His name is Olivier. Both he and his wife, Martha, are human. They shared the hobby of hunting. When my pack slaughtered each other, Olivier and his wife were caught in the cross fire while on a hunting trip. I found them wounded in the aftermath. Olivier, who's ex-military, injured many of the pack members I fought, and inadvertently helped me and Blaise in our scourge."

Lucien turned to meet my gaze fully now. "It made me realize that maybe, if only humans knew of our existence, they could've come and helped my pack members when I was away, just like Olivier and Martha did. What if so many atrocities that happened to Otherborne could've been prevented by getting help from humans?"

He cupped my face suddenly, tracing my cheeks with his thumbs. "Like when you helped me when I was on the verge of death."

My heart broke at his words, and at his touch too. It reminded me of the conversation we'd had only an hour ago, about my emotions being manipulated as his Eteria. How selfish he felt for finding me and keeping me close despite everything he knew. The kiss . . .

"What happened to them?" I asked in a whisper, focusing on his story. His words. "To Olivier and Martha."

His hands slid down from my face and held my own. He stared at my palms, almost studying them. "The French equivalent to the American Supernatural Society called it a breach of protocol, and much like Chase, the sorcerer, almost did to you, they erased the couple's memories."

He grew quiet then, and I did too. For a few long seconds, neither of us said anything as we held each other's hands, as though trying to comfort and console one another. I felt raw and bleeding on the inside, and could only imagine how Lucien felt.

"I promised I would never let something like that happen again." He suddenly spoke, breaking the silence, and caught my gaze. His eyes almost pleading with me to believe him. "When I was offered the position of an Alpha here in California, I promised that I would always be there for my pack members. That I would never be far. That I would take care of them."

I nodded, leaning my forehead against his. "I know. I believe you."

"Yet Kate was afflicted by Wildlight only four months into my job," he said in a strained voice, "and I was blindsided and betrayed, yet again, by a Beta of my choosing. And now, one of the very few pack members I truly trust . . . Anaïs . . ."

His voice trailed off, and he pulled me close, burying his face in my neck and holding me tight. I held him just as tightly back. No more words were needed. I understood everything now.

Lucien was as much of a broken person as I was.

And maybe together, we two broken pieces could make a whole.

CHAPTER 28
THE HUMAN PART

My heart was heavy as I watched Lucien holding Anais down by the shoulders, while Remi and Blaise were on each of her sides, restraining her as well. Not that it did anything much—she was thrashing against them, rattling the bed in the process, her sharpened teeth biting air.

Thayer and I stood by Enoch, who was stationed at the end of the bed, his face grim while his eyes took on a chilly look. He stretched out his hands and gently curled them around Anais's ankles. Then he grew still.

A moment later, I gasped as something flared beneath her skin in violent pulses. It spread all over her body, coloring her veins an eerie, acid-like green. It flickered on and off, and there was a hum in the air, like a soft, barely audible whistling sound, that disappeared when Anais began to scream.

Aside from Enoch, who kept focusing, everyone else flinched at the bloodcurdling, inhuman shrieks coming out of Anais's elegant throat. I snapped my gaze to Lucien, whose jaw locked tight, his knuckles white due to the force he held down Anais with.

"I see you behind the rising tide, Anais Verdin," Enoch said suddenly, his voice low, steady, and almost priestlike. *"Rise from the deep and come forth."*

The reaction was instant: Her flickering veins caused her body to recoil like something struck. A rippling shock wave rolled under her skin, the luminescence collapsing inward before flaring again, almost as if it was confused. Enraged.

Enoch closed his eyes. When he spoke next, his voice took on an edge of something else. As if something other than Enoch was talking through his throat. *"Take back what you have forsaken."*

The screams stopped. Anais froze.

Tension spread through the room, along with something else. Something I couldn't quite see, smell, or taste, but I could feel. As though another existence was present beyond what the eye could see.

Then, a soft light spilled from Enoch's hands—not too bright, more like the soft glow of the sun reflected in a lake. It sank into Anais's skin through her ankles and rapidly crawled up her thighs to her waist, torso, neck, arms, and head, engulfing her entirely, before her body jerked once, sharply, as though shocked by an invisible defibrillator.

Enoch let her go, but the light stayed. The others released her as well when Enoch gave them a confirming nod, his eyes still closed, and we all watched as the light seeped into her skin, melting within it, taking over the hellish green that colored her veins and instead turning them a soft white, like scars all over her body.

Her eyes snapped open, and they were no longer lost and gone. They were soft and terrified.

"Thayer?" she whispered in a voice turned raspy from her screams, as though surfacing from a dream she'd been drowning in. "Enoch?"

Thayer rushed to her side, taking her hand in his, face so pale, it was a wonder he didn't pass out. "I'm here," he whispered. "Thayer. I'm here."

I turned to look at Enoch as he opened his eyes. For a moment, they weren't the fragile brown of an ordinary man's. They were silvery, translucent—as if a soul's light was shining through his pupils from the wrong direction.

Then he blinked and it was gone, and I couldn't help but think I might've imagined that.

Enoch moved toward Anais's other side and drew her wide-eyed deer-caught-in-the-headlights gaze. "You've been afflicted with

Wildlight," he said, gentler now, but in a hurry. "I've pulled your humanity forward, but it's a mere thread. I cannot hold it long."

Her breath steadied. The slight shimmering of her veins beneath her skin calmed, as if tamed by the strange gravity of Enoch's presence.

Lucien, whose eyes were still on Anais, asked hoarsely, "How long?"

"Five minutes," Enoch said. "Maybe less. The Wildlight cannot be held at bay for much longer than that."

Anais swallowed, blinking tears away. Thayer, too, seemed so crushed, I felt myself on the verge of tears again. None of it was fair. Wildlight wasn't fair. While I didn't know Anais that well, she did not deserve this. No one did.

"Show me your back, Alpha," she suddenly said, voice shaking but clear, as she turned to stare at Lucien. "Before I disappear again."

Lucien hesitated, but Enoch shot him a warning look. He sucked in a breath and took off his shirt, showing Anais his back.

"Scalpel," Anais ordered, and Remi handed her one from the cabinet near her bed. "I'm sorry, Alpha, but we don't have time to put you under—"

"Just do it," Lucien cut her off through gritted teeth. Blaise had brought over a chair, and Lucien propped himself on it, leaning his elbows on its back, facing away from Anais, who, with Thayer's help, was now sitting. Thayer did not release her, with his hand behind her back, keeping her steady.

Wordlessly, Anais dug the scalpel into Lucien's back.

Instinctually, I rounded the bed toward Lucien and held his hands, sick with worry at everything that was happening. But Lucien didn't move. He sat as still as a statue, his muscles tight, and not a muscle moving on his blank face.

Blood poured from Lucien's back as Anais carved new lines over the Spellscript. I did not understand what she was doing at all; obviously, she was overwriting the Spellscript with a new one, but the lines of the new one were odd, jagged, not as symmetrical as other Spellscripts I had documented throughout the years.

"Two minutes," Enoch's voice echoed in the silent room, and his voice was a little strained now. Glancing at him while still holding Lucien's hands, I realized he was leaning against the wall, sweat glistening over his face. He seemed dizzy.

Anais murmured something unintelligible as she carved more lines into Lucien's back. His blood was creating too large a pool under his chair—so much that I feared this was more than his body could handle.

With a sudden movement, Anais threw the scalpel on the floor and put her bloody palms over Lucien's messed-up back. She closed her eyes, and a soft light poured from her into Lucien's skin. The light was different from Enoch's: brighter, more purple in color.

Lucien's back soaked in the light, and Lucien's hands suddenly clenched mine—the only time he'd moved in the past couple of minutes. His face remained expressionless, and the rest of his body didn't move, but he was holding me tightly. And when I saw the raw, tattered skin was being woven together, closing the wounds, it looked so painful, I squeezed his hands right back.

"Thirty seconds," Enoch said, his voice a soft whisper. From the corner of my eye, I saw he had slid down to the floor, almost as if he couldn't keep himself standing.

Anais suddenly took her hands off Lucien. His wounds, I saw, were closed. All that remained were the scars of the Spellscript carvings and the new ones Anais had inflicted.

"Done," she murmured, sagging back against Thayer, who wrapped his arms around her, face a little ill, though his eyes were lit with a horrified kind of wonder.

The same kind I was feeling right now too. Because Lucien sagged against the chair, not falling to the floor only because I was still holding his hands, and Blaise, who'd stood next to him, caught him in time.

"Lucien!" I called, hovering over him when I saw his eyes were closed. My heart fell as terror filled me, and I turned to Anais. "What's wrong—"

But Anais was no longer human.

Everything happened in a blur. Blaise practically peeled Thayer off her and shoved him back as he and Remi went to restrain her. Anais growled and thrashed against them, but she seemed a little weaker than before, and Blaise and Remi shackled her successfully to the bed again. She growled and growled, trying to bite into everyone who came close, and Blaise had to physically hold Thayer back. My stupid brother had tried to reach her.

"I'm sorry," I heard Enoch faintly say, before the hospital director succumbed to his own darkness and lay still on the floor.

I stared at Lucien's sleeping face as I held his hand, wondering when he would wake up.

Remi, who wasn't just his cousin but also a healer in the Concordian Ward, said it would take a few hours. Having his Spellscript overwritten, along with Anais's unplanned deep healing, would've taken a big toll on anyone, but since Lucien was an Alpha, Remi believed he would awaken after a good few hours of rest instead of staying unconscious for days.

It didn't sit well with me either way, and so I stayed by his side after Teya and Blaise helped him get back to his cabin in the woods so he could sleep soundly in his own bed.

I told Thayer he should come back to the cabin with me, but he refused. "I want to stay here," he'd said, face calm, though his eyes showed his distress as he sat next to Anais.

Despite his dislike for her, I understood why this whole thing hit him so hard. It hit me hard too. Seeing someone you knew, even for a short time, losing their humanity like that, with no hope of ever returning, was a lot to process. Thayer had spent most of his time since we arrived at the Ward with Anais and Enoch, as the two searched for a way to neutralize Lucien's Spellscript. Beyond their mutual dislike, I believed Thayer respected her. And that must've been even worse, seeing someone you respected turning into an incoherent beast in human flesh.

"Here you go."

Blaise's heavily accented voice made me snap out of my dark reveries, and I looked up to see him holding two cups of coffee. I could only nod as I thanked him, taking one cup from him.

He took a seat next to me, right near Lucien's bed. "He's going to be okay, you know," he told me, dark eyes reassuring. "Lucien is strong."

The way he pronounced *Lucien* was almost musical. It made me give him a weak smile. "I know he's strong," I said softly, "but I can't help but worry."

He nodded with a heavy sigh, his eyes fixating on Lucien's serene face. "Did he tell you about Montvoilé?"

I nodded, feeling a heavy weight on my chest. "Yes. It . . . it's awful. I'm sorry you had to go through this."

Blaise leaned back, sipping his coffee. "When we first moved here six months ago," he suddenly said, "Lucien, as the newly appointed Alpha, was given the choice to either keep the pack name or change it. It's a choice every Alpha has, and it carries a lot of weight in the werewolf world."

He gave me a sad look. "In French, *Montvoilé* translates loosely into 'the veiled mountain.' Our pack back then kept this name for many centuries, to enforce our secluded lifestyle. We refused to let Otherborne mix with our pack, through friendships or mating. Humans, obviously, were out of the question."

I remembered Lucien had said werewolves were very homogenous. That seemed to track.

"When we came here," Blaise continued, returning his gaze to Lucien and tightening his hold on his coffee cup, "the pack name was Suncrown Ridge. A very bright, sunny name, fitting for a California werewolf pack." He smiled a little. "But Lucien didn't like it. It sounded too rigid. Too bright. It was like everything Lucien didn't believe in stuck in a name."

"But *sun* is supposedly a positive word," I said, frowning.

He shook his head. "It's more about the whole rather than every word on its own," he said quietly. "Put together, *Suncrown Ridge* gave Lucien the feeling of a dry, cutthroat, isolated place. So he changed it."

"*Montrevere*," I murmured, thinking it through. "What does it mean in French?"

"'Mountain of revelations and dreams,'" Blaise replied at once, a soft smile stretching his lips. "A name fitting for a pack led by an Alpha dead set on ushering in a new era for not just werewolves but all Otherborne as well."

I couldn't help but smile at that, feeling warm inside as I looked at Lucien's sleeping face. He wasn't just a beautiful man on the outside; Lucien was just as beautiful on the inside too. He was a good man who'd been through a lot, but also a man who stuck by his moral code, and who refused to let his own idealism put his people in danger again.

He harbored the same guilt I did regarding his pack in Paris, and his family. He couldn't save his sisters either. That's why he understood when I told him about Willow and Julianna. Why he held me close and just let me cry until I had no more tears left.

Blaise's voice drew my gaze back to him. He was now looking at me intently, emphatically. "I've known Lucien my whole life," he told me. "He's like a brother to me. I swore to fight for him, and protect him in my own way too. That's why I know when he's in true danger."

My eyes widened, but Blaise didn't stop. "You sound like a good woman, Drew," he said, face serious. "It's quite obvious to me why Lucien caught feelings for you."

I froze, jaw on the floor.

"My Alpha is a man who puts his heart on his sleeve," Blaise continued like a bulldozer making its crude way into my very soul. "It shows even in something like changing a pack's name to fit his vision."

Everything in my mind screeched to a full stop as I stared at Blaise, entranced.

"He has never given his heart to a woman before." His words hit like a hammer on my heartstrings. "But it seems he has given it to you."

A few splashes of coffee hit my fingers, and I realized my hands were shaking.

Blaise plucked the cup from my hands and put it down along with his empty one before he returned his gaze to me. Then he said, "I'm afraid I can't approve, because you're going to break him."

My head shook from side to side at once as I felt my throat constrict. But I had to force the words out. "Is it . . ." I tried to clear my throat and failed, so I croaked, "Is it because I'm human?"

Blaise's gaze was pitying. "If you were *just* a human, then no," he said grimly. "But you're his Eteria."

I hugged myself, unable to stop shivering. I couldn't think. I could barely even breathe. "The magical mind control," I gasped out, feeling so cold, yet also hot, because Blaise's words were like sharpened knives filled with hope.

Did Lucien really have feelings for me? Could it really be possible?

Blaise suddenly took my hand, snapping my attention back to him. "There is a way for you to stop being his Eteria."

I froze again. My shivering stopping too. Everything came to a halt. "What?"

"An Alpha has the power of Transference," he said, his hold on my hand tightening. "It's a special magic carried by Alphas only that can transform a human into a werewolf."

I tried to process his words and failed.

"If you become a werewolf," Blaise continued, eyes almost pleading with me, "you will no longer meet the criteria of being an Eteria, because you will no longer be human."

My mouth hung open. My mind raced with so many thoughts I completely blanked out. I couldn't believe what he was saying. I couldn't believe such a thing was even an option.

"You seem to have feelings for Lucien too," Blaise said now, letting my hand go and rising to his feet, eyes as dark as the night sky. "They may be the product of your Eteria status, or they may not. Wouldn't you want to find out?"

I had no words. I could hardly even think about what he was saying.

Seeing I was at a loss, Blaise put a hand on my shoulder, squeezed, and stepped back, grabbing the cups of coffee. "I'm going to go now," he said quietly, glancing at Lucien briefly before returning his gaze to me. "Think about it, Drew." He paused, grimaced. "At least for Lucien's sake. *Please.*"

Before I could respond, he left, closing the door behind him.

My heart was beating in my ears as I slumped against the chair, confused and shocked, and turned to look at Lucien.

And suddenly, I was filled with pain. Because if Lucien did have feelings for me like Blaise assumed, then why didn't he offer to transform me into a werewolf to begin with?

If he cared for me even a little, why didn't he tell me this was an option? That I could stop being his Eteria? That would've solved all our problems!

But maybe there was a reason he didn't say anything. A reason Blaise wasn't privy to. Maybe this wasn't possible with an Eteria. Maybe I was doomed to not being able to trust my own emotions. My own attraction. My own feelings.

Hesitantly, I looked at Lucien again and let myself truly feel. All the feelings I had suppressed. Everything I told myself was nothing. All the emotions I tried not to acknowledge.

The pain I felt for him when he told me his story.

The way my body felt when he kissed me senseless.

How every touch of his made me feel safe.

How being in his arms was like finding an oasis in the middle of a big, lonely desert.

Every moment we'd spent together since I found him outside my apartment building on the verge of death was meaningful. Every moment I caressed his beautiful coat, or cupped his face, or wished I would be in his league so he would notice plain old me . . .

A pair of brilliant blue eyes suddenly entered my vision, and I stared for a long moment before I realized Lucien was awake.

And staring right at me.

I jumped to my feet, not knowing what to do, feeling vulnerable, as if everything I was feeling was written all over my face. "Lucien—" I blurted without meaning to, having no idea what I wanted to say, or if I even wanted to say anything.

But I didn't have time to think because a moment later, everything became a blur.

One moment, I was standing near his bed, not knowing what to do with myself.

The next, Lucien had jumped out of the bed, grabbed me by my waist, and thrown me on the bed, settling between my legs, his hands caging my face.

My lips parted as heat and confusion pooled in my stomach. With my heart beating like an incessant war drum, I stared at Lucien and tried to speak, but found that I couldn't utter a word.

He pushed deeper into me with his hips, and when I flicked my gaze down, I saw a huge tent in his pants pressing against me.

I could feel myself getting wet at the sight, at the feel of him pressing his cock against my jeans-covered entrance, until I realized, belatedly, what kind of position we were in.

"Lucien," I gasped, finding my voice, snapping my eyes to meet his. "What are you doing?"

Lucien didn't speak. An unnamed emotion shone brightly in his eyes as his muscles grew stiff, his jaw locked, and I could almost hear him gritting his teeth as a soft yet animalistic growl rumbled in his chest.

The contradiction between his expression and the hot, mouth-wateringly stiff cock hidden underneath his pants threw me off. On one hand, my mind was scrambled as my own arousal roared to the surface, while on the other, I was so fucking confused.

Then he spoke. And his voice was as guttural as it had been the night before, when the full moon still lingered in the sky. "You smell like *him*."

I stared at him, frozen.

He lowered his face so our noses almost touched. "Why did he touch you?"

For a long moment, I had no idea who he was talking about, but then I remembered Blaise had grabbed my hand. But he couldn't possibly be talking about that, could he?

And suddenly, I was filled with frustration. "What the hell do you want from me, Lucien?" I snapped at him. "Why do you care?"

He growled louder as his lips hovered over mine. "I want to pump my scent into your skin until everyone knows you're mine."

I tried, and failed, to respond.

And Lucien, the sexy asshole, grinned smugly. "Is that a yes?"

"A yes?" I squeaked, feeling my chest growing heavy as my nipples hardened under my shirt. My loins clenched, my panties instantly drenched, and my breaths stuttered.

His eyes flashed, and this time, I could read his expression completely. His hooded gaze on my lips, the way he rocked his tented cock between my legs almost uncontrollably, the need etched in his face.

Lucien wanted me.

Feeling like I was in some sort of a dream, I pressed my hands against his chest, and his growl grew louder at the touch. His eyes flared, and he repeated the question in a gravelly voice. *"Is that a yes?"*

Hazily, I wrapped my legs around his waist and arched my back, pressing myself against him, which made his growl reverberate even more under my hands. "Lucien," I whispered, catching his gaze.

He seemed on the verge of snapping. *"Answer me, Drew."*

Nothing made sense. Logic ran out the window. Right then and there, all I was able to do was succumb to whatever this madness was.

"Yes," I whispered, and whatever restraint Lucien had, it snapped before I could even finish my sentence.

His lips crashed against mine as he devoured me, biting my tongue, my lips, licking and sucking until I could no longer breathe. His hands ripped—literally *ripped*—my shirt off my chest, throwing the tatters away as he grabbed my breasts and fondled them so hard, I gasped, feeling myself getting more soaked within the second.

My jeans and panties met the same fate as my shirt before he kicked off his own pants and aligned his naked, veiny, precum-dripping cock against my slit, the fold cradling his thick, long erection, wetting it with my juices. The feeling was so intense, I bit his lip hard enough to draw blood.

But Lucien didn't seem to care. In fact, this only spurred him on. His hand grabbed my hair and forced me to arch my neck as he pressed his lips against the spot where my pulse pounded so fast, it was a wonder I didn't suffer a cardiac arrest. It seemed Lucien found that spot full of wonder, too, because he sank his teeth into my skin and bit. Hard.

I half screamed, half moaned at the feeling of him licking and biting that spot over and over again, while rubbing his cock between my soaked folds. I practically saw stars. I could do nothing but hold on to his shoulders and try to ride that overwhelming onslaught of feelings he unleashed in me.

When he finally released my neck, he moved down to my breast and bit my stiff nipple, sucking it, while playing with the other, his cock suddenly pressed harder against my clit and rubbing it, hard, and the never-ending sensations became too much.

I broke apart as the orgasm was torn out of me with such sheer strength, I screamed, my entire body shaking and trembling. But far more than that, I could feel myself squirting over and over against his cock, coating both his erection and his magnificent abs with my juices.

But I couldn't bring myself to be embarrassed about it. In fact, how could I be, when he let me go and sat up, showing me his delicious pecs, his bulging biceps and corded arms, his hazed, glowing eyes, and his messy auburn curls?

Just the sight of this devastatingly gorgeous man, with his big mouthwatering cock, made my inner muscles squeeze, causing me to squirt directly at his belly.

He stared at my pussy with maddened eyes, watching as I still trembled in the aftermath of my release, and he stretched his hand toward my entrance and rubbed his finger against me.

I jolted and tensed at the brief sensation, and watched, wide eyed and filled with need, as he brought his wet finger to his mouth and licked it.

The sight almost made me cum again.

But I didn't have time to even process the sight because, as though I weighed nothing, he flipped me onto my stomach in a sudden, swift move, grabbed my thighs, and pulled me onto my knees, before his hands held my ass, parting it.

When he nudged the tip inside me, my trembling turned into fervent movements of trying to get him to just impale me. My breasts felt heavy, my mouth was dry, my skin glistened with sweat, and my need to have him take me, the need to find release again, as if I hadn't just experienced the greatest, most absurd orgasm of my life, was so overwhelming, I actually whimpered.

Without warning, he pushed himself to the hilt inside me, stuffing his huge, thick cock in my pussy, and that one movement almost made me black out, it felt so outlandishly good.

Holding my waist up so I wouldn't fall, while I grabbed the sheets with all my might, he unceremoniously powered in and out, gliding easily inside thanks to my preposterous amount of wetness, fucking me in a way I had never been fucked before. His movements were so strong, and coupled with how big and thick he was, he stretched my insides to their absolute limit, making me feel as if he was literally reaching my womb.

There was nothing I could do other than to hold on to the sheets, moan, and scream as he fucked me into oblivion.

I could feel the orgasm building inside me, so strong, so powerful, unstoppable, until it, too, was almost forced out of me, taking my breath away so I could barely even moan, it was so overpowering. I squeezed around him as the orgasm didn't end, but came in wave after wave, consuming me over and over again, while Lucien kept penetrating me hard and deep, his fingertips digging into my skin.

And apparently, he couldn't handle all the squeezing, because he leaned down, pressing his front over my back, somehow moving even faster than before, while his growls filled the air, reverberating from his chest to my back, making me shudder as the orgasms kept cascading down my body, and I could feel him coming, filling me with his cum, the warmth of it spreading across my entire body, as he pumped me until I milked him to the end.

He buried himself one last time inside me, and, without taking his cock out, enveloped me in his arms and rolled to the side, spooning me.

I could barely breathe, barely think, as I felt my juices, mixed with his cum, dripping down my inner thighs. He didn't let go, though.

And to my shock, I could feel he didn't go any softer, even after he came.

He only seemed to grow impossibly harder.

"Lucien?" I breathed out in question, my heart, still beating fast, somehow stuttering at the feel of his hardness.

Lucien didn't respond for a few seconds.

Then he leaned down and pressed his lips against my ear. "Drew," he said quietly, and I realized he was no longer growling. Instead, his voice was dark and raspy.

I shuddered. "Lucien," I almost cried out, trying to make him move, fuck me again, push me to the brink of ecstasy.

But his next words were like a cold bucket of water over my head. "I love you, Drew," he whispered hoarsely, "and it's killing me inside."

CHAPTER 29
HOW TO CONVINCE AN ALPHA

Lucien was off me the second after his soft, painful, heartbreaking confession. Slowly, I rolled around to my back, staring at him with wide eyes, full of disbelief.

But if I thought I heard him wrong, the moment I saw his agonized face as he sat back on his knees, looking at me as though I was the best and worst thing that ever happened to him, I knew I couldn't deny it.

Lucien told me he loved me.

Lucien told me he loved me.

"I l-love you," I blurted out in a stuttered whimper, tears welling in my eyes, and shook my head, sitting up when he looked at me with frustration. "I love you, too, Lucien—"

"You don't!" he cut me off with a desperate expression that felt like a knife to the gut. "You don't really love me, Drew! You're my *Eteria*—you're *magically wired* to fall for me, even if I were the worst person in the world!"

His words were true, but they hurt nonetheless. "But you aren't," I begged, lifting myself to my knees before him and cupping his face in my hands so he wouldn't be able to look away. "You are a good person,

Lucien. The best man I've ever known. I love you. I really do." My voice broke as the tears I tried to hold in burst out.

He grabbed my wrists, face twisted in unbearable pain. "How can I trust your words when you don't trust them yourself?" he asked in a devastating whisper.

I traced his face with my shaky fingers, unable to answer. Because he was right. I couldn't trust my own emotions. That was the logical way to think.

But in truth, the way I felt when he was looking at me like he did now, when he claimed me with his cock, when he touched me, and still did, as if I were precious and fragile . . .

He'd protected me from Chase when he was still heavily wounded.

He treated me with respect and affection like no one ever did before.

When he smiled at me, I felt like I was ten feet tall.

When he laughed at my jokes, I wanted to see him laugh all the time.

I hurt when he hurt. Both physically and emotionally.

I cried when he cried.

He comforted me when I didn't even realize I needed comfort.

He looked at me as if I mattered. As if I was important. As if he needed me.

And I needed him too. I needed him so much that it took my breath away.

How could all these emotions be the result of some magical manipulation, when they felt so fucking real?

"I love you," I said, feeling like a broken record, and pressed my lips against his. "I love you, Lucien. *I love you.*"

His hands were around my neck as he kissed me, and I could feel the pain in him when he murmured against my lips, "Who are you trying to convince?"

I pushed at his chest, angry at him but even more at myself for being unable to refute his words. "What about you, then?" I snapped, wiping my tears as I glared at him. "Do you actually love *me*? Do you think I believe it?"

He growled, glowering back, as he pushed me down to the mattress, his naked body pressed against me, his arousal still hard, hot, and thick near my wet entrance. "I've wanted you from the moment I first saw you," he almost snarled, eyes holding mine. "Your kindness, warmth, beauty . . . I couldn't help but be drawn to you from the start."

I shook my head, even as my body betrayed me, my legs widening up on their own to accommodate his heavy, gorgeous body between them. "You're lying."

"You must be clueless, then," he hissed, eyes clouding with lust as he rested his cock along my slit, making me gasp as arousal rose within me again. "You have no idea how extraordinary you are, Drew. How beautiful of a person you are, both inside and out. You are everything I have ever wanted. Everything I've ever needed."

I cried out as his lips pressed a kiss to mine. "I love you so much, and knowing that your emotions aren't your own . . ." He leaned back, his gaze filled with sadness. "It's fucking *killing me*, Drew."

My heart was racing at his words. My entire body ached for him even more now. "Lucien," I pleaded with him, rubbing against him and making him groan in agony. "Turn me into a werewolf, then. Blaise said you could do it. That it would solve my being an Eteria—"

"Blaise knows shit," he interjected with a bitter smile before he pressed his lips to my throat, his hands grabbing my thighs. Even though we were almost fighting, we couldn't stop touching each other. Wanting each other. Longing for one another. "You have no idea what it means to become a werewolf."

"I don't care," I whispered, moaning as he licked at my throat before biting into it. "If . . . if that's what it takes—"

He leaned back to look at me, his cock probing at my entrance and making me gasp. His face was both grim and full of need. "Do you want to suffer every full moon, Drew?" he asked, his brilliant blue eyes catching my own brown ones. "Do you want to have the unavoidable risk of being afflicted with Wildlight? Do you want to be forced to live under a different set of rules than the ones you grew up with?"

Tears fell down my face as I grabbed his shoulders, digging my nails into his skin. "Lucien," I whimpered, knowing his words were important. That his worries were valid.

I'd seen the effect of Wildlight, after all.

But did it all matter when the man before me was everything I'd ever wanted too?

He lowered his face so he could lean his forehead against mine. "It would be selfish of me to ask you to forsake your humanity and transform into a werewolf for me, just to prove your love. Not just selfish; it would be absolutely inhuman. I will never ask that of anyone. Least of all the woman I love."

And that right there solidified my decision. Because up until now, I'd thought Lucien didn't have any sort of feelings for me. I thought my feelings were unrequited. If I'd known I had the option to transform into a werewolf before he told me he loved me, I would've thought it an absurd, far-fetched idea.

But he loved me. The fact he refused to put me at risk, even if it meant never knowing how I truly felt, was enough for me to believe it. His touch, his words, his warmth . . . It all told me everything I needed to know.

And so I pushed at his chest, catching him off guard, and flipped us over so I could straddle him as he lay down, staring at me with eyes wide in shock. But I was determined now. I refused to cry and beg him to believe me.

Because I knew what I wanted to do.

"For the last eight years I've been both lonely and alone, Lucien," I told him, putting my hands on his chest. "Alone in my convictions, and lonely in my life. I had no one to call my own. I'm estranged from my parents, and up until a few days ago, I hadn't spoken to Thayer. My precious sisters are long gone too. I have no remaining friends, not after Chase proved to be nothing more than a spy. I have no one. Or so I thought.

"It might not have been so long since we first met, Lucien, but you flipped my world upside down," I confessed, my determination overriding my fear of showing him my vulnerability. "You don't make me feel lonely. You make me feel like I matter. Before I even realized it, I couldn't see how I would ever be able to go back to my life from before meeting you. My life would be miserable without you in it.

"You are my everything, Lucien," I said softly, "and I want to show you I'm your everything too."

His expression broke. "Drew . . ."

"Transform me into a werewolf," I said—commanded, really—as I lifted myself up to place my entrance over the tip of his hard cock. "That way, you'll give me everything I've ever wanted: a home. *You.*"

Before he could respond, I plunged myself down, burying him deep inside me, and moaned at the feeling of him filling me up to the brim.

Lucien groaned, his hands on my hips, his scorching touch sending electric shocks to my heart and my pussy.

So I started moving, riding him hard, fast, and deep while he held on to me, disarmed and undone, shame, guilt, defeat, and relief, too, written all over his face.

And I knew I had finally gotten through to him.

Because my stubborn Alpha flipped us again so I was on my back and drove in and out of me with both power and tenderness, kissing me with affection and love, passion and desire, and pure, unadulterated need, until we both saw stars.

Lucien and I looked like we had just had sex. Which we had.

And Blaise, Teya, Callista, Ren, and Oz noticed.

After the last round of sex, Lucien and I had no time to discuss anything else because we heard people entering the cabin. At first, Lucien and I were tempted to ignore them, preparing to go another round, when there was a knock on the door, and Blaise's voice called, "I've got the portals!"

Now, after hastily putting on clothes without even brushing our hair, Lucien and I sat at the round dining table with the Betas, looking like we'd just rolled out of bed and smelling like sex.

Blaise and Teya didn't hide their knowing smiles, while Oz seemed disgusted. Ren and Callista seemed slightly uncomfortable.

While I shifted awkwardly in my seat, Lucien didn't seem troubled as he spread out on his chair, his arm resting on the back of mine and his fingers twirling my messy, knotted hair. "Tell me about the portals," he now instructed Blaise in a drawling voice that made me clench my thighs together.

Stop it, I admonished my stupid libido.

Clearing his throat, Blaise grew serious as he pulled out five flasks filled with liquid I recognized very well. The muted, grayish-brownish color of the shadow mark. "One of my contacts in the Underearth came through," Blaise said, drawing my gaze back to him. He was looking at Lucien. "We received a formal invitation from the Syndarch."

Lucien froze, his fingers leaving my hair, and he straightened in his chair. "Tell me everything."

Blaise nodded and complied. "According to my contact, the Syndicate became aware of Mack Page's death soon after you"—he glanced briefly at Oz, whose face was dark—"dealt with him."

"It's fine, Frenchy," Oz hissed. Apparently, his vocal cords were healed. "You can say that he killed him."

Lucien ignored him and nodded for Blaise to continue, and he did. "The Fae whom Mack contracted was indeed from the Syndicate's Covert Umbral Neutralization Taskforce. The Syndicate, however, claims that the Fae operated on their own, without the Syndicate's knowledge."

"Of course they claim that," Lucien murmured, grimacing. "What about the Fae that attacked me in Drew's apartment?"

"My contact confirmed it was the same one who almost killed you," Blaise said with a heavy sigh. "They said the Fae hasn't returned to the Underearth since after they tried to kill you that first time, which, according to my contact, was because they were tracking down Mack to receive the payment."

Lucien's lips thinned. "Did they get the payment, then?"

Blaise shook his head. "My contact wasn't clear on why, exactly, but the Fae was delayed, and by the time they found Mack, he was already dead. That's when they realized you must be alive."

Something about this didn't add up. "Why didn't the Fae make sure Lucien was dead to begin with?" I asked, frowning, and flushed a little when everyone turned to look at me. "Lucien was still alive, albeit barely, when I found him."

"That's a good point," Blaise murmured, "but from my association with the Fae through my various contacts, I've come to know they are a very conceited, arrogant bunch. Most likely, the Fae believed they finished the job without finishing the job."

"But that's too sloppy," Teya chimed in, folding her arms. "Umbral Fae aren't sloppy."

Blaise shrugged. "Either way, that's all I know."

"So the invitation?" Lucien prompted, voice contemplative. I knew he was still thinking about what we'd just discussed too.

"The Syndicate wants to negotiate a deal with you as a gesture of good faith, or, in other words, for the sake of sweeping this whole thing under the rug," Blaise replied and motioned toward the flasks full of shadow marks he'd put on the table. "My contact gave me these portals. We are to use them in an hour, Overearth time."

"Overearth?" I repeated, surprised.

Lucien smiled a little when he replied, "That's what the Fae call our time, since time runs differently in the Underearth."

"One hour in the Underearth is about a day in our world," Blaise supplied. "That's because the Underearth is considered by the rules of space and time as a different dimension."

Before I could ask questions about *that* intriguing piece of information, Lucien rose to his feet. "In that case, we need to get ready," he said, and turned to look at his Betas. "Blaise, Oz, and Teya—you're coming with me to the Underearth."

Everyone nodded, even Oz, despite his permanent look of distaste.

"Since it can take a few days, Overearth time," he continued, turning to look at Callista, "I appoint you as temporary Alpha until we return. If anyone has a problem with that, you have my permission to punish them accordingly."

Callista let out a sigh and nodded, while Ren raised his hand. "I'm in charge of the trainees' field trip tomorrow. Is that still going to happen?"

With a shake of his head, Lucien said, "While all other pack activities should continue as usual, anything that requires leaving the pack territory is postponed until we return." He grimaced. "I don't want to take any risks until I make sure the Syndicate is no longer a threat to anyone here."

Ren nodded, and Oz scoffed. "The trainees are gonna *love* that."

Lucien's eyes snapped to the annoying Beta. "Do you want to have your vocal cords severed again?"

Oz folded his arms and looked away, jaw tight. "No, *Alpha*."

I could tell Lucien was pissed at Oz's tone, and it made me wonder why he'd decided to take him to the Underearth. With his attitude, Oz might be more of a threat to Lucien—and this mission as a whole.

Lucien turned to me then. "Since the Syndicate has also threatened your and Thayer's lives, you'll come with us, too, Drew," he said softly. "Callista will let Thayer know so he won't worry."

"Is he still in the Ward?" I asked quietly, turning to look at Blaise.

He nodded grimly. "I don't think he's planning to leave there anytime soon."

"All right," I said and sighed. "Then to the Underearth it is."

CHAPTER 30
THE UNDEREARTH

"Why did you choose Oz to come along?" I asked Lucien quietly as we walked through the forest. We had just finished showering and putting on fresh clothes, and it was time to meet our other companions for the field trip.

So I used the time to voice my concerns.

"Despite his hatred towards me, Oz cares about the pack, and he knows that a threat to me is a threat to the pack as a whole," Lucien replied in a calm voice, though his face was troubled.

And this didn't make me feel any better. "I still don't like him," I informed him. "He's picking fights for no reason, acting rude and disrespectful towards you, and generally being a humongous asshole."

Lucien let out a breath. "Oz and Mack used to be best friends," he said. "I believe Oz's anger isn't really directed at me, but rather at Mack, for betraying not just the pack's trust, but Oz's too. But since Mack's gone, he directs his fury at me." He smiled bitterly. "Of course, if his behavior persists after we're done with the Syndicate, then I'm going to take serious action. Let's just say this is his chance to show me he is fit to remain a Beta, or a pack member in general. But let's talk about something more important now."

I knew what he wanted to talk about, so, looking straight ahead, I decided to speak first. "Once we come back, you're transforming me into a werewolf. It is settled."

My voice was defensive, and I was prepared for a fight—only this time, without the mind-blowing sex, which was quite unfortunate. But when Lucien said nothing, I glanced at him and saw a gorgeous smile on his face. It was a genuine smile, so beautiful, so breathtaking, I found myself unable to look away, entranced by the sight.

"Okay," he said softly, glancing at me with a tender look that made me weak in the knees.

"Okay?" I repeated, eyes wide in disbelief. "You're not going to talk bullshit about being selfish and whatnot again?"

He chuckled and wrapped his arm around my shoulders, pulling me to him. "When it comes to you, Drew, you could ask me to pull my heart out of my chest and give it to you, and I would say yes."

I wrapped my arms around him and huddled closer. "Lucien . . ."

He kissed my forehead. "I just hope you don't come to regret it," he said quietly. "That's all I'm really worried about."

"I won't," I said at once, pulling back to catch his gaze. "And in the zero chance I ever do, I will never, ever blame you."

His gaze softened, and I could see it. His love for me. It shone bright in his eyes now, when before it never had. As if he didn't want to hide it anymore.

But I could also see the hesitation still lurking there too. He couldn't fully trust my words yet because I was his Eteria, after all. An emotional slave whose soul belonged to him, and who was destined to love him, and only him.

That only made me more determined to go through with transforming into a werewolf. I couldn't wait to show him—and myself, too—that what I was feeling was real. That it had to be real.

Nothing else mattered to me more than showing the man I loved that I truly loved him.

After a few minutes of walking in silence, wrapped around one another, we arrived at a clearing in the forest where Blaise, Teya, and scrunch-faced Oz were waiting.

Wordlessly, Blaise handed each of us a flask filled with a shadow mark and said, "It might look like there isn't a lot of liquid inside, but it's an optical illusion. There is enough to drench you fully in the portal for it to occur safely, but make sure to not leave even the smallest part of your body dry."

Blaise motioned for us to uncork the flasks, and I was suddenly nervous. The first time I saw Lucien's human form was when he stopped me from touching the shadow mark. He'd told me later that if the portal wasn't applied right, it could cause single and even multiple dismemberments.

Lucien must've noticed my anxiety because he lowered his head toward me and murmured, "Don't worry, Drew. It's not like when you had a few drops; there is enough here to cover you whole without leaving even a pinky out."

I swallowed hard. "All right."

"Follow my lead," Blaise now said as he placed the flask over his head and began pouring the liquid.

But it wasn't really liquid, or rather, not entirely. It poured down almost like some sort of glaze, yet when it made contact with Blaise's skin and clothes, it turned into liquid. The liquid spread smoothly all over his body as if it knew what to do on its own, as if the shadow mark was actually sentient in a way, and once the last drop hit his head, Blaise evaporated into thin air, leaving a small trail of fine white smoke behind.

I blinked, staring at where Blaise had just been, before turning to Lucien. "What . . ."

Lucien shrugged and surprised me with a sexy wink. "Welcome to the world of magic, Drew Colter."

Smiling a little, and relieved to see him joking like this—despite everything that had happened and everything that would happen soon—I took in a deep breath and mimicked everything Blaise had done.

The shadow mark felt like warm mud on my skin as it crawled all over it, and my clothes, evenly. All I had to do was leave my flask above me until the last drop. The liquid found its way to every spot without me needing to do anything; it even crawled up my raised hand, the one holding the flask.

Once the last drop landed on the tip of my nose, I felt as if I was being yanked forward forcefully, even though I didn't move. I shut my eyes as I felt a sudden sense of nausea before the yanking feeling disappeared and my nausea retreated, leaving me breathless.

Feeling disoriented, it took me a moment to comprehend that I was no longer at the clearing in the middle of the forest of the Montrevere werewolf pack near LA. Because what I was seeing before me was far too unbelievable.

It seemed the Underearth wasn't called an Underearth for nothing. This place, the city that sprawled down the hill the Betas, Lucien, and I were currently standing on, was literally built under the ground.

The ceiling was far too high for me to actually see, but I could see the walls were made of the very earth this place was named after. The city itself, while I couldn't see the end, only the few blocks ahead, looked like an ominous version of Venice, with canals between blocks and houses, bridges to get from one place to another, and boats parked near the houses as a means of transportation.

The city was mostly dark but for the lanterns hung on the walls, dimly lighting up the roads. The smell was that of mud and ocean water, and the freshly cut grass we stood on as it covered the hill.

"What do you think?" Lucien murmured now, looking at me with piercing eyes, after he appeared out of thin air just like the others and me.

I returned my gaze to the city. "It's beautiful," I said quietly, "but eerie."

He nodded in agreement, it seemed, before he looked at Blaise, who stared at the city ahead. "Lead the way."

Blaise nodded and began climbing down the hill. The other two Betas, Lucien, and I followed, and as we did, an uneasy feeling crawled into my gut, as if my instincts were trying to tell me something.

But since I had no idea what they were trying to tell me, I ignored them for now.

We walked among the bridges, passing by people who seemed human, but each had a certain feature that differentiated them from any normal human I'd ever seen.

For instance, we passed by a family of four, with one of the mothers having long pointy ears, like an elf, and the other sporting shiny dark scales over her bare arms. Their son and daughter seemed like a mishmash of the two mothers, with both scales and pointy ears, though the son also had something akin to a tattoo framing his face, which had to be some sort of a birthmark, since the boy was merely four or five years old.

Most people we passed, though, had pointy ears in different lengths. When I asked Lucien about it in a low voice, he replied, "The Underearth is considered the most Fae-centric city in the Otherborne world."

Meaning each and every person with pointy ears had to be Fae, or of Fae heritage.

I tried not to stare at the people we passed by, so as to not seem too out of place, like a human in a zoo, but it was hard—especially when some of the passersby had horns, or sported tails and animal ears, or were covered in fur in their human form.

The deeper we went into the city, the more bustling it became. Booths, shops, and individual traders were hanging around the streets, and people engaged with them, purchasing and selling their things. It felt like a scene out of a fantasy movie, one of those Willow loved so much. The only jarring difference was that the people here were dressed in modern fashion like the average human and were using phones and electronic devices to swipe credit cards.

At the end of what seemed like the main road, Blaise, who led our group, came to a stop before a shop that seemed like an apothecary from outside. He then turned to us and said, "This is the meeting point. My contact should be here soon."

Lucien nodded and leaned against the shop's vitrine, folding his arms, face relaxed but his eyes on full alert.

I stood next to him, fiddling with my shirt nervously and continually readjusting my glasses as I watched the crowd of people milling about, the families talking in a mix of American English and some sort of foreign tongue I didn't recognize.

Another thing I noticed was the Spellscripts. There were many of them everywhere—carved on the building walls, the bridges' bricks, statues, even on trash bins. Some of those Spellscripts seemed similar to those I had recorded in my notebook, but most were foreign to me.

A man suddenly approached our group, wearing torn jeans and a shirt that hung off his shoulder, with long blond hair split by his pointy ears and eyes the color of pure violet. He was a beautiful man, but unlike Lucien, whose beauty might be heavenly but was still human in a sense, this man seemed as perfect as a marble statue. With his flawless, hairless porcelain skin, symmetrical face, and those violet eyes, he would've seemed entirely alien to human eyes had it not been for his surprising hipster fashion sense.

Blaise came over to the man, and, shockingly, the two gave each other a manly half-hug, half-pat-on-the-back kind of greeting. "It's good to see you face-to-face, for once," Blaise said afterward, and the man, the obviously Fae man, nodded, his face starkly empty, which made his resemblance to a statue even more acute.

Turning to us, Blaise introduced him. "This is Zairos," he said and motioned toward Lucien. "Zairos—this is Lucien Delterre, the Alpha of the Montrévère pack."

Zairos—what an odd name—walked toward Lucien and offered his hand. Wordlessly, Lucien shook it, his gaze scanning the Fae man, assessing him.

When the formalities were over, Zairos stepped back and spoke in the lowest voice I'd ever heard, which contrasted with his elegant statue-like looks so much, it felt as if he was being dubbed. "The HQ is a few blocks away. They are expecting you. Follow me."

There was an odd lilt to his words, an accent I couldn't pinpoint, but I ignored it and, along with Lucien and the Betas, followed the Fae man down the block and over the bridge toward our destination.

The walk was silent. Before, the Betas made small talk with one another, but now everyone kept their mouth shut, seemingly on high alert. Oz especially seemed jumpy, glancing around with a scowl on his face, as if something would attack us at any moment.

After a few minutes, Zairos stopped in front of a huge castle. A true, honest-to-God *castle*, with turrets, a moat created by the surrounding canals, and a flag blowing at the top of the highest spire.

While it was large, I realized why we hadn't been able to see it until now: The castle was surrounded by equally tall buildings, as if it was meant to be both conspicuous yet somehow concealed.

The castle was built with what seemed like actual onyx stones—the stones gave the illusion of a sun shining on the castle walls and reflecting back, which couldn't have been done by concrete painted black.

To my surprise, though, there were no guards standing near the entrance gate leading to the short bridge to the large black entrance doors. What kind of a castle didn't have guards? Especially since it was the Syndicate's HQ, apparently.

Either way, Zairos hovered his hand over the gate's lock until it clicked and opened as if it was an automatic door, though the chill in my spine told me otherwise. Still, we followed him inside, across the bridge, and over the moat, and reached the entrance doors.

I expected Zairos to simply walk in, but to my surprise, he paused and turned to us, his eyes narrowed, the first motion I'd seen his face make. But he still lacked an expression and seemed to be merely giving us a warning with his gaze.

Then he spoke in that oddly accented bass-tone voice. "The Syndarch will see you in the Hall of Aelir," he said flatly. "The Syndarch speaks first. That is the rule."

I glanced at Blaise, who seemed to be the only one in our group to have any idea about the Underearth, the Fae, and the Syndicate, and when I saw his face darken in an angry kind of caution, I suddenly felt alarm bells going off in my head, and that something from before that had been shifting uneasily in my gut bloomed into a full-on bad feeling.

But we had already come too far, and we had no choice but to follow Zairos through the opening grand doors and into the black castle of the Fae Sable Syndicate.

"Do not utter a word."

Blaise murmured those words to Lucien, Oz, Teya, and me as we walked through the dimly lit corridor, following Zairos to wherever he was taking us inside the castle.

Teya and Oz nodded, and Lucien did, too, while exchanging meaningful glances with Blaise. It seemed like the two were reading each other's minds or something, because Blaise gave a small shake of his head before returning his eyes forward.

I couldn't help but feel extremely nauseous due to the ominous feeling cooling my veins. It reached a point when I couldn't take it anymore and grabbed Lucien's hand, needing his touch to anchor me before I spiraled even more.

Lucien seemed to need it, too, because he gently pulled me close, linking our fingers together.

Zairos stopped at the end of the corridor, where another pair of big black doors awaited. This time, he didn't simply open it; he knocked in a certain offbeat rhythm, as though it was a code.

And apparently it was, because a second later, the doors were pulled open, this time by two men with pointy ears, whose faces were just as blank as Zairos's. But unlike Zairos, those two were dressed in black tactical gear that seemed more fitting to Fae who belonged to a Mafia-like organization called the Sable Syndicate.

The moment I stepped through the open doors, I felt all my bad feelings reaching their boiling point, and it took everything in me not to double over and puke my guts out, what with the nausea growing almost unbearable.

At first glance, it seemed like a throne room. It was certainly spacious enough to be one, with high ceilings, Gothic glass windows viewing nothing but a pitch-black void outside, and a long carpet reaching the stone stairs leading to an actual throne.

But the more my eyes darted around, the less fancy the room became. About twenty Fae men and women stood on the sides of the carpet, their eyes following our group as Zairos led us to the throne, while behind them, all over the walls, a bunch of cabinets rested, filled with all sorts of artifacts.

In all honesty, it looked like a throne-room-turned-museum rather than an actual active throne room. Especially with some of the artifacts being oddly shaped jewelry.

Zairos stopped near the stairs and moved to the side, bowing his head. "Syndarch, I present Alpha Lucien Delterre of the Montrevere pack and his entourage."

Lucien let go of my hand, which made me feel immediately unstable on my own two feet, and as he walked toward the stairs, I felt a sense of panic. I knew that if I didn't hold on to something, or someone, I would keel over, and so I took the hand of the Beta closest to me.

Unfortunately, that Beta was Oz, who froze when I grabbed his hand, but I couldn't let him go. He might be a rude asshole, but I needed him right now, while Lucien took care of this meeting.

Oz glanced down at me, bewildered, and I gave him a pleading look. I might've looked as ill as I felt, because Oz's face grew grim as he gave me a sharp, miniscule nod and returned his gaze forward.

Relieved he was letting me hold on to his hand, I looked up to watch the Syndarch as he rose from the throne.

The Syndarch, which I guessed was the leader of the Syndicate, probably holding a status akin to that of a don, was a child.

And by *child*, I mean a seven-or-so-year-old boy with a mop of black hair, violet eyes similar to Zairos's, and a round face filled with faint freckles. His pointy ears were a little short, barely peeking through the mass of his hair.

One other major difference between this boy and a normal one, though, was the fact he wore tactical black gear like the other Fae in the room, aside from Zairos.

It seemed I was the only one taken aback by the Syndarch's age, though. The Betas seemed unsurprised, and so did Lucien, who now stopped near the end of the stairs and stared at the much-shorter boy.

The boy stared down at Lucien and spoke in a serious, toneless kid's voice. "I have yet to meet a man, specifically a wolf, who survived the Mathenio."

Something told me I didn't want to know what the hell the Mathenio was.

Lucien didn't speak, didn't respond, and I realized he was following Blaise's instruction.

The boy smiled, and it sent a chill down my spine. This wasn't a normal smile. There was no joy or humor in it, but there was nothing else either. It was a smile devoid of emotion. A mere stretching of the muscles.

Such a smile on a boy's face was maniacal.

"Tell me, Lucien Delterre," the boy said, staring at Lucien with that creepy smile. "How did it feel?"

I tightened my hold on Oz's hand when Lucien spoke, now that he was given permission. "It felt like death," he replied plainly, almost as if he was talking about the weather.

The boy's smile widened, which made him seem far more sinister than before. "What does death feel like?"

"Pain," Lucien responded in that same dry voice, as I swallowed hard and didn't even blink as I stared at him. "Excruciating pain."

There was a short pause before the boy's smile disappeared, and he held his hands behind his back, beginning to descend the stairs. Seeing him drawing slowly closer to Lucien made my horror rise impossibly higher.

"The Mathenio is a mysterious power," the boy said as he descended one stair, then another. "Once in every few centuries, a Fae is born with that power, you see."

The boy reached the end of the flight of stairs and stood mere inches away from Lucien, who glanced down without tilting his head forward. The boy took notice of it, I could tell, because a sudden light entered his eyes.

"The interesting thing about the Mathenio, however, is that this time, no Fae was born with it," the boy continued as he passed by Lucien, approaching Teya, who, like Lucien, kept her head straight while glancing down at the boy. "So I wondered if the effects were the same."

And if I went by his previous smile, whatever this Mathenio and its effects were, they were the same. Which made me wonder—if a Fae wasn't born with this power, whatever it was, then who, or rather, *what*, was?

The boy raised his hand suddenly and twirled a strand of Teya's waist-long platinum hair. Teya visibly tensed, but she said nothing, and did nothing, as the boy played with her hair. "You have Fae heritage," the boy claimed now, staring at Teya. "Who was it?"

Teya's response was said in a tight, terse voice. "Great-great-grandmother. Thalira of Morn."

"Ah," the boy said, eyes widening—again, without emotions, just as if to mimic a human's expression. "I heard of her defection a long time ago." He paused, cocking his head. "Is she still alive?"

Teya gave a sharp nod.

The boy hummed, contemplating something, before he let go of Teya's hair and moved to Blaise. I could see Teya's shoulders relax, though she was still tense and on alert.

Blaise didn't move as the boy sized him up. To my surprise, he said nothing and walked around Blaise to reach Oz and me.

I was sweating and trying to gasp for air as quietly as I could the entire time, and when the boy drew close, I felt like I couldn't take it anymore. It was as if the boy had an aura of pure suffocating malice, so much so I could barely remain standing.

But Oz's grip was tight, and I clung on to it, thinking about it only, to try and keep still.

The boy gave Oz a once-over and seemed to dismiss him before his violet eyes landed on me.

Something bizarre happened just then.

The boy put his arms around my waist, barely reaching there, too, and hugged me.

I couldn't move. Could hardly even breathe. I dug my nails into Oz's palm, but he didn't flinch and held my hand still, as if he knew that if he let go, I would crumble.

Because the boy's hug felt like being caged inside Pandora's box.

"Drew Colter, the Alpha wolf's human savior," the boy said now, tightening his hug. My eyes snapped to see Lucien staring at me with the color drained from his face. "How interesting that it was *you* who disrupted Mack Page's plans."

My heart stopped.

What did he mean by *interesting*?

He leaned back but didn't let me go, his hands holding the hem of my shirt. I glanced down at him, meeting his wicked violet stare, and felt my sight swarming, as though I was on the verge of passing out.

"I tried to warn you," he said, and as if by magic, my nausea, my weak state, and everything else disappeared. It was like the boy flipped a switch. I could let go of Oz's hand now, which I did, and remain standing without fearing falling to my knees.

The boy smiled again, that strange, sinister smile, and released my shirt as he stepped back to take me in. "I didn't want you to get involved," he said, his gaze sharpening. "Especially after my people looked through your apartment and found what it is you do for a living."

He raised his hand, and to my horror, I saw one of the Fae standing on the sides, a woman, handing him a stack of papers clearly printed from the internet.

The Hallowing Hour's latest volume.

"You see," the boy said, smile gone, as he flipped through the paper and paused on a certain page, "you were tracking our movement without knowing that's what you were doing, and wrote about it in this magazine, which, luckily for you, hardly anyone reads."

He showed me the volume I hadn't yet seen. On the front page was the story I'd finished writing a week ago, the one describing every place I'd found the shadow mark, the Underearth portal, with the latest one being at the crime scene on Sunset Boulevard almost two weeks ago.

The boy then threw the magazine on the marble floor and, with that empty expression, pointed at it and shot a literal flame out of his finger to the paper, setting it on fire.

When his violet gaze met mine again, I could tell he was no longer expressionless. There was something akin to disgust burning deep in his eyes. "You know too much," he said flatly now. "As a Proctor of the Council for Regulation of Arcane Phenomena, I adhere to clause 3(iv) of the Motion for Irregular Threat Removal and sentence you to immediate execution."

His words didn't compute at first.

Not until Lucien was suddenly grabbing the Syndarch's throat from behind, his fingers turned into sharp claws, and aiming the claws on his other hand at his chest. "You are not going to touch her," Lucien said, voice as flat as the boy's had been but with rage written all over his face.

The boy's face remained impassive, though his eyes flashed again with what seemed like disgust. "You've done so well until now, wolf," he said in a somewhat condescending tone that made my skin crawl. "It's unfortunate you're determined to ruin our negotiation."

Lucien's hold tightened on the boy's neck. From the corners of my eyes, I saw the other Fae in the room, including Zairos, preparing to attack, though none of them did. I wondered why, considering their very young leader was at risk.

"That's funny," Lucien murmured now, voice low and a growl reverberating in his chest. "I don't recall you trying to negotiate."

Blaise, Teya, and Oz seemed extremely alert now, ready to defend Lucien and me at any moment. My heart suddenly raced as I realized, belatedly, that the situation had taken a turn for the absolute worst.

"I don't mind negotiating with you about your little pack, wolf, as a gesture of good faith after our slight mishap," the boy said now, and I could see him rolling his eyes despite the fact Lucien's claws dug enough into his neck to draw a small amount of blood—blood that was the color purple, like his eyes, rather than red. "But the human has to die."

"This is nonnegotiable," Lucien said through gritted teeth. "Proctor or not, I won't let you kill her."

The boy gave a long-suffering sigh. "Why must you make things so difficult?" he asked, and if there wasn't a genuine questioning tone in his voice, I would've thought he was being sarcastic. "You're acting as if she's your Eteria."

It wasn't just the boy who scoffed disbelievingly at the word *Eteria*; the Fae surrounding us, who hadn't made a sound until now, let out similar sounds of disbelief. Teya, Blaise, and even Oz exchanged horrified looks, as they all knew what the truth was.

My heart pounded loud enough, I swore I could hear it echo in the hall.

I looked up at Lucien, who stared back, fury, worry, and fear in his eyes. And I knew just then that he didn't want to reveal that to the boy, or to anyone else in this room, for that matter. He didn't want to reveal what I was to him.

Or rather, he was scared.

Why? Because it would put me in more danger or something? But I was already *in* danger—if the boy wanted to kill me, I had no doubt he could with a mere fling of his hand.

And the frustration and helplessness I could now see on Lucien's face made it seem as though he'd reached the same conclusion.

"Killing her would make you the one who ruined any potential relationship between us, not the other way around, Syndarch," Lucien now said in a low voice, face grim. "Because she *is* my Eteria."

CHAPTER 31
ON THE SYNDARCH'S TERMS

The whole situation did a one-eighty after Lucien uttered the two magic words: *my Eteria.*

First, the boy tapped on Lucien's arm, indicating he needed to let him go. Lucien was reluctant, but he did, and the boy landed on the floor, wiped his blood, and flicked his fingers without saying a word.

A few moments later, a simple square table was carried into the room by one of the Fae, followed by two chairs placed on each side of the table. A pair of Fae drew the chairs for Lucien and the boy to sit down on, and once they did, another Fae brought a stack of stapled papers, along with two pens.

The boy lifted a pen and said in a monotonous voice, as if he hadn't just threatened my life or had his own life threatened by Lucien, "The contract between my Fae and Mack Page is already null and void, considering Mr. Page's untimely demise." He delivered this observation dryly as he scribbled something down on the paper. "I suggest we negotiate a deal between us with that in mind."

Lucien grabbed my hand, lacing our fingers together, much to the Betas' shock, as he leaned back and said, "I would like to know the exact details of that contract."

The boy shrugged. "It's very simple," he said, tapping on the desk with his pen. "Mack wanted you gone. He offered to pay my Fae with five favors in return once you were dead, and gave them an advance of two favors."

That didn't seem to sit well with Lucien. "What kind of favors?" he asked, eyes narrowing.

"I am not so uncouth as to inquire of any Fae of mine what kind of favors they ask for in their private contracts," he replied, sounding almost offended at the idea that he would know such private information, and so we were left to wonder.

Seeing he wouldn't be able to get an answer for that, Lucien moved on. "I want a nonaggression agreement between the Syndicate and the Montrévère pack," he said now, grabbing the other pen. "You won't come for us, or for me, as the Alpha, under any circumstances, and we will not come for you."

The boy smiled. "This is not how it works, wolf," he said in a lecturing voice that made me scowl. "I require payment."

"In the form of favors," Lucien added with evident distaste.

The boy shrugged. "We are Fae," he said matter-of-factly, as if that explained everything.

And it seemed it did, because Lucien gave a curt nod and said, "Then I would like you to pay us with favors in return."

"Ah." The Syndarch's smile widened. "Now you're talking."

The next few minutes were a back-and-forth between Lucien and the Syndarch, as each changed, added, and removed terms for the contract. A lot of it I didn't quite understand, but since Lucien obviously did, it didn't matter.

I was no longer feeling sick, no longer sweaty and anxious, as if my body felt the danger had passed now that Lucien had declared me his Eteria. Yet some part of me was still uneasy, as if something wasn't quite right still.

"To seal our agreement, the contract requires a member of your pack to stay here as a liaison," the boy now said, leaning forward in his chair, his eyes falling on Teya. "I would like to add that I shall choose the liaison I see fit."

Lucien didn't seem to like it one bit. "I refuse to leave a member of my pack down here for an indefinite amount of time, Syndarch."

The boy sighed again. "Under the agreement, I am not allowed to harass, abuse, or touch even a strand of any of your wolves' hair," he said, folding his arms. "This is a necessity for our mutual nonaggression relationship."

It seemed Lucien couldn't refute that, even though he didn't like it one bit, as revealed by the curl of his lips. "Fine," he grated out. "So in this case, I will choose the liaison of the Syndicate as well."

"This is fair." The boy nodded. "How many are we talking about? One?"

Lucien glanced at Teya, who seemed a little pale, and said, "Two."

"Two," the boy repeated in a murmur while making a face, another rare show of emotion. "No. Let's make it three."

"Fine," Lucien said, blue eyes flaring in barely hidden hatred as he looked at the boy. "We choose today, then."

The boy nodded and pointed at Teya, like a kid in a candy store. "I want her," he said plainly. "I don't care about the other two. Zairos can choose them."

Teya's pale face fell now, but I saw her trying to collect herself, to not show how distraught she obviously was. It made me feel sick, seeing her so out of it. While I didn't know Teya, never talked to her, either, I couldn't help but feel sympathy for her. She obviously didn't want to be the liaison, and yet she had no choice.

Lucien didn't seem happy about it either. "You chose one of my Betas," he said in a warning tone. "That means you owe me a high-ranking member too."

"This won't be a problem." The boy shrugged, a secretive smile on his lips. "I'll do you even one better: I'll give you the Mathenio."

The silence that followed the boy's words could have been cut with a knife. Everyone seemed shocked, holding their breath, at what the boy just said—including the Betas, and Blaise in particular, who seemed downright flabbergasted.

The shock didn't bypass Lucien either; he stared at the Syndarch, almost disbelieving, and with a healthy amount of suspicion. "The Mathenio," he repeated slowly, breaking the silence.

With another cold smile, the boy nodded. "Yes. You'll get the Mathenio and two others of your choosing."

As if he still couldn't believe his ears, Lucien nodded before he turned to Blaise. "You choose the other two."

Blaise, whose shock was still palpable, gave a sharp nod.

"Then if that is all, I think we are done here," the Syndarch said as he signed the contract and pushed it toward Lucien. "It's *very* nice doing business with you, Alpha wolf, and congratulations," he added, glancing at me, "on your Eteria, that is."

Lucien signed, too, his muscles tense, and rose to his feet, grabbing my hand. "Teya needs to pack," he said, not acknowledging the latter statement, "and Zairos needs to pick the other two members of my pack. I'll take them both with me and leave Blaise here to pick your members."

The Syndarch rose to his feet, his face suddenly bored. "I'm looking forward to it," he said, voice dry, before he turned his back to us and left the hall as if nothing had just happened.

We stood in the clearing deep in the Montrevere pack's forest, after Zairos had given us shadow marks and we had all poured them over us and arrived safely. We'd been in the Underearth for about two hours, which meant it had been two days up here.

Oz was the first one to speak after we reappeared in the clearing. "Zairos will come with us, Alpha," he said, and for the first time, the way he said the word *Alpha* wasn't sarcastic or rude. "To see potential pack members, that is."

The only indication Lucien noticed the change was the slight widening of his eyes, but he schooled his face and nodded. "Let's meet back at the office."

It was only after Teya, Oz, and Zairos took off, when Lucien and I were walking back toward his cabin, that I could finally breathe. "What's going to happen now?" I asked quietly.

"Now our pack and the Syndicate owe each other ten favors, to be fulfilled within five years," he murmured in response, voice tired. "This is the best possible outcome."

I scanned the profile of his face. "So why do you look like you lost?"

His lips pursed. "Because Fae are dangerous, and leaving Teya and two other pack members in the Underearth makes me sick to my stomach with worry."

Considering how unbothered, yet arrogant, the Syndarch was, I could somehow understand. "Teya is strong, though, right?" I said, squeezing his hand.

"She is, which is the only reason why I didn't fight the Syndarch over this." He sighed before stopping in his tracks. I stopped, too, and turned to look at him, frowning. "What bothers me the most, however," he said quietly, "is that the Syndicate now knows not only that I have an Eteria, but who my Eteria is."

I tried to smile. "Then it's a good thing you're going to transform me into a werewolf, isn't it?"

He didn't smile back. "All it means is that even if you didn't insist on transforming, I would force you to anyway." He seemed tired and angry then. "Because if you remain human, powerless and easy to kill, the Fae will certainly come after you sooner or later."

His words should've scared me, but I wasn't scared. "Then it's a good thing you're going to transform me," I said again, narrowing my gaze when I saw his hesitance. "Right?"

"This shouldn't be the reason why you choose this path," he murmured, but I knew he wasn't disagreeing with me. Instead, he seemed infuriated at the situation rather than anyone specifically. "You shouldn't . . . become a werewolf because of *me*."

"Lucien," I said, taking his hands in mine.

He searched my gaze. "You have to be sure, Drew," he said quietly.

"And I am." I smiled, my love for Lucien overwhelming me until I almost couldn't take it. And this was precisely why I was ready. "So do it. Now."

His expression shattered and he pulled me into a deep, warm hug. "All right," he said, holding me close. "As you wish."

CHAPTER 32
ALL THE SAME

Lucien's bedroom was dimly lit as I sat on the edge of his bed, fingers twisting in the blanket, trying to breathe normally. It didn't work; my pulse was too loud, my skin felt too tight, and Lucien kept watching me like he was memorizing every last second of who I was before this.

"You can still say no," he said quietly, reluctantly, but resolutely too.

I couldn't help but smile at him. As if I could ever say no to him. I couldn't wait to prove to him—and myself—that it was *not* because of some sort of twisted magic. That it was for him. Just him. The man, rather than the werewolf. "I want this," I told him softly. "I'm sure."

A muscle in his jaw ticked. Not in anger but in something like fear. As if he wasn't sure this was right, even after everything we'd discussed.

But he didn't protest or try to convince me not to do it. Instead, he stepped closer, slow and careful, as if approaching something fragile. I felt the heat of him before he touched me, the tremor in his restraint. The shift in the air made my breath catch when he finally crouched in front of me, eyes level with mine.

"When I bite," he murmured, "your body will fight the change. You will feel pain, but it should pass. Afterward, you will lose consciousness for a while." He grimaced. "I'm not sure how long. It differs. On average, it should be a few days, until your body acclimates to your new . . . state."

I nodded, swallowing hard, not looking away.

His hand rose and brushed my hair back from my neck, his gaze following the movement. "Lie back," he whispered.

I did, trembling now.

Lucien leaned over me, bracing his weight on one arm so he did not crush me. His breath whispered over my throat, hot and uneven, and I realized he was shaking too.

He was afraid. Lucien Delterre, Alpha extraordinaire, was afraid for me.

And it made me love him even more.

"I am ready," I said. "Lucien, do it."

His eyes locked onto mine, stormy and sad yet full of impossible tenderness. "I'm so sorry," he murmured.

Then he opened his mouth, his teeth sharpening unnaturally, and sank them into the skin of my neck.

And the world shattered.

Not from pain, though there was pain, but from the rush. Heat tore through my body while lightning splintered my bones. My blood grew molten as my vision exploded into white particles. My heartbeat tripped, then surged, then thundered—so deafening, I couldn't hear anything else.

I could not breathe.

I could not think.

I could not be.

Lucien held me through all of it, his hands firm and his voice low as he murmured my name again and again, like a prayer. Something protective wrapped around me, even when I felt like I was dissolving from the inside out.

Then the pain folded inward, and the heat cooled.

Everything softened, as if a warm tide rolled over my body and pulled me back from the deep end. My senses expanded so much that

I could hear Lucien's heartbeat like a second one beating rapidly inside my chest. I could smell the cedarwood on his skin, the stormy, wild essence that lived inside him, that made him *him*, and the faint hint of fear he still had not shaken.

Slowly, I blinked up at him. His face hovered over mine, breath unsteady, arctic-blue eyes bright with worry. "Drew?" he asked hoarsely, voice breaking. "Are you . . ."

I managed a tired smile. My body felt heavy, but my mind was crystal clear—and not just because I didn't feel pain now.

Because whatever sort of magic my being an Eteria had on me was gone.

I had never felt that magic before now, but a moment ago, I'd felt this foreign something in my head. Something that didn't belong.

Yet now, that something was gone, and for the first time in my entire life, I felt like I could actually *breathe*.

It was like shackles that tied me to something beyond my reach had been snapped open, broken, setting me free.

My emotions surged, uncontrollable, overwhelming, and absolutely, heartbreakingly beautiful.

"Yeah," I whispered, reaching for his cheek, as tears, happy tears, filled my eyes. "I love you all the same."

The last thing I saw was his expression. Relief poured all over him, making his entire body sag back, as if he could no longer hold on, and softened something on his face I had not realized he'd been keeping tightly guarded all this time.

My hand fell, and, with a smile, I closed my eyes as I welcomed the darkness of a deep, long sleep.

EPILOGUE
LUCIEN

When I told Drew Colter that I had wanted her from the first moment I laid eyes on her, I didn't lie.

If anything, I downplayed what truly happened.

The moment I opened my eyes—in so much pain I could hardly breathe, still in my wolf form from when I tried to kill my attacker—and saw Drew's beautiful chocolate brown eyes, I was a goner.

That feeling hadn't changed. The more I got to know her, the stronger that feeling grew, and it became much harder to restrain. But I had restrained it nonetheless.

Because she was my Eteria, and I was terrified that any action I took would make the Eteria magic force her to love me.

Yet I couldn't help myself. I couldn't stay away. I needed her like I'd never needed anyone.

And I selfishly claimed her.

I didn't believe her when she told me she loved me. I wanted to. I wanted to so much it had taken everything inside me to shake me out of this impossible delusion.

But the moment I bit her, I could feel it. I had felt the connection between her soul and me, the connection I had felt since I had first laid eyes on her, sever, the tether gone.

And I was terrified all over again. Because what if she opened her eyes and realized it had all truly been mind control? That she had transformed into a werewolf only to find out everything was a lie?

It had made me sick to my stomach, thinking that after telling me she loved me, she would take her words back.

But what she said instead was that she loved me all the same.

She loved me.

Not as an Eteria. As a woman.

My woman.

And for the first time, I allowed myself to trust her completely. To believe her.

To truly, fully love her.

Watching her beautiful face now as she rested, eyes closed, her wavy chestnut brown hair spread all over my pillow, a sense of possessiveness filled me. *She's mine,* I thought, tracing my knuckle over her face. *Mine. Mine. Mine.*

I was following the trail my knuckle made down to her throat when I stopped, hovering over the dark bite mark I had left there a few hours ago. The Transference that had turned her into a werewolf.

My own wolf couldn't wait to meet the one who'd been born inside her.

Sweet, kind, beautiful Drew, I thought, pressing a kiss against her forehead, wishing I could stay in bed with her until she awoke.

But she wouldn't awaken for another day at the very least, and I was an Alpha with duties I couldn't postpone, and so reluctantly, I got off the bed and exited the room.

Thayer, Drew's older brother, was in the living room. He'd spent most of his time in the Concordian Ward, but when I sent word about Drew, he had rushed back. He seemed distraught, as though he hadn't slept in days. He was obviously haunted by Anais's condition, and now by Drew's decision.

My heart felt heavy when he looked up and stared at me in that suspicious, distrustful manner of his, which I tried not to take personally. He was protective of his sister, and like any protective older brother, he didn't like me. Not yet, at least.

Which was why I was a little wary when I said, "I'm heading out. Keep an eye on Drew and call me immediately if she wakes up."

Unsurprisingly, Thayer's eyes narrowed. "Is she all right?" he asked through gritted teeth.

My phone vibrated in the pocket of my jeans, and I knew I didn't have more time, so I walked toward Thayer, put a hand on his shoulder, and said, "She will be all right. I promise. So try not to worry, and call me when she wakes up if I haven't come back yet."

Before Thayer could reply, I left the cabin and headed to the pack's Heart.

Zairos, the Syndicate Fae, had made his choice as to who would be part of the liaison team along with Teya.

His choices, though, were extremely odd.

Teya and Oz had told me they would take him through all pack facilities so he could find someone of a suitable circumstance and age to choose. Of course, one of those facilities was the Penitentiary, but I hadn't thought they would want a criminal.

The Syndicate might be made of Fae assassins and similar criminal-type personnel, but with the Syndarch also being a Proctor—one of the twelve high-profile people who made up the Council for Regulation of Arcane Phenomena, the global organization that oversaw all the world's Otherborne—the Syndicate didn't associate with *actual* criminals.

But the contract with the Syndicate said they could choose whoever they wanted, like I could choose whoever I wanted from their ranks. Whether she was a criminal or not didn't matter.

So they chose two wolves from the Penitentiary. A young werewolf woman called Rowenna Ashtros, who'd been incarcerated and awaiting trial for the murder of another pack member, and, somewhat unsurprisingly, Dianna Rook. I was sure Zairos had chosen her under orders from the Syndarch, seeing as she had been one of Mack Page's assistants.

What they would gain from taking Dianna, however, I didn't know. And that made my Alpha instincts tingle in suspicion.

"Are you sure about your choice?" I asked Zairos now.

The pale Fae man nodded. "They shall come with me."

Teya, Rowenna, and Dianna were already packed. None of the three looked at me, seemingly occupied with their own thoughts. I could only imagine; they were chosen to be the liaisons. And with Kate, Dianna's sister, barely holding on to life due to her Wildlight, I knew the last thing Dianna wanted was to be whisked to the Underearth, so far away from her.

This was out of my hands, though. Which made me both angry and resigned.

I walked toward Teya and grabbed her shoulders. She raised her eyes to me, rueful yet resilient. "You're strong," I told her in a quiet murmur only she could hear. "You can handle this. I know you can."

Teya nodded silently and gave me a small sad smile. "When my family returns, tell them I'm sorry I didn't get to say goodbye, and that I love them."

My chest tightened when I thought of Teya's family. Her parents, two of the oldest werewolves I ever knew—who gave birth to Teya in their fifties, against all odds, considering their age—were extremely overprotective of Teya, their only daughter. They were now traveling through Europe after retirement, and the notion of telling them what had transpired while they were away made me feel an overwhelming amount of guilt.

"I will," I told Teya now nonetheless, and she gave me a quick hug, which I returned.

Then I turned to Rowenna and Dianna. "You're lucky," I told the two of them, as they avoided my gaze. "You get to start fresh without any consequences to your actions. Thank Zairos and the Syndarch for your good fortune."

The two young women had the decency to look somewhat ashamed.

Relaxing, I nonetheless gave each of them a pat on the shoulder, startling them into snapping their gazes toward me. "Do a good job there," I told them. "Despite everything, you're capable enough for that."

They nodded, seemingly stunned, and tensed when Zairos finally spoke. "I'm taking them now, then."

I looked at the Fae man and shot him a serious look. "Not a hair on their head," I reminded him, the threat in my voice undeniable.

But the Fae man, like every damned Fae, simply blinked back and nodded, as expressionless as a bulk of stone.

When Zairos, Teya, Rowenna, and Dianna were gone, I walked into the meeting room next to this one, where Callista, Oz, and Ren were sitting.

Callista looked like she'd been crying. Teya had been her best friend, after all. Ren and Oz seemed grim as well. "They're gone," I told them now, not feeling much better. "Any word from Blaise?"

Oz nodded and turned to look at me. His attitude from the past few days disappeared after our visit to the Syndicate, which was a relief. It seemed as if he finally realized what I'd tried to tell him about Mack, and why I had to do what I did. "He's on his way with the prisoners," Oz now said, spitting the word *prisoners*.

Of course, he wasn't referring to the Fae liaisons Blaise picked, but rather to the fact that our pack members had become prisoners of the Syndicate too.

"All right," I said, sitting down. "Let's wait for them, then."

But it was hours before Blaise entered the room, due to the difference in the flow of time in the Underearth. "Alpha," he greeted me formally, nodding, before he turned around. "Come in."

Other than the Mathenio, which the Syndarch shockingly "gifted" us, I didn't know what to expect. First, I didn't know *who* had the Mathenio, since the Syndarch mentioned something about it not being a Fae, exactly, or something along those lines, but also, I wasn't sure who the other two should be.

But other than Drew, Blaise was the only one I trusted out of the entire pack. He'd been with me since Paris. He'd stuck by my side. He hadn't joined a new pack after the demise of ours, despite the many packs all over Europe that were eager to offer him a position, considering his reputation.

Instead, he came with me all the way to Los Angeles, to a new pack, in a new country, across the ocean.

And he had never failed me before. Which was why I trusted him to choose well.

Yet his choices made no sense. At least not at first glance.

Much like Zairos's didn't. Because this group included three young women who didn't seem very highly ranked, or powerful, like I somewhat expected.

Blaise, though, kept a blank face as he motioned toward the first woman. "This is Ivoria," he said, introducing the first Fae woman, who seemed just as apathetic as the rest of them. "She is part of the Syndicate's messenger team."

The words clicked, and I realized what Blaise wasn't saying. Because *messenger team* was a covert term for information traders.

Meaning this woman could be a really good asset.

Blaise then walked toward the other two women, and I noticed something I hadn't before. One of those two women was unconscious. The other woman was keeping her standing, even though she was obviously passed out.

I watched as Blaise gently pried the unconscious woman from the one holding her, even though the other woman at first refused to let go. But Blaise murmured something to the woman that made her freeze and retract her hands, letting him carry the unconscious woman in his arms.

"These two Fae women are sisters," Blaise now said, glancing at the conscious sister, whose face was curtained by a mess of dirty, tangled curly hair so long it reached her knees. "This one has the Mathenio," he added, pointing at the conscious one, before jutting his chin toward the one in his arms. "This girl is . . . her sister."

I narrowed my eyes at Blaise's hesitation. Blaise never hesitated. He spoke with precision, explained his decision thoroughly, and didn't bother talking in circles. He was one of the most straightforward men I knew.

But his hesitance now, about the qualities the unconscious sister brought as a liaison, gave me pause.

"Names," I said, trying not to growl as I caught Blaise's look, trying to decipher, despite my irritation, what he was getting at.

Before Blaise could speak, the standing sister suddenly took a step forward and pushed her hair away from her face, revealing a pair of familiar gray eyes. "I can talk for myself, though I don't like your tone," she said bad-temperedly, glaring at me.

I frowned, trying to figure out why her eyes seemed familiar to me. "I'm the Alpha here, Faeling," I said quietly, not threatening, just warning. "Here, what I say goes."

If looks could kill, the woman's glower would have. "We'll see about that," she murmured ominously before she straightened and said, jaw locked in stubbornness, "I'm Willow Colter. And this is my sister, Julianna."

AUTHOR'S NOTE

Dear new and old readers,

Writing has always been a means of escape for me. When the world seems to crumble down, it is books that I turn to for comfort—both reading and writing them. I'm sure a lot of you can relate, at least to the reading part.

The way I see it, the difference between being a writer and being an author is whether anyone reads your material or not. I would've forever remained a writer if it weren't for you, dear readers. I managed to become an author because of you, and for that, you forever have my gratitude.

Whether you like my books or criticize them, I appreciate each and every one of you.

And you are the reason I wrote this book to begin with.

My first werewolf book, *The Millennium Wolves*, has seen huge success thanks to your love, and I knew that I would want to revisit the werewolf genre in the future—if not for me, then for you.

This was the main driving force behind the writing of this book.

I wanted to go back eleven years, to when I first wrote *The Millennium Wolves*, and give both you and me a nostalgic callback to the genre that brought me to where I am today.

I truly hope that my hard work wasn't for naught and that you enjoyed reading. I hope that this book managed to bring you a few hours of comfort in the crazy world we live in.

With love,

Sapir x

ACKNOWLEDGMENTS

I want to thank Georgia McBride, my amazing literary manager, who trusted me with the turbulent process of writing (and rewriting) this book, even when I didn't trust myself. Without your encouragement, none of this would've been possible.

I would also like to thank the Montlake editorial team for your continued support and dedication to my books.

To my family and friends—I appreciate your patience when you listened to me whine endlessly until I finished writing this book. I love you all beyond words.

ABOUT THE AUTHOR

Sapir A. Englard is the author of massive digital hit The Millennium Wolves. Published in 2019 on the Galatea app, the twelve-book series has amassed more than 210 million reads. The series is also available in French from Hugo Publishing. Englard's success has been documented in *The Boston Globe* and *Forbes*, as well as on TechCrunch and other websites. A graduate of Berklee College of Music, Sapir is a full-time writer and musician.